ALL THE TINY BEAUTIES

All the Tiny Beauties

A NOVEL

Jenn Scott

ACRE

CINCINNATI 2022

Acre Books is made possible by the support of the Robert and Adele Schiff Foundation and the Department of English at the University of Cincinnati.

ISBN-13 (pbk) 978-1-946724-53-3
ISBN-13 (e-book) 978-1-946724-54-0

Designed by Barbara Neely Bourgoyne
Cover art: Tailor mannequin stock photo, iStock by Getty Images

The press is based at the University of Cincinnati, Department of English and Comparative Literature, McMicken Hall, Room 248, PO Box 210069, Cincinnati, OH, 45221–0069.

Acre Books books may be purchased at a discount for educational use. For information please email business@acre-books.com.

For Shane. There is none of this without you.

Jack is in his corset, Jane is in her vest.

—LOU REED, "SWEET JANE"

I

WEBB, 2001

*H*e'd wanted a single egg, its shell cracked against the fine edge of the bowl, yolk and white slipped into the swirl of simmering water while his soap played in the living room. This had been his ritual for days; weeks, months, years. Time elided, blurred them together. Countless things could occur during an egg's poaching: a character inflated with self-importance could sail his boat toward a stormy horizon (never to be seen again). A man could impregnate his sister-in-law—*oopsy!*—while his wife waded into a river intending to drown. On this particular day, a character had a premonition and took the train not to work but to her fiancé's apartment. There, she found the fiancé in bed with her best friend. The sweaty couple, upon discovery, had first fumbled inside and then extricated themselves from the tangle of sheets. The affronted woman raged. A lamp was thrown. Webb went to poach his egg.

Minutes later, lifting the pot from the burner, he accidentally dragged the dishtowel through the blue flame. Fire lapped the fabric. Surprised, he dropped the dishtowel on the rag rug at his feet. Normally a fastidious man, he had inexplicably, the day before, used this rug to clean an oil spill on the kitchen floor and then left the oil-soaked rug piled before the oven. Now, watching as the fire leapt at the oil, he understood: nothing in his life had converged as perfectly as this intersection of laziness, fire, and oil. His had not been that kind of life, success glinting at him like pieces of tinfoil. He recalled Hila whispering into his ear, "Webster. You will do anything you want in this beautiful world."

His only thought, however, was a bumbling caveman's—*Look, fire!*—though he wore not a furry loincloth but a teddy. *Sea Breeze Silk Step-In!* the catalog had exclaimed, unable to contain its enthusiasm. *A true classic,* *the teddy is also called a camiknicker! A silken piece of luxury, perfect for the boudoir! A must-have for those sleepless nights! $49.95!* A person could wear the Sea Breeze Silk Step-In inside the boudoir, or he could wear it inside the kitchen (!) while poaching an egg (!). In this process, he might ignite a dish towel (!), which, in a moment of panic, he might drop on a rug he'd cleaned up oil with (!) and hadn't bothered washing (!).

The small fire grew larger with a rush of orange beauty. Mesmerized, Webb stood watching it. He imagined the flames swallowing him, taking him from this life as smoke thickened, seared his lungs, and he was reminded of his mother's lessons, years ago, in this very kitchen: "This, my darling boy, is how you make a roux. This is how you begin. Like so."

Beginnings begat endings. Endings begat beginnings. Inside him, confusion swirled. His chest burned. And then, fear parted the unavailable air like the abrupt thing it was. Told him, *Get out! Go!* Panic seized his heart. He bolted through the side kitchen door into his overgrown lawn. He heard someone screaming. *He* was screaming, his voice gnashing the air as he stumbled across the yard, once his square of paradise, but now a source of consternation to the neighborhood.

"I've come to talk about your yard." The horrible woman across the street had rung his bell, ignoring his negligee with its foam bosom. "How many fairies does a man *need*?" she'd asked.

"You'd be surprised," he said. "But in this particular instance, there are seventy-four."

"You've counted?"

"Any self-respecting man knows how many fairies he shares his home with."

"At least forty-six are faceplanted," she said. "Like they've had all-night benders."

"You know those crazy fairies," said Webb.

"I don't, actually," said the neighbor. "We don't *all* live in LaLa Land."

Webb did not know what LaLa Land was, but guessed it was small and exclusive, like a hotel elevator that rode only to the penthouse suite.

"You have *bamboo*," the neighbor said, and Webb remembered planting it, Hila's rush of words as he dug into the earth. "Oh, Webster, not bamboo! A fence you can rip down if you're angry. Bamboo will remain, reminding you of your poor choice to plant it, until the day you die."

"This is Rockridge," his neighbor continued. She meant: this neighbor-hood possessed higher standards than debaucherous fairies and insidious bamboo, men dressed in the women's lingerie. Rockridge wasn't, for God's sake, West Oakland, with its couches abandoned in lawns, its discarded mattresses and refrigerators, its loitering thugs. Webb had not told her he'd lived in this neighborhood since 1933. He'd been born, squalling, inside this very house, in the back right bedroom later belonging to his daughter. This woman, cawing at him like a godforsaken crow, might consider herself the neighborhood's nouveau watchdog, but his mother had been the originating heartbeat of this community, welcoming new arrivals with her best butter-cream layer cake, inviting the wives to the neighborhood gatherings. "We meet Wednesday afternoons! Please, join us!"

Inside the chronic dim haziness that Beverly had hated in him, but Hila had forgiven, Webb paused in the street, deciding what to do. He could not tell this crow woman about the dish towel, the oil-soaked rag rug.

Moments later, he rang the bell of his neighbor to the right. He pressed his face against the door's square of polished glass and peered inside. The neighbor stood at the end of the hallway, deciding whether to answer. His face flattened against the little window; their eyes met.

"I believe I may have set my kitchen on fire," Webb said when she opened the door.

"That's a lot of conditional tense," the woman said.

Webb said, "My kitchen is on fire."

She ushered him inside, dialed 911, spoke calmly to the dispatcher. Webb admired her newfound composure. He'd seen this woman drop a carton of eggs onto the pavement while unloading groceries, had seen her cry when the bottoms of moving boxes gave out. She'd appeared incapable of grace.

Poise, Beverly had called it, not grace.

"Thank you," the neighbor said into the receiver, as casually as phoning for takeout. As if his life had not just been cracked open.

Later, she stood beside him, watching as his kitchen burned.

Flames tongued the air angrily. Neighbors accumulated, nudged. Of course, he'd set his house on fire in broad daylight. Of course, he'd been wearing his Sea Breeze Silk Step-In when he'd done it. His man parts—

for this was what Beverly called them, voice clipped with derision, when she wanted to put reflective distance between *her* and *them*—lay curled behind the lacy crotch like a rat that had died in the walls. Spreading his fingers, Webb obscured the fact of his crotch, remembering Uncle Frank from countless years ago. He told himself the firefighters were too busy fighting fire to fixate on a man's lacy crotch, but he knew. These were brawny men who probably drank lattes made with heavy whipping cream. They'd recount this story to their wives over steak still bloody: *We went to the call, and there was this man in a teddy, you know, those lacy ones I'm always asking you to wear. Guy had foam boobies.* These men would afterward have vigorous sex with their non-teddy-wearing wives, desperate to prove their masculinity. Webb watched now as they dragged hoses, shouted commands. Sweat quivered on his upper lip and behind his knees like something spilt. It collected on his broad back, and he imagined the pattern it left on the smooth silk: a makeshift butterfly with an impressive wingspan.

The neighbor stood beside him. A mass of bangle bracelets slid and clattered on her arm, suggested she wanted someone to keep tabs on her; she wanted to be noisy and not lost. Though she'd lived next door to Webb for several months, he barely knew this woman; he did not know this woman. And yet it was she who stayed with him until the fire was out, who skirted the edges of his burned house to survey the damage. It was she, for he had no one else.

"Is that your daughter?" a firefighter asked.

"Absolutely not!" said Webb, but surely this woman and Debra were close in age. She *could* have been his daughter.

The firefighter told him they'd contained the damage to the kitchen, dining room, and staircase. *No*, he could not stay there. *No*, he could not go inside for his things. (The firefighter studied the wispy sky as he said this, determined not to see Webb's lack of adequate clothing.) The neighbor, hearing this, ran to retrieve a blanket, which she draped over Webb's shoulders; it barely hit his pasty thigh, barely hid his crotch. He was not cold, but he shivered beneath the blanket covered in sunflowers. His entire life, he'd hated sunflowers' determined good cheer. Their happiness at any cost, even when a man burnt up his kitchen.

He and the neighbor studied his blackened house as if it were a museum exhibit. A memory rushed at him: taking Debra to see an art exhibition in San Francisco. This was during one of those weekends they'd been left alone while Beverly tended her sick mother. Debra had regarded the paintings the way his neighbor now looked upon the remains of his kitchen: politely, with feigned investment, her mind elsewhere. Thirty years later, he still remembered his daughter's sigh as he tugged her arm, urged her to step back.

"Here, stand here. Beside me. See how the details emerge. The people, their hats."

She didn't care, didn't yet know: some things you see best with distance.

But that was a different lifetime, the sort of thing a man either struggles to remember or to forget, depending on his mood.

WEBB, 1939

*T*hat beast," his father said throughout Webb's childhood. "That terrible beast. That remarkable conflagration of 1923."

Webb's father told the story of the Berkeley conflagration at every dinner party, despite the apathy of those who'd heard it at previous dinner parties. Webb listened from the kitchen, falling in love, every time, with the word *conflagration*, rolling it on his tongue like the suckers he bought from the Rockridge five-and-dime, swirled purple and blue and almost too large to fit inside his boy's mouth. He listened as Charlotte, always willing to help his mother, plated butter lettuce salad or arranged roasted beets onto platters. He imagined his father lording over the dining table as he spoke, the places set meticulously with the family china and silver, the crystal passed down through generations until Webb, at age thirty-seven, smashed it all against the asphalt until nothing remained save a pile of variegated shards. Hila had swept these shards into a box and then he, Webster, had formed a fist with the hand that had signed the papers. With this fist, he punched the bits of beveled glass and gilded china repeatedly.

"Good God," Hila said when he removed his blood-covered hand from the box. "Webster, that is the behavior of an asshole. Only a giant asshole would ruin such beautiful and sentimental things. People get divorced, Webster. They just *do*."

"That beast," his father began. It was Thanksgiving, 1939. The china and crystal still existed, whole, on the polished table set by his mother. "That terrible beast. The remarkable conflagration of 1923."

Uncle Frank sighed heavily. Beside him sat the fidgeting neighbors. Because it was a holiday, Webb sat at the table with the adults, hands resting neatly in his lap. That is, *presumably* it was a holiday. This, like a bruise, was a sore point. His father had already subjected the guests to his monologue regarding the ever-shifting values in *this going-to-shit, this goddamn country*. What did it mean when a man could change a national holiday whose date had been in effect since the great Abraham Lincoln declared it so? What did it mean when a president could disregard the entirety of his country's history on a whim, changing it to suit himself because the few weak-minded, whimpering jack-asses making up the National Retail Dry Goods Association wanted people to behave like ladies and *shop*? ("*Yes*," he'd narrowed his eyes at Webb. "Isn't it the truth, Webster, you'd like nothing more than to join the pretty ladies for shopping and tea.")

His father said, "That terrible day, our team was on the field, doing wind sprints for punishment because we couldn't execute a goddamn play to save our lives. That day, we fumbled on snaps, kicked the ball across the turf like a comedy routine. We were a black cloud of disaster."

Black cloud of disaster: the bad poetry of bravado. Here came a digression detailing the miraculous Cal football teams of that era. The Wonder Teams. Those glorious—magnificent!—years. "Fifty games without a defeat. Such a magical, wondrous time in the history of California football." His father waxed nostalgic: Oh, the deafening roar of the crowd. The frenzied shaking of the pompoms. The lingering glances of the girls who idolized them.

The Thanksgiving turkey Webb's mother had toiled over grew cold at the table's center. Uncle Frank interrupted, "A fifty-game undefeated streak is different than a fifty-game win streak, Genie. Shall we move on to something *actually* important and carve this bird?"

The tie against Nevada. The memory of it, the impertinence of Frank, caused Webb's father to turn his chair. He sat staring at the wall, a brooding clam drinking bourbon. This was his house. He was supposed to carve the Thanksgiving turkey, to serve it, graciously, to his guests, but when his wife offered him the carving knife, he shooed her away. Webb's mother carved the turkey herself, smiling as if it were perfectly normal for her husband to sit with his back toward the Thanksgiving guests.

"Eugene, love," she addressed his broad back when she'd finished carving. "Will you lead us in grace?"

A tenuous moment passed before Webb's father turned his chair back toward the table with a loud clattering. He blessed himself and bowed his head. Webb readied for thanks and praise and talk of daily bread.

His father sang:

Our sturdy Golden Bear
Is watching from the skies
Looks down upon our colors fair
And guards us from his lair.
Our banner Gold and Blue
The symbol on it too
Means FIGHT! for California
For California through and through!

His father sang the song in its entirety, both choruses, ending, "In the name of the Father, the Son, and the Holy Spirit." The guests blessed themselves with loose-hinged smiles. The next-door neighbor's wife flattened her hand against her mouth, suppressing her nervous laughter. Webb's father sipped his bourbon and picked up his story.

"I was struggling," his father said. "But I would have rather died on the thirty-yard line before quitting on those sprints."

"We're back to *this*?" Uncle Frank appeared more good-natured now with a plate of turkey before him.

"We all waited to see who would cave first. No one wanted to be that person, that *loser*. It was an exceptionally hot day. We'd all been denied water as a result of our disastrous practice. Just when I arrived at that pivotal juncture—when I believed I couldn't do anything more, that *I* might be the weak and pathetic bastard who quit—the campanile bells rang. We all stopped dead in our tracks, because why were the campanile bells ringing? Let me tell you, emphatically, that the ringing of the campanile bells was a godawful sound. The sound of bells has never enticed me like it does others. It's the first cousin to the sound of fingernails scratching against the chalkboard. It's the discordant sound of hell."

"Now, Genie," Uncle Frank interjected around a mouthful of meat. "That seems a bit indulgent. We're talking about *bells*."

"It's true!" Webb's mother said. "At our wedding he demanded no church bells be rung before our ceremony, or he'd leave me at the altar. I begged the priest: *please*, no bells! This man is my destiny!"

"Can you imagine?" his father said. "Having just run wind sprints without any water, the ache in your stomach nearly splitting you in half, and now the campanile bells are ringing and you're being told to gather along Hearst Avenue and fight this beast of a fire, this terrible conflagration? *You men are all we have*, they said. *This city will burn without you.* We tossed our helmets onto the field and went to fight that fire! When we'd finished, our faces looked as if they'd been dipped in tar, but we'd saved the city."

"Oh, Gene!" The neighbor's wife set down her butter knife so that she might concentrate solely on regarding Webb's father with admiration. Her husband, monosyllabic since arriving, reached for the gravy.

Uncle Frank said to the neighbor's wife, "Genie became a man that day. Next, he'll regale us with magnificent exploits about building *the bridge*. The steel was like ice, you know."

The neighbor's wife sat, rouged and confused. The next afternoon, Webb would hear his mother tell Charlotte, who came over for coffee and day-old pie, that bewilderment didn't do much for that poor woman's features.

"You didn't know?" Uncle Frank asked. "*This man* helped build the iconic Golden Gate!"

"The Golden Gate!" the neighbor's wife exclaimed.

Leaning close to her, Webb's father said, "When the fog rolled in, the steel was like ice."

"You're Californian, Genie," said Uncle Frank. "What relationship have you ever had with ice?"

"It's frozen water, Franklin. A man doesn't need to be Einstein to understand it."

For the duration of dinner, his father and Uncle Frank skirted the edges of their chronic disaccord. Finally, they arrived at the Roosevelts. Webb's father hated *those goddamn, those terrible people with their views.*

"And that hideous woman!" his father declared. "Her voice makes my skin crawl!"

Webb himself adored Eleanor's voice. It made him feel both bereft and comforted, impossibly lost but also found, a speck on the ocean, too tiny to disappoint anyone, so tiny that surely his secrets, exposed against the backdrop of great expansive sea, mattered little.

"Oh, come now." Webb's mother was setting the table for dessert: newly polished spoons and forks, fresh plates and cloth napkins. The pies had already been placed on the table. Webb had helped make all of them. Together, he and his mother had rolled the crusts, cooked the fillings. English deep-dish apple pie. Mince pie. Chocolate cream pie. Lemon meringue, pecan, pumpkin. A pie for every person, because his mother loved baking pie and he loved helping her.

His mother said, "Eleanor is such an accomplished woman!"

"Her calves are fat." His father tapped his empty glass. "I look at her and think I can never bring myself to touch another woman again."

"I'm sure every woman is thanking her lucky stars for that," Uncle Frank said. "Have you even seen her calves?"

"I've seen her face. It resembles a foundation that hasn't settled properly."

The neighbor's wife laughed. Or, as Hila would later say about the laughter of women she despised, the neighbor's wife *guffawed*. "Harhar!" She threw back her head as if riding a carnival ride, this guffaw dissolving into a fit of coughing. Her husband shoved a glass of water at her. She drank, and Webb noticed a smear of lipstick on the woman's front tooth. He knew his mother, observer of every minuscule thing, had also seen this lipstick. She smiled and pretended she hadn't, and Webb understood his mother didn't like the neighbor's wife.

"Gene, you're awful!" the neighbor's wife exclaimed, and her husband, noticing the smear, caught her eye and tapped his own tooth.

Uncle Frank excused himself. Throwing down his napkin, he disappeared down the hall. Webb's mother refolded her brother's napkin. ("Corner to corner," she had instructed Webb. "Careful. You don't want your germs on the guest's napkin.")

"Edna." The neighbor's wife, having picked up on her husband's signal, spoke with a half-closed mouth.

"Della," said Webb's mother.

"You've outdone yourself."

"It's a pleasure having you," his mother said. "You've outdone yourself so frequently on our behalf."

The table fell silent as everyone wrestled with the inaccuracy of this statement.

"Webster," his father said. "Stop fidgeting."

(He'd been sitting perfectly still.)

Uncle Frank remained in the bathroom for quite some time. Webb didn't blame him: the bathroom, safe and contained, smelled of lilac and possessed clean towels that beheld no animosity. Webb's father huffed. Here were the pies, beautiful, with their golden crusts and deftly woven lattices. Here was his coffee growing cool with anticipation. The room, heavy with silence, resonated with the *tick tick tick* of the grandfather clock.

"Where the hell is Franklin?" Webb's father asked. "Keeping a man waiting inside his own home!"

"He'll be here in a moment, love."

"The pies are impatient!" his father declared, and the neighbor's wife tittered over the concept. Her husband sat beside her like a miserable raisin. Webb's mother placed a fresh coffee before his father.

"Pumpkin," Webb's father demanded.

"Franklin's our guest, love. We need to wait."

Webb's father shoved away from the table. His napkin fell to the floor, and he stalked into the hallway. Webb's mother stood. For a moment, Webb believed she would follow his father, but she only folded his napkin neatly, placing it on his clean dessert plate. She ignored Uncle Frank's surprised yelp.

For years afterward—an entire lifetime!—Webb wished that Uncle Frank had locked the bathroom door. Their family history might have been utterly different. Webb, in his short existence, had seen his father break down doors. In this case, his father didn't have to break down anything. Moments later, Uncle Frank stood in the threshold of the dining room, pants gathered around his ankles, his shirttail barely covering his man parts. Webb's father's hand clamped Uncle Frank's neck like a vise. He announced, "Frank is leaving! Everyone, say *Goodnight, Frank!*"

They sat, stupefied. Webb would later wonder how they had arrived at this convoluted moment. Mere seconds ago there had been talk of pie. Now Uncle Frank cowered before them, trying to obscure their view of his genitalia with his hands.

"I said, say *Goodnight, Frank.*"

Their response was a broken chorus of tin-sounding words, cans trailing a newlywed car.

"That won't do!" Webb's father said. "That was only lackluster!"

"Goodnight, Frank," they said, this time like zombies.

"Say it like you mean it. Frank is *leaving*."

"*Goodnight, Frank!*"

His father forced Uncle Frank, tripping on his bunched trousers, back down the hall. Uncle Frank's pale buttocks mooned them. They heard his protestations as the front door opened and closed. Moments later, Webb's father returned with the look of someone who'd handled malodorous garbage. He rattled his plate.

"Della, is there something you'd like in particular?" His mother's voice betrayed nothing. "Webster?" She touched his cheek, communicating, in this touching, that everything would be okay. "Edward, what about you?" she asked as the front bell rang. "Excuse me." She turned toward the door. Webb's father ensnared her wrist, his hand circling it like a bracelet he'd never given her.

"It's Franklin," his mother said. "At the door."

"*Of course* it's Franklin," his father said.

"Well, let's ask him inside. It's Thanksgiving. Let's just have some pie together."

"We'll have pie," said Webb's father. "But without Franklin."

"Love."

"Ever since I've known him, he's goaded me. If I had a tail, Franklin would cut it off for fun."

"Genie," Webb's mother said, "surely we can ignore the past for today."

"Do I seem the sort of man to ignore the past?"

He certainly did not seem the sort of man to ignore the past; everyone stared at their plates devoid of pie, contemplating this.

"All we *have* is the past," he said loudly.

"Right now, here, is the present." The neighbor managed these pea-sized words.

Webb's father stared at the neighbor as if, inflicted with leprosy, he'd begged for alms. "The only thing we can be sure of," he said. "The only thing there's any certitude of, is the past. And in the very recent past I told Franklin, with certitude, that I never wanted to see him again in the present."

Seconds passed in silence. Again, the bell rang.

"Did he think I was bluffing?"

Webb's father disappeared. A sigh of relief pressed through someone's teeth. He returned, grasping the sleek wooden handle of his .38 revolver.

"*Gene*," the neighbor said, his voice a pinprick.

"*Edward*," said Webb's father.

"This isn't the Wild West. Let's be reasonable."

Webb's father said, "I've always been most proud of my excessive reason."

Nodding, he went down the hallway. Again, the sound of the front door opening and closing. The grandfather clock registered time's passage: *tick tick tick*. Between the ticks, an indiscernible argument, muffled, like tears into a pillow.

"Edward," said Webb's mother, "would you like more coffee?"

A shot rang out. No one moved. Not even as the neighborhood dogs abandoned themselves to barking. A car could be heard, speeding away. Moments later, Webb's father entered the dining room.

"I've worked up quite the thirst," he announced. "Who else needs a beverage?"

"Actually." The neighbor's voice quivered. "I forgot. We must. We have an engagement."

"An *engagement*?" Webb's father said.

"Yes. We, Della." The neighbor paused, and his wife chimed in, "We need lemons."

Webb's father waved the gun dismissively. "There's a tree in the yard. Take whatever you need."

The neighbor adopted a new tactic. "We promised friends we'd stop by."

"Friends!"

"Yes, our good friends."

"*Your* good friends?"

"Yes."

"But you have no friends! That's why you're always over here. You're like the barnacles on a boat's bottom, clinging to us." He pointed the gun at the neighbor. "Pow!" he said, before pointing the gun at the neighbor's wife. "Pow, pow!"

Her sudden sobs only irritated him further.

"Dear girl," Webb's father said. "Your emotions are really working my last nerve. Now shut up and let's have some pie."

"*No*," said Hila when Webb told her this story. "Tell me you did *not* eat pie."

But yes, they'd eaten pie served on the china that Webb later flung onto the asphalt after signing his marriage away. They ate pie, staring intently at the plates as they chewed, finding comfort in those pretty blue flowers, those gilded silver edges. Thirty years later, Webb smashed those plates to bits, crying over the dissolution of things not meant to dissolve. He punched their broken pieces, and Hila wrapped his bloodied hand in a towel. She salved his wounds, dabbed his tears.

He told her the rest later. Cool tangle of skin and sheets. The sharp pronouncement of her clavicle demanding to be touched. Her lips, whose texture was a story in Braille as he drew his finger across them. Vibrato of fan, for Hila loved fans, their incessant thrum lulling her as she lay awake. Like that man of war, Napoleon, Hila did not sleep, though she planned menus rather than covert military operations. There was nothing covert about Hila. She looked you dead on and said what she thought. Talking of pie while staring at Hila's aghast mouth, he realized he'd never told Beverly this story. He and Beverly had brought a child into the world. They'd been man and wife, and still he'd erased this day from his life's history. He'd taken vows with her as though he were a happy man, not damaged but instead whole, like the perfect sun warming an afternoon. Tangled amid the cool sheets, his omission seemed damning.

"What kind did *you* eat, Webster Eugene Jackson?" Hila asked, having worked through her surprise. "What pie did *you* choose beneath the barrel of a madman's gun?"

Hila loved quotidian details others shrugged at. Obsessed with French history, she read books upon books about Versailles. She cared less about political maneuverings and intrigues. She wanted to know: how did the household run? What did Marie Antoinette eat (hot chocolate and plain chicken with broth) and who served it and where were the kitchens and how was the food transported by these people from these kitchens to the great dining halls? *Courtesans*, she'd sigh, and then tell him of the filthy creatures who crapped in the halls. Behind pillars, she said, on those black and white tiles you see gleaming in the pictures, a man would crap and pull his pants up, and with crap still smeared in the crack of his ass, he'd get right back to courting. Several times, walking outside, Marie Antoinette was doused with the contents of someone's chamber pot tossed out a window.

But now Hila was asking what pie he ate. Did he remember?

"I remember everything," said Webb. "Unfortunately. Always."

She touched her hand to the place his heart lived. He longed in that moment to palm her own heart like a ripe and tropical fruit, something a man still craved even as it filled his mouth.

"Pumpkin," said Webb.

"*Pumpkin*," said Hila.

"My mother's recipe."

"Ah, yes," Hila said. "I don't usually care for pumpkin pie, but that recipe bespeaks fall without banging you over the head with it. Certainly," said Hila, "it's the pie *I* would choose if a madman were pointing the barrel of a gun at me on a day designated for gratitude. There is positively no other pie I'd want."

He felt her beckoning finger against his hip, his thigh.

Afterward, he listened to the steady *beat beat beat* of her heart, memorized it like the lines of a poem, committed it to his perfect memory.

Webb's mother never told her version of the 1923 conflagration at dinner parties. Only once did she tell Webb. He was seven and hovering beside her as she made pineapple upside-down cake, his favorite, for a treat. It was 1940. Wartime rationing had not begun. There was as much sugar as a woman desired. There were eggs, butter, meat. A woman need not shorten her hemlines. She did not (yet) have to paint seams down her calves to replicate the stitching on a pair of nylons. Her sleeves could possess a cuff and pandemonium would not ensue.

"My mother had always been a histrionic woman," his mother said, creaming butter. "As the fire came closer, she walked room to room, crying, while others moved the valuables outside. We carried her favorite hats to the yard, and the hat boxes were large enough to sit on."

Her father and brother Frank struggled with the antique dressers and chairs, the velveteen love seat from the parlor. They dragged these things onto the front lawn, ruining the precious sod, while Webb's mother and her sister sat on the elegant dining chairs eating sugar cookies. They tilted their chins at the approaching smoke, identifying patterns and pictures inside it as if it were a cloud, Frances singing in her silken voice,

Yes, we have no bananas
We have no bananas today
We've string beans, and onions
Cabbageses, and scallions
And all sorts of fruit and say
We have an old fashioned to-mah-to
A Long Island po-tah-to
But yes, we have no bananas
We have no bananas today

The song was typically sung up-tempo, but Frances slowed it to a sultry dirge, lengthening the words like taffy while she stared dreamily at the darkening sky. "*Yes, we have no bananas,*" Webb's mother sang to him as she poured the batter into baking tins. "It remains one of my finest memories of my sister. I still hear her lingering on the phrase *old fashioned to-mah-to.* How I loved that expression! Her voice was like the crystal we carried outside, clear as day. In high school, you know, she sang in the choir."

Neighbors dragged their children down the street by the elbows, struggled with family portraits and landscapes, family heirlooms, things worth saving. Dogs loped beside them. The dogs' and the people's eyes were glazed red from the smoke. They walked, coughing. The sky crackled. Trees burst spontaneously into flame. Strewn across the ground were countless dropped and forgotten things: fur slippers, an iron skillet, a baby's silken bassinet.

"A man carried an urn beneath his arm. Much later I heard of someone dragging a piano from a house—a piano!—and a girl sat and played it while everything around her burned. Afterward, people baked potatoes over the glowing embers. What uncanny behavior! People lose themselves when disaster occurs. They lose their heads." Webb knew his mother thought of Frances, of whom she rarely spoke, and when she did it was only to say, "She had a bout. But didn't come through."

Cake in the oven, his mother stared thoughtfully out the kitchen window. Later, Webb's wife would stare though this same window. "My father struck my mother that day. He was typically a docile man—*too* docile, some might say—but tensions ran high, and when she wouldn't stop crying and moaning and carrying on, he pulled her aside to what he mistakenly believed was a private place. He slapped her right cheek. She still cried, and so he turned her head and slapped the left check. He slapped her into silence. It isn't right, of course, for children to see their father hit their mother. That's something that stays with a child. But it had to be done. Afterward, she sat peaceably on the lawn, the red marks from our father's hand on her face. She didn't make another peep until after the house burned down. And then, oh, lord. How she wailed! You would have thought she was the only one who lost her home that day, but six hundred homes burnt to the ground. Fifteen hundred people, displaced. We spent that first night huddled on cots in a makeshift sanctuary. The sheets smelled heavily of bleach, and I pressed my nose into them, inhaling to avoid the scent of smoke. To this day, that smell makes me weep. The smell, the sound. Unless you've experienced it, you cannot imagine the din fire makes. It's the sound of the sky cracking open, like a Christmas nut. Oh, Webster, that you never experience such a thing."

COLLEEN, 2001

*H*er neighbor came to her door with a polite knock, as if he wanted to borrow baking soda or cooking oil, something easily lent. If he hadn't pressed his face against the door's window, she wouldn't have answered. Their eyes met; she answered. Colleen had endured twelve years of Catholic school: the constantly slipping knee socks and shifting plaid skirts, the communion wafers that tasted of paper on her tongue. Having been reprimanded by stern nuns for slight transgressions, she was scrupulously honest, rule-following. "But the sign says no left turns between four and six!" she would tell her husband, who lacked her commitment to dictums. "But the menu says no substitutions!" Guilt manifested inside her, as dense as a nodule. *That word.* Nodules were now inextricably woven with lies, indistinguishable from one another, like the seeds the young man had confused before he died inside a school bus in the Alaskan wilderness. He'd studied the seeds, read up. No matter.

When she opened the door, the neighbor stood before her, large and barefoot, wearing a silken teddy. A foam bosom strained the lacy neckline.

"I believe I may have set my kitchen on fire," he said.

Such a weird entanglement of language: had he or hadn't he?

He had.

In her own kitchen, Colleen dialed 911, speaking in the level voice of a woman who'd once been married to a police officer who became a detective, a woman taught to keep extra running shoes in the car's trunk in case of earthquake or apocalypse, who'd been taught (despite her acute disinterest) to shoot a bullet squarely at an intruder's chest.

The firefighters arrived in the calamitous way of firefighters. Busy connecting of hoses. Guttural commands, broad gesticulations. Colleen stood beside the neighbor. From the sidewalk, they watched his house burn. They felt the heat in swells, like they'd wandered too near a campfire, then wandered away. Their shoulders accidentally touched, touched again.

And then it was over. Smoke hung thickly in the air. The neighbor betrayed no emotion as the firefighters explained his home was off limits. Since their arrival, he had been covering his crotch with his hands. Colleen ran to get a blanket. Sunflowers: obnoxious. The only thing she had. She'd left most of her things—their things—behind in LA. The firemen left; the gathered people dispersed. In the newfound silence, the neighbor sat in Colleen's living room while she made tea, searched the yellow pages. This man could not stay with *her*. Over earl grey she told him she'd found a room at the Extended Stay America.

"With kitchenette," she said, feigning brightness.

They drove in silence, and as Colleen pulled into the parking lot, the man hunched over, making himself small. She remembered that time at the cafe in Brentwood. A couple had tied their dog to a post but allowed too much lead. The dog had stepped into the road and been hit by a car. The impact hadn't killed him, but he had lain on the road, curling in on himself. His owners ran to him, knelt. The woman, inexplicably, still held her latte. Colleen had never forgotten the incident. Years later, she still imagined the terrible guilt the owners must have felt. It was an easy mistake to make, but one that couldn't be undone simply, or at all. It took a mere moment to ruin a thing; it took days, weeks, months, an entire lifetime to repair it—and if not to repair it, to diminish its terrible accompanying emotions.

Colleen reached through space and touched the man's knee. She found it smoother than her own, meticulously devoid of hair, akin to her knee at age fourteen, when she'd been excited to draw a razor over its awkward curves. The man jerked away.

She understood: at their best, some things were only manageable.

When Colleen had moved in, the woman across the street informed her the neighbors to her right were fine. The neighbor on the left was, obviously, another story.

"I'm not sure what you mean," said Colleen.

For one, the woman said, he wore women's lingerie as bold as you please, rolling out the garbage bins in clothing too trashy for Victoria's Secret, things prostitutes wouldn't deign to wear. Second, his yard was an abomination, covered with dandelions he couldn't be bothered to mow. He'd made some bad decisions regarding vines. He'd planted *bamboo;* surely Colleen knew how insidious bamboo was.

Colleen did not know how insidious bamboo was.

"Peek inside his yard and see for yourself," the woman said. "Bamboo and ivy and morning glory and all the damn fairies."

"Fairies?"

Yes, *fairies*. Not gnomes. At first she thought he had a granddaughter, a little girl, but no, he lived alone. A grown man obsessed with *fairies*. Once, she'd looked over his fence and counted twenty. They were pretty enough, the woman supposed, with their wings, their bright smiles, but when his morning glory threatened to overtake the neighborhood, she'd gone to talk to him. She told him his yard was a blight. His house needed repainting. People could scarcely sell their homes at full value with his occupying space on the street. *Please*, she said. *Tend your affairs!*

Yes, he said. *Of course.*

She'd felt better about the situation, but that afternoon, she saw him in his front yard, wearing flowered pajamas, bending over the grass with a ruler and a pair of scissors. He made a great show of measuring the blades of grass to two inches and snipping them to an exact height.

"Can you believe that?" the woman asked Colleen. "Cutting the lawn with a pair of scissors!"

"I can't," said Colleen.

She was renting the house next door to this man's—a house in Oakland, miles away from her former life in Los Angeles—because her husband had conducted an affair with a young woman. He'd told this young woman that she, Colleen, who had her entire life possessed effervescent good health, was dying of cancer. He'd told her, his lover—Colleen hated the word *lover*, as she hated the words *panties* and *moist*, as she hated the words *noodle* and *chunk*—that she had a nodule. This nodule had metastasized. His wife was riddled with cancer, in the exact way a target was riddled with bullet holes at his shooting range. His wife had cancer in her lungs. In her bones and kidneys. Their marriage was not a happy one, he'd said. He stayed because he'd taken vows to love and protect his wife, *'til death do us part*, and because his wife needed his excellent healthcare. He was living in their guest house and went to the main house only when his wife felt ill after chemo. Then, as an act of kindness, he tucked her hair back when she vomited into the plastic tub.

Of course, Colleen and her husband didn't have a guest house. They were a childless couple with no need for extra space. The young woman lived in San Francisco; Colleen's husband had at least known to keep physical distance between them. She imagined him laughing heartily with the men at the station, declaring, Oh, *no*! He didn't shit where he ate! Surely there had been others, but this one was a coltish blonde. Colleen met her only because the young woman, visiting Los Angeles for a bachelorette, had brought the gaggle of revelers, drunk off cosmopolitans, to the house on a reconnaissance mission. Colleen thought, *This* was what girls did nowadays at bachelorettes? At her own, she and her friends had downed slippery nipples and fuzzy navels. They heckled the male strippers and shouted *yeah, yeah!* in time to their pelvic thrusts, the way self-respecting girls did at bachelorettes in the '80s. Colleen had suspected, even then, beneath the strobe lights, that she should not marry this person. Her doubt had seemed a normal part of the process.

Finding no guest house, this woman and her friends had trampled Colleen's flower beds, her dahlias and ranunculus. John was working the night shift, so Colleen had taken an Epsom salt bath. She'd just donned her freshly laundered bathrobe, started water for chamomile tea. She planned to read, as a treat, the newest issue of *People*. Carb cutting! Was Jennifer Aniston's new diet plan safe? Colleen heard a screech, muffled laughter. Someone saying, *Shhhhhh*. Going to the front window, she pulled the curtains aside. At least five barelegged women stampeded over her lawn in high heels. They wore, all of them, glinting tiaras and excessive sequins. Colleen watched with a vague sense of amusement—*ah, youth*—until one of the women tried to pull Colleen's camellia from the ground. The young woman struggled, landed on her ass, got up and struggled some more. Finally, she held up a branch of the shrub triumphantly before throwing it onto the grass with disgust, as if it were not a plant but the severed horse head in *The Godfather*.

"Excuse me!" Colleen stood in the front doorway. Because they didn't hear her, she advanced down the front walk. She'd forgotten she wore her bathrobe. At some point, she'd become the sort of woman who forgets she's wearing a bathrobe.

A blonde in a dress that could easily have been confused for a shirt—Colleen realized a young woman's dress is an older woman's shirt—paused. "*You're* the sick wife!" She spoke in the tone Colleen should have used to accuse them all of trespassing, of floral destruction. Later, the phrase *the sick wife* would pierce Colleen the most. Standing in the bathroom she shared with her adulterous husband, she would press her face in countless directions before the mirror, searching for telltale signs of illness.

Colleen said, "I don't know what you're talking about."

"The cancer." The girl repositioned her tiara.

"You've confused me for someone else," said Colleen.

Her friends surrounded her protectively, like greasers surrounding the single greaser who'd started a fight. "Stage four. It's metastasized in your lungs. You're dying. He told me."

Instinctively, Colleen touched the place where her lungs lived. "*Who?*"

"John."

Though a strange weight had settled, not in her chest, but in her stomach, Colleen invited them in, this coterie of would-be showgirls, shoulders dusted with glitter, lips hot pink. Their dresses seemed no more than wrinkled handkerchiefs, insubstantial, but the tiaras remained affixed to their heads, unmoving. *Future Mrs!* declared a satin sash slung around one girl's torso. Colleen brewed strong coffee, set out brownies. She spoke as if conducting a job interview. "*How* do you know John?"

The blonde, like all young women who believed themselves in love, talked readily, wanting her story—she believed it a love story—to be heard. The others collected around her, though clearly they'd heard countless iterations of this tale. The woman and John had met in a bar in Palm Springs. He'd intervened when a different man wouldn't leave her alone; it seemed the blonde possessed myriad suitors. She and John had been seeing each other for two years. (Two years!) They'd taken trips to Napa, to Mendocino. Had dinners in San Francisco. Gone to baseball games. They'd even—Colleen's heart stalled, like a plane's faulty motor—traveled together to New York City, a place Colleen yearned to visit.

"You knew he was married," said Colleen.

"I knew you were dying."

"I'm really not."

"He stayed with you because he wanted you to have the best care imaginable!"

The woman took a brownie from the platter on the table. Colleen had become a woman who served dessert to her husband's lover.

"He said we'd get married after you died."

Inside Colleen, impatience swirled. "It wasn't odd to you that I never did? I mean, shouldn't I have succumbed pretty quickly to this terrible cancer? But here I am, well enough to serve you brownies."

"He wanted us to be together, make a family."

"And you believed him?" Colleen tamped back her agitation. She herself had never questioned him. Had taken, at face value, those work dinners, those work trips.

"Of course I did! He loves me! He wants children, but you said no."

Colleen stood shakily and called a cab. There was no point in more talk. This woman wouldn't understand the loss of something fiercely desired, but again and again denied. This brownie-eating girl—yes, she was a *girl*—had years of fertility, pink and blossoming, ahead. Her eggs remained inside her, ready and waiting, like candy inside a dispenser. Colleen ushered the girls outside. The blonde still held Colleen's coffee mug. Fine, she could have it. Waiting for the cab's arrival, Colleen asked, "How did you know where we live?"

She knew, the girl said, because she had followed Colleen's husband home from work the day before.

"You trailed a detective to his house?" Colleen asked. "That was stupid."

She knew then that her husband had gotten bored with this girl, had wanted to be caught. He'd let her discover what she needed to discover so he would not have to tell her there was no guest house, no sick wife. Colleen realized that she, too, was part of the plan. She, too, was meant to know the truth. He'd let the girl do his dirty work. Colleen understood her husband no longer wanted to be married.

"For two years," the girl said, "you noticed nothing. Who's stupid?"

The cab pulled up, and Colleen watched as the five of them struggled into the sedan. "Goodbye," she said.

The man's name was Webster Eugene Jackson. At the Extended Stay America, Colleen spoke to the desk clerk on his behalf. She ushered him through the convoluted hallways to his temporary apartment. It was obvious that he was simply too *large* for the Extended Stay America. Not metaphorically, like men who frequented the Ritz-Carlton, with their Rolexes and silken ties, but actually. Physically. Colleen waited in the kitchen while he examined the other rooms. She opened cabinets, peered inside. They'd been constructed cheaply and quickly, like shanty towns. In one cabinet was plastic drinkware. The pots and frying pans were as thin as a child's play set. The Extended Stay America was only a rough approximation of home. The lightweight facsimile of home.

Colleen was relieved to leave, to shed responsibility for this man she barely knew. Driving away, she felt buoyant. Webster Jackson was not her problem; why had she thought he was? But the next morning, the scent of smoke still hung in the air. She sat drinking her coffee while another day stretched before her and stared out her kitchen window. She'd left LA with no plan, no prospects, choosing Oakland because it was both far and near. Upon arriving, a lethargy had overcome her. She read, watched tv, fed herself. She rarely left her sparsely furnished rental. Now, as she noted the caution tape surrounding the house next door, the burned-out hole where the kitchen had been, Catholic guilt quivered inside her. Webster Jackson lacked access to his clothing. He had no family, no food. He had nothing save a loveseat which could barely support him, a shower so tiny Ken and Barbie couldn't have coupled inside it. He had the teddy he wore, the sunflower blanket she'd given him. Remembering the sidelong glances of the hotel patrons as he stood like a streetwalker in the lobby, she reached for her purse. What else did she have to do—besides wait, patiently, for tomorrow and hope that it felt different than today?

Colleen drove to the Long's Drugs on 51st Street. There, she bought stiff blue jeans and boxy t-shirts, white tube socks. Plain underwear. Orthopedic-looking athletic shoes. She guessed at the sizes, just as she guessed at what food he'd want for his cupboards. Ramen noodles. Cans of condensed soup. Chef Boyardee. In shopping for a lonely man, it occurred to her that she, too, was lonely.

He opened the door still wearing the foam-green teddy. She unloaded her gifts onto the kitchen counter.

"This is wonderful," he said. "Thank you."

At the tiny formica dining table, they drank weak coffee made in the kitchen's shuddering coffee maker. She asked if there was someone she could call? A family member? A sister or brother? A son or daughter? A friend?

"I have none of those things," he said.

On her third visit, she brought chocolate croissants from the bakery in their neighborhood. She brought coffees so they wouldn't have to drink the wretched stuff from the coffee maker.

Wearing his stiff new denim and flannel like a woman laced into a corset, he reminded Colleen of herself, a child at Easter, constricted by dresses her mother insisted she squeeze into. He said, abruptly, "I have a daughter."

"A daughter!"

"We haven't spoken in thirty-one years," he said. "Not since she was twelve. I wouldn't know how to contact her. And anyway, she shouldn't be involved in this."

Webster Jackson had a daughter. Colleen had not spoken to John since her arrival in Oakland. She dialed his number, hung up. Dialed it a second time. On the third try, she let it ring.

"No," he said when she asked.

"Remember your affair? And how the girl and her tiara-wearing friends came to our home and ripped my plants out of the ground?"

"Fuck, Colleen."

"It's just a phone number," she said. "An address."

Webster Eugene Jackson's ex-wife was now Beverly Murdoch, currently living in Los Angeles. His daughter was Debra Johnson, once Debra Jackson, formerly Debra Murdoch. She lived in Santa Monica on a lush street that Colleen knew. She and her husband had once attended a dinner party in the neighborhood, had admired the homes. "We should live here," her husband had said, and Colleen nodded yes, but felt the truth pinching inside her. Even then, she'd known their relationship would not survive long enough for change.

Colleen called the number. A machine picked up, and a woman's lilting voice said, "The Johnson family is not currently in. Please leave a message." Colleen left a message: she was calling for Debra Johnson on behalf of her father, Webster Eugene Jackson. Would she please call back? Thank you. Colleen hung up, hopeful. When a week passed and she'd heard nothing from Debra Johnson, Colleen called a second time, thinking the woman hadn't received the message. She called a third and a fourth time. Groveling in the face of defeat was a specialty of hers. Colleen left a fifth message. In the middle of this fifth message, it sounded as if someone picked up the phone.

"Hello?" Colleen said. "*Hello?*" The response was a click and then a dial tone. Calling back, she got a busy signal. Debra Johnson had taken the phone off the hook.

Lies, her husband had told her in defense of himself, were spontaneous. They simply occurred, much like a natural disaster, and the aftermath was unwieldy, inextricable. At the time, she'd been scornful. She was not, and had never been, a liar.

Colleen told the first serious lie of her life to Webster Eugene Jackson. It occurred without warning, like lightning forking through a desert sky. Spontaneous, just like her husband said.

"I found your daughter," she said. This, of course, was not a lie. His face creased with emotion at the news.

She could have stuck to the truth: I found her, yes, but she refused to speak to me. Instead, she quaked at his expression of raw exposure.

Debra was polite, Colleen found herself saying, but guarded. She wasn't ready for a reconciliation, but in time, if he proved he was doing well, that his life was in order, she'd consider it.

"If I prove my life is in order," he repeated.

"She mentioned a caretaker," said Colleen.

"A *caretaker?*"

"Someone who can stay with you, ensure you're doing well."

"I *know* what a caretaker is. Why would she think I need such a thing?"

"I told her about the fire."

"That was an accident!"

"I'm sorry," said Colleen. "She won't consider seeing you otherwise."

"What about *her*?" he asked. "How is she? How did she sound?"

"It isn't like we had a heart to heart," she said. The gravity of her deception hardened inside her. Lying, her husband had not told her, obscured all other things.

DEBRA, 2001

My husband had obtained, for my birthday, tickets to see the Dodgers play the hated Giants. The game had an evening start time. We'd miss dinner but see the sunset, the dusky California air announcing to us the arrival of spring. Spring! The beginning of things. An origin story, whatever that was.

"Nice," I said, without thinking it so. He patted my shoulder like he might a dog.

We took few family excursions, so I felt the weight of making this one right with countless superficial details meant to lure us into a sense of fun: footlong hotdogs, soda in sweating plastic cups. Peanuts and Cracker Jacks because the song declared we should have them. Anything Jamie wanted, anything to make this a moment in his childhood that he'd remember with warm nostalgia. He slid into his seat without even the hint of a smile. He'd brought his portable CD player along; he closed his eyes, kept beat to music only he heard. He hated being here, his hatred nothing a churro could solve. He'd played three uncomfortable years of Little League, stepping up to the plate as though it were a ship's plank. He'd never hit a single ball, hadn't even lobbed one foul. He swung his bat like a drunk flailing at a piñata.

"Your son sucks," a woman told the nape of my neck during one of Jamie's at-bats. He was seven, maybe eight. Boos from the parents of his own teammates swelled from the bleachers. From the parents of the opposing players rose a scattered applause.

"Are you kidding me?" I wanted to ask but didn't, and felt for weeks like I'd failed him. I'd carried this boy, my son, inside my womb. I'd acknowledged his perpetual restlessness inside it, and when he finally existed in the world, I gave up on him.

Though my husband insisted his son play baseball, he never attended Jamie's games. In the overbearing Santa Monica sun, in the ever-rising dust of whatever neighborhood diamond Jamie struck out on, I felt relieved my husband was a hypocrite. I'd known, when we married, that I had taken vows with a man who'd name his son after himself, a man who'd be incapable of containing his disappointment over the birth of a daughter. (Regarding lineage, what use was a daughter?) I could have guessed he'd be a man who didn't let his son win at anything. Not checkers, not chess, not air hockey. Not Monopoly, not the game of Life, literally or metaphorically. These wins that were inconsequential to my husband might have built Jamie's confidence.

I'd wanted to name him David, the fifth most popular boy's name in 1989, the year of his birth. A name that translated from Hebrew as *dearly loved*. But James the father preferred tradition, wanted James Thomas the Fourth, a doppelgänger. In the sleepless nights before my son's birth, I paged through the baby name book and saw that James was Hebrew for *supplanter* and English for *replace*. Thomas was Hebrew for *twin*, but it was obvious long before Jamie stepped up to the plate in an ill-fitting uniform that we'd either chosen the wrong name or deeply valued irony.

At the Dodgers game, my husband stared with venom at Barry Bonds the way girls stared at other, hated girls in the high school cafeteria, with that imperfect glowering that mattered little to the person being stared at and everything to the person staring. Peanut shells accumulated at our feet. The scent of spilled beer permeated the air. My husband inundated us with statistics: Chan Ho Park finished the 2000 season with three consecutive starts and no runs allowed. He'd gone 18–10, had a 3.27 ERA. My husband had not forgotten, however, that in 1999, the man had allowed two grand slams to the same player in the same inning, a certain Fernando Tatis of the St. Louis Cardinals.

"That guy," my husband said, pointing him out. He confiscated Jamie's CD player, handed him a baseball mitt. My husband believed that boys hungered for mitts, hungered to catch balls. Jamie hungered for nothing except to be left alone. He touched the mitt as if it had been formed from excrement. In the setting sun, he appeared mealy and pale, like strewn bait. When, in the bottom of the third, Mark Grudzielanek hit a home run, and

Shawn Green followed shortly with another, Jamie refused high-fiving the revelers in celebration.

In the top of the fourth, Russ Davis hurled a foul ball high above our section.

"Jamie, you've got this," my husband said as the ball began its downward arc, white against the darkening sky, picking up velocity as it traveled toward us.

My son pressed his hands against his legs. The ball nailed his right eye with an audible crack. The people surrounding us gasped collectively, but when the ball bounced and rolled left, they descended on it like lions upon a starved gazelle.

"Are you all right?" a man, a perfect stranger, asked my son while my husband watched the man who'd retrieved the ball coddle it like a baby bird. Jamie stared stoically at the sky. The bruise above his eye had not yet bloomed, but would. While I touched the area tentatively, checking for damage, security arrived. They'd pinpointed our whereabouts and now stood at the end of the aisle, waiting to escort us to the infirmary.

"Are you coming?" I asked my husband, who yanked on his fanny pack. The act appeared to soothe him, like the curious rituals of the batters inside the batter's box. Eyes directed at the field, he shook his head.

The infirmary was sterile and depressing, my kind of place. Jamie's, too, sunless and cool like a defective womb. Here, the ballpark losers festered. People who had fallen down drunk, eaten spoilt hotdogs, forgotten to drink water. Inside the room's stark sterility, the crowd noise was muffled, the stadium music muted.

A nurse tended my son like Alice Waters handling a young lettuce. She pressed a cold compress to his eye and poured us paper cups of water that tasted of paper cups. Soon, she closed a curtain around us, and we sat for a long time on a hard cot not speaking, instead listening to the distanced sounds of the stadium and the immediate, echoing sounds of the infirmary. A welt had formed above Jamie's eye, and inside this welt could be seen the stitching of the baseball where it had hit him. He touched these marks as a blind man would. I thought: he is not a happy child. I'd suspected this his entire life. Inside the Dodgers' infirmary, I knew it.

We stayed until the nurse, grown impatient with our silent misery, ousted us to make way for a woman who clutched her thumb, dripped blood on the white tile. I realized there had not been a single man in the infirmary and wondered if Jamie had noticed it, too.

"Be safe out there!" The nurse spoke cheerfully, as if to diminish the fact that she was kicking us out.

We should have left with our despondent son, but we stayed to the bitter end. The last pitch, the final out. We stayed even though the Giants were down six runs by the seventh inning. Their players exited the field wearily, reeking of a dejection that endeared them to me. I waved goodbye.

"They're not embarking on a cruise," my husband said. To Jamie he said, "Next time maybe *catch* the ball."

My mother had organized my birthday celebration: dinner at the country club the following night, Sunday. "Nothing fancy," I told her. "Of course not," she said. "Just the five of us." I believed her, until the maître d' escorted us to the private dining room. Twenty people I had no inclination to be near on an ordinary day, let alone a day celebrating myself, shouted out, "*Surprise!*"

The menus declared we'd be eating six courses, including lobster tail and filet mignon. There would be mixed lettuces served with goat's cheese, charcuterie: cured meat and loaves of meat and whipped meat made from parts of animals my mother didn't eat but understood lent a party respectability. My mother had an affinity for sorbet palate cleansers. Tonight's menu featured two. In the corner of the room loomed my birthday cake, a four-tiered monstrosity adorned with cascading fondant lilies. This party would drag on until my next birthday. In crumpled brown linen, I was the most underdressed guest.

"You look like a potato," my mother said. "Or like the woman who lived in the shoe."

"Mother, you agreed. Nothing special."

"What? These are your closest friends."

"Right," I said. "Speaking of potatoes, Jamie is trying to become a vegetarian. Is there something we can get him, a vegetable plate of some sort?"

"There's mashed potatoes with the filet. And, you know, the garnishes are vegetables."

"Something more substantial," I said.

Someone interrupted to snap our photo. We smiled dutifully.

"Lobsters are extremely pain sensitive," Jamie said at dinner as I passed him my decorative radishes and carrots. "More so than even us."

"Is that so?" A man directly across the table pierced his lobster tail with the tiny fork, emulating the presumably high-pitched squeal of a lobster as he did so. Everyone dissolved into laughter just as I placed him: an acquaintance of my husband from the club, a man he stayed late drinking manhattans with, a man to whom I'd never uttered more than a passing *hello*.

"Here, son." The man gathered his own decorative radishes and carrots on a bread plate, which he passed across the table. Soon others were passing their decorative radishes and carrots to Jamie, laughing as he collected bread plates in a stack.

"I see you have baseball stitching on your face, son," the man said.

"You just called me *son*," Jamie said. "Twice."

"It's a term of endearment."

"I don't even know you." Jamie stared at him with a bored gaze I admired. "There's no endearment."

After dinner were toasts. My mother told the story of my birth at Cedars Sinai Hospital, a story whose only thimble of truth was yes, I had been born. Because I stood before her, flesh and sinew, blood and bone, she could not flub this detail. She and Clive had rushed to the hospital like madmen! Clive, so anxious, had thrown up in a bush outside the hospital door! He parted the branches, *and*. Soon, I'd arrived. Five pounds, perfect. (I'd been, actually, nine pounds, seven ounces. My mother had cried upon seeing me, feeling robbed of an infant. She'd told me this one evening after too much champagne, words she could never take back.)

My mother held her champagne flute with the tips of her fingers, as if fearful it might give her a disease. "*Happy birthday!*" Glasses clinked.

Waiters served coffee and cake. Pound cake, despite my aversion to it. I took my plate and found my father. He hadn't spoken, it seemed, since this party began. I ate the frosting from my piece of cake. My father ate his cake, leaving a line of abandoned frosting, one cracked fondant lily. We traded plates, a thing we'd done with our plates of cake and frosting since I was twelve, my age when he'd *actually* met me, the moment we became the hostages of my mother's hijacked history.

"If she doesn't stop talking," my father said, "I'm going to miss *Who Wants to Be a Millionaire?*"

"Maybe you should call your lifeline," I said.

"That." My father shrugged. "I used that years ago."

"That dinner cost a fortune," I said on the ride home. "And still, our son ate garnishes."

"*Hmm*," my husband said.

"Can we stop somewhere?"

"For what?"

"To get Jamie some *food*."

"We just ate a six-course dinner. Your son chose to eat radishes instead of lobster," he said, ignoring the fact that Jamie was in the backseat.

"He's our son."

"What?"

"*Our* son," I said.

At home, Jamie shut himself inside his bedroom. My husband shut himself inside his office. Left alone, I made a grilled cheese. I imagined the monologue I'd be subjected to if my husband saw me making this grilled cheese. I was babying Jamie, he'd say. Spoiling him. Still, I left the sandwich on a tray outside Jamie's bedroom, knocking sharply to announce its arrival. Then I scrubbed the pan, dried my hands on my burlap skirt, cleaned the counter, realigned its things. My husband had left a stack of papers on the kitchen island. Buoyed by residual champagne, I marched this stack of papers into my husband's office without knocking. I found him talking on the phone, feet propped on his expansive walnut desk even though he chastised Jamie for leaving accidental thumbprints on it.

"Debra!"

Wavering in the doorway, I understood my name wasn't a greeting but an announcement to the mysterious person at the other end of the line: *she's here*. I was supposed to turn around, return from whence I'd come. I crossed the room and sat on the leather sectional, tossing my husband's papers onto the coffee table without regard for their order. I clicked on the tv. Airing was a program about bees. Bees swarmed across the television screen. People in beekeeping suits tread carefully amongst them. The narrator's soothing voice reminded me, inexplicably, of pleated khaki pants. Across the room, my husband still pressed the phone to his ear. The tension of his body told me he was considering how to proceed.

"Okay," he said finally into the receiver, his voice reluctant, almost gentle. "We'll talk soon."

I braced myself for his anger: what was I thinking, entering the blessed sanctum of his office, turning on a nature program while he conducted serious business? *His* hard work, *his* tenacity, allowed us to have this lifestyle, these things.

Given my husband's love of soliloquy, it surprised me he'd never done theater in school. Lecturing me or Jamie, he arranged his body like a prism meant to catch the light, appeared overly conscious of his hands. Predictably, he'd played sports, though I wondered who he would have become had he been given even the corner of a stage, several earnest people to listen to and admire him. He would have failed at projection. My husband's voice didn't rise like the voices of other angry people, those I'd seen on *Judge Judy* and *Court TV*. When he was angry, his voice pinched itself, as if his fury proved so intense even he cowered before it.

He sat beside me on the sectional, ignored his scattered papers. On the screen, bees buzzed. Though I stiffened, he said merely, "Bees fascinate me."

The only relationship I'd known my husband to have with bees was swatting them away from his turkey clubs.

"I like the way they work inside their little groups."

"Colonies."

"What?"

"They're called colonies."

"Right!" my husband said with undue enthusiasm.

For a moment we watched a beekeeper in his suit hold his arms out like Jesus welcoming the little children, and his arms, in Jesus position, were soon covered in bees.

"Did you like your birthday?" my husband asked.

"It seemed maybe excessive."

"You know your mother," he said.

"Yes," I said, but did not.

His hand palmed my knee. "Is this all right?"

"I guess so," I said, but he seemed to think I said *yes, go!* because then he was kissing me with a dog's sloppiness, his mouth tasting of the after-dinner cigars the men had smoked, with an inflated sense of importance, on the country club's back patio. He yanked my dress various ways as if it were a curtain refusing to slide along a rod. His removal of my clothing had the frenzy of ER technicians in the moments before lifesaving surgery. He created a flurry of distraction before I could ask questions: who had been on the phone? Why had he spoken with such softness? Had he really put his feet on his walnut desk? My husband wrapped a hand around each of my breasts before pressing them against his eyes like a pair of binoculars. I asked nothing. And then, perhaps because it was proximate to his mouth, he bit my right nipple. Laughter rose inside me. I bit the inside of my cheek to distance myself from it.

My husband proceeded to have sex with me on the leather sectional. This was unusual. That is, we'd never had sex on the leather sectional, but also we hadn't had sex on top of any object for months. Nary a bed, a floor, a countertop. Our coupling in this moment felt like a business transaction, akin to the signing of a document, as if, in having sex with him, I agreed I hadn't noticed whatever telling thing I'd noticed. Nothing was amiss. We were normal. *Look!* We were so normal we had sex! He pumped away, desperate to jam some normalcy inside me.

I remembered my mother's advice, dispensed over lunch several weeks before my wedding day. Smoothing her black napkin on her black-clad lap, she said, "Sometimes, a man will just want a hole. Any hole will do. Give him whatever hole he wants. This is a fine moment to consider what remains to be accomplished for the week. Did you make your nail appointment? Did you arrange the hors d'oeuvres for the party? Did you, for instance, accommo-date the terrible woman with the nut allergy? If you engage, if you *reciprocate*, he'll want all of you. An ear to listen, a shoulder to cry on. Encouragement, support. It's easier to lend out the hole and be done with it."

"Lend it out," I said. "Like a library book?"

"Exactly," my mother said.

The bees still buzzed behind my husband's bare shoulder as he finished, his back arching dramatically. The camera zoomed in: translucent wings, shimmying bodices. Honeycomb, honey. I'd lent out the hole; we could move on. Watch the twitching antennae, not talk. "Shockingly," the voice-over informed us, "the average worker bee produces only about one-twelfth teaspoon of honey in her lifetime."

I was contemplating this startling fact when I felt my husband's mouth traveling the length of my pale stomach. Down, down to that inexplicable nether region. This descent was the true tipping point of his guilt: he was having an affair. In the twenty years of our lackluster sexual history, he'd never done *that*. My laughter interrupted the program's soothing narration.

"Is it ticklish?" my husband asked.

I would crack myself open with laughter, cleave myself in two.

"Deb, come on. We were being *intimate*."

His use of the word only spurred me on. He muttered into the hollows of his pant legs as he turned them right-side out. A moment later, in his anger, he tripped on a cuff and pitched forward onto the floor. I laughed harder.

"Who are you?" he asked, leaving me alone in his office, a place I'd never been left alone. His self-imposed banishment from his sacred space seemed a magnificent reversal of roles.

I stared for a long time at the ceiling.

Who, he'd asked, and my mind echoed: *who, who, who.*

I'd told no one that weeks before, a woman had left a hesitant message on the answering machine.

"This message is for Debra. My name is Colleen Crane."

This Colleen Crane's words sounded as carefully chosen as chess pieces.

"I'm calling on behalf of her father. It's important she call me back."

Colleen Crane gave her phone number twice, ensuring that Debra, whoever she was, would get it right.

Jamie was still at school, sitting in seventh period social studies, memorizing details about the pecking order of Mesopotamia or the political climate of Ancient Greece. I listened to the message five times, ten times. Soon, Jamie would arrive home. Writing her phone number on a tiny piece of paper, I deleted Colleen Crane's message. Neither my husband, nor my son, knew of my biological father. They had no clue I'd spent my first twelve years in Oakland, a different girl entirely. No clue that I'd waited, waited for this phone call; had imagined its possible iterations. And here, it had arrived, the voice on the other side not my father's, but that of a stranger.

"Go ahead," I remember him saying, words roughened by bourbon and nicotine. His voice scraped silence, got to the bottom of things. "Open your mouth and smell it." He proffered his glass of bourbon. "It seems ridiculous, but with an open mouth, you'll take in its nuances. Through nuance, your life will change." Together, we inhaled bourbon through the misshapen circles of our mouths, the television rattling its game shows behind us.

BEVERLY, 2001

She woke thinking about the cake, whose memory gave her a flush of self-consciousness. The cake, more extravagant than most wedding cakes, could have fed one hundred people. They'd had twenty—people she'd worked hard to dredge up, for Debra was not a social creature. Beverly gave the cake remains to the waitstaff, who surely descended like vultures upon it, with little regard for fondant-sculpted flowers, their white shirts stained from the evening's work. Beverly had complained several times to management: theirs was a high-end club. Must the waitstaff look so slovenly? Their shoulders slumped when they realized she was sitting in their section. As a result, she ran them ragged, sending them constantly for elusive things. *I said warm water, not hot. I said cooked through, not cooked to oblivion. Yes, I wanted lemon, but what use have I for seeds?* Last night, as the guests raised their cocktails and shouted, "Surprise!" Beverly saw the disappointment on Debra's face. She'd expected just the five of them, eating dinner with little fanfare in the main room. Her daughter wore brown linen, as if she were a contestant in the three-legged race at the county fair. Beneath the dress's sagging hemline were those hideous sandals that were a trend recently. Despite them looking like shoes Moses might wear as he parted the sea, starlets appeared in the thin pages of the celebrity magazines wearing them. They wore these shoes not trekking rugged landscapes as one might expect, but pushing their grocery carts or holding lighters at rock benefits. Incomprehensibly, Debra paired them with every outfit.

"Dear, it's a formal party, not a picnic."

"Funny, no one told me."

Her grandson, too, appeared disfigured; welts marred his pallid face. At dinner, Beverly's son-in-law told the too-animated story of Jamie's being clobbered by a baseball at the Dodgers game the night before. Of course, Jamie had failed to catch a baseball; that anyone had believed he'd catch a baseball was as ridiculous as a wedding cake at a birthday party. Her son-in-law was in denial about the sort of boy he'd raised. Laughter rose from the table at her grandson's expense, providing Beverly the first inkling that something intricate occurred just below the surface between her son-in-law and the blonde sitting beside him. Her son-in-law was not a funny man. Still, laughter wracked the woman's body; it went on and on. James was a man you laughed on cue for only if he'd given you an orgasm, or several. Beverly studied this woman, surely the daughter of an Olympian and a *Sports Illustrated* swimsuit model. In addition to the laughter of a walrus, the blonde possessed the exceptionally dextrous mouth of a horse. She was a zoo unto herself. Her husband, a business associate of James, sat on her other side, a man in desperate need of shoulder-opening exercises. His posture told Beverly he was as miserable as Debra—no small feat—who now picked her fingernails (at the dinner table!) without the slightest inkling regarding her husband and this trophy piece.

The time arrived for Beverly to give her toast. "I remember, plain as day, rushing to Cedars Sinai in the night, Clive so anxious beside me as we drove!" she began, then elicited laughter of her own, telling of Clive emptying his stomach in the bushes. "When my beautiful baby girl arrived, she was so tiny I believed I'd break her. I was terrified to hold her, but Clive never put her down. It was the first I'd seen him cry."

Unlike her son-in-law, *she* could tell a story, molding the shifting mass of so-called history into whatever necessary thing. Debra had been born in Oakland. She had not been tiny, but had weighed almost ten pounds, causing Beverly—*not* Clive, for he had not yet existed in their lives—to cry over an infant who, swaddled, resembled a snow boulder large enough to kill a person should it roll down an embankment. Beverly had sobbed, but Webster pressed his snow boulder of a baby against his chest. He trembled, his husky voice lulled into sweetness. *"You're really here."* He acted as if he hadn't existed—not truly—until Debra's arrival on this earth.

After her toast, Beverly watched as Debra and Clive shared two pieces of cake. They switched plates, leaning close as Debra ate two servings of icing, and something suddenly banged inside Beverly: Debra disliked poundcake. Yet Beverly had chosen it for this party. Birthdays were always disasters. Once you passed the age of ten, they all felt like bombs sending shrapnel into your face.

She remembered her fiftieth, a surprise party planned by Debra and Clive, cancelled at the last minute because Beverly had told neither of them she'd scheduled a celebratory facelift. (*Do not go gentle into this good night*, she thought as the anesthesia lumbered over her.) She recuperated in a private room, swabbed in gauze, only her eyes and mouth visible. When she called Debra to retrieve her, her daughter broke the news: they'd planned a surprise party for her two days hence. "Absolutely not," Beverly said, insisting Debra call each guest to cancel, reading from a paper the words Beverly had asked her to say: "My mother has a stomach flu so miserable she's been sent to the hospital. You know she's terrible at caring for herself."

"Actually," Debra mused between calls, "you're excellent at caring for yourself."

Face afire, Beverly reached across the white sheets for her daughter's hand. "Thank you for planning me a beautiful party."

Debra snatched her hand back. "It was Dad's idea."

There'd been a time when Beverly wanted nothing more than for Debra to call Clive *Dad*. When it happened, she thought, this single word would signify the solidarity of their family unit, would validate Beverly's decision to leave Webster. But when the moment finally arrived, she saw she'd been wrong. There was no solidarity to speak of. Only the allegiances had shifted.

The morning after Debra's birthday celebration, Beverly drove to Santa Monica and let herself into her daughter's house. On weekdays, Debra volunteered. She held cats at the SPCA, played card games with the elderly, adjusted pillows beneath lonely chemotherapy patients as liquid dripped into their veins. When she wasn't helping others, she veered toward self-improvement: yoga, meditation. Something called qigong. Like Beverly's once-upon-a-time husband, like her former mother-in-law, her daughter tended toward depression. Debra had received both Webster's girth and his unshakeable sadness. Was it any wonder her son-in-law was tempted to stray?

James had stared at that trophy blonde—Beverly had learned her name, Janie Walsh—as if he wanted to rummage her like a transient would a recycling bin. Beverly was here to find evidence of his philandering; James had a history. Just off the den was his office, a place Beverly had never ventured. As she opened the heavy door, the morning light exposed floating particles of dust. Everything appeared tidy except the cockeyed couch cushions. Beverly rifled James's desk drawers, searching for anything incriminating: love letters, credit card receipts, Janie Walsh's crumpled panties. She found papers printed with dull columns of dull numbers, ChapStick. Of course her son-in-law had dry lips.

Curiosity pressed her upstairs, to Debra and James's bedroom, a room emitting the sterility of a vacation home before the renters settled in. Their bed, despite its rash of pillows, appeared inhospitable, not a place where people in love did shameful things. She entered Debra's walk-in closet. A space any artist would be pleased to starve inside, it possessed a room for Debra's clothing and connected to a sitting room where she could ponder, from the comfort of a formidable pale-blue Louis XIV armchair, which clothes to wear. Beverly doubted Debra had ever sat in that chair. Despite owning a vast array of clothing, her daughter tended toward jeans and t-shirts, sacks with convenient holes cut for the head and extremities. Beverly went hanger by hanger, touching everything. Items she'd gifted Debra hung untouched, tags still connected. Seeing the burlap dress of the night before returned to its hanger, Beverly felt a sharp pang in her chest. Moved by a feeling she refused to examine, Beverly ripped it down, stuffed it inside her purse, which took it hungrily, bulging like a snake who'd just swallowed an exceptional mouse.

Relieved, Beverly inspected the built-in drawers, finding a glut of that terrible costume jewelry Debra had sold briefly. She'd brought the catalogs to the ladies' locker room at the club, pestering women just emerged from the hot tub, before they'd even blown their hair dry. Their wet hair hanging against faces devoid of makeup—occasionally, these women were *naked*, their bosoms swinging ponderously over the glossy pages—they regarded Debra's inventory of junk. Beverly took Debra to lunch, where she poked casually at her lettuce and informed her daughter she wasn't some trailer wife. Wasn't some destitute woman on government assistance. She didn't *need* to sell cheaply made jewelry that called to mind plastic trinkets children choked on. She didn't *need* extra pennies to buy tins of sardines for her malnourished family. She needn't bother with such frivolous endeavors.

"This is a career path," said Debra.

"It really isn't," said Beverly. "You're only taking sales from the women who need them."

Debra had stopped then, but apparently not before amassing quite the stockpile. Beverly slipped a bejeweled noose of a choker into her purse before moving on. The sitting room shelves had been carefully arranged with an excess of knickknacks. Webster had given their daughter, not just girth and depression, but a hoarder's desire to save every inconsequential thing. "With a knick knack paddy whack, give a dog a bone," Webster had sung to his daughter, who reached for Edna—always Edna—as Beverly, overwhelmed by her inadequacies, bit down until she tasted blood. *Knick knack paddy whack*. What did that even *mean*? Debra, like Webster, saved everything for fear of losing the quick heat of its memory inside her: letters and concert programs, wedding invitations and dime-store prizes. She treated everything as a talisman, worried that if she discarded any of it she'd hurt someone's feelings, bring doom upon those she loved. As a young girl, she'd carried three dolls everywhere rather than neglect any. "Dolls don't have feelings," Beverly told her daughter, who cried and struggled not to drop them on their heads. She clutched all three dolls inside the remarkable wingspan she'd inherited from Webster. Her daughter, angel of the inconsequential, the superfluous.

And then, amid the knick knack paddy whacks, it caught Beverly's breath.

On the third shelf, to the left of her daughter's wedding photograph, appeared Edna's jewelry box. Victorian, gilded, made of beveled turquoise glass. Inside this jewelry box, Edna had kept the pearl earrings loaned to Beverly on her wedding day. How had Debra gotten it? Fingers trembling, she opened its delicate lid. There were the earrings, which Beverly tucked into her pocket. But also a newspaper article folded into a neat square like an old-fashioned handkerchief. The headline jumped out: LIGHTER POPS, BEAUTY QUEEN CRASHES! How had Debra gotten *this*?

Beverly still remembered, in the aftermath of this accident—*her* accident—sitting with the intimidating Miss Margaret at the dining room table. The lacquered mahogany tossed up her muddled reflection as Miss Margaret chastised her: "Why were you driving so fast? Were you smoking? Poise "—Miss Margaret elongated the word—"isn't something one abandons for a cigarette."

Printed with this article were two images. Beverly hadn't seen these photographs in years, but here they were. The first showed her sitting at her bedroom vanity surrounded by trophies and sashes. As an adult squinting at this grainy photograph, Beverly saw these sashes—juxtaposed against the girlish scene of her bedroom, canopied bed in the backdrop—not as signs of victory but as materials used to bind a person, like bandages; or worse, they suggested sadistic behavior. In the second photo, Beverly stood before the billboard she'd driven the car through. She wore a tiara and a pageant sash declaring *Miss Real Cool*. "A useless title," her mother said, but Beverly had admired the sash's lush purple color. Adorned, Beverly pointed at the billboard's gaping hole. "Your mouth is wide enough to fit a grapefruit inside!" Miss Margaret had said, appalled by the other large hole in the photograph.

Several days after this article came out, someone slid an envelope inside Beverly's locker. Opening it, she discovered clipped-out copies of these images, amended with cartoon bubbles bursting from her O-shaped mouth. *Boil my cabbage*, said one. On another, an arrow pointed: *Enter here!* In the shot of Beverly at her vanity, a giant penis sat amid the trophies. This penis drooped over (this penis was not poised!), the tip brushing Beverly's shoulder like an unhappy tulip. Horrified, Beverly had taken these clippings into the girls' bathroom, where, with poise, she flushed them down the toilet.

Now Beverly stared at her young face. Then, moved by a spontaneity that hadn't blossomed inside her in years, she entered her daughter's ensuite bathroom, its many mirrors producing a sudden slew of mimicking Beverlies. Passing the neatly folded hand towels and scalloped bars of soap, she flushed the strip of newspaper down the toilet as easily as a dead goldfish, just as she'd done at seventeen at Santa Barbara High, wearing a skirt so large she could barely fit in the bathroom stall.

She watched the paper spin inside the bowl: swirl, swirl, and gone. These tiny bits of history. What was life, really, except the constant kaleidoscopic reiteration—the insistence—of memory, of things you preferred to forget?

COLLEEN, 2001

Nights while everyone slept, Colleen picked up Webster Eugene Jackson—"Webb," he said, "just call me Webb"—from the Extended Stay America. Together, they passed his house so he could see the contractor team's progress, afterward driving down College Avenue toward Berkeley. As she drove, he pointed: that building had once been the Chimes Theatre. He and his mother had walked there from the house, his mother clasping his hand despite his being too old for handholding. Inside the theater, they shared popcorn, his mother eating kernel by kernel with a flash of red fingernails while he shoved large handfuls into his mouth. It was the War with a capital *W*. Sugar was rationed, candy rare. Nail polish, too, but women, his mother said, had to keep up morale, had to bolster the downtrodden spirits of men. At that young age, he told Colleen, he had not yet identified the sarcasm in her voice.

"Women are building guns! They're building airplanes!" she'd say when they returned home, recounting what they'd seen on the news reels while his father snorted over the absurdity.

"Remind me," his father said, "never to ride those airplanes."

He never accompanied them on their outings, and when Webb and his mother chattered about the new stools at the Chimes Pharmacy Soda Fountain (they had backs! they swiveled!); when they dissected the china beauty of Elizabeth Taylor in *Lassie Come Home*, or the incessant dipping of Humphrey Bogart and Ingrid Bergman's hats and lips toward one another in *Casablanca*, his father waxed nostalgic about how things used to be. A farm, he interrupted them, sounding like an angry English poet. *A farm* had once existed where the Chimes Theatre now stood. A farm with a barn, the way farms had, and a pond. As a child, he'd thrown rocks into this pond. In this pond, he had fished. Remembering the darting movements of the fish inside this pond made his father wistful.

"I appreciate sentimental men," Colleen said.

"That was bourbon," said Webb. "Not sentiment."

"Well, a pond sounds nice."

"At least it wasn't another rendition of the Berkeley conflagration."

"I don't know that one," said Colleen.

"The city caught fire. The campanile bell rung like a death knell, and the football players rallied to save the burning city."

"I guess I missed that one," said Colleen.

"I didn't," he said and gestured toward a building. "That's a bar now. But once upon a time it was the Rockridge Improvement Club, and no matter what it is or what it becomes, it will remind me of my mother."

Pointing out these places that had once been other places, he told Colleen: despite their differences, all generations were fundamentally the same. They lamented what was gone, abhorred what had taken its place. This attitude ambushed a person, turned him old overnight. *He'd* become old. Had become his father, cantankerous regarding even the slightest change, ambivalent toward the future.

What had compelled her to lie to this man? How would she ever explain it? His daughter did not want to see him. Colleen had seized upon the idea of a caretaker because she doubted his ability to care for himself. Because he'd set his own house on fire, a convoluted story she didn't understand about a dish towel and an oil-soaked rug. She'd told this lie because she couldn't possibly take responsibility for another human when she could scarcely manage responsibility for herself.

A new restaurant had opened several doors down from the Chimes Pharmacy. *Grasshopper* declared the sign above the door.

"What does that even mean?" asked Webb.

"It's an Asian tapas bar."

"A who?"

"They serve Asian small plates."

"Huh."

"We should go. Have dinner, drink too much sake."

"I don't drink sake."

"You eat," said Colleen.

"I do."

"It'll get you out of the house."

"I'm not *in* the house. All I want is to get back in the house."

"Right," she said.

They'd found a girl to move in with him. They'd interviewed her at the Extended Stay America, at Webb's tiny formica table, drinking Lipton tea served from flimsy teacups. The girl was young—mid-twenties, Colleen guessed—with a messy bun, ripped oversized jeans, and a t-shirt declaring she had survived Bob Novak's fiftieth birthday.

"Who's Bob Novak?" Colleen asked, trying to make conversation.

"I don't know," said the girl. "He's probably dead."

A palpable malaise surrounded her; she moved as if through the thick of something. The teacup, plastic, had the heft of a dumbbell when she lifted it. Yet she answered their questions politely: *Yes*, she was quiet. *No*, she didn't smoke. *No*, she would not be inclined to have visitors. *Yes*, she had a job, working in an Italian restaurant at the corner of University and Milvia in Berkeley. Colleen knew the restaurant. It had a charming staff; how had this girl gotten hired?

Webb stared into his tea and asked: did she care if a man wore women's clothing?

She did not.

Did she care if *he* wore women's clothing?

She did not.

"Not just dresses and skirts," Webb said. "Women's lingerie."

Her eyes were dull. "I don't care."

"A man wearing *brassieres*."

"I use pronouns," she said.

Webb shrugged. "Doesn't everyone?"

"I don't want community. I don't need a family."

"My entire life, I have been thoroughly unable to provide either of those things," Webb said.

Her name was Hannah. Colleen hadn't considered Webb would choose this girl. Colleen had imagined, when she used the word *caretaker*, someone older, upbeat, and inclined toward order. A person who'd fill his days with tasks to distract him from his depression. A person to emphasize a regular schedule, to encourage the consumption of vitamins and the daily practice of meditative breathing. Someone to hunker down with him, to watch whatever romcom played on the television. She'd not imagined this girl, secreting sadness from her pores. This girl, with her bitten-down nails and unmoisturized face, continually chewing the inside of her cheek and crossing and uncrossing her legs.

This girl would not save him from himself.

Just days before Webb returned home, Colleen's phone rang.

"May I speak to Colleen Crane?" asked the voice on the line, sounding vaguely familiar.

"This is she."

"My name is Debra Johnson. You called me a while back regarding Webster Jackson."

"Yes! I've been wanting to talk to you. *Needing* to talk to you."

An uncomfortable silence resonated. Colleen heard the slight catch and release of Debra Johnson's breath. She pictured this woman inside a beautiful home, inside a kitchen scrubbed by someone hired for the purpose. She pictured Webb, living at the Extended Stay America. He stared over the top of the refrigerator when he reached inside for milk. His feet dangled off the end of the bed. He'd broken the handle from a dresser simply by opening the drawer.

"Your father," Colleen began.

"Biologically, yes, he's my father."

"You're his only living relative, not counting your mother."

"Don't count my mother."

"You're his only blood relative," said Colleen.

"I can't help that."

Colleen said, "He caught his kitchen on fire."

"Was he playing with matches?"

"He's living in an extended-stay hotel."

"This has nothing to do with me."

"You're his daughter."

Debra Johnson laughed a maniacal laugh. It occurred to Colleen that she'd been drinking.

"Obviously, you know nothing about it."

"I guess I don't," said Colleen. She said, "I don't."

"I haven't seen or heard from the man in thirty years."

Colleen struggled with what to say. "I'm sorry."

"Did he ask you to call because he's afraid to do it himself?"

"No," said Colleen.

"He's not afraid?"

Colleen wavered. "No, he didn't ask me to call."

Debra Johnson asked, "Does he know you're calling?"

"Sort of," said Colleen.

On the other end of the line, Debra Johnson said nothing. Colleen considered the things she might say but couldn't. She didn't say that from her own kitchen window, across the span of grass between their homes, she could see his. Didn't say she'd helped select the new countertop, the backsplash and appliances; had brought tile samples and paint swatches to the Extended Stay America, where at the tiny formica table, he and Colleen compared colors, debated. She'd told Webster Eugene Jackson his daughter wanted to see him . . . in time. Had led him to believe there was the possibility of making whatever he'd destroyed right again; that there was a clear path away from his melancholy.

"You shouldn't have called," Debra Johnson said.

"You called me," said Colleen.

"I called you back."

"If you have nothing to say, why did you call?" Colleen spoke gently, with words like kid gloves. But Debra Johnson had hung up.

"I'm sorry," Debra Johnson said when she called a second time. A week had passed.

"There's nothing to apologize for," said Colleen.

"You were right. I called you."

"I shouldn't have put you in that awkward situation."

"I was inappropriate. I'm sorry."

"Are you Catholic?" Colleen asked.

"Yes, why?"

"You have the trademark guilt."

"I still don't want to talk about him," Debra Johnson said. "I just wanted to apologize. It was a bad day, a bad week, and I called you looking for a fight."

"You're not very good at it."

"What?"

"Fighting."

"My husband would tell you differently."

"They usually do," said Colleen.

Silence bloomed between them.

"When you called, had you been drinking?"

"Did I seem drunk?"

"Pretty drunk," Colleen admitted.

"I'd opened up some wine. An important bottle my husband had been saving."

"Cheers to that," said Colleen, and Debra Johnson laughed.

When she called Colleen several days later—just to talk, it seemed— Colleen wondered what they were scraping up against, but felt pleased to laugh, feign normalcy. Their friendship occurred accidentally, gradually. Webb provided the distinct boundaries of their conversations, the abrupt line drawn in the sand. Talking about everything except Webster Eugene Jackson, they discovered they'd lived separate but simultaneous lives, like water ballerinas performing singularly but in unison. They'd each gone to high school in Los Angeles, had graduated the same year. They might have passed one another in shopping malls as teenagers, sucking Orange Julius shakes through wide straws, testing lipstick colors against their wrists. They might have searched for albums at the same record store. Wild Cherry. Paul Simon. Seals and Crofts.

"I was a cheerleader," said Colleen.

"I was not."

"I mean I was an *alternate*. Mostly I ran to get the other girls Cokes, or the menstrual pads they'd left in their lockers."

"I tried out once," said Debra. "My mother made me. She thought I needed more extracurricular activities. Or, well, any. They made me take off my glasses. I couldn't see anything and got nervous and cheered myself right off the stage."

"Were you hurt?"

"Not physically."

"My mother was a cheerleader," said Colleen. "I was very disappointing to her."

"Mine was a beauty queen."

"Yikes," said Colleen, spontaneously and with feeling.

Together, they laughed.

HANNAH, 2001

When Hannah first moved to Oakland, she'd asked her new housemates if they needed anything from scary market. "No," they
said. "Thank you." But when Hannah returned carrying her
Grape Nuts and milk, they waved her to the dining table.

"You've offended us," the angry housemate said.

"What? How?"

"*Scary* market," the housemate who never stopped smiling said.

The market was in a rundown area, was rundown itself, frequented by
rundown-looking people, and Hannah's simple question, with its careless
adjective—*scary*—subjected her to a monologue regarding her apparent
hatred of the poor and disenfranchised.

"You're lazy with language," the angry housemate said.

"I don't mean to be."

"No one *tries* to be lazy." Like a woman drugged, the smiling one smiled.
"That's paradoxical."

"I've heard you," said the angry one, "calling me *she*. My name is Mason.
Gender pronouns are conveniences, crutches. Your language choices have
repercussions."

"My language," said Hannah, "seemed adequate. That place is scary
as hell!"

She'd witnessed, her first time there, a skirmish in the aisles. Cans of
condensed soup and Spam clattered to the ground. Liters of orange and
grape and cherry sodas fizzed onto the cracked linoleum. Two men brawled,
knocking into boxes of Fruit Loops, smashing four-dollar bottles of chardonnay. "Come on, now!" a woman wearing a bathrobe yelled into the

fray. She wore a towel wrapped around her still-wet hair, clutched a frozen burrito to her chest. "Before I miss my program!"

"I just wondered if you needed milk," Hannah said. "Cereal. Snacks. Maybe a Slim Jim. Or should I say, Slim *Him*?"

Hannah believed this a funny joke. The angry one did not.

Another day, as Hannah sat at the solid oak dining table, they informed her she was not a team player. She was not *present*.

"I'm right here." Hannah remembered grade school, raising a thin arm when the teacher called her name.

"Physically, yes." The smiling one smiled. "Bodily."

"That's important," Hannah said. "Isn't it?"

"We're interested in building community," said the angry one. "We thought you wanted the same thing. Right now, you're the weakest link. We feel misled. Duped. You've been *duplicitous*."

Under other circumstances, Hannah would have been pleased to be called duplicitous. She'd not suspected she had it in her.

"You've been eating my pecan sandies." The smiling one no longer smiled.

"And my string cheese," said the angry one.

These things were, unfortunately, true. Her housemates' sole redeeming quality was keeping the kitchen stocked. On several occasions, having nothing to eat, Hannah had concocted a haphazard dinner for herself, sneaking a pecan sandie from the package in the cabinet, a handful of crackers from the cracker box. She'd pilfered several carrots from their plastic bag. With the stolen carrots, she took several digs of hummus from the angry one's tub of garlic Sabra. The garlic's aftertaste lingering too long on her tongue, she ate two sticks of string cheese, a spoonful of chocolate Tofutti ice cream. She took a second spoonful in an attempt to smooth away the evidence of the first, double-dipping into the container. The smoothing of the Tofutti, like Hannah's insistence, as a child, on cutting Barbie's hair, did not go well. Soon, half the container was gone, smoothed forever away. She took a second pecan sandie. She took a third.

"No!" Hannah infused as much indignation as possible inside this tiny word. She understood she had just lied about *cookies*. She had just lied about *string cheese*. She understood such lying was an indoctrination into something larger. She'd turned a sharp and strange—a necessary—corner in her life. She was no longer the person she'd been.

The smiling one produced the empty bag of cookies; she'd held the package in her lap. Hannah considered game shows, first the drum roll and then the announcer's cool voice saying, *And behind door three!*

"Hannah," the angry one said. "Did you eat Maggie's cookies?"

I ain't gonna work on Maggie's farm no more, Hannah thought, and wondered who Maggie was before realizing it was the smiling housemate.

"Did you?"

"No." Because it was important to commit to the lies one told, she added, "I most certainly did not."

"Here's the thing," Maggie said. "We need to see an improvement from you."

"Or," said Hannah.

"Or it will be time for you to leave."

Afterward, Hannah avoided her housemates, staying inside her room when she wasn't at work. She ate bowls of Grape Nuts in bed or huddled beneath the covers, listening through the window to the neighbor talk heatedly with the man he called his "houseguest." The houseguest lived in a small cottage behind the main house. He spent a lot of time talking loudly to the neighbor in the yard just outside Hannah's bedroom. Hannah had never spoken to the neighbor or the houseguest, had only heard their conversations, watched their calamitous comings and goings.

The neighbor drove a convertible whose license plate declared HOT TAN. Hannah's housemates, ever generous with people who were not Hannah, believed this license plate ironic, a sign of the neighbor's acute wit. Generosity, Hannah understood, frequently obscured people's abilities to see. The man who called himself Hot Tan did, actually, possess a dark tan that gave his skin the look of a rotisserie chicken. He had a grandmother's coiffed hair, which explained why he never drove with the convertible's top down.

She woke one night to his shrill voice. "Nah, dude. Palm trees *are not* indigenous to California."

"But I'm looking at one *right now.* Right there. That's a palm tree."

"Yeah, dude, but someone brought it over. Some guy put it on a boat and got it here."

Either Hot Tan or the houseguest picked up a guitar and plucked the strings. Hannah had noticed Californians, like Elvis in his movies, frequently had guitars at the ready. Either Hot Tan or the houseguest strummed as Hot Tan sang, "Jane says, 'I'm done with Sergio. He treats me like a ragdoll.'" Hannah waited for the next line, but Hot Tan sang again, "Jane says, 'I'm done with Sergio!'"

He continued like a skipping record. Hannah considered opening the window and yelling out the next lines: *She hides the television. Says, "I don't owe him nothing."* In her previous life—in Pittsburgh, with Max clutching cans of Iron City, back when they'd still been a couple—Hot Tan's voice, off-key and snagging on this single line would have proven hilarious. But here, alone in this state she'd heard was golden, she felt only blankness, as if the dark reaches of outer space had taken up residence inside her.

Hot Tan's angry voice sliced through the night. "Dude! You *did not* just pour a bucket of piss on me!"

"Dude, I did."

"Why *the fuck* would you do that?"

"Because, dude. You're a fucking asshole."

Hannah heard the scraping of chairs against concrete, the shattering of glass, a dog's barking. Through the window, dark figures wrangled in the night. They grappled, smacked one another's heads. One figure tugged the other figure's ear. They yanked each other onto the ground and rolled, grunting, across the patio.

They tired quickly and lay unmoving. Then they drunk-cried, uncomfortable tears sounding like the routing of pigs in the muck.

"Dude, I'm just saying you need to be grateful."

"You haven't given me a pot to piss in—"

"Dude, I gave you that."

Hannah heard the roughly hewn laughter of men.

In the morning, she watched from the living room window as they left the house. Hot Tan's roasted face resembled a baseball mitt; the houseguest dragged his left leg like a sack of laundry. They opened the convertible's doors, chattering, demonstrative songbirds, and Hannah realized she knew nothing about human relationships. This reminded her to call her mother, though none of it explained why there'd been a bucket of piss in the first place.

"How are you?" her mother asked.

"You know," said Hannah.

Her mother had not cried over Sam's death. Her mother was not, as she described others, with honed derision, *a crier*. "Never trust a person's tears," her mother said. "Tears are manipulative, a sign someone wants something from you." Hannah knew she meant Fran, Sam's mother, who was an equal-opportunity crier, weeping over things small and large: an over-poached egg, a run in a pair of pantyhose, curdled cream, a used syringe forgotten on the bathroom vanity. Fran's tears were as familiar to Hannah as a family cat taking up space in her lap. The sound she'd made, calling Hannah to say Sam had died, had been ear-shattering. Fran made that sound, and once she'd purged herself of it like a poison, she spoke calmly. "This is your fault, Hannah."

Her mother said, "There's something I need to tell you."

"Okay," said Hannah.

"Something I should have told you sooner."

"*Yes.*"

"Fran died, Hannah."

A wallop in Hannah's heart. A gobsmacking.

"I read it in the paper several weeks ago."

"And you're telling me now?"

"This is the first time you've called since it happened. Call your mother more, Hannah."

Silence swallowed them.

"How?"

"We both know how. I'm guessing pills. A quiet death, not terrible."

"They're all terrible."

"I'm sorry," her mother said, and Hannah could not discern what she was sorry for: that Sam had died, or that Fran had died, or that Hannah was upset by these things. Her mother asked, "When will you be coming home?"

"I don't know."

"There's nothing for you there."

"I guess."

"How is everything else?"

"There is nothing else."

"Hannah."

"I'm late for work."

Hannah was not late for work; she didn't have to work for several days. She was thankful for this, if nothing else. She hated her job, still another thing she could not have told her mother. Her mother believed life was composed of steady hard work pierced by momentary joy. She would not have understood Hannah's acute hatred of the restaurant. But Hannah hated it. Hated the buzzer she wore clipped to her apron, buzzing angrily when her tables' food was ready. Hated the sullen faces of the cooks on the line, the woman chef who mewed like a cat in heat whenever Hannah passed her. Hated the manual floor sweeper that regurgitated everything she'd just swept back onto the carpet. Hated the carpet; what restaurant had *carpet?* Hated the gurgling fountain at the dining room's center, the kitschy murals of an Italian piazza painted on its walls. Hated the gawking clay pigeons squatting on the ceiling rafters. Hated the clothesline stretching across the dining room, the brassieres and underwear and bathing suits hanging from it. Hated the customers who asked, "And *whose* speedo is that?" Hated the bug-eyed assistant manager who drank espressos in quick succession. It was his speedo; a photo of him wearing it on an Italian beach hung in the hallway leading to the bathroom.

"We've been open twenty-one years," the general manager said during Hannah's interview. He had a goatee, a woman's padded hips. The goatee looked like dirt Hannah wanted to wipe off. Above him, boxers hovered from the clothesline. "We're family. We sit down for dinner every night. People have worked here for decades. They fall in love, get married, have babies. This job isn't a stopgap. If you want a revolving door, this isn't the place."

"I'm determined not to evolve," Hannah said, before realizing she meant *revolve.*

In the days and weeks after Sam died, Hannah walked. She walked the two-and-a-half miles to work. After her shifts, she walked the two-and-a-half miles home, south through Berkeley, into north Oakland. She returned home hungry, having declined sitting with the others for staff dinner. Locking herself into her bedroom, she ate bowls of Grape Nuts in bed, sore but soothed by the exertion. She woke and walked some more, trying to outpace an ominous feeling she couldn't pinpoint but that existed inside her, making her walk harder, faster. Needing a destination, she walked to work when she wasn't scheduled, past the barbecue joint with the dog chained out front, past the Ethiopian café and its men sipping iced coffees in the parking lot. Past billboards, the Raiders and their commitment to excellence. Past a particular house where, after a while, a man leaned out the upstairs window as she passed, raising his tallboy to toast her and shouting, "Hey, girl, hey!"

She walked to the laundromat, sitting near the circle of men who gathered to sip bottles of Crown secreted in brown bags. They drank Crown and ate Cheetos purchased from the vending machine, watched *The People's Court* on the mounted television. Their ceaseless commentary comforted her. "I'd be hella pissed if someone's boa constrictor ate my chihuahua." Or, "What's that dude's problem? He's mad at the stripper gave him whiplash?" Or, "Hell, no!" during an episode in which a laundromat manager wanted money from a woman who'd spent hours in the bathroom without doing laundry.

After Sam's death, Hannah skipped several weeks of laundry herself, cycling through her dirty clothes, cycling through them again. When she finally returned, the men nodded agreeably, offered her a sip of Crown. "Girl. We wondered where you were at."

Someone had noticed she was gone. This implied they'd noticed she was present. In Pittsburgh, she'd known everyone: people in line at the grocery store, at the post office. She'd walked down the street nodding hello. People nodded back, affirmed her existence. Here, she spent entire days in silence. She walked, walked. Once, on University Avenue, she passed her work's large windows, through which she waved at a coworker bussing a table. The coworker waved halfheartedly at her, and Hannah understood he had no idea who she was. Unknown, she walked toward the Berkeley Marina, where she stood staring at the sweeping expanse of the bay. She felt restless, disappointed by its largesse. She needed something smaller, more contained. She needed to be walking; she needed to be still. She needed both noise and silence, water and booze, a meal that was not fiber-laden breakfast cereal. Her various conflicting needs made her bones ache. Turning, she walked the miles back to the house, inhaling the unpleasant scent of herself.

The day her mother told her Fran had died, Hannah walked down 51st

Street, which became Pleasant Valley Road, which became Grand Avenue, which brought her to a body of water—a lake! She'd had no idea Oakland possessed such a thing. Ducks, hungry for worms and stale bread, poked their bills into the scant grass. A painter squinted intently at the lake before turning to his easel. On the canvas, Hannah saw, was a giant marijuana leaf in blistering technicolor. The painter dabbed carefully at the leaf's center. The water glinted in fine afternoon sunlight. Hannah realized she did not revolve or evolve. She needed to be present. *Here. I'm here.*

That night, weary from walking, she overheard the angry housemate talking about her to a friend. Hannah listened with detached interest from her bedroom, jaw aching as she chewed Grape Nuts.

"She's weird," the angry housemate was saying. "She walks like ten miles a day and comes backs sweaty and crazy eyed. She eats like seven boxes of Grape Nuts a week. She *lied* about eating Maggie's pecan sandies. I might start counting them, to see."

"Unless you want to look insane," said the friend, "you probably shouldn't do that."

"She has zero social life. She claims to have moved here to be near her best friend, but I've never seen her. I think she's imaginary."

Hannah counted the angry housemate's use of pronouns (five!) before opening her bedroom door. The angry housemate and her friend shifted uncomfortably on the couch.

"My friend is real." Hannah's voice cracked the silence. She realized this was no longer true, was in fact a lie to add to the others.

"Okay," said the angry housemate. "Sure."

"I don't need a pronoun for you," Hannah said. "Cunt is a noun. You're a cunt." She shut herself once again inside the bedroom.

In the morning, she found the note slipped beneath her door, written in erratic penmanship. *You are no longer welcome in this house. We are asking, in writing, that you leave.*

Pittsburgh, Max told her in the days before she left that city, had more bridges than Venice, more registered boats than Miami.

"That's not true," she said.

"It is."

She didn't tell him the bridges in Pittsburgh were brief, underachieving things. They took you across placid brown rivers and called it a day. The Monongahela, the Ohio, the Allegheny: confluent, but not beautiful.

According to Pittsburgh lore, Bruce Willis had refused filming an action sequence in these rivers. He'd claimed the Monongahela was too polluted with muck and debris for even a badass like himself. "What a prima donna!" people said of Bruce Willis, shifting inside their Steelers parkas. "Bruce Willis is a little bitch!" Pittsburghers knew they were far more resilient than Bruce Willis, afraid neither of pollutants nor of cancer. A group of people who called themselves the Polar Bears Club jumped into the Monongahela every New Year's Day. On the news were flashes of exposed stomachs, sagging swimsuits: they didn't need wetsuits! Afterward, men and women shivered inside t-shirts declaring *It's a 'Burgh Thing!* They celebrated with Primanti's sandwiches, dripping water onto the floor as they ate kolbassi and knockwurst.

"This sandwich is historical," Max said the last time they ate there. There had been the familiar heaving crush of fraternity boys and sorority girls, a plethora of exposed ass cracks, residual stickiness of spilt beer and ketchup.

"Testosterone on a bun," Hannah said and saw his disappointment.

"You understand nothing," said Max, a man defensive about a sandwich, and Hannah understood why animals in terminal pain must be shot quickly and efficiently. Suffering things should not be allowed to linger; failed love was much the same. He'd grown distracted when he kissed her, knocking his teeth against hers with the sound of an eggshell cracked against a porcelain bowl. She had doubted the truth of the matter but saw it was true: she would go to California.

"California?" Max said when she told him her plans. "To live? With your friend, the heroin addict?"

"She's sober now."

"She's been sober for, like, a day."

"Six months."

"If you ask me, it will be a disaster."

"I didn't ask you."

"You'll hate it," her mother said. "That dull brown landscape. No green. How expensive it is. California is a place devoid of history."

"Every place has a history."

"You won't have a job, a car. You won't know anyone."

"I'll know Sam."

"I give you three months," her mother said.

"And then what?"

"You'll be back."

"Thanks," Hannah said.

"She wouldn't do this for you."

"She would," Hannah said, and knew she wouldn't.

Still, when Hannah arrived, Sam waited at the gate, bundled up as if for Pennsylvania winter. She looked different than Hannah remembered, her face excavated, as if someone had persistently chipped at its once-large features, diminishing them. Handing Hannah an avocado, she spoke in a voice as placid as a Pittsburgh river: "You live here now. It's necessary to like these pronto." She stared behind Hannah as she said this, at an advertisement for Bermuda. An exuberant woman in a scant bikini kicked her photoshopped hamstrings behind her. *Fun and Sun!* declared the advertisement. Sam's ensuing words gave way to something akin to anger. "Thirty grams of fat in a single avocado, but don't let that deter you. They have lutein. They have cholesterol. They have vitamin E. Go ahead, be a Californian and eat the fucking avocado."

Lutein and *cholesterol* felt like arrowheads hurtling through her dermis. Did Hannah know, then, how it would end? The avocado was as soft in her palm as the spot on the crown of an infant's head that you weren't supposed to touch. She considered what to say. She did not say, *I'm happy to be here.* She did not say, *You look good.* These were lies, things Sam easily detected.

Hannah was still searching for words when Sam drew near her. She pressed her lips to Hannah's cheek and then—briefest ode to the past, portent of the future—she dipped and bit Hannah's bottom lip.

"Oh!" Hannah said loudly, and others at the gate paused in their own kissing and welcoming to stare. Hannah touched her finger to her lip. Blood crowned her index finger when she pulled it away.

"Welcome home," Sam said, breath hot against Hannah's ear.

II

DEBRA, 1969

*M*y mother took the business of womanhood seriously, showing the gifts God gave her to their best advantage, not unlike owners of poodles in heated competition. She attempted any trend rumored to make one thinner, younger, brighter. Never more intelligent—she didn't care about *that*—but brighter as in cheery, ever-beckoning, like linoleum scrubbed vigorously with vinegar. Weekly, my mother treated her hair with mayonnaise, massaging it into her scalp for upwards of an hour while she remained locked inside the bathroom paging through *Vogue*. She admired mayonnaise's conditioning properties, though remained leery of its fat content in a condiment capacity, slapping my hand if I dolloped too much on a sandwich, or ate too many deviled eggs at a picnic.

In the mid-1950s my mother had been a beauty queen, beautiful but with a girl-next-door quality, a wholesome affability, that pained her. She longed to be exquisite. As a child, I spent afternoons lingering over the pageant photos my mother safeguarded in a velveteen box. In my favorite, taken just after she'd won Miss Long Beach 1954, my mother poses with the runners-up, plain girls who may as well have been gargoyles standing on either side of her, their presence amplifying my mother's natural beauty.

Perhaps this was the moment my mother learned ugly girls—better yet, fat girls—were her best accessory, better even than diamonds shucked from mines and pearls dredged from the ocean's deep. I studied my mother's dark hair and porcelain skin, her graceful hands folded *just so* beside a corsage placed in her lap. In this photograph, her neck and the pearls encircling it are gorgeous things, the sweetheart neckline of her bathing suit exaggerating the angle of her breasts, but from the photographer's awkward vantage, my mother's thighs appear enlarged. In different light, there might have been evidence of cellulite. Still, her teeth and the whites of her eyes have a persuasive brilliance. Here she is: Miss Long Beach 1954. Healthy, genial, sweet.

"That girl had terribly hairy arms," my mother said once of the runner-up smiling so forcefully her cheeks looked stuffed. "Also, look how jagged her teeth are."

"What's she supposed to do about *that*?"

"That's not the smile for her. Something less toothy would work better."

"She's trying."

"Yes. Too hard. Beauty should look effortless."

My mother spoke with scorn of the lesser local titles a girl could have: Miss Sea Legs, Miss Frozen Food, Miss Home Freezer, Miss Letter Carrier. The winners of these pageants posed in kitschy promotional photographs depicting their titles. Miss Smog Fighter might gape openmouthed at the wisp of smoke rising from the open jar she held. Miss T-Square might be measured with a giant T-Square by a dashing man in a bowtie as they stood, inexplicably, on a boardwalk. Miss T-Square might wear a bathing suit and stilettos, and one might wonder if the bathing suit was worn to justify the boardwalk, or if the boardwalk was a convenient excuse for the bathing suit. In her photograph, Miss Shoe Tree might sit on a chair surrounded by countless pairs of shoes, some stilettos, some not, and in this way, Miss Shoe Tree, willing to be associated with flats, proved herself more well-rounded than the other girls.

My mother sought bigger titles. Miss California was the preliminary requirement for competition in Miss America, and Miss America was, my mother believed, her destiny. As someone possessing destiny, she preferred to hold the titles of places, not things. Miss San Fernando Valley was fine. Miss Christmas Tree was not. Miss Southern California Motorcyclist, referencing both places and things, was borderline. My mother claimed never to have won a local title. She simply wasn't the sort of girl who sought to be Miss Plumbing. Titles involving menial tasks—those suggesting the troublesome mysteries of *toilets*—were off limits. She claimed never to have posed in front of an open refrigerator beneath a sign declaring *Gas Is Dependable!* the glint of her smile suggesting *yes*, it most certainly was.

In the velveteen box, my mother kept two clipped newspaper articles. The newsprint had begun to fade, the occasional bottom of a *g* or *y* missing entirely, but I read and reread these articles, fascinated by this glamorous person who'd given birth to me. A story printed in the *Santa Barbara News Press* in May 1956 detailed her preparations for that year's Miss California pageant:

What, exactly, does a beauty queen's intensive training look like? To keep herself trim, the reigning Miss Santa Barbara performs calisthenics, in addition to advanced tapping classes several times weekly. Daily, she practices turning and gliding. It's important the toes go first, she tells us! On Saturdays, Miss Laurenzi works with a pageant coach. "Miss Margaret selects the clothing I'll wear in competition. She plans everything right down to the shade of lipstick! She considers the shape and finish of the jewelry I wear. We certainly don't want to annoy the judges because my earrings are too shiny or loud!" As for her beauty regime, Miss Laurenzi soaks her hair in mayonnaise weekly to moisturize it. She follows with a beer rinse to add protein and body. She describes her skin care routine, with a single coy smile, as "rigorous."

The second article recounted my parents' wedding:

Santa Barbara News Press, Saturday, June 29, 1957
FORMER MISS SANTA BARBARA WEDS FORMER CAL BEAR IN FAIRY TALE WEDDING.

New York City is the honeymoon destination of Mr. and Mrs. Webster Eugene Jackson (formerly Beverly Laurenzi), whose wedding was an event of last Sunday. Our Lady of the Snows Church provided the scene of the noon nuptials.

Mr. William Laurenzi escorted his only daughter down an aisle adorned with white roses and white cymbidium orchids. The bride wore an imported Chantilly lace gown with a low-cut square neckline and full-length Chantilly sleeves. The gown's fitted bodice extended into a bouffant skirt, also Chantilly lace over silk. The bride's full-length veil was affixed with a custom jeweled tiara, a nod to Miss Laurenzi's past participation in beauty pageants. She carried a large bouquet of white roses, additional white cymbidium orchids, phaleaenopsis orchids, and stephanotis. "Something Old" were pearl earrings passed down from the bridegroom's mother and previously worn by four generations of brides on the groom's side.

Following the ceremony, two hundred guests celebrated with luncheon at the bride's childhood home, dining beneath a white tent at tables set with white linen and silver-edged china. The tables' centerpieces were lush cascades of white roses and white hydrangea. The wedding cake, four tiers, was also adorned with white roses and additional white phaleaenopsis.

The bride's attendants wore matching frocks of pale-pink crystalline styled with long torso bodices and full skirts. They carried complementary bouquets of white roses. The mother of the bride, Mrs. Mary Laurenzi, selected an ivory-colored frock with ivory accessories, while the mother of the groom, Mrs. Edna Jackson of Oakland, wore Dior blue Italian silk set off by pink accessories. Sent on her honeymoon beneath a sea of rice, the bride wore a pale-green suit accentuated by gold.

Beverly Laurenzi represented Santa Barbara in the statewide Miss California competition in Santa Cruz last summer. A 1956 graduate of Santa Barbara High School, she was that class's Valedictorian. Webster Jackson was a former All-State Cal Bear who started Defensive Back for Pappy all four years of his tenure at Cal, from 1951–1954. Upon returning from their trip East, the couple will make a home in Santa Barbara, where Mr. Jackson will teach English at Santa Barbara High School.

"My own mother," my mother would say, reading this article over my shoulder. "*Ivory-colored frock.* She should have just worn a wedding gown."

I'd lived years in the same house with my paternal grandmother, but had had little dealing with my maternal grandmother, she of the ivory-colored frock, a woman whose face was set in a perpetual expression of angst. An asphyxiating cloud of perfume accompanied her everywhere. Her hair, mercilessly teased and sprayed, was the size and shape of a soccer ball and dense enough to bruise a man's shins. Incapable of washing her own hair, she attended the beauty parlor thrice weekly so her "lady" might wash and style it. She and my mother spoke hours on the phone discussing trivial matters, but a frostiness rose between them when they were physically together. Still, when I was twelve and my maternal grandmother became very ill, my mother announced she would travel to Santa Barbara over the Labor Day weekend to visit and care for her.

"*You?*" I asked. I was eleven, but I'd learned early that sick people annoyed my mother, who was, at best, an indifferent caretaker.

"Of course. She's my mother. One day you'll do the same for me. It's your inheritance."

"I thought that meant a house," I said. "And jewelry."

My mother said, "You don't want this house."

"I love this house."

My mother rolled her eyes.

Labor Day weekend, 1969. On Saturday morning, my mother materialized in the kitchen with a clatter of heels and impatience. She wore white slacks and a pattered tunic, an oversized sunhat more appropriate for the exotic places I'd seen on television, those with flickering torches and burgeoning flora. Labor Day weekend, 1969, my mother's beauty still radiated a creamy ease. She had not yet begun working at it. Beneath the kitchen's straining fluorescent light, my father and I admired her. We didn't question the practicality of white slacks proximate to illness. We did not acknowledge that her hat looked ridiculous indoors, nor that the morning was still so new there was not yet sun worth blocking. We knew, but did not declare: there was no sunshine in caretaking.

We drove as a family to the airport. As a family, we walked through the terminal's broad entrance, my father carrying my mother's suitcase. The suitcase was new, bird's-egg blue with gold trim. My father ferried it effortlessly to the ticket counter.

"Give your mother my regards," my father said at the gate, his voice the voice of someone trying to sound sorrier than he actually was.

"Yes, *yes*." My mother's voice was the voice of someone trying to sound less impatient. When my father leaned to kiss her goodbye, she turned. His lips met her cheek, and she slipped away from us.

"Well," my father said after the plane had departed the gate. We stood looking at the space where it had once been. "Are you hungry?"

In eleven-and-a-half years, I'd never been to breakfast alone with my father. He ordered us both coffee. I'd never drunk coffee. The first sip was a hurdle. Wrapping my hands around the mug, I felt adult, indoctrinated into a thing I didn't understand. I studied the menu. My mother would have insisted I order from the Calorie Counters section, where the unappetizing choices included a half grapefruit served with cottage cheese and something called Dieter's Catch: canned tuna inside a gutted tomato. My mother would have ordered this, attacking her makeshift bowl with glee. Watching her, I would wish such simple things could please me, though I knew, at heart, she was not easily pleased. I did not see the point of wasting happiness over something as mundane as a tomato.

I ordered eggs and hash browns, bacon, white toast. My father sat across from me, unfazed by the caloric excess. My mother's neurosis regarding my size had everything to do with my father, a large man who unabashedly took the space he needed. Rumor declared him handsome. Dreamy, mysterious. Girls at school, those with older sisters in my father's English class, whispered that my father was the reason their sisters read the difficult sentences in *The Grapes of Wrath* twice, three times. He was the reason they answered the essay questions with precisely indented paragraphs and careful penmanship.

What these girls called mystery was actually a fog that refused to burn off. Despite the physical magnitude of his body, my father always seemed elsewhere, untethered to place or circumstance.

My father said, "There's something I want to discuss. I have a plan."

"A plan," I said.

"Something I've considered for a while."

His plan was to take the neighbors' swing set from their backyard.

Every day, my mother stared out the kitchen window across the neighbors' bedraggled yard at that rusted, crooked object while she washed dishes. Every day, yanking off her rubber gloves, she declared that swing set an eyesore, an abomination. While the neighbors were celebrating Labor Day weekend, dipping their pale toes into the cold Pacific—their last hurrah before hunkering down to winter and rainy season—we would dismantle this corroded debacle, cart its pieces to someplace other. We would banish this hideous object from our present; relegate it to our past.

"You want to steal it," I said.

My father said, "I prefer to think of it as a beautification project. It will be our gift to your mother, our love song, while she is away doing an admirable thing."

He had already done reconnaissance, wandering over to make small talk as the father grilled sausages. The neighbor, wielding his tongs, waxed poetic about who produced the best bratwurst on the market, the merits of ketchup versus mustard as a condiment, while my father observed that the swing set had not been properly set with concrete. The poles had been dug into the earth without reinforcement; they wobbled continuously whenever the youngest son pumped his legs on the swing, proof that the neighbor, in addition to being a tedious man, was also lazy, more concerned with bratwurst than the safety of his family. My father felt certain he could pull those poles from the ground.

"You're serious."

"Of course."

"When?"

"Tonight." My father snuffed his cigarette in the ashtray. "After midnight. So eat your breakfast. Gather your strength. We have important work to do."

At home, my father did not demand I practice reading aloud—*elocution*, my mother called it—snapping the consonants like fruit pulled from the vine. The time to attend ballet class in a snug leotard, to look with shame upon my bulging stomach as the class pirouetted poorly, approached without mention.

The minute hand tick, ticked on the clock. Terrified of my mother's wrath I said, "I have ballet class."

"If you would like to attend ballet," my father said, "absolutely, you should go. A late dramatic entrance never hurt a ballerina. I suspect, however, that dance may not be your calling. There's no shame in this. There are other destinies."

We frittered the day away in a manner that would have appalled my mother. We ate in front of the television, dropping crumbs in the crevices of the couch. We gutted Ring Dings with our index fingers, embracing the self-declared bona fide good health they would provide us, their bodybuilding vitamins and iron. I peeled the chocolate sheath from a Yodel, felt the jagged pieces of chocolate like pills on my tongue. I imagined myself an unhappy lady who'd had enough. These pills set to dissolve on my clamoring tongue were the pills that would kill me. I imagined this unhappy woman was my mother and that, before her final heaving breath, as her eyes rolled hideously backward, she would believe herself fat and ugly, unloved.

For dinner, we drank Bubble Up and heated TV dinners inside their compartmentalized trays. On the television was *Untamed World. Locusts swarm land! Ant armies locked in battle! Caterpillars devise ingenious twig armor!* We dug into our TV dinners, swapping desserts—apple cranberry cake cobbler for apple cake cobbler, minuscule but significant distinction—turning our attention to *Tarzan and the Trappers,* circa 1958, the year of my birth. A scantily clad Tarzan with pectoral muscles larger than his loincloth barked, "Stop drum! Do not make war on trappers!"

"I've never understood," my father said. "Tarzan has no clothes, but inordinate amounts of pomade. Hollywood is magical yet paradoxical. Someday, we'll go there. I'll stroll with you and your mother along the Hollywood Walk of Fame. People passing us will turn their heads, certain your mother is an actress with her own star along the boulevard. We'll have aperitifs and shrimp cocktail. We'll toast ourselves, admire the setting sun in a fiery sky."

"I'm too young to drink aperitifs," I said.

"It will be our secret. What's life," my father sighed, "without a few sly secrets?"

That night, I stumbled behind my father across the grass to the neighbors' swing set, the flashlight he'd given me making concentric patterns on the grass. The moon—a quarter moon—eyed us, complicit with our plan. Stopping, my father stared at the contraption through the dark. Just when I wondered if he lacked follow-through, as my mother had always declared, he slung his toolbox onto the grass and got down to business.

I aimed the flashlight as my father completed the methodical task of unscrewing every tenuous screw holding that hideous swing set together. Simultaneously, he directed the stream of light: "Here, there. No. To the left. To the right. Thank you, Debra, you are an excellent accomplice." The rusted pieces accumulated in a heap: poles, braces, the chains holding worn swing seats, the set's decrepit slide. I'd watched the neighbors' children forcing themselves down that slide, disappointed every time it did not bear out the promise of its name. My arm grew tired from holding the flashlight. I switched hands. My other arm grew tired. I shivered in the night, waiting for something unexpected to happen the way it did in made-for-tv movies: a dog's sudden bark calling attention to us. A bedroom light yanked on abruptly, a neighbor's appalled face pressing the window. I did not yet know the most damning things occurred right beneath your nose with little fanfare; you had no idea they were happening.

The neighborhood slept soundly, resting up for whatever Labor Day celebrations awaited. I watched as my father worked—strong, capable man. How I loved his word, *accomplice*. I whispered it to myself, a mantra, holding the light steady.

When he'd finished, my father collapsed onto the cold grass, gazing at the dark sky. I lay beside him, memorizing this moment we would never experience again. We would be forever moving further from it: the scratch of the grass against our necks, the slight pressure of my father's shoulder against mine. Beside me, his breath had the slightest incriminating rasp of exertion. Staring at the quarter moon, the stars, I imagined my mother's joy over the swing set's disappearance. I imagined our own pleasure—mine and my father's, as if it were a singular pleasure—at her delight.

I asked, "Do you believe mother will provide comfort to grandmother?"

"I have no doubt," my father said.

I didn't believe my mother could provide comfort to anyone.

"Your mother," my father said, reading my thoughts, "does her best. Someday, maybe you'll be a mother and you'll do your best. You'll want your child to understand that."

"Maybe," I said.

He said, "I wish you could have seen her onstage at Miss California, how lovely she was, how well spoken. Her grace. You'd have been awed by her."

"I guess."

My father heaved himself from the grass, lent his hand to pull me up. "Let's get this stuff hidden."

We carried the dismantled pieces of the swing set to the shed, where my father buried them beneath tarp. We shook hands, congratulating ourselves on a job well done. We had effected change, however slight, and we slept the sound sleep of criminals who'd pulled off their caper.

Monday afternoon, Labor Day, we retrieved my mother from the airport. She emerged from the jetway as burnished as a copper pot.

"Mother," I said. "Did you forget to apply sunscreen in grandmother's sick room? Or did you misplace your sunhat?"

"A wind snatched it." My mother fluttered her hand. "Your grandmother preferred to be outdoors. She liked the sun on her face."

My father kissed the bloom of my mother's cheek. "The color suits you," he said. "Very nice, indeed."

"I forgot," my mother said. "The sun is a beast in the south. It's far more effective than this negligible northern sun."

"It's the same sun," I said.

"It isn't. One day, you'll acknowledge the difference yourself."

"We rotate around a singular sun."

"It's *rhetorical*." My mother snorted.

"You just *snorted*," I said.

Typically, the verb *snort* in relation to herself would have annoyed her. Pigs, not women, snorted. Now she appeared unfazed, and she uncharacteristically rolled down the passenger window, angling her chin into the wind without any regard for her hair. Into this rush of wind, my mother declared, "I *do not* like fog!"

"There's no fog," I said.

"There's *frequently* fog. There's frequently *a great deal* of fog."

She declared these things emphatically but cheerfully. Her excellent mood unnerved me. My mother wore many things well others couldn't: minuscule swimsuits, lipstick the color of succulent cherries. Happiness, she wore like a burlap sack. It was ill-fitted to her contours, a thing as easily collapsed as a lung.

At home, she moved lightly around the kitchen. My mother never moved lightly around the kitchen, a place she despised. As a result, her cooking involved slapdashery, dishes thrown into the oven, forgotten until the timer reminded her that such quotidian things as casseroles existed. Her culinary skills consisted of combining and pouring. The distinction between simmering and boiling confounded her. She never clipped out recipes instructing the cook to braise, poach, brine, truss, deglaze, caramelize, or sweat, and she either avoided ones requiring chopped onion or garlic or omitted these ingredients entirely, saying, "It's just *onion*."

By the time I was eight, my mother cycled through the same handful of recipes each week, never veering from the allotted course: Monday was Italian-Sauced Fish. Tuesday, Scalloped Deviled Ham. Wednesday, Yam and Sausage Skillet. Thursday, Oriental Casserole. Friday, Bologna Noodle Bake. Saturday, Smoked Beef and Macaroni. On Sundays, she demonstrated a modicum of improvisation, alternating between Mexican Supper Casserole and Mexicali Casserole, depending on whether canned chicken or sausage had gone on sale at the grocery store. Occasionally, in a moment of either grandiose aspiration or residual Catholic guilt, my mother attempted Creamy Ham Towers or Seafood Bake, the latter adding sophistication to our family dinner by dint of canned crab and shrimp, condensed cream-of-celery soup.

Upon returning home on Labor Day, my mother began preparing Italian-Sauced Fish. Why, I asked myself, couldn't we grill hamburgers like a normal family? Slinging peas inside a pot then a bowl, she proceeded to Italian sauce the fish. Several times, she glanced out the window that looked upon the neighbor's yard, but her oversized happiness obscured the view. She did not notice the absence of the swing set.

We ate dinner beneath the unnerving stares of the figurines in the curio cabinet. My father dished dry gray peas onto a plate, asking, "And how is Mother?"

"Not well." Tears at the corners of my mother's eyes. "I've made arrangements to return in two weeks." She added, "If that's all right."

"Of course," my father said.

"It's a terrible thing to see your mother incapacitated, Debra." She looked at me. "I hope you'll be spared that experience."

I nodded in a manner I hoped appeared sympathetic, but already I grasped that I preferred my life when my mother was not in it. We chewed in silence, listening to the *tick tock tick* of the grandfather clock. My mother stabbed at the fish without eating it, which was her way. Soon, the doorbell interrupted the infinitesimal space between *tick* and *tock*.

"What on earth?" Pushing from the table, my mother went to the door. We waited for her return. We waited some more. I realized something existed worse than Italian-Sauced Fish, and this was cold Italian-Sauced Fish. My father touched his fork to the congealed mozzarella on his plate.

Returning at last, my mother said, "It appears someone stole the Russells' swing set while they were in Santa Cruz. The youngest went to play before dinner and found nothing but four holes in the ground. Dennis was asking if we noticed anything. I told him I was away myself, but maybe you'd noticed something."

"If I remember correctly," my father said with a slight smile, "that rusted debacle was an eyesore."

"What kind of person steals a swing set?" my mother asked. "It's an assault on the notion of family. Their boy is devastated."

"He'll recover," my father said, sounding uneasy. Our eyes met. His skittered away.

"I had no idea we live surrounded by criminals!"

"I'm sure it wasn't true criminality," my father said. "Only a matter of self-preservation."

"I don't know what you're saying! I don't understand this confused philosophy!"

My father stood stiffly, poured himself a bourbon from the decanter stashed in the cabinet. When he returned to the head of the table, I went to him. He held his left arm around my waist, lifted the glass with his right. We stood like this until my mother, clearing the table with impatient clanging, shooed us to the living room. I lingered as she washed the dishes with more care than usual, ran the sponge along the curves of the plates. She hummed into the pots, never once looked out the window.

My mother spent an increasing number of weekends in Santa Barbara. While she was presumably serving my grandmother applesauce and lukewarm water, proffering the bedpan when she needed it, my father and I grew closer. We hiked in the hills, went to museums, watched movies. We cooked Julia Child's boeuf bourguignon and sole meunière, her tarte tatin and mousse au chocolate. On one of these weekends together, as I relished my mother's absence, my father told me: when my mother turned sixteen, my grandfather bought her a new car, a white Cadillac convertible, sleek and beautiful. My mother loved this car, but in 1955, when she was seventeen, she crashed it. She was driving to her boyfriend's house at the time, singing along to whatever song played on the radio. My father didn't know the exact song. It could have been "If I Give My Heart to You" by Doris Day, or "That's Amore" by Dean Martin, or "Little Things Mean a Lot" by Kitty Kallen. These were songs to croon to, my father said, and in her crooning, my mother accidentally pressed the car's lighter into the socket with her knee. A moment later, as my mother skimmed down the road in her white convertible, the lighter finished heating and popped out, landed against my mother's thigh. It was January, my father said, but unseasonably warm. She wore shorts. Startled by the sudden searing pain, my mother lost control of the car, which careened off the road and into a billboard. The billboard was a low-lying number propped up by stakes; my mother drove the Cadillac right through its center. Days later, the local newspaper printed a story about the incident. My father produced the carefully folded clipping from his pocket and handed it to me, watching as I smoothed it open.

Santa Barbara News Press, Thursday, January 27, 1955
LIGHTER POPS, BEAUTY QUEEN CRASHES!

A local pageant Queen is recovering and has resumed her training following a dramatic roadside crash last Sunday.

Beverly Lorenzi, 17, of Santa Barbara, daughter of Mr. and Mrs. William Laurenzi, crashed her automobile into the Arden Diced Cream billboard just off Highway 5. The incident occurred late morning when, the teen says, the car's lighter launched itself from its socket and into the car, landing against her leg. Questioned regarding how the lighter began its damaging trajectory, Miss Laurenzi had no real answer, saying only, "It happened so fast!"

The teen's mother, Mary Laurenzi, who heads the local Kiwanis chapter, expressed concern over her daughter's injury, for Miss Laurenzi's right thigh is now marred by a circular burn as a result of the wayward lighter. Beverly Laurenzi does indeed need her legs in perfect condition! The teen, currently the reigning Miss Real Cool 1955, represents Munroe Appliances and will compete for the title of Miss Santa Barbara in several short weeks. (In related news, please see our article on page 7 summarizing Arden's legal troubles regarding its diced cream product.)

Several grainy images appeared beside this article, including a photo at the scene of the accident in which my mother posed before, and pointed at, the gaping hole in the Arden Diced Cream billboard. She wore pageant attire: tremendous dress, affixed tiara, her mouth an O of feigned dismay.

I touched the grainy face. "She gave you this?"

"Your grandfather did when we got engaged. He thought it was hilarious. You know your grandfather. But also he may have wanted to dissuade me. I was certainly not the man they'd hoped for her. But nothing—nothing on earth!—could have torn me away from your mother."

I'd seen my grandfather sparingly in my eleven-and-a-half years. I did *not* know him, just as until that moment, I did not know about my mother's car crash. Didn't know about Miss Real Cool, or Arden Diced Cream. I knew only that when my mother returned from her weekends in Santa Barbara, she was a stranger.

Those nights, I waited for her to join us after the washing of the dishes, to sit with us, watch *Gunsmoke* or *The Avengers* or *Mayberry R.F.D.* Instead, she took baths. I heard the rush of the water through the pipes, signaling she'd chosen, not us, but a lukewarm soak. Lukewarm because that temperature was best for a woman's skin. It delayed a woman's inevitable decline, preserved what demanded preserving—though it's possible she drew a scalding bath. It's possible she plunged in without regard for even her hair. Maybe she held herself beneath the water, counting how long she could hold her breath. Anything was possible. The woman who'd left us Labor Day weekend, 1969, was not the woman who returned. We had no clue, it appeared, about the person who'd stepped off the jetway.

WEBB, 1956

He'd met Beverly Laurenzi by chance when she'd visited her cousin at Cal one weekend. House party, crush of people. She, a buxom beauty, all lipstick and lash and perky breasts he couldn't stop admiring. He'd graduated the year before and was attending this party with his fiancée, still a student, who clung to his arm like a drowning person grabbing flotsam in a raging sea. Betsy surely felt the current that tugged him as Beverly Laurenzi's hand touched his in introduction. The wedding was scheduled for sultry July. They still found themselves inside the remnants of winter yielding to spring, the last drops of rainy season. Betsy, absentminded, had forgotten her umbrella. She stood rain-splattered beside him, as wilted as a used tissue dredged from someone's pocket.

"And who's this?" Beverly asked, staring at Betsy.

"This is my fiancée," he said, remembering her.

"Hello, fiancée," said Beverly. "Do you have a name?"

Webb's throat was thick with mortification. He said, "This is Betsy."

"Betsy," said Beverly, who shamed Webb further: "Let's find you a towel."

Wrapping her hand around Betsy's wide middle, Beverly steered her down the hallway to the bathroom. Betsy had worn heels to this party. Her ankles caved inwards like a child new to ice skates, but her waist had never looked as attractive as it did in that moment, with Beverly's arm ensnaring it. He doted on Betsy the rest of the evening, touching the small of her back, offering drinks and canapés, but neither could he stop watching Beverly, as if she were a bee let accidentally into the house, threatening to sting.

She telephoned him the following week—*she* phoned *him*, a man with a fiancée!—asking, did he remember her? Her voice, cool as peppermint candy, scraped his insides raw. He'd cataloged every moment she appeared at the corner of his eyesight that evening: "You stood at the punch bowl with Jimmy Sanders, who said something that made you laugh. You drank the punch he poured you. In the living room, later, you sat on the couch with crossed legs. You arranged a curl in your hair and ate one bite of a sugar cookie."

He joked, "I guess I remember you."

Her flustered silence told him she didn't know he was joking. (Years later, hearing this story, Hila would say, "Oh, Webster. There's no intimacy to be found with a woman who doesn't understand a man's humor.")

As they conversed, he imagined them protagonists of a modern fairy tale: football hero, beauty queen. For Beverly Laurenzi—sipper of Jimmy Sanders's poured punch, laugher at Jimmy Sanders's lackluster jokes—would compete in the Miss California pageant this coming June. Webb had never known a beauty queen; had only seen them on television, his mother mumbling about painted floozies as they turned in their swimsuits. A beauty queen! He asked a great many questions regarding Beverly Laurenzi's clothing selection, her beauty regime, couching the questions as if they stemmed from a pure interest in her rather than his own preoccupation with beauty tricks and tulle. What color bathing suit? What cut of evening gown? How did she choose what to wear for the interview? How did she approach accessorizing? For the four months they spoke on the telephone, the topic was almost exclusively the Miss California pageant. Webb could not have said, *Well, Beverly Laurenzi prefers smooth peanut butter to crunchy.* He could not have said, *Beverly Laurenzi sneezes at the scent of freshly mown grass.* He knew, however, that yellow made her skin appear sallow. (Yellow, Webb would later learn, was a tricky beast.) He knew that Beverly Laurenzi preferred Mango Passion for everyday lipstick, and Crimson Crime for evening competition. He knew that during breakfast interviews, she checked her distorted reflection in the bright silver of the coffee pot. That once, before a dramatic recitation, she stuck a pepper into her eye so that onstage, she might appear appropriately teary. Having scant talent for dramatic recitation, she'd given it up for tapping, whose costumes were shorter and more heavily sequined.

A week before the pageant, Beverly said, "You should come to the competition."

"Why would I do that?" Webb asked, his voice a flirtation, as if he were not scheduled to be married to a woman whom, months earlier, urged on by his mother, he'd declared his absolute love for. Betsy—studious and steady, shy and deferential, devoted—would, his mother claimed, make a worthy partner.

"Because, well." Her words were wisps, tickling. "I'd like you to."

Webb had never left the Bay Area, but now he would drive to Santa Cruz to see Beverly Laurenzi of Santa Barbara crowned Miss California. He knew she would be.

The morning of his departure, his mother turned her cheek before he could kiss it goodbye. "Does Bets know you're wasting money and gas to see this doxy put herself on display?"

"Mother." He'd told Bets nothing, but he spoke with enough reproof to suggest he had.

The contestants in the Miss California pageant were forbidden contact with the male gender; chaperones followed the so-called floozies like train cabooses. As a spectator, Webb saw Beverly from a careful distance as she and the others paraded through the business district Friday afternoon. Crowds on either side of the street cheered them on. *Oh*, Beverly—wearing a lilac frock covered with white eyelet, its skirts so full the other girls couldn't wander too near. She walked the entire length of the welcome parade in stilettos, reminding him of Betsy and her ankles quivering like Jell-O. His fiancée was likely at home, bent over her biology books, chewing her lip in concentration. His guilt proved both annoying and fleeting. He concentrated instead on the swish of Miss Santa Barbara's skirts, a direct correlation, he knew, to the lusty movement of her hips.

He found his way into her orbit that evening at the Cocoanut Grove, where a dance was held so pageant attendees might meet the girls in their swimming attire, pose with them for photographs. Beverly wore a fiery red swimsuit with black embroidery—a questionable choice, Webb thought. Its halter top gave her breasts an unnatural perkiness even for the current trend. The embroidery perhaps overemphasized her thighs. But what a clever actor she was beneath the chaperones' watchful gazes!

"Good to meet you, Miss Santa Barbara."

"And who are you?"

"Webster Jackson, from Oakland."

"Hello, Webster from Oakland. Do you attend college?"

"I graduated from Cal."

"I bet you played football!"

"Strong safety."

"Do you have a girlfriend to keep you company at night, Webster from Oakland?"

"No."

Technically, this was true. Her eyes buzzed at him. Crimson Crime on her lips. Hair so shiny from those mayonnaise marinades she'd detailed to him during phone conversations; who knew mayonnaise could be so titillating? He yearned to touch her clavicle, glinting like costume jewelry above her bathing top. The contestants posed, blinking at the camera as a man snapped their photo. Her hand casually brushed his hip. Inside him, an inferno.

The next day, Saturday, was the talent competition. Miss Sacramento read a religious poem, verse she claimed to have written after waking from a powerful dream. Her many strained pauses suggested she needed more fiber in her diet. Miss Lakeport twirled a baton to "Standing on the Corner" by Dean Martin. ("Brother, you can't go to jail for what you're thinking," sang Dean while Miss Lakeport twirled, twirled.) Miss San Jose performed a lighthearted hula about a car ride. Miss Castro Valley presented her own paper sculpting. Miss Los Angeles recited a composite of poems she'd written on the topic of kissin'. ("Easy now, boys!" declared the emcee.) Miss Albany presented a mottled film of herself swimming, set to narration she too had written: "Stroke through the chlorine water / stroke through the makeshift sea." Webb had not known beauty queens were such a poetic bunch. Where was Beverly? Where *was* she? Miss San Diego sang a jaunty medley of French tunes. *Yes*, that was a baguette she whirled into the air. Finally, Miss Santa Barbara appeared onstage in a red costume, tapping to "Puttin' on the Ritz." (*Oh* no, Webb thought. She wore red twice.) Beverly tap-tapped, the fringe on her skirt shaking. She wore a black top hat, black fishnet stockings. Despite her poor color choice, he wanted to swallow her whole, wanted to feel the contours of her inside him—her elbow against his spleen, her knee against his lung. Her this against his that. He would regurgitate her, swallow her again. These thoughts frightened him, but what had Dean Martin just sung? *Brother, you can't go to jail for what you're thinking.*

The next morning, the contestants walked in a pastel herd to the chapel. Webb stood on the corner, part of a mob trying to glimpse the beauty queens. Snatch of Beverly in cotton-candy-pink chiffon. (Dusty rose would have been better for her coloring, and her pearls hung too low for that square neckline. Miss Margaret was useless!) An hour later, the mob broke into applause as the competitors exited the chapel with pious expressions suggesting they hadn't just prayed to the Lord God, Heavenly Father to please let them win. They smiled and waved at the crowd as they walked to their hotel rooms to prepare for the finale, where before thirty thousand spectators, the five finalists would be announced and brought onstage for interviews.

Awaiting the announcement of the finalists, the shoulders of other men pressing him, Webb felt sick; what if Beverly wasn't selected? But there she was, the third girl called onstage—deep exhale—standing in a pewter-colored dress beside two less beautiful girls. Soon, the emcee was shoving his microphone into Beverly's face and asking his questions.

"With all the modern modes of transportation, where would you like to spend your honeymoon?"

"I'm sure anywhere would be a wonderful place to visit with my one true love, but I'd most like to visit New York City. I'd like to see the Empire State Building! I'd like to meet that loveliest of ladies, Lady Liberty! Speaking of ladies, I dream of seeing *My Fair Lady* on Broadway."

"Has the time arrived for a woman to serve as president or vice president?"

"Historically, women have been granted a special place inside the home. They provide restful homes so men might feel focused and rejuvenated to do their important work outside the home. Men have run this country for hundreds of years and done a fine job of it. I believe women should cherish their work inside the home and leave presidency to the men."

"How has participating in the Miss California pageant enriched your life?"

"Here at the Miss California pageant, I've learned the *true meaning* of female community. I've met girls who will be my forever family. These girls will sustain me through thick and thin. They will be aunts to my children. *I'll* be an aunt to *their* children. This community is something I will cherish my entire life."

"Thank you, Miss Santa Barbara!"

The tension waiting for the judges to name the winner was not unlike that of watching football games: praying the defense would solve the riddle of the offense, praying the offense would elude the defense. Onstage, the final five leaned into one another, held one another's hands. The emcee cleared his throat; Webb's breath wavered, suspended.

Later, he would think it odd that the first runner-up, the closest thing to the winner, was so lost inside the fray. Better to be fourth runner-up; everyone at least looks at you, claps politely. Better to be third runner-up, second runner-up. The first runner-up is simply shoved aside to make way for the winner. Beverly, first runner-up, smiled and clapped and kissed Miss California 1956 as Miss California 1955 affixed the tiara to her bouffant. Looking at Beverly's ceaseless smile, Webb thought, *There's a woman with grace. There's a woman to spend an entire life with.*

The crowd dispersed. Rather than return with the throng back to the Boardwalk, Webb walked instead toward the ocean.

Throughout his life, he'd seen the Pacific but never touched it; had never frolicked in its waters as he'd seen others do. He walked now through the hot sand toward the surf, mesmerized by the swells, the waves' constant rush and recede. He removed his shoes and socks, tucked them into the sand. Like a tongue, the water lapped his toes. Colder than he expected, it caused him to yelp. The residual pageant-goers stared at him. He waved, and they turned away. His toes sank deeper into the wet sand.

He inched forward, water swirling around his ankles, then continued on until it lapped his kneecaps. Soon, it hugged his waist. Waves crashed against him. His sodden pants clamped his legs. The pull of his clothing terrified him, threatened to drag him under. *The ocean* terrified him, with its countless things he couldn't see, existing beneath its dark surface. This surface, in the lull between waves, quivered like the skin on a custard. He considered rushing back to shore but decided he would stand waist-deep in the cold ocean for a full minute. He consulted his watch. Stupid! He'd forgotten about it, and time had stopped.

He thought, *There's time enough for you, Webster Jackson. The watch is a goner, but you can still change. You can marry this beautiful girl, be man enough for her. She can be woman enough for you.* Standing in the swollen ocean, he imagined a life with Beverly Laurenzi. He had never been much interested in the world, nor in being a man. The tedious tasks surrounding manhood made him weary—but for this graceful beauty, Beverly Laurenzi, he would relegate these truths, dark and swirling like an ocean, to the furthest reaches of himself. He would heed his mother's words, years ago, as he stood in that beautiful floral apron: "We must often be very quiet about the things which make us happiest."

To seal this pact with himself, Webb ducked beneath the water, holding his breath until his lungs threatened to burst. He emerged flailing, gasping for air, a different man.

Hila was the only one he'd told. Years later. They sat in the yard, drinking bourbon amid the jasmine.

"Oh, Webster," she'd sighed. "A man can't baptize himself."

"It's a metaphor."

"Love. Never make promises to yourself you can't keep. They'll only return to haunt you."

He found Hila beautiful, sitting in the yard, wrapped with blankets, cheeks rosy with either whiskey or cold. His heart banged wildly inside him. He thought, *I should marry this perfect human.*

"I had an epiphany," he said. (To himself: *I am* having *an epiphany.*)

"Epiphanies are dubious bitches. Sometimes, yes, they're truths, things a person has been too oblivious to see, but usually they're just projections of what the person wants to believe, the story he needs to tell himself so he might move forward."

Because she sat before him doubting epiphanies, he did not tell her: *I love you. I will always love you. Let's go, together, to the courthouse. Tomorrow, as soon as it opens. Let's go now. I'll break down the doors. I won't take no for an answer.*

"Webster, you taught English. You should know to avoid epiphany just as you do overwrought metaphor."

Slipping his glass from his hand, she went to get more bourbon, so he did not tell her she was right. He'd trusted his epiphany inside the cold sea because he had no other recourse. Had no choice *but* to emerge from the ocean a different man, his wet clothes clinging, his mouth dry from the salt water he'd inadvertently swallowed. His pants had chafed his legs. He thought he might scream. *Webster,* he reminded himself, *men don't scream.*

Showering at his spartan hotel, he scrubbed himself raw and emerged cleansed. Scrubbed, raw, cleansed—these words, their implications, would have proven problematic to Hila but were all he had. Cleansed, *raw,* he waited for Beverly Laurenzi on the Boardwalk still clogged with pageant-watchers. Screams from the Giant Dipper warbled; the air smelled thickly of funnel cake.

She came to him very plain. Cropped pants and t-shirt, face devoid of makeup. He felt dizzy with the obvious metaphor of it—here, again, was metaphor—that he was seeing her now so clearly, without powder and crimson lips, without dark and beguiling lashes. A short time earlier, she'd stood onstage in her feathery pewter dress, and he'd believed this woman was the woman he'd spend his life with, or else. He knew it now with less certainty as his thoughts leapt ahead to the ugliness that lay before him. He saw the hideous crumpling of Betsy's face, felt his mother's sharp disappointment. Webb could pay for the cancelled wedding out of his own savings. Writing checks for the hall, the dress, the flowers would be easy enough. Betsy's sadness, his mother's judgment: these were things for which he'd never finish paying.

On a bench facing the ocean, he sat wordlessly with Beverly Laurenzi, first runner-up to Miss California. Casting her a sidelong glance, he realized she'd been crying. He said, "Should we eat some funnel cake?"

"I don't want funnel cake."

"What is it you'd like?"

He'd asked an impossible question, harder than anything the emcee had asked earlier. A question he himself would not answer, at least not aloud. Perhaps she felt the same, for she remained quiet. Then, taking his hand, Beverly Laurenzi led him silently to a darkened place beneath the pier. Carnival music swelled. Stink of seaweed, buzz of gnat. Beverly Laurenzi unbuttoned his slacks. From too near came the sounds of children on the beach. Webb thought, *We are going to fornicate in a public place.* She yanked his pants down to his ankles, knocked him onto the sand effortlessly, and straddled him. Webb thought, *Who is this person? Did Beverly Laurenzi like creamy or crunchy peanut butter? Did she sneeze at the scent of freshly mown grass? Was she opposed to or titillated by Elvis Presley's hip gyrations?* Beverly Laurenzi moved her own hips on top of him. She looked unwaveringly into his eyes, and in that dark underbelly of the pier, had her way with him.

Despite its brevity, the act allowed for a whirligig of confusion. The seaweed's sour scent gagged him, but he felt good. Good, *good.* Then reality impinged, as though a curtain had been drawn back, exposing it. He had a fiancée. They were to marry in one month. They'd chosen wedding bands, selected cake. When he'd proposed, she cried, declared herself the happiest, luckiest girl. "I don't deserve you," she said, and she didn't, but for reasons opposite those she thought.

Beverly Laurenzi of the pert breasts stretched her neck and emitted a high-pitched moan. In the surprise of her ecstasy, she jerked her head forward just as he was craning up to kiss her. She knocked her forehead against his chin with a crack.

"Webster," his mother would say when he broke his engagement. "Who are you?"

"Your son."

"My unrecognizable son," she would say.

Beneath the pier, he took Beverly Laurenzi's head between his hands and soon realized he held her like a child holds a kitten, too tightly, until he accidentally suffocates it.

"Marry me," he said, and she nodded.

BEVERLY, 1957

*H*e never stopped talking about his mother. Not as he and Beverly walked in the dappled afternoon sun, nor as they waited in line at the theater. Not even at the soda fountain, when Beverly pivoted on the stool to show her best side. There was nothing the ever-talented Mrs. Edna Jackson could not do!

"She has a flair for the beautiful," Webster said, not undramatically. "I can't wait for you to meet her."

To Beverly, sipping chocolate Coke daintily through a straw (on which she left the prettiest of lipstick kisses), what Webster described sounded not like flair but rather neurosis. His mother sounded like a nut job! *You'd be wise to marry a man who loves his mother so dearly*, Beverly told herself. *His father died recently. She's alone, and he's protective of her.* A whisper of doubt responded, *A grown man so attached to his mother is unnatural! His relationship with her will doom yours.* Still, she smiled brightly, intermittently exclaiming, "How wonderful! Marvelous!" at things she believed neither wonderful nor marvelous.

In the days before the War, his mother threw countless dinners, overseeing (neurotically!) every special detail. She measured—with a *ruler!*—the tablecloth's overhang. She meticulously squared plates, ironed the cloth napkins before folding them. She gathered roses from the garden (*of course* she'd grown them) and arranged the centerpieces herself (*of course* she'd arranged them), selecting harmoniously hued flowers and the correctly shaped vessel for whatever mood she sought. (Beverly stopped herself from asking: did she form the vase herself using clay she'd dug from the yard with her bare hands?) Mrs. Edna Jackson made cards for each place setting, painting the edges of the paper with gold ink, writing the guests' names in calligraphy. Chancery and uncial were her go-tos, said Webster, but certainly, if pressed, she could do Gothic and Old English lettering. (Beverly's Catholic-girl penmanship, of which she'd always been proud, now appeared as elegant as urine sprayed onto a bathroom wall.)

Edna cooked the dishes for these parties with her friend Charlotte ("Charlotte is a second mother to me," declared Webster), serving her guests with an open, graceful hand. For Edna knew about left-hand service *and* right-hand service. She remained inflexible on the concept of the ever-present plate. Guests' water glasses were kept three-fourths full. Cold dishes were served on cold plates, hot dishes on hot plates. The rim of every plate, hot or cold, was wiped free of fingerprints. She was passionate about finger bowls.

"There was never a cook as good as my mother," Webster said, sucking down a vanilla milkshake. Beverly reminded herself: *a man who respects women's work within the home is rare and wonderful.* Beverly's father grunted when her mother placed dinner on the table, a grunt not of appreciation, but an acknowledgment of food's presence before him. Her own mother combined ingredients halfheartedly, serving dishes with a clatter, and if that wasn't enough to bring Beverly to the table, she yelled, *Dinner!* But Edna boiled and pan-boiled and poached and oven-poached. She braised and fricasseed. She larded. She preserved and pickled. Using only a potato, she clarified and purified cooking oil for reuse. She chopped the backbone from a chicken as she discussed *Our Gal Sunday*. She was a saucier, a master baker. Probably even a candlestick maker. Possibly, she could foretell the future, sing arias, pirouette endlessly, scale the highest of mountain peaks, survive without oxygen. Levitate.

Said Webster, "My mother has poise."

Something ugly tugged inside her, but smiling her pageant-girl smile at this man she'd agreed to marry—this man she barely knew—Beverly said, "How wonderful! Marvelous!"

One afternoon, in the dawn of their marriage, when Webster was teaching and Edna out being a pillar of the community, Beverly let herself into Edna's bedroom.

Dear Edna kept her bedroom like a church: quiet, dark, devoid of dust. Spread across the bed was the ubiquitous chenille spread of Edna's generation. On the nightstand was a candy dish filled with Richardson After

Dinner Mints. In the dim hush, Beverly opened the nightstand drawers with hollow thunks: nothing. She moved on to the dresser, thumbing Edna's silken things folded carefully inside the top drawer. These silken things emitted a cloying scent she associated with purple. Lavender, lilac. Beverly shoved the drawer shut.

Opening the beautiful beast that was Edna's armoire, Beverly touched the hanging dresses one by one. She would have liked to try Edna's pretty things on her own body (even Beverly could admit Mrs. Edna Jackson had excellent taste in clothing), but Beverly couldn't have fit in Edna's clothes if she tried: she still possessed the hourglass figure that had failed her in Santa Cruz. Edna's hips, a metaphor for Edna herself, were straight and narrow, like an apartment building's unwelcoming hallway. If Beverly could have gotten Edna's dresses over her own hips, she might have pretended she was a different woman entirely. Happy, topped off like a gas tank with her joy! She'd be everything she'd promised and had been promised: an envied wife, an admired homemaker, a sought-after lover. She wasn't *just* a failed beauty queen with a mediocre talent for tapping. She was capable of actual conversation, something more than the breathy utterances with which she'd boggled the pageant judges.

Instead, Beverly strapped on a pair of Edna's shoes. Walking with mincing steps across Edna's tasteful bedroom rug, she performed her best impersonation, hitting the notes of Edna's speech as if they were a song: "Webster! What is it you need? Beverly, don't trouble yourself. I'm his mother, I'll get it. How many sugars in your coffee this morning, my darling? How would you like your eggs? One poached, one sunny side up, one scrambled? Yes, of course."

Beverly had just latched Edna's pearls around her neck when, inside the armoire, inside a box slipped inside a different box in the bottom drawer, she discovered a collection of letters, small bundles tied together with beautiful ribbon, as if they'd been painstakingly sorted. They smelled of perfume. Joy by Jean Patou, to be exact. The world's so-called costliest perfume. Beverly's mother presided over the perfume counters at the department stores; had trained Beverly at a young age to dab a bit languidly on her pale wrist, to identify abelmosk and absinthe, bergamot and bigarade; to push the tiny vial back to the saleswoman, saying with derision, "Sandalwood." It surprised Beverly that Edna—who made *headcheese*, who seemed always elbow-deep in animal innards, a woman who handled the chicken manure for the garden *without gloves*—that *she* possessed letters spritzed with the world's costliest perfume.

Edna was at the Rockridge Improvement Club having tedious conversations about community. Climbing into her bed with the box of letters, Beverly stole a Richardson After Dinner Mint from the candy dish, untied a bundle. The letters each began in meticulous penmanship devolving into a loose, shoddy hand as they gained momentum. They were, all of them, signed *Your C.*

Dearest Edna—
On the coast at Sea Ranch today with Alfonse . . .

Here, Beverly paused. There were men actually named Alfonse?

On the coast at Sea Ranch today with Alfonse and inside the briny air . . .

Beverly considered the craggy Northern California coast she'd heard tell of but hadn't seen. This northern coast belonged, presumably, to the sweater-wearing seagoers rather than the bikini-clad seagoers Beverly had grown up with. As someone who looked remarkable in a sweater, Beverly yearned to visit the coast wearing one. She imagined herself, smiling beguilingly as the northern Pacific air tousled her hair and lifted her skirt, but Webster, wary of adventure, insisted he couldn't leave his dearest mother alone, even briefly. He would worry too much. So summer had passed, and he'd not yet taken Beverly to the coast. He'd not yet taken her anywhere.

. . . inside the briny air, I thought of nothing except you. I picked blackberries along the bluffs and emerged with blood smattering my hands and wrists. I imagined you, capable, tending my wounds. I made pie with the berries because it's your favorite, my darling. I was of course careful not to overhandle the crust, just as you showed me.

Beverly skimmed, caring little for culinary advice, though she now had a deep craving for blackberry pie.

You would have been proud, though my efforts went unnoticed by Alfonse. That man couldn't discern a tender pastry crust if his life depended on it, and unfortunately his life does not depend on it.

As a pageant girl, Beverly had maintained overwrought female friendships. She'd been one girl in a pastel sea of girls resembling the after-dinner mints in Edna's bedside candy dish. The particularities of competition demanded they get fresh with one another: Beverly yanked girls' bosoms into sweetheart necklines, stuffed their buttocks into swimsuit bottoms. Posing shoulder to shoulder in bathing suits for promotional photos, Beverly couldn't have determined whether the sweat on her thigh was her own, or the sweat of Miss Sacramento sweating profusely beside her. Her relationship with these girls was superficially close and critically distant. Amiable, but strung with tension. Standing with her leg cocked jauntily beside Peggy Sue or Patty May—hers was the generation of girls with two first names—Beverly compared her leg's girth and coloring to those of the legs bracketing it. Hugging these girls at day's end, she gauged their thinness, their firmness, this touching a litmus test rather than an affectionate gesture.

During interviews, Beverly claimed to have extravagant feelings toward these girls; a glut of emotion regarding sorority was expected of her. Catching glimpses of herself in the polished coffee thermos (yes, her curls were holding!), she spoke of the camaraderie they all shared. Ten years from now, she told the judges sitting across from her, even twenty years from now—no, for the rest of her life—these women would be her friends.

It was all false, of course. As Beverly, married just four months, lay in Edna's bed reading her letters, she realized she had no fierce female friendships. Edna did, and while it humanized Edna-the-paragon to some extent, it also rankled. Here, again, her mother-in-law had outstripped her. She was putting down the pages, intent on returning them to their hiding place, when the next passage caught her eye. Reading on, Beverly emitted a sharp "*Oh!*"

I imagine your mouth [the mysterious C wrote of her blackberry wounds] *soothing the scratches. I imagine your lips traveling to the private crevices of my body. The ensuing ecstasies.*

Beverly bolted upright and hunched over the letter.

I try, when Alfonse lies on top of me, to imagine that I am with you, my dar-
ling, except the weight of him is so unlike yours, his body so unlike yours. His
lips, nothing like your lips. Afterward, I lock myself in the bathroom and draw
a hot bath. I rid myself of his touch and imagine you. I touch my thigh, my
stomach, the unspeakable places. I imagine my fingers are your fingers. I close
my eyes and believe it's you.

"It's hard for you, I know," Edna had said one afternoon, instructing
Beverly in the proper scrubbing of the bathtub. "It's nothing your mother
ever taught you. But unlike with pageants, you have to get in and get dirty.
You have to put in some elbow grease."

You have to get in and get dirty. Well, it certainly seemed Edna had. Beverly wanted to burst with disgust at her newfound knowledge. Though she'd
heard tell of lesbians, she assumed she'd be fortunate enough never to meet
one. Edna, ever capable, had brought another woman to so-called ensuing
ecstasies. Throwing down the letter, it came to her: Edna was a lesbian with
Charlotte. C was Charlotte. Edna's lips had traveled the private crevices
of *Charlotte's* body. Edna had brought *Charlotte* to ensuing ecstasies—this
woman who still made her grown son peanut butter and pickle sandwiches,
cutting them into triangles as if he were a kindergartner. "Lesbian." Beverly
said the word out loud as she returned the letters to the drawer, remade the
bed, shook the candy dish so it seemed nothing had been eaten. The word
clogged her throat like a fistful of hair inside a drain, gave her tongue a
leaden feeling. Reflected in Edna's vanity mirror, Beverly's face appeared
distorted, ugly. She thought, *This is how a person pays for a rash decision, for*
treating her life with frivolity.

Just weeks into her marriage, Beverly had understood she'd made a terrible mistake. Then for months after that realization, her insides had been
the shaken scene inside a snow globe. When the flurries settled, the core
truth remained: in choosing Webster, she had been wrong.

"Where will you be spending your honeymoon?" asked the wedding
guests.

"New York City!" she'd answered, filled with wonder over the prospect. She'd never been to the East Coast. She'd expected to travel there as Miss California; well, she would go as the newly minted Mrs. Webster Eugene Jackson. She'd selected a new suitcase for her travels, bird's egg blue with gold trim. She had arranged the prettiest outfits, made dinner reservations, purchased tickets for Broadway shows.

On the car ride from the reception, Beverly plucked rice grains from her hair, from the folds of her pale-green suit. She felt a grain on her tongue, another inside her bra, and realized that nothing was as romantic as what a person either wanted it to be or had been told it would be. At least in the car, she could remove her heels.

The following morning, Webster spent a long while speaking quietly on the telephone before pulling her aside. "Mother is having a bout."

"About," Beverly said.

"A *bout*." Webster emphasized the space between syllables.

"I'm sorry, I have no idea what that is." Beverly spoke in her airy pageant girl's voice, but a bout sounded ominous, threatening.

Webster said, "Sometimes Mother gets deeply sad."

"Yes," said Beverly. She meant, *don't we all?*

"She locks herself in the bedroom, refuses to eat. She'll emerge from this, stronger than before. Until then, we just need to manage."

"We?"

"You, Mother, and I."

We. The three of them, we.

Was it all right, Webster asked, if they postponed leaving for New York and instead accompanied mother to Oakland, to help her situate? They could fly to New York from San Francisco.

The word *situate* confounded Beverly. Hadn't the woman lived in that house for years? Hadn't she situated herself long ago? Beverly considered for a moment but saw no other option.

"Yes, of course," she said.

A kiss at her neck. A hot whisper: "Thank you."

Edna did not emerge stronger than ever. Two weeks later, before their departure from San Francisco, Webster pulled Beverly aside, asking, *please,* could they delay their trip until Mother got her bearings? Beverly felt the burgeoning of anger. She'd been promised the glamour of New York City. She tamped back her emotions, telling herself this was her first wifely test.

"Yes," she said stiffly. "Of course. I wasn't positive about my clothing selection." She hoped her husband, the man she was bound to for all eternity, *'til death do us part*, would recognize her obvious disappointment. He did not.

"Only for a little while." Webster kissed her, and she pressed into him. This was the only surety in the dawn of their marriage: their bodies belonged together. In Webster's childhood bedroom, encased in flannel sheets, as the baseball bobbleheads nodded their approval, Beverly found solace in her hunger for him. She wanted only to move across the space of the bed with him, shifting in enough directions so that she might feel, when it was finished, dimensional. Whole.

They did not travel to New York City. They went no place at all. When it was decided they would stay in Oakland—they would *live* with Edna, permanently—Beverly's meticulously chosen crystal, the floral sheets she'd selected, too large for Webster's double bed, remained at her parents' house. "There just isn't room!" Edna declared when Beverly asked could she please send for their things. They remained with her mother, glinting at Beverly from various corners and shelves when she visited.

On the afternoon of the day she read Edna's letters, Beverly donned the dress she'd chosen to wear to *My Fair Lady* on her honeymoon, a wonderful pink organza with a fitted bodice and full skirt. She curled her hair and applied lusty red lipstick. After admiring how pretty she looked—too pretty for this life—she scrubbed the bathtub in her dress and makeup. She scrubbed until her back ached, using the so-called elbow grease Edna spoke of. She found that the bathtub refused to become clean, as if her dark, tangled emotions had spewed across its porcelain. She was not equipped to clean *that*. She lacked the elbow grease for *that*. She hated this life, and it had only just begun. Entire decades remained before her. She then climbed into the bathtub still wearing her dress. She closed the drain, turned on the faucet. Water crashed around her. Organza billowed like a balloon on the verge of bursting.

This, she realized. There was only this life.

Beverly remained in the bath until it grew cold and Webster was knocking at the door, saying, "Love, it's time for dinner."

She stood, stepped from the tub and, sodden, walked to the dining room, pink organza clinging to her torso and legs. Her hair—she'd caught a horrified glimpse in the mirror—was a bird's nest. Her mascara swooped across her face like war paint. Her lips appeared bludgeoned. Beverly took her place at the table, water collecting in a puddle beneath her chair.

"My love." Webster reached for her. "What's happened?"

"She's fine," said Edna sharply. Webster drew back while Edna addressed her: "Beverly, darling, would you like butter?" Though Edna's words were spun sugar, her tone conveyed the truth: she believed Beverly overdramatic, a spoiled child. Neither she—nor *Webster*—would pander to such a person.

Making no response, Beverly sat listening to the sound the water made as it dripped from her hem to the floor. As though her daughter-in-law were not a spectacle, a disgrace, Edna passed Webster the butter. With lowered eyes, Webster passed Edna the salt.

WEBB, 1970

At age fourteen, one day in the continuum of bored, lonely days of summer, Webb played with matches and set a field alight. This was his introduction to living, breathing, *actual* fire. A different beast, he learned, than the nostalgic blaze recounted at dinner parties or over the baking of pineapple cake. Above him, the hills quivered in the gauzy sunlight. The sky was a stolid, unrelenting blue. In a moment that proved to him how long a moment could be—*an eternity*—Webb waited for time to resume. He had two options: cry or get help. Historically, he'd chosen tears. On this occasion, he ran for help. Finding it, he did not say he'd started the fire, and days later—a lesson in irony—he was given a dull medal attached to a red, white, and blue ribbon as a testament to his bravery, his wonderful act of valor.

"Let me tell you what my Webster did!" his mother told Charlotte over the phone. "It involves an act of valor!"

This was Webb's indoctrination into that murky space between his reality and others' perceptions of it.

At the dinner table, turning Webb's medal to and fro, his father said, "It's tarnished."

Webb's mother said, "I think it's incredibly beautiful!"

"This ribbon is *frayed*."

"Genie, love. Webster is a hero. He committed an act of valor."

Genie, love. Webster is an arsonist. Webster is an unfathomable liar. In the heat of the moment, literally, Webb had constructed his flimsy story: he'd been walking to a friend's house when he first smelled smoke, then noticed it snaking upward from the grass. Recounting this story to the fire marshal, Webb suggested he *may have seen* a shadowy figure at the corner of his vision. (Here, he learned the noncommittal power of conditional tense.) He imagined his hypothetical arsonist with a hunched back and a trench coat, though he did not share these details with the fire marshal. Instead, he remained vague, saying he did not want to mistakenly incriminate anyone.

The fire marshal said, "Of course not, son." He laid his hand on Webb's shoulder, and *then* Webb wanted to weep. No one except his mother had exhibited such clear belief in him. Only his mother called him *son*.

A small article ran in the local paper. Bottom right-hand corner, fifth page, with blurred print and a grainy photograph in which Webb resembled a confused squirrel staring into the barrel of a gun. This was a look he wore for much of his life. It said, *Please! Don't shoot me!* at the same time it said, *Please! Shoot me!* as though Webb couldn't decide which outcome he preferred.

"Thanks to Webster," his mother told Charlotte, "only three acres burned!"

"Thanks to the wind," his father said when she repeated this at dinner. "Or lack thereof."

Later, when his mother was doing the dishes, his father turned to examine Webb, sipped bourbon and cleared his throat. "You say you were walking to a friend's house?"

"Yes, sir."

"What friend is this?"

Staring at his father, Webb spoke the first name to stumble into his mind. "His name is Eugene."

"He has my name?"

"Yes, sir."

"How coincidental. Am I familiar with this boy's father?"

"I don't believe so."

"What's his surname?"

"He never told me," said Webb. "Or I forgot."

"I see." A terrible pause ensued. His father said, "I don't wish to get into it with you, Webster, since it would greatly upset your mother. She and that fat fire chief believe you. But countless details in your heroic tale fail to make sense. Certain details are grossly amiss."

"Yes, sir."

"The most glaring anomaly is that you do not have friends. Webster, you've never possessed a single friend, and I believe this Eugene character is a construct of your imagination, just as this entire story—your so-called heroism—is a construct of your imagination. If you tell an outright lie, Webster, you need to ensure that lie is believable. As it stands, your credibility is tenuous. When your credibility appears tenuous, Webster, mine also appears tenuous. When my credibility appears tenuous, I find myself an unhappy man. Do you understand?"

"Yes, sir."

"What's more, Webster, at this rate I find it unlikely that you will ever have a friend."

"Yes, sir."

In his life, he'd had one friend, one true friend, and her name was Hila.

ARSON! the newspaper declared in September of 1970, the fall their friendship took root: 37 HOMES DESTROYED!

"Houses burst into flame," Hila read, "spontaneously. From the sheer magnitude of the heat. Before the fire ever reached them."

She brought the newspaper with her each morning that fall, ironing out its creases with her flattened palm because she was meticulous in this, in every, way. She brewed strong coffee, arranged sugar cubes into pyramids that rivaled those of the Egyptians. She served cream inside tiny milk bottles she'd brought back from Germany, a tiny bottle for each cup. "All kitchens," Hila said, never once spilling cream as she poured it into the bottles' slim necks, "need their darling milk bottles for the dainty serving of cream."

Beverly had never cared for darling things until she'd begun collecting those porcelain figurines. Here, a child whispering secrets to a goose; there, a girl with an oversized watering can, everywhere a sad slumped little harlequin. Webb believed himself a happy man until he looked into the figurines' unnerving—they were always blue—eyes. *You fool*, their eyes declared as he poured himself an innocuous glass of milk. *You fucking asshole. You piece of shit.* He imagined them whispering amongst themselves in lilting British accents. *He wears women's panties. Last week, when his wife visited her sick mother, he scrambled eggs wearing a flimsy negligee. His daughter was upstairs sleeping!*

There had been no advance warning of Beverly's leaving. Of her *abandonment*. If it hadn't involved his beating—desperate—heart, he would have pressed a gold star onto Beverly's collar for her masterful orchestration of the event. The day that everything changed, he left for school as he did every morning, wearing clothes selected by Beverly: a brown plaid jacket over a brown turtleneck that threatened to swallow his confused face. A thick brown belt had been involved in this fiasco, brown pants, brown shoes, brown nubby socks. He looked, literally, like a giant piece of shit; but this, Beverly declared, was fashion. She sat at the kitchen table with hot rollers in her hair, her face smeared with menthol-smelling cream in broad flourishes like cake frosting. Wearing her maroon housecoat, she sat peaceably at the table eating Stella D'oro breakfast treats, turning the thin pages of the *TV Guide* with a deliberation that would, in retrospect, unnerve him. Nothing about Beverly in that moment suggested action or impetus. In fact, nothing about Beverly had suggested action or impetus for a long, long while—not since the end of her pageant days.

He had not said goodbye to Debra. Poking his head inside her room, he found his daughter still sleeping, mummified inside her blanket.

"Debra isn't well this morning," Beverly explained. The pink rollers sectioned her head, exposing intimate scalp. The *TV Guide* fluttered closed; a cartoon image of Carol Burnett with an unconscionably large mouth grinned from the cover. "If she feels better when she wakes, I'll drive her over myself."

Their kiss—the last—was inconsequential. Beverly turned just before his lips met hers; he received a mouthful of face cream that stung a shaving cut like a bee sting.

"Don't forget, I'm making cacciatore tonight!" she said as the door closed behind him. Technically it was Monday, Italian-Sauced Fish day. The night before, she had cooked something called Pampered Beef Filets despite its being Sunday, Mexican Supper Casserole day. The pampering of the beef filets had not gone well, but perhaps—he hoped, he prayed—Beverly had turned a culinary corner. He loved cacciatore, and she had never before made it. Of course, he realized later, she had no intention of making it. Looking back on these farewell words, Webb felt their chiseled cruelty.

At school, he discussed *The Grapes of Wrath* with his ninth graders and *Beowulf* with his tenth. He brushed chalk dust against his tight brown pants; extreme tightness in the ass of one's pants was supposedly a hallmark of fashion. ("Mr. Jackson," someone sniggered. "There's chalk on your rump.") He ate a bologna sandwich for lunch, graded essays. He oversaw seventh period study hall without admonishing the whispering students; who had energy for such a thing? When the final bell thankfully rang, he ducked into the gym for a snippet of that day's theater rehearsal, a thing he'd been doing since he'd first heard the songs wafting into the hallway. Students were rehearsing *The Pajama Game*, a musical Beverly adored. They'd seen the film version in the theater, mere months after their wedding. Today, students playing the roles of Hines and Mabel rehearsed "I'll Never Be Jealous Again." Their respective voices cracked on the high notes, Hines giving the air a lackluster punch after each of his lines.

"No, *no!*" The woman who would be Hila clambered onstage like someone struggling up a highway embankment after a car accident, waving her arms for assistance. "*Good God*, you two are simply terrible today!" she announced with a cheer that belied her words. "Awful! I'd say this is torturous, wouldn't you? I'd slit my wrists, but there are no knives in this gym. Only bouncing rubber balls and nets and painted lines and the residual scent of greatness of these people called *athletes*. Can you smell it? We feed off this residual greatness as if it's a bowl of stale porridge."

The students onstage stared at her silently. The woman who would be Hila smiled an exuberant smile, slung her arms onto the shoulders of the despondent Hines and Mabel. "Let's do it again, shall we?" To Mabel she said, "My dear, Reta Shaw is rolling over in her grave. She's a very large woman who can't be doing this."

Mabel said, "Reta Shaw isn't dead."

"A minor detail." The woman who would be Hila shrugged.

"Isn't it slander?"

"I'd prefer you weren't so sensitive. Theater is a rough-and-tumble business. Do it again, please."

Arriving home that afternoon, Webb didn't notice anything amiss. The astronauts would soon broadcast from outer space. Turning on the television, he did not remember the promise of cacciatore. Later, it would strike him that an entire hour had passed before he realized his family was missing. Well into the television program he watched, a character expressed anguish. The sound of this man's anguish competed with the growl of Webb's stomach. Only then did he consider dinner (cacciatore!) and realize it had not been started. It had not been started because there was no one to start it. He was alone in the house. He then noticed pictures were missing from the living room walls. Gone were Beverly's pageant photos; gone were Debra's bucktoothed school photos. Gone were her studio baby portraits, naked Debra laid smiling across a fur block. What remained, like remnants of a pox, were pictures of *him*. He, Webster, appearing perplexed in nearly every one, as if the photographer had just screamed at him in gibberish.

His ever-present fog lifted. He jumped from the couch, stumbled. The television played its jaunty music as he righted himself. Guns were fired. Their distinct reports rang out as he rushed upstairs to his and Beverly's bedroom. Gone was Beverly's tailored clothing from the closet; gone, her meticulously arranged tubes of lipstick and vials of perfume from the vanity; her lotions and creams and swabs from the bathroom. Gone was her silken underwear from her top dresser drawer. Gone were her pageant sashes, her crowns. She'd left, on a hanger, the maroon housecoat, that hideous thing! He wrangled it off the hanger and onto the floor, emitting a sound like something rabid that had stumbled into the mayhem on the television program, needing to be shot.

Maroon, marooned. He'd been marooned.

She had not taken his family's china, passed down from Webb's great-grandmother, his grandmother, his mother. Of course, she'd left that. From the first, she'd sniffed with derision every time she'd set the table with it. *Bluebells*. On the dining buffet, he found their bent-edged wedding photograph. She'd taken the gilded frame, but left the photo—Beverly wide-eyed and beautiful, he broad-shouldered beside her. Webb still remembered the taking of this photograph. He'd pressed his hand into the small of his new wife's back, trying to step close, closer to her, the bouffant skirt of her dress denying him proximity, the photographer's sharp command drawing him to attention. "*Smile!*"

She'd left those terrible figurines behind. He'd thought she adored them. This was one of many things he'd been wrong about. *So she left you*, their blue eyes said nonchalantly. *Your mother warned you she was a two-bit floozie*. Webb poured himself a glass of whiskey. He swept the figurines off their glass shelves and into a box, which he carried outside. Standing in the street, he drank whiskey and smashed figurines onto the pavement: the shepherdess with the lamb tossed over her shoulder as casually as a gym towel, a shepherd playing a flute, harlequin after harlequin. The pieces skittered across the asphalt like stones across an expanse of water.

His neighbors—man, wife, and two small boys dressed in matching fucking pajamas—stood on their lawn, watching him.

"Hey!" He flung a contemplative fawn to the ground. "How's the show? Do you want some popcorn? A goddamn sodie pop?"

The mother hustled the boys inside as they craned their heads over their shoulders. The father made his way across the lawn to Webb, surrounded by splintered figurines.

"You should know, Webster," he began, "Carol says a truck was at the house this morning. Loaded up a bunch of things, took them away."

"We needed to downsize. Give to those less fortunate. Others have nothing."

"Before that, a man came."

"Beverly's father." Webb felt dizzy.

"He was younger. Drove a blood-red Cadillac. A really nice car, Carol said. Took off with Beverly and Debra."

"Her brother," said Webb.

"Webster, are you okay?"

Late that night, as he drank tumblers of whiskey, Webb discovered a letter in the bottom drawer of his bureau, where he kept his special things tucked behind his ordinary clothing. She'd written it on pink monogrammed stationery scented with perfume, as his mother had once scented her letters. The monogram ended with her maiden initial, a cursive *L* that could be confused for a noose leading invisible things away. She must have ordered this stationery weeks ago; her usual stationery included a stolid, dependable *J* at the end. Jackson. Beverly Jackson.

Webster.

By now you know that Debra and I have gone. You've found this letter in your drawer of disgusting things.

This life I have with you is unacceptable, very different than the life you promised me. My mother has assured me I am deserving of more than you will ever offer. I am taking Debra to Santa Barbara to care for my mother, who is dying. This is something I should have done months ago, as leaving you is something I should have done years ago.

A lawyer is arranging the paperwork.

Also, I disagree. Pale peach does not wash out my skin tone, as you have frequently insisted.

Beverly Laurenzi

Of course Beverly had gone to her mother's house. Her mother had been ill for months. Webb felt ashamed that he had never asked about the particulars of this illness, had not accompanied his wife on these trips. Beverly hadn't invited him, but neither had he offered. Healthy, his mother-in-law terrified him. He could not fathom her sick.

The next morning, dawn cracking the sky, he called Beverly's parents. He hadn't expected her mother to answer—wasn't she laid up somewhere, tangled inside a slew of bedsheets? But her tinkling *hello* was the same as always, reminding Webb of knives *tap, tapping* against crystal glassware. The tinkling dissipated when she realized who was on the line.

"Mom," he said, "please. I need to talk to Beverly."

"Don't use that word." Her voice had become a thing so sterile he could eat from it.

"Need?"

"*Mom.*"

"Mother?"

"Mrs. Laurenzi."

"Mrs. Laurenzi," he repeated.

"Webster, Beverly has made it quite clear she doesn't wish to speak to you."

"Please, then let me speak with my daughter."

"Webster."

"Put my daughter on the line!" he yelled, before realizing he should not speak to a sick woman in a voice so loud. He added, in a voice that might fit through the eye of a needle, "Please."

"I don't think so."

"*Please!*"

"I will not put Debra on the phone with a maniac. Exhibit an iota of control. Don't you have a pair of women's panties to busy yourself with?"

Heat filled his face. "She'll think I don't care!"

"I'm hanging up now. Goodbye!"

"*No!*" he shouted. He wanted to say he was sorry, so sorry. He was sorry he hadn't once visited during her illness. He was sorry he hadn't sent flowers, not even carnations with an excess of baby's breath filler. He was sorry that for thirteen years he believed her to be a hateful woman whose presence he found intolerable. He had failed as a son-in-law. He had failed Beverly, her beautiful daughter, whom he had pledged to love and protect. He had not provided even a remote portion of the happiness he'd promised her on that sweltering June day in 1957. He had not kept the promises he'd made either to Beverly or to himself.

In the days that followed, he drank whiskey during school hours, pulling secretive swigs from the silver flask he forced inside the pocket of his tight brown pants. This flask felt like a mass against his ass, malignant, as he lumbered through the echoing hallways. In the faculty bathroom, he sat on the toilet, drinking whiskey and more whiskey, staring at the peeling stall door as the whiskey disappeared. He still wore the outfit he'd been wearing the day Beverly left him; he would wear this outfit until Beverly returned to him. He would not bathe—he would not remove this clothing—until she returned.

After school hours, having no ill-prepared dinner to rush home to, he stayed for theater rehearsal.

At some convoluted point during the week Beverly left, a small girl wearing a blonde wig—it sat lopsided on her head, like a wide receiver's helmet after a brutal play—rehearsed the song "There Once Was a Man" with the loser playing Sid. The girl playing Babe looked constipated as she hit her notes. Sid botched his. Their yodeling at the ends of stanzas reminded Webb of the sounds a man makes when another man punches him repeatedly in the gut.

There once was a man who loved a woman.
She was the one he slew the dragon for.
They say that nobody ever loved as much as he—ee.
But me—ee,
I love you more.

Doris Day and John Raitt's rendition made a person want to cartwheel and sing jaunty tunes heavy with metaphor, to skip down the aisles of the grocery store warbling about the beauty of an apple! Here, when the boy playing Sid lifted the girl playing Babe, he took several bumbling steps before his arms collapsed and he first dropped, then tripped over her. Babe's meaty thigh flashed like a beacon at Webb sitting in a distant row. The scene screeched to a halt.

"Did you seriously just drop me?" Babe asked.

"You're heavy."

"Did you just call me *fat?*"

"Keep going!" singsonged the woman who would be Hila. "No one cares about your inane personal drama! We care only for Sid and Babe's burning love!"

Listening to this song Beverly had loved and sung offkey into his ear, the memory rose: Beverly beside him in the darkened theater with her bright lips and perfected curls, the competing scents of her perfume and powder, she all rosy hue and beauty. Now, in the school gymnasium, he clambered from his seat and into the aisle, dropped to his knees. His own breath threatened to suffocate him. When he raised his head, the woman who would be Hila stared at him. Their eyes caught, held. A sock puppet could stare him down; Webb slunk from the auditorium. In the hallway, he leaned against the cool wall and heard the woman who would be Hila saying, "John! Sid isn't supposed to behave like a dumbstruck birdie!"

He, Webster Eugene Jackson, should not behave like a dumbstruck birdie. He had to get it together, had to emerge somehow, reenter (had he ever resided there?) the land of the living. Beverly would not return to him otherwise; he would not see his daughter.

He attended baseball practice, a yearbook meeting, a meeting of the senior prom planning committee. The baseball team, fit and ruddy, reminded him of his inadequacies. The prom committee, plump with seriousness, devoted an hour to discussing how many balloons were required to festoon the gym for the festivities. ("Three hundred seventy-eight," said a girl with a balloon-piercing chin. "I'm sure of it.") The prom theme this year was Tangled in the Stars, whatever that meant; it sounded painful. He remembered, with a start, the summer Beverly had participated in the Miss California pageant. The pageant theme had been Stairway to the Stars. (What was this obsession with stars?) For the pageant, an actual staircase had been built onstage. From the ceiling hung shimmering foil stars. The staircase led nowhere, but Webb nonetheless saw an expanse of beckoning future. *Come,* the staircase had whispered. *Here, where the rest of your bright life resides.* The yearbook committee spent their hour-long meeting discussing prom.

"How many balloons do you think it would take to festoon the gym?" he asked, and the yearbook committee stared at him.

Webb decided he preferred the uncomfortable teenagers at theater rehearsal with their oversized and undersized foreheads. Their alien necks, their pimples. The theater students all wanted, desperately, to be someone different than themselves for an afternoon. Webb appreciated this. Also, it was easier to drink from a flask inside the darkened auditorium. He returned to theater practice.

When he arrived, the woman who would be Hila demonstrated choreography.

"Bum, bum, bum, *bum.* Like so." The woman who would be Hila bent herself backward in a feat of pliability. "Stop looking like a bored fish and do it correctly, please, with a hunk of dark chocolate."

"This day is going to be all picnic." The loser playing Sid bumbled his line.

"This picnic is going to be all day!" the woman who would be Hila corrected cheerily.

They were rehearsing the group number "Once-a-Year Day." Webb remembered the scene from the movie, the actresses in their frothy dresses, the actors in their cropped white pants exposing colorful socks, everyone leapfrogging, skipping, flitting, cartwheeling like delirious confetti. The students bumped into one another like confused shoppers at the grocery store, laughing nervously. The woman who would be Hila yelled, "I didn't tell you to channel people on quaaludes!"

Afterward, standing in the chaos of students rushing to cars and buses, the woman who would be Hila approached Webb. Horns honked. She nodded at him, lit a cigarette, held out her hand, rolled her eyes. He would later understand: she was the queen of doing myriad things in effortless succession. She said, "Hila Firestone."

"Webster Jackson."

"Yes, I know."

An elongated silence passed.

"Excuse me," Webb said. "There's a Cheerio in your scarf."

"A what now?"

"A Cheerio. In the folds of your scarf." As he resisted the urge to pluck it out himself, Hila's slender hand felt contemplatively along her scarf. The lone Cheerio disappeared inside her mouth.

"Breakfast." She gave an easy shrug. "Toasted oats, vitamin B. I gather you're a fan of musical theater."

"Yes," he said lamely.

"Well, you look and smell like excrement." Inhaling her cigarette, she stood before him, all angles and style, unbridled energy. Her suit—cerulean, a color to get lost inside—emphasized her dark hair, her porcelain skin. Her eyes were the sort of blue that gave the impression of transparency, like the eyes of a husky. Her wrists were slivers of flesh and bone. In relation to Hila Firestone, Beverly would have been described as *meaty*, a word that would have spurred her to hysterics and compulsive lettuce-eating.

"There was a time," Hila said, "when every woman in this joint wanted to bed you. We believed you a Renaissance man! An English teacher with movie-star good looks. With those shoulders, you probably played sports."

"I played football."

"*Football.*"

Her tone made him defensive. "Do you know what that is?"

"Snideness, sir, does not become you. It makes you palpably unattractive, more so than even the odious scent you're emitting."

(He would learn Hila's father had coached high school football in Texas. She'd grown up sitting behind the players' bench during games, watching her father's wild gesticulations. As a testament to her acting ability, she'd eradicated the lone-star drawl from her speech, but it returned when she dissected dime and nickel defenses and man-to-man coverage.)

"I'm sorry," he said, and was.

"Subconsciously," Hila said, "every woman wants to draw the attention of a man with a beautiful wife."

"A man with a beautiful wife," Webb echoed.

"I've seen her," Hila said, "at holiday parties. Once, she shoved me aside to reach the eggnog."

"She really likes eggnog," said Webb, despite having never seen Beverly drink eggnog.

"I would have expected more from a pageant girl. Miss California, isn't that right?"

"She was first runner-up."

"Did they knock off points for shoving the judges? Still, impressive! If I were a beauty queen, I'd be delighted with myself. I'd carry the sash in my purse in case I needed a tourniquet."

"No," said Webb.

"No, I wouldn't be a beauty queen?"

Studying her, he thought she would not be a beauty queen. He'd once been surrounded by them, a contagion of powder and lace, plump cheeks, obvious affability. Hila's delicate features brought to mind a miniature, something wrought with meticulous care by a person wielding a magnifying glass. Hers was not an obvious beauty, not the kind that accosted a person but rather compelled them to look, *look* until they found they couldn't turn away from her slender, reaching neck, her sharp knees, appearing just below the hem of her dress.

"No," he said. "Runner-up wouldn't be enough."

"I suppose not." She suffocated her cigarette beneath the formidable heel of her shoe. "Maybe I'll shove *her* at the next holiday party."

"Probably not."

"Never doubt my ability to shove!"

"Beverly is through with faculty parties."

"Who can blame her? All those overwhipped deviled eggs the chemistry teacher's wife makes. Doused with so much paprika they look infected with measles! And let's not forget the ceaseless array of pigs in a blanket."

"She left me." His voice cracked. "She took our daughter. No notice. Just gone."

This was the first time he'd uttered it aloud. He said nothing about the letter Beverly had written, her parting words left in the drawer of silken things. He waited for Hila to speak. She only reached her thin arm through space, laid her hand on his shoulder. Her hand possessed surprising weight, and he recalled, abruptly, the fire marshal's kindness all those years ago. They stood like this for a long moment inside the students' waning frenzy.

"There's always notice," Hila said. "Sometimes it's just impossible to see."

Webb said, "You're very talented."

"Not very," she said.

"You do a great job with those kids."

She tilted her chin to the sky, the intentional movement of a person trying not to cry. "I love those kids," she said. "And no, it isn't enough."

The students finally gone, they sat on the curb, passing the flask, and when they'd finished the whiskey, Hila went with Webb to his house, where they drank more whiskey from the tumblers Beverly hadn't taken. Between sips of bourbon, Hila convinced him to wash his clothes. He knew how to do laundry, just as he knew how to scrub the toilet and bake a charlotte russe. Just as he could sew a button and hem a pair of pants. He was not actually the bumbling and incompetent man he pretended to be so as not to draw attention to himself. He left the room and changed into another tight selection of Beverly's.

"I admire your devotion to this particular *ensemble*." Hila shoved his brown outfit inside the washer. "It's your version of a hunger strike, but with clothes. Admirable, yes, but all good things come to an end." She wrenched the washer dial around noisily. *"Voilà!"*

He realized he had no idea what subject Hila taught. Something cultured, he assumed. He'd heard her slinging French phrases at *The Pajama Game* actors when they mauled their lines. She told him she was the school's home economics teacher.

"You're joking!" Webb said.

Her face grew long, and he grasped this meant she was angry. "Why on earth would I be *joking?*"

"I just meant you're a natural onstage. I thought you were the theater teacher."

Hila lit a cigarette. The washing machine thrummed.

"Beverly doesn't allow smoking inside," Webb said.

"Yes, but darling Beverly doesn't seem to be present, does she? How long, might I ask, since Beverly the Beauty Queen left you?"

"Twenty-three days."

"Whom did she leave you for?"

"Excuse me?"

"Was it a family friend? A childhood acquaintance?"

"What are you implying?"

"I'm not trying to be stealthy about it." Hila plucked tobacco from her pink tongue. "I'm asking outright: whom did she leave you for?"

"No one!"

"A woman who leaves her husband furtively, without words, is usually a whore with a plan."

"My wife isn't a whore!"

"She's barely your wife."

"Beverly has never had a plan in her life!"

"All right." Hila gave a nod.

He interpreted this as a kindness. She did not seem a woman who placated. She seemed above pleasantries. Just as she understood things Webb did not.

It had grown dark. They sat waiting for the wash cycle to end, and when it did, she maneuvered his clothes into the dryer with one hand, holding her cigarette in the other. She explained to Webb the dryer settings and poured herself another whiskey. When she'd drunk it down, her slender neck lengthening as she swallowed, she left.

Webb felt tremendous relief when she'd gone, though he watched through the peephole as she made her way down the front walk to meet her taxi. Even having consumed all that whiskey, she did not teeter on her formidable heels. She held her own as far as whiskey, as far as a great many things, were concerned.

He avoided her after that, though once, struck by an inexplicable urge, he passed casually by the home economics room at the far end of the hall. Through the door's small window, he saw Hila in a black dress dusted with flour, bending over students' mangled pastry.

"*Yes*, it's a galette." Her voice traveled easily through the door. "It's meant to be freeform, certainly. It's a rustic pastry, but it's traditionally somewhat *roundish*. Marianne, can you please draw a circle on the board?"

A gaping circle, an aching hole, had opened in Webb's chest. He wanted to climb inside this hole, disappear there.

He did not attend the final production of *The Pajama Game*. As curtain time came and went, he sat watching television and drinking whiskey. He imagined Hila joining the cast onstage for their standing ovation. In his imaginings, she held flowers. She wore a short black cocktail dress with sheer sleeves, curtseying not once but twice, three times. She wrapped her arms around Babe and bumbling Sid, whispering jokes in their ears with an intimacy he'd be jealous of. But what did he care? She'd called his wife a whore!

He didn't see her at prom; she'd chosen not to be tangled in the stars. Ignoble chaperone, he drank surreptitiously from his flask, studying the moving sea of bare shoulders and shiny fabrics, baby's breath and ruffled tuxedo shirts. He popped five of the three hundred seventy-eight white balloons festooning the gym. Countless homemade stars and meticulously curled ribbon hung from a lopsided trellis beneath which students posed for photographs. They said *cheese* and clutched one another like drowning people amid the ribbons, swatting at the various decorations. These teenagers, Webb saw, were literally tangled in the stars. He wished Hila were there to laugh about it.

At the graduation ceremony, across a field of red gowns, he spotted her wide smile. Later, he bumped into her. She carried a glass of punch in one hand, a paper plate filled with pigs in a blanket in the other. The plate buckled beneath their weight. Hadn't she spoken scathingly about pigs in a blanket? And here she was, carrying at least twenty of them!

"Don't look so embarrassed to see me," she said. "It's not as awkward between us as you think. How's your laundry going? I see you ended your brown clothing strike."

She offered the paper plate to him. Clumsily, he pinched up a pig in a blanket, but before he could take even a single polite bite, Hila had disappeared into the wash of red. It swallowed her up, and she was gone.

Summer, unseasonably warm, began with an itch. Webb had given Beverly time. Time was up. He called his mother-in-law's house every day asking for Beverly, swallowing down the emotion rising in his throat. His mother-in-law was a woman easily annoyed by tears, by raw, unfettered feelings. "Good God!" she said about crying babies, as if these babies should control themselves. The few times she and Webb had been together, they'd barely spoken. On his and Beverly's wedding day, just before husband and wife made their rice-strewn exit, she approached Webb, who anticipated her kind congratulations. She said, "The halibut was very good." Beverly's father added, "Yes, very moist." Later, Webb counted the words of Beverly's mother on his fingers. Five words; words contained on a single hand. *The halibut was very good.* Webb supposed it had been. As for the word *moist*, it made him feel like he had just seen Beverly's father naked.

"Please," he said. "Please, let me speak with her."

"Webster!" Beverly's mother said, every time, before hanging up. "Stop groveling! Act like a man!"

Men had determination. His calling became a compulsion; he would prove to Beverly he had remarkable determination. He sat on the couch, drinking whiskey, listening to the phone ring on the other end of the line while he watched the summer reruns without volume. Scenes of *The Doris Day Show* flashed before him: the Golden Gate Bridge; a cable car; Doris in a bright yellow rain hat; Doris in red, pattering shoes. Despite how radiant she wanted to look, despite the luminous California scenery unveiled in the backdrop, Doris was no longer the young woman from *The Pajama Game*. Doris had gotten old. *He* had gotten old. "You old hag," he told Doris's face on the television, but speaking to Doris in this manner only made him feel worse.

One day he called and the number was disconnected. He dialed the operator, who confirmed in a lemony voice: "Sir, that number is disconnected." The new number was unlisted. No, she could not provide that number. On the tv screen, *The Mod Squad* blinked—a show Debra had neglected her homework to watch. He yearned for his daughter, for her wit and smile. She was always hunching over. He wanted to straighten her, remind her to stand tall, to face things. He wanted to remind her she was beautiful.

"Sir? Please don't cry." The operator's bewildered voice swept over the line, and he realized he was, actually, crying, a thing he hadn't done since he was probably Debra's age.

He would drive to Santa Barbara. He would bring his family home.

His car was a Chevrolet Impala bought at Beverly's behest, the pea-green of a soup she wouldn't have had the patience or inclination to make. Pulling into the gas station, he felt a shimmering positivity, the first he'd felt in four months. There was something to be said for action and impetus. Leaning jauntily against the car, he filled her up. At the grocery store, he bought snacks for the road, choosing things Debra would want, without caring what Beverly would say. Beverly fretted over Debra's weight, forbidding her to have sugar, overseeing portion control, championing minuscule bites and methodical chewing. Sometimes, Webb saw, she made Debra feel badly about herself. He'd chosen not to intervene, never to rock the boat. Things would be different now. He accepted the grocery bag from the cashier with a happiness disproportionate to the act of a man accepting a grocery bag from a cashier.

For the drive, Webb dressed in the layered sort of outfit Beverly admired, an outfit whose components demanded an ironic authority or else suggested he was very cold: turtleneck, vest, jacket, too-tight pants threatening at any moment to split up the ass. The Chevrolet Impala did not have air conditioning. He sweated and drove, thinking the brown humpbacked California hills looked like sad animals waiting to be kicked. Moisture pooled at the backs of his knees. He rolled down the window, stuck his head into the gritty heat. He rolled the window up, rolled it down. Twice, he pulled to the side of the road, clasping the steering wheel and breathing deeply. Telling himself there was nothing to feel anxious about. He was only restoring things to their natural order.

Beverly's mother, opening the massive front door and discovering Webb on the landing, said, "Oh." Her taut face suggested she would never again fail to look through a peephole.

Struck by a sudden feistiness, he said, "You could have begun with *hello.*"

"Yes, well."

She reduced the width of the door's opening to a crack, through which her lips appeared as red and polished as a poisonous apple. She said, "*You* could have called first."

Laughter barreled out of him. Beverly's mother reduced the crack in the doorway further.

He said, "I'd like to see Beverly."

"I'm sorry, Webster."

"Mom," Webb said. "Mrs. Laurenzi. Mary. *Lady.*"

The crack disappeared. Her voice sounded muffled from behind the door. "She's not here."

"I'll wait!"

"It will be a while."

"I have time!"

Her heels clacked away from the door.

He waited at first on the stone front steps so that when Beverly pulled up the drive (Why would she be *out?* Who would she be out *with?*) she would see him sitting with excellent posture, his chin angled like a man in an Olan Mills portrait. He needed only a hideous carpeted block to overlap his hands on, an impressive column to lean against, a hazy pastoral backdrop. Hours passed, and he began to feel like a stray cat who, having been fed once, now refused to leave the property. He ate Oh Henry! bars, throwing their shiny wrappers onto the manicured lawn. He gutted Twinkies, sucking the sweet cream from his index finger before eating the spongy cake (this was how he'd seen Debra eat a Twinkie, several Twinkies, when her mother wasn't looking). He'd brought Jif peanut butter, an utterly inappropriate road trip-food. He stuck his busy little pinky finger into the jar, sucked peanut butter from it like a teething Debra had once sucked rum from this digit. Where, in this giant mess, was his daughter?

Having nothing better to do, he ate an entire container of Pringles, sending the empty tube clattering down the asphalt drive. He drank six bottles of Bubble Up, tossing the empties into the grass. Because he'd drunk six bottles of Bubble Up, he then urinated into the rose bushes pressing against the house. This provided such a supreme sense of satisfaction, he urinated again in a morning glory climbing a trellis. Shaking himself off, he walked the perimeter of the house, looking for the faintest suggestion, the glimmer of proof, that Mary, Mrs. Laurenzi, Mom had lied and Beverly was, in fact, upstairs in the pink lacey bedroom of her childhood, debating when to see him. She was the queen of making a man wait, of drawing out his patience like a tenacious piece of taffy. It turned dark, and Webb stationed himself beneath what he believed was her bedroom window. He felt along the ground for small rocks to toss against the glass. He pitched them up and away. Lights turned on. Beverly's father yanked open the window, his bald head appearing like a beacon.

"Hey, Romeo! Did you just throw rocks at my window like a goddamn child?"

"Yes," Webb said. He added, "Sir."

"I'll call the police if you don't get the hell out of here!" The window crashed shut.

Webb slunk back to the stone steps.

He fell asleep with his back pressed against the front door. Some time later, he jerked awake. Moths pulsed nervously around the porch lights. He dragged himself then—aching shoulders, once again full bladder—to his car, where he crushed himself into a fetal position on the backseat.

A pounding against the passenger window woke him. A balding man beat rhythmically on the glass with the palm of his hand. "Come on, now! Up and out!"

The man opened the back door. Reaching inside, he grabbed Webb's ankles, one in each hand. The man tugged, tried to pull Webb through the door's tiny opening. Webb held tightly to the seat cushion and kicked.

"Hey!" the man said.

Webb said, "Remove your hands from my ankles."

The man's hands remained.

"I swear to God," said Webb, "if you do not remove your hands *right now*, I'll lose it."

The man released first one ankle, then a second. He backed up several steps, watching as Webb maneuvered stiffly from the car.

"Let's make this quick," the man said when Webb had extricated himself. "I have an important meeting this afternoon."

Webb studied the man standing before him: pressed suit with sharp pant creases, a large shirt collar, polished shoes with tassels. The severe sweep of the man's part emphasized rather than disguised his thinning hair.

"They knew you'd show up eventually," he said. "Took you longer than expected. They'd call the police, but they don't want a scene."

Webb asked, "Who are you, the Laurenzis' handler?"

He sighed. "Come on, now."

"Did they find you in the yellow pages?"

"We can make this hard," the man said. "Or we can make it easy."

"We're getting nowhere," said Webb.

"I'm Clive," the man said.

"Okay."

"Clive Murdoch. I'm him."

"Fine," said Webb.

"Don't play stupid!"

"I am not, as you say, *playing stupid*. I sincerely don't know you."

Clive Murdoch shook his head. "She didn't tell you."

"Who?"

"Beverly. I'm the man she left you for."

Webb's hands clenched into fists. "She didn't leave me for a man."

"What," said Clive Murdoch. "She left you for cattle?"

"That's unnecessary." Webb spoke in the sharp tone he reserved for inappropriate students. "She's staying with her sick mother," he explained. "Here."

Again Clive Murdoch shook his head. "We've been living together for months now. In Los Angeles."

"That's not true," Webb said. "Where's my daughter?"

"In Los Angeles with us. We're a family now."

"You're a family now." Webb repeated, and wanted to punch himself in the face for it—for saying, for affirming, those words.

"She said she explained everything. She said you understood."

Clive Murdoch rested a hand on Webb's shoulder—as the fire marshal had, as Hila had. Without thinking, Webb lunged at him. Webb had never before grappled, but suddenly he was grappling with Clive Murdoch on the neat, dewy lawn. As his hands clamped on Clive Murdoch's shoulders, a neighbor's dog yipped in the distance. Trying to throw the man off balance, Webb grunted with exertion. Clive Murdoch did not. He watched Clive Murdoch's tasseled shoes stepping gracefully in the grass and realized Clive Murdoch was speaking—*instructing* him.

"Drive with your left foot, now, harder, there you go. Like that. Shift your weight forward. There you go. Head up, keep your head up. Don't look at my shoes. When you do that, I know I have you."

Clive Murdoch's tie swung like a pendulum before Webb's face. Its pattern was elaborate, gyrating circles and stripes. Looking at this tie was not unlike looking into the shifting depths of a kaleidoscope. Webb understood: Beverly had chosen this tie. Her color combinations were reckless, bold. He remembered the faculty dinners, his colleagues' sidelong glances. True love meant enduring the embarrassment of an ugly tie. Looking at Clive

Murdoch's very ugly tie, Webb knew Beverly had not left him for cattle. She'd left him for a man, for *this* man. He wanted to wrap Clive Murdoch's hideous tie around his neck and choke him with it.

But surprisingly, Clive Murdoch, who was not a tall man, nor a wide one, had gotten him to the ground. Dew seeped through Webb's shirt, his pants.

"I told you not to look at my shoes," he said.

"You've done this before."

"Former Missouri State wrestling champion. First in my weight class. I wrestled one sixty, went fifteen zip my senior year."

"You've put on a few since then," Webb said, and Clive Murdoch pressed Webb's face into the grass, pulled his arm sharply backward. Pain radiated into Webb's shoulder. He gasped for air, was spun toward the sky, then faceplanted back into the grass.

"That was my signature move." Clive Murdoch gave Webb a final shove. "The Surfboard." He stood up. Despite the green stains on the knees of his pants, he appeared invigorated.

Webb's lungs felt collapsible. He made his breath as shallow as possible, pressed a palm against his bruised heart. "I'm glad you relived your glory years," he said from the grass. The morning sky was just coming into itself.

"My glory years," said Clive Murdoch, "are yet to come." He extended a hand to help Webb up.

It was painful to realize that Clive Murdoch wasn't an asshole. More painful that Clive Murdoch believed his life—with Beverly at his side—would only improve. Webb had once felt the same.

From one of the large picture windows, Beverly's parents had witnessed the entirety of this debacle. They looked unconcerned. Impassive. *The halibut was very good.* Though it hurt, Webb lifted his right arm and waved limply. It was an act of defeat. Of surrender.

They allowed him inside to clean himself up. He washed in what had once been Beverly's childhood bathroom with its Italian tile and gleaming fixtures, with its hand towels a person wasn't actually supposed to use. Beverly's mother would rather a man dry his hands against his dirty pants than against her monogrammed hand towels. With toilet paper he rubbed at the dirt and snot and grass on his face and clothes. He'd remembered Pringles and Twinkies and Bubble Up, but hadn't thought to bring clean clothes. He'd planned on collecting his wife and daughter, on bringing them immediately home. He hadn't imagined staying overnight. He hadn't imagined they wouldn't return with him.

Webb sat at Beverly's parents' dining table in his soiled clothes while Beverly's mother served coffee. Implied was the understanding that this was the last coffee she would ever, in his lifetime, serve him. She offered him Danish—store bought, served on plates as if she'd made it herself. Finishing his coffee, Beverly's father cleared his throat and left the room. In this way, Webb understood that he too knew about the women's panties.

Beverly's mother said, "Now, Webster. Clive works in television. Think of the life he can give her! You teach *English*."

"We do speak it," he managed to say. "It's what allows us to communicate our thoughts and dreams to one another."

"Thoughts and dreams!" Her tone suggested these things were hilarious.

"We took vows," said Webb. "We said for better or worse."

"Neither of those addresses the issue of mediocrity."

"I *love* her."

"Webster. Love is never enough. In books, maybe. But not in life."

"How long has it been going on?"

With a sharp motion of her chin, she turned away from him.

"And I suppose," Webb said, "you're the epitome of health?"

"It's a miracle, really," Beverly's mother said, pouring cream into her already white coffee.

"And Debra?" An invisible band tightened across Webb's chest.

Clink, clink, clink went the spoon inside the cup. "She's free to contact you, if that's what she wants." Beverly's mother shrugged. "I'm afraid she hasn't expressed any interest."

An alien feeling rose in Webb—a desire to damage, to hurt. "Your daughter," he said, "is a whore." These words, an iteration of Hila's, made him feel not better but worse, as though he'd punched himself. Standing abruptly, Webb spilled the jug of cream, white expanding across the table's dark wood.

Reaching Oakland's border, he stopped at a phone booth inside a rutted parking lot to look up Hila's number. She did not seem the sort of woman to have a listed number, but he turned the pages of the phone book to F and saw her name in tiny type: Hila P. Firestone.

He had meant to sound very casual, but when she answered the phone after many rings, he found himself making a ratcheting sound into the receiver.

"*Oh*," she said. "Webster."

He did not start school the following week. He no longer cared about thoughts and dreams, their iterations and articulations. He no longer wanted to read poorly constructed sentences on the overarching themes in *The Grapes of Wrath*, nor did he want to hear students' ceaseless titters accompanying the final moving scene of that book. He no longer cared how or why or wherefore. He would never go to that goddamn, that *fucking* place again. His mother had left him money, and though it wasn't enough to support a family, he no longer had one. His needs were meager. His *life* was meager.

He stayed home, spending his days on the couch. Hila visited every morning before rushing off to teach the dullards who couldn't crack an egg without getting shell inside it. Shell inside egg white offended her tremendously, he learned. As did an over-poached egg, an under-poached egg, white pants, commemorative plates featuring the stern faces of Royals, plastic cutlery, the illogical lyrics of ballads, the syrupy bits of maraschino cherries waiting at the bottom of a tin of fruit cocktail. Fruit cocktail itself offended her. Finding stacks of it inside the kitchen cabinet, these last remnants of Beverly, she swept the tins into the garbage.

Hila tended him, brewing coffee, bringing baguettes and jam and unsalted butter for breakfast. Salted butter was another thing she hated, preferring to sprinkle the salt herself. During these mornings, she did not expect him to entertain her, nor even speak. She read the newspaper, smoothing the pages as she read, sighing over the neat printed columns. When news particularly bothered her, she gnawed her lip and stared at the left corner of the kitchen ceiling. It occurred to Webb that Beverly had probably never glanced at that corner of the ceiling, which entranced Hila. There were a great many things Beverly had never bothered seeing; that he had never bothered seeing.

When the fire started in late September, Webb did not see the smoke from the living room window but heard the rattle and roar of approaching fire engines.

That afternoon, he and Hila stood on the front lawn. The smoke caused their lungs to itch; they coughed deep, dry coughs.

"It's like a roux!" Hila declared. "Growing slowly thicker!"

The words reminded him of his mother, of a time before Beverly. Webb looked around, realizing this simple outing to his front lawn was the first time he'd left his house since he'd returned from Santa Barbara. How was it possible that weeks had passed? How was it possible that he could hate so many things? Himself. His life. The world. He inhaled the smoky air, Hila standing silent and thoughtful beside him.

The next morning, she read aloud from the paper. "Thirty-seven homes, gone!" she said, her remorse as tangible as condensation on a window pane. "Just like that, gone! It could have been even worse!"

"Worse!" he said, and could not imagine it.

She called in sick that morning. There would be no sewing of sleeves, no baking of casseroles. She poured them another coffee and said, "There are days when a girl can drink it black, and days when she's weak, needs the comfort of sugar and cream."

"And today?"

"Today demands cream!"

"I can't imagine you weak," he said. "I can only imagine you exuberant and kind and strong."

"Well, you barely know me."

"I know you." He did not say he knew her well enough to grasp she was a goddamn angel. (Perhaps his mother, in an act of forgiveness, had sent her.) He told her, instead, the story of the 1923 fire—that remarkable conflagration—as recounted by his father. She poured herself still more coffee, added more cream. Listened. Beverly had never listened when he told these stories. She'd never understood: history, this passing down of these meager stories, was all that remained. They were all he had. Someday, they would be all that remained to Debra, her children and grandchildren.

"Do you know," Hila said. "They believe arson caused the fire yesterday." She imbued the word *arson* with meaning.

Webb had not told a soul about the fire he'd started at age fourteen, his supposed act of valor. He'd surely never mentioned it to Beverly, who would have thought him criminal.

He told Hila all of it. In the pause afterward, he awaited her judgment, her disavowal of him, her renegation of friendship; just *who* had she been brewing this coffee, preparing these breakfasts, for? She'd grocery shopped for an asshole! She'd shared coffee with an imposter! He waited, and Hila— lover of irony—surprised him by laughing. She doubled over, spilling her coffee into the saucer that shook happily in her hand. Hers was a genuine laughter, was in fact contagious, and Webb, by default, found himself laughing as well, not reluctantly. In the rush of his emotion, he could do nothing but take her beautiful face between his hands and kiss her, kiss her.

WEBB, 2001

*T*he day he returned to his house, Webb stood in the kitchen where as a child he'd watched his mother trying out scraps of fat with milk, and where as a husband he'd watched his wife eat Stella D'oro biscuits. The space, once familiar, now felt foreign with its gleaming new appliances, its cheerful paint. Colleen stood beside him, and because he could not explain the intricacy of his emotions—how tangled they were, like strands of holiday lights—he said nothing. When she'd gone, he sat at his new kitchen table staring at the wall, swallowed by an inarticulate blankness.

Days later, he heard the girl moving in using the key Colleen had given her. Sound had always reverberated in these old walls. He listened as she unpacked in Debra's former room, though there was little of Debra left in it.

He knew he should greet her. Say, *glad to have you.* She lived here now, with him, a man who'd spent the last eighteen years alone. It was morning. He hunkered inside his bedroom. Once she left, he could eat something. He could piss! When she didn't leave, he searched his bedroom for a vessel to relieve himself in. His bedroom was remarkably devoid of such vessels. He considered urinating out the window. This would surely enrage the neighbor across the street, perpetually complaining about his bamboo, his drunken fairies.

Morning became late morning became early afternoon became late afternoon. Finally, nearing three o'clock, he heard the front door close. Webb rushed into the bathroom. A sickness gnawed inside him. He now shared his house with a stranger. A girl he didn't know, sleeping in what had once been his daughter's room. *Webster,* Beverly had written during the thick of divorce proceedings. The gold monogram on her new stationery read BM; how unfortunate. *I know what's been arranged. Still, I cannot force her to do something she doesn't want to do.*

"The mind cannot wander on an exhale," Hila would say in Webb's bleakest moments, when he rose in either the dark of night or blink of morning, saturated with yearning for his daughter. Hila's hand pressed the place where his heart presumably lay, coddled by this thing called his body that she loved, with its failures and foibles. "See?" Her hand rose and fell, proving that neither he, nor his heart, was lost.

Listening for the girl's return, he made peanut butter and pickle sandwiches, filled thermoses with water. He brought these things to his bedroom, now a fortress. The thermoses of water would soon be a problem, he realized. Returning to the kitchen, he shook the remaining pickles and brine into the garbage, bringing back the empty jar. That night, hearing the girl move about, he held the jar delicately between his hands, considering: was he *really* this man? Was he truly so frightened by a girl's presence that he refused leaving his bedroom? He was indeed. He pissed into the pickle jar. He'd returned home, but his home—his life!—now pulsed with anxiety like a strobe. Months ago, his home had contained him as sweetly as a cocoon. Now, he was a hostage hugging a jar smelling residually of pickles. Yet another mistake, for he'd discarded the pickles and now wanted to eat them. There appeared to be no limit to his bad decisions.

He soon discerned the girl's schedule. During the day, she left her bedroom only to shower and eat morning cereal. Standing at the top of the stairs, he heard the *clink clink clink* of her spoon against the bowl. At three o'clock, she left the house—for work, presumably—at which point Webb ventured from the confines of his bedroom. Their first week together, he tiptoed into the kitchen, searching for clues. Inside the cabinet whose interior still smelled of sawdust, he found two family-sized boxes of Grape Nuts. In the refrigerator was a gallon of nonfat milk. The girl ate alarming amounts of Grape Nuts; he discovered the flattened boxes hidden beneath other things in the trash can, as if she knew the amount of Grape Nuts she consumed was suspect.

In his experience secrets were, every time, relegated to the waste bin. As a child, Webb had watched his mother stalk across the yard to the neighbors' house—the same house where Colleen Crane now lived—and deposit an entire failed charlotte russe in their garbage. This, when butter and sugar and eggs were nearly impossible to obtain, an extravagance. His mother's perfectionism was a disease. *Waste nothing*, the newspapers declared.

When you take more than you can eat, you cheat your buddies in the fleet. His mother lifted a finger to her red lips—*shhh*—and Webb felt frightened by the lengths good people would go to hide what they did not want known. His father's reprimand when the neighbors asked about the cake—they'd discovered it the following morning—bristled with the energy of a nuclear experiment. "We don't waste things in this house." Webb understood his father did not care about wasting things. Certainly, he cared little about cheating his buddies in the fleet. Webb's father had no buddies, in the fleet or elsewhere. His father was only mortified that his wife had rifled inside the neighbors' garbage can like a raccoon. He cared that they *believed* she'd undermined the war effort, not that she'd actually undermined it. They *believed* his wife clandestine in a time when everyone was instructed to report alarming, secretive behavior. *Keep watch!* the advice in the pamphlets went. *Be alert for spies and saboteurs!*

Nights while the girl slept, Webb baked cakes. The baking soothed him, as it had when he was a boy. Sifting flour, whisking sugar into bright yolks, he briefly forgot he was sharing his house. He remembered, instead, his mother's instructions: "Never dip the measuring cup into the flour. Spoon the flour. Level it, like so." At night, baking, he forgot he'd dropped that kitchen towel, had changed the course of his life so abruptly. He could wear his favorite pink chemise, low cut and lacy, its sheer skirt exposing matching panties. Hanky Panky Chemise, the catalog had called this beauty. *Hanky Panky*, a film he'd seen with Hila, her shadowed face transfixed by the movie screen.

In the quiet just before dawn, as the cakes cooled, he'd sit on the couch, watching television.

And then one day, the girl stood in the doorway staring at him with a blank expression. On the tv, a Frenchman in a camouflage suit sold ugly sweaters with typical Basque finesse. Webb's breath snagged as if it were one of those sweaters, poorly made. His heart plummeted as she came toward him. She sat beside him on the couch, her shoulder pressing his.

"The long black quiver of dying," she said. "The steady drip of it."

Webb concentrated on the television screen.

"That pasture with too many cows and bales of hay we pushed down the hill onto the road. If cars had been coming, there would have been trouble!"

She was sleepwalking! Never wake a sleepwalker, he'd heard. He wanted to inch away but feared startling her. "Coming up," the television announced, "two-tone poodle sweaters!"

The girl sat watching the segment in her sleep state. The camouflaged Frenchman exclaimed, "Go ahead and show some skin! Wear this little number without a bra!"

The woman assisting him added, "I would suggest perhaps a nude cami underneath."

The ticker on the bottom of the screen counted time elapsed, sweaters sold. Six minutes, forty sweaters. Poodles stared from the sweaters' woolen fronts. Surreptitiously, Webb studied the girl. He'd known, sitting across from her at the Extended Stay America's tiny table, she understood sadness. She would live in his house without judging his own. They'd draw a circle of respect around one another, two sad people with no expectation of camaraderie.

The girl burst into loud loon's laughter, which brought to mind *On Golden Pond*, still another movie he'd seen with Hila. "Too sentimental," she'd declared as they came out of the theater, blinking into the sunlight. She asked Webb, "Do you know they hate each other, father and daughter?" He said nothing. Fathers and daughters were too sore a subject for him. He soon felt the comfort of her lips against his neck. "I'm sorry. Forgive me."

The girl laughed her demonic loon laugh. He wondered if he should have stayed in his bedroom, pickle jar at the ready. *No*, he'd had to bake cake. The girl's laughter stopped. Abruptly, she stood from the couch and left.

A memory rushed at him: Beverly, calling Debra fat. He'd known his daughter would grow tall, grow out of her childish body; but did it *matter* if Debra was fat? She was who she was. Still, her appearance as judged by Beverly worried him: Debra's glasses, too thick; her body, too custardy. How would she navigate her mother's demands, her criticisms? How would *he* negotiate between them? Though she might appear sturdy, his daughter had not been built to withstand pressure. Her insecurity might cause her to become someone she was not; *Beverly* might cause her to become someone she was not. He'd held his daughter close and promised himself that under his watch, Debra would be who she was meant to be.

He'd promised, but he had not maintained his watch. Had not managed. As a father, he had failed.

HANNAH, 2001

At work, Hannah did the things expected of her: she mixed elaborate Italian sodas for demanding children, filled baskets with staling ciabatta, recommended cannelloni al forno and malfatti con funghi. She lied outright about the wines on the list, montepulciano d'abruzzo and nebbiolo and verdicchio and vermentino and dolcetto and barbera, which she pronounced, to the manager's mortification, Barbra, as in Streisand. In Pittsburgh, she'd worked at BYOBs, pressing bottles against her knee for leverage when she opened them, angling them like rocket ships. Now, she tossed out descriptors with gusto, unsure if they applied to the particular wine: jammy, earthy, integrated tannins, lively acid, good mouthfeel, bright, round, fruit forward. "*Yes*," she said regarding primitivo. "Primitivo is the supposed mother of zinfandel." She sold a bit of primitivo, having latched onto this detail. She knew nothing about dark fruit and tobacco and spice-box overtones, but something about mothers and daughters. *Primitivo is the whore mother of zinfandel*, she wanted to say. *Primitivo ruined zinfandel's life. They're currently checking paternity for zinfandel's punk-ass daddy.*

Inside the wait stations, servers laughed and drank strong coffee and made plans for after work. These people did everything together. This group dynamic proved elusive to Hannah; she had only done everything with Sam. These people went out every night after work, drinking late, then meeting the following morning for wholesome breakfasts of grain-free pancakes and real maple syrup diners paid extra for. After breakfast, they dispersed, made art and music, studied anatomy and pedagogy. Hannah knew these things not because they invited her; they did not. She gleaned details as she polished silverware or folded napkins after service. They were a group. She was other.

Only one person—a cook, dirty but handsome—appeared as unable as she to navigate social situations. He never sat with the chattering lot of them, but ate dinner leaning against the metal prep counter. They worked few shifts together. Occasionally, they passed one another on University Avenue, he leaving work, Hannah arriving. Experiencing a need to speak to this awkward person, she lingered, peering inside storefronts, daring their paths to cross. A tiny happiness burgeoned inside her when they did, a feeling she hadn't felt in so long it seemed unnatural. One day, he stalked toward her, hat angled low over his face. She'd practiced what she wanted to say, something vaguely poetic about the glimpse of the bay seen from University Avenue; how had she taken this route so many times without having noticed it? As he came closer, never looking up from the concrete, she began speaking. He shooed her away, kept walking.

She watched as he continued up University. He wore pants too short to be pants but too long to be shorts. Watching him stalk off, she was returned to her state of acute alienation. She decided she hated that guy. He was an asshole with unwashed hair, wearing nonsensical pants.

Entering work through the back door, she saw that the entire dry-storage area had been burned to a crisp. A giant hole remained where the bins of pasta and flours and beans and large boxes of frying oil had once been. This hole brought to mind the blast sites in sci-fi movies, what remained after the aliens blew the dumb, uncooperative earthlings to bits.

The restaurant's owner ranted before this hole. Hannah gathered from his tirade that the dirty handsome cook had placed a hot pan on a cardboard box while fumbling through dry storage for garbanzo beans. This box had, regretfully, contained several gallons of cooking oil. This cooking oil had, regretfully, ignited.

"Who puts a fucking hot pan on a fucking box filled with oil?" the owner shouted at Hannah. "That fucking guy, that's who!"

Hannah decided she liked that fucking guy, this dirty handsome cook who appeared as fucked in the parameters and particulars and polite cordialities of life as she was. She guessed she'd never see him again. A person couldn't set a restaurant on fire and remain employed there. Upstairs, she searched for his number on the employee phone list. His name appeared without a number. Of course this person lacked a phone number, just as surely he lacked a bank account and a comfortable mattress with back support. Most likely, he couch-surfed, subsisted on beer and ramen. Disappointment shook her; she would have liked to know him.

He returned the next day, moody and repentant, cautious regarding the placement of hot pans. He approached her, looking at her feet as he spoke. She saw not his eyes—days later, she would notice their startling greenness—but his jaw, which resembled a primitive weapon. The way his part cut his hair resembled abstract signage.

He said, "I was rude to you."

"You were," Hannah said.

"I had a bad day."

"I heard about that."

"I mean, that isn't an excuse."

"We've all had them," Hannah said. "Bad days."

The dirty handsome cook turned back to the kitchen.

Hannah thought, *Nothing changes.*

Midway through the night, her buzzer buzzed. None of her tables needed food. She went, confused, to the kitchen, where the dirty handsome cook stood with two dishes of hazelnut gelato. He passed one dish to her, kept the other for himself, rummaging in the dish pit for two clean spoons. They sat on the metal prep counters behind the line, eating their gelato as if there were no prawns to grill, no meat to salt, no diners requiring more parmesan, more bread, more olive oil.

"I started a fire." He motioned towards the hole.

Hannah said, "I'm living with a man who caught his kitchen on fire." She had told no one this; there had been no one to tell.

"Really."

"Something about a dish towel. Olive oil. I didn't really understand it."

"A friend of yours?"

"No."

"Someone you know."

"Not really."

"But you live with him."

"Right."

"Why?"

"I needed somewhere to go."

"I get that," he said.

They finished their gelato without speaking. Hannah appreciated the dirty handsome cook's reluctance to fill the air with meaningless words. Together, they stared at the gaping hole where dry storage had once been, and then they returned to work.

HANNAH, 1989

S he and Sam became friends at the end of eighth grade, during the class retreat to a camp named Little Flower Camp. There, they shared the bottom beds of neighboring bunks beneath the rheumatic eyes of Sister Grace.

Sam was the only girl picked after Hannah in gym class that year, a remarkable feat. No one wanted a girl on his dodgeball team who took intentional hits, nodding thankfully at whoever had hit her. Afterward, blue and violet bruises staining her skin like ink blots, Sam sat alone on the bleachers, staring into space with the air of someone who heard God muttering in her ear. She and Hannah first spoke during breakfast in Little Flower Camp's rattling cafeteria. As Sam opened packets of sugar onto her Froot Loops, she ran on about Patty Hearst and the Symbionese Liberation Army, neither of which Hannah had heard of.

"She was an heiress," Sam said impatiently, "taken from her apartment in Berkeley. They beat her fiancé, poor Steven Weed, to a bloody pulp. One minute she was eating a tuna fish sandwich and watching *Mission: Impossible*, and the next, some urban guerrillas were shoving her inside the trunk of a car. For weeks they forced her to live blindfolded in a tiny closet, eating nothing but mung beans."

"*Mung* beans?"

"For the first days of her captivity, she wasn't given access to a bathroom."

Sam talked about Patty Hearst as they wobbled unconfidently in their canoe; as they stood in the cafeteria line for various ambiguous meats impaled on sticks; as they drank tepid milk; as they singed marshmallows over the campfire (what fun!); as the nuns recited the night's prayers into the darkening sky.

"She was forced to have sex with members of the SLA," Sam said. She spoke too loudly of things like mung beans and rape, fecal matter and fascists. When she wasn't speaking about Patty Hearst, Sam talked instead about her father and his new wife—*She's amazing, more like a sister*—as well as her half-brothers, two young boys spit out in quick succession, close enough in age to be dressed alike despite not being twins. Her father lived in Connecticut but owned a summer home in the Hamptons. She was going to visit this summer. For a month, maybe two. *Fuck*, maybe she'd stay. Her mother—she rolled her eyes—was fucking crazy. Fucking exhausting. Needy for attention. Worse than the women on talk shows. "She dresses like a street walker. I've seen my mother's nipples more times than I can say. That woman loves a low cut-shirt."

The other girls inched away from Sam when she wandered too near. Hannah felt oddly drawn to her. She'd never heard anyone say *fuck* so frequently. She'd never heard anyone talk about her mother with such derision. Hannah knew nothing about Patty Hearst. She knew even less about fathers—she'd last seen hers when she was five—but she understood these other girls didn't want her near, either. She walked with Sam everywhere, so close their shoulders touched, and touched again.

This retreat was meant to form their characters, to build the necessary spiritual resources for whatever difficulty lay ahead. "Be kind," the nuns said. "As you move through God's world, be always kind."

When Sam and Hannah arrived at their public high school, the memo on kindness, unlike Patty Hearst's vague manifesto demanding food for the poor, had never been issued. When either Sam or Hannah approached, girls scattered like a flock of birds after a gunshot. Hannah had not seen such a thing in nature—birds rushing against a pallid sky—but rather on television, in the movies she and Sam rented on Friday and Saturday nights because they were neither popular nor social creatures, never invited to the distant edges of parking lots to drink warm bottles of Schlitz and make intrepid sexual discoveries. They spent weekends in Sam's darkened basement, watching tv and eating Duncan Hines frosting straight from the container, Sam's mother, Fran, forcing her hips between them on the couch. Like the sea, they parted, made room for her.

Smoothing her daughter's sleek black hair, Fran asked, Did they *need* anything? *Want* anything? Were they too hot? Too cold? Were they hungry? Thirsty? Why was it so *dark*? Why were they opposed to light?

"If it's dark," said Sam, "we can't see you. We can pretend you aren't here."

"Samuelle, that isn't how the nuns taught you to treat people." Fran smoothed Hannah's cheek as she said this. Her hands were soft, the non-working hands of a woman with too much time to moisturize. A woman whose wealthy husband had run off with another woman, assuaging his guilt with a hefty divorce settlement. Her fingers massaged Hannah's earlobe. The willingness to touch another person's earlobe, Hannah suspected, was the true token of a lonely person.

"Fran, stop fondling Hannah."

"I'm not *fondling* Hannah."

"I *see* you, Fran."

Hannah had never heard a child call her mother by her first name. "I'm your mother, not your friend," her own mother would have clarified had Hannah ventured to call her Karen. Fran watched movies with them, thumbed the thin pages of the tabloids with them. She took them shopping, bought Hannah gifts her mother made her return.

"Tell her *thank you* for her supreme generosity, but your mother can clothe you just fine on her own."

Hannah, initially baffled by Fran's constant attention, soon understood Sam's tolerance of it. Fran's presence was the tradeoff for the things she provided them: boxed wine, Smirnoff Ice, bottles of vodka kept in the freezer and mixed with concentrated orange juice. The three of them watched *Gleaming the Cube* and *Heathers* for the umpteenth time, Fran filling their glasses with Sutter Home white zinfandel, saying, "Shannen Doherty is *not* an attractive girl. I know people find the space between her front teeth sultry, what have you, but really, her mother should have done something about that while she was young. Samuelle, be glad you have a concerned mother who refuses to let you walk around like a gap-toothed yokel."

New Year's Eve, 1991. Hannah and Sam, sophomores in high school, celebrated the turn of the year in Sam's basement, with the couch opened into a bed. The three of them—Sam, Hannah, and Fran—drank gin and pineapple juice and watched standup comedy late into the night. Fran's laugh sounded like pneumonia. Hearing it, Hannah pressed her hand against her chest.

New Year's Day, they woke in the still-darkened basement, having missed Dick Clark and the dropping of the shiny ball, the arrival of 1992. The angry red numbers on the digital clock declared it midafternoon. Hannah's mother had already left ten messages on the answering machine, each one mounting in irritation. The phone rang midway through playing them; Fran ripped its cord from the socket. In the kitchen, she closed the blinds. She donned sunglasses. She stuck Eggos in the toaster, frozen pancakes in the microwave. On the table she chucked the tub of margarine, the syrup. Beside Mrs. Butterworth's clasped hands, she stacked several packages of Lunchables and said, "There! Now it's officially brunch."

On each of their plates, she placed pills too formidable and colorful to be innocuous. They frightened Hannah with their faux cheer, but Sam swallowed hers and Hannah's easily with her orange juice as she watched the muted cartoons on the kitchen tv. In the next moment, she was slathering her pancakes with margarine.

Hannah's mother told her, every year, that New Year's Day was a day she should experience with careful intention, spending it the way she'd like to spend the entire year. Hannah would later think that the entirety of 1992 had been absorbed into oblivion, a dusky expanding cloud of confusion with muffled voices like the persistent hum of a radiator. She was only glad she hadn't swallowed those pills before her mother came. (*This is your brain*, the commercial said. *This is drugs. This is your brain on drugs. Any questions?*) Hannah was determinedly chewing an overtoasted Eggo when they heard her mother banging on the door. She'd come in the cold sans coat, her hair a confused net, looking like the homeless women who warmed themselves in the steam from the sidewalk grates in Center City.

"This is ridiculous!" Hannah's mother swept both literal and figurative cold into the warm kitchen. "It's three o'clock in the afternoon! I left messages!" Her eyes rested on the telephone's disconnected cord.

"Please," said Fran, flinching from the volume of her voice. "The girls were just having breakfast. They need nourishment to conquer this wonderful new year. Would you like some juice? A pancake?"

"No, I don't want a goddamn *pancake*. Hannah, it's time to go."

Months later, Fran invited twenty girls by engraved invitation to Sam's seventeenth birthday party. Only Hannah had shown up, pecking at canapé and crudité, yanking at her tights as she navigated around the duck liver pâté.

Fran loitered by the door for half an hour.

"No one's coming," Sam finally told her.

Washing down some pills with a shot of golden liquid, Fran assembled plates for the three of them: duck confit, cassoulet, ratatouille.

Sam said, "I don't get the party theme."

"French!" said Fran.

"*Why?*"

"Because, Samuelle, you study French!"

"I'm *failing* French." Sam asked, "Is there any wine?"

Fran poured glasses of pink wine. Pink was the secondary theme. Fran had selected pink satin tablecloths, pink flowers, pink shiny napkins that slid easily off a person's lap and onto the floor.

"I hate pink." Sam swilled her wine and said, "I'm sure the Frenchies don't drink this shit."

"Well," said Fran with forced cheer, pouring Sam another glass, "it's the shit we have."

The birthday cake was two cakes, one shaped into the number one, the other shaped into the number seven, both cakes frosted in lush pink rosettes. Beside the cake, the party favors were arranged: twenty tiny boxes wrapped in pink glossy paper, each containing a gold necklace with a dangling Eiffel Tower pendant. Fran lit the candles on the cake, and together she and Hannah sang a lackluster version of "Happy Birthday," followed by Fran's shrill instruction, "Blow out the candles! Make a wish!"

Sam blew out the candles. She closed her eyes for a moment. She opened them and said, "I wished you'd die. So I could live for a moment in peace." Plucking each candle from the cake, she made a pile on the dining room table. "Fran, why the fuck are you crying? You got the party you wanted."

"Samuelle, that's no way to talk to your mother."

"I hate you," said Sam. "I don't care how I talk to you."

"Samuelle."

"No wonder he left you. No wonder he wanted someone different."

Hannah had only ever seen Fran cheery, like a cardboard cutout grinning from a department store window. Now her mouth sagged down, even as she lifted her chin. "He didn't want you either, Samuelle."

"Fuck off."

"He didn't even want you for a *summer*."

In response Sam lifted the number seven cake, carrying it from the dining room and through the wide foyer, gaining speed as she climbed the stairs. From above, she held the cake over the railing that overlooked the house's grand entrance. She paused for a dramatic moment before releasing it, watching it smash onto the polished floor below. Rushing forward, Fran fell to her knees over the obliterated cake, weeping and shoving handfuls into her mouth. Hannah watched, appalled. Fran had gotten pink frosting in her hair, across the front of her elegant black dress.

When Sam motioned at Hannah to come upstairs, Hannah hesitated. *Your mother*, she mouthed.

Sam gave a dismissive wave, and Hannah climbed the stairs, leaving Fran with her legs splayed indecorously on the floor, her arms wrapping her middle.

Inside her bedroom, Sam locked the door. This seemed to Hannah excessive, but soon Fran was rattling the knob.

"You ungrateful bitch, Samuelle! After everything I do for you!"

Sam pushed play on her tape deck. She turned the volume loud. Fran's fist pounded the door.

Hannah said, watching the doorknob twist back and forth, "Is she okay?"

"She's fine."

"She doesn't seem fine."

"She'll get over it." Sam shrugged. "She always does."

In 1993, they graduated, their white commencement gowns appearing stark without the golden lapels of the honor society, their graduation caps sitting slanted. Both Hannah and Sam had overapplied their eyeshadow the way the Merle Norman associate had shown them. ("Begin by making a darkened V in the corner of the eyelid," the heavily eyeshadowed woman had instructed.) Their mothers maintained careful distance from one another in the heat. They were graduating the last weekend in June, thanks to an interminable teachers' strike, thanks to the Blizzard of 1993.

The bodice of Fran's dress squeezed her breasts, hoisted them upward like an offering.

"I'm bummed," Sam told her between gulps of fruit punch. "You dressed like a prostitute for my graduation."

Fran, busily eating deviled eggs, said, "Don't say *bummed*. You know my feelings about bummed." She held up a deviled egg. "Can people think of nothing better to serve? It's disgusting, how long these sit in the heat!"

Sam said, "No one's holding a gun to your head, saying, 'Eat the fucking eggs!'" To Hannah she said, "So you won the French award! Congratulations!" Sam's mouth formed an ugly smile, and Hannah understood as she sipped diluted fruit punch that Sam was not actually congratulating her. Hannah had won the award by default, as the only senior studying French. Sam wanted to hurt her.

"Let's toast your magnificent success!" Sam raised her glass, flung its contents into the air. Fruit punch rained on the students loitering near them. Girls in white gowns screamed and scattered.

"Mademoiselle." Sam wrenched Hannah's arm, pulled her close. "You won't achieve anything in this life. You'll fail as effectively as I will. You can have your stupid French award. It's the best you'll ever do."

When Hannah received her yearbook in August, late because of the teachers' strike, it appeared thrown together, as if the yearbook committee only wanted to put high school behind them. Several seniors had been omitted from the graduating class entirely. An editor must have noticed this after the book was printed; photographs of the missing students had been xeroxed on a sheet shoved inside the book as an addendum. Sam had not ordered a copy of the yearbook for herself. She paged through Hannah's, pausing at the graduation-day collage and tapping the photo. "I threw fruit punch on this girl."

"You sound nostalgic," said Hannah.

Sam pressed her thumb over the girl's face. "If things don't at some point appear retrospectively rosy, what's to prevent us from hauling off and killing ourselves?"

"Is that your official yearbook quote?"

"Alas," Sam said, "I'm not in the yearbook."

"Of course you are," Hannah said, but she wasn't. She had not submitted a senior picture of herself; had not provided a mortifying child photo or a last will and testament. She'd not answered inane questions about her favorite colors and foods; did not appear at the periphery of any club shots, her face blanched by poor photography. Nothing indicated that Sam had been a member of the class of 1993. She'd erased herself from school history. The girl in the punch-stained graduation gown would not be able to locate Sam's face; would not be able to point and say, *This girl. This one here.*

Two weeks before their departures for college, Fran swooped into the darkness of the basement and said, "Come on, girls! Let's be fancy lunching ladies!" She clicked the television off.

"I hate lunch." Sam clicked the television back on.

"Samuelle, I didn't raise you to hate lunch."

"What does that even *mean?*" Sam asked.

"It means we're having lunch," Fran said, but once inside her Jaguar, they didn't drive to any restaurant. Fran merged instead onto the Pennsylvania Turnpike, taking her ticket jauntily and driving over the tremendous bridge jutting a hundred sixty-three feet over Clarks Summit, passing countless uninspired places where they might have eaten. Fran drove, wind whipping through the Jaguar's open sunroof, tousling their hair, save Fran's, which remained as unyielding as a papier mâché planet made in a kindergarten art class. Hannah suspected Fran was taking them to lunch somewhere in Wilkes-Barre, a restaurant with carved radish garnishes and flaming desserts, salads tossed tableside; this seemed generous of her. Passing the last Wilkes-Barre exit, Hannah wondered if Fran was taking them to lunch in Hazleton; this seemed odd of her. But just beyond the last exit to Hazleton, Fran pulled the Jaguar onto the side of the highway.

"Girls," she said.

"Fran," Sam answered. Cars clipped past at an alarming speed. "Is it truly necessary to have a tête-à-tête on the side of the highway?"

A semi rattled past.

"Girls! We're not *actually* going to lunch! Though if you'd like lunch, you can have it. Starving you isn't the point of this excursion! The point is, we're going to Gettysburg!"

"*Gettysburg?*" The derision in Sam's voice was as dense as clay.

"*I had a dream,*" Fran recited.

"You're fucking kidding me."

"No, I am *not* fucking kidding you," Fran, so cheery, said.

"That's not even the right speech!"

"It's an approximation. You understand my point."

"No," said Sam. "I do not!"

The car idled. "Since you were very young, I've wanted to take this trip together. I hear it's very beautiful."

"It's a *battlefield.*"

"Site of the most casualties in the Civil War. A turning point in our country's fine history."

"How impressive; you've been reading something besides *People*," Sam said. "We don't have *clothes* for this happy jaunt."

"But you do!"

Fran had, actually, packed them each a suitcase; had loaded these suitcases into the car's trunk several days prior. She had considered everything. Inside the room of their colonial-era hotel (est. 1797), Hannah and Sam dumped their bags onto the garish floral quilt covering the fourposter bed. Inside each suitcase were tiny bottles of expensive toiletries lined like soldiers inside a zippered compartment; silken makeup bags brimming with new cosmetics; overalls with the tags still attached. *"Hideous!"* Sam tossed them aside as Fran argued that overalls were making a comeback this fall. (When Hannah arrived at the University of Pittsburgh two weeks later, the freshman girls were a swarm of confusion and half-buckled overalls.) Fran had packed pajama sets. She'd packed *underwear.*

Sam twirled a shiny metallic pair of panties on her finger. "Did you buy these at Frederick's of Hollywood? Were they buy-one-get-a-one-night-stand-free?"

"Girls, you're of an age when you need to consider underthings more intentionally. They're not *just* some flap of fabric to conveniently cover your vagina and prevent chafing."

"That's exactly what they are," Sam said.

"In college, you don't want to scare boys away with baggy underwear. Also, what if something happens to you, a terrible accident, and you're rushed to the hospital? Maybe there's a handsome doctor in the emergency room. You don't want such a man cutting off your ugly briefs and thinking, *Here's a woman who doesn't value herself. Here's a woman not worth saving.*"

"I just vomited in my mouth," said Sam.

"There's a new toothbrush and toothpaste in that suitcase. Also, some mouthwash. And floss. Whatever your beautiful mouth needs, Samuelle, your mother has considered."

Fran had thought of everything, but she had not told Hannah's mother about the trip. "I didn't *forget* to ask her." Fran ushered Hannah to the telephone. "I chose to forget. She takes herself—she takes *mothering*—too seriously. She can't stop us now that we're here."

Hannah dialed her mother's work number and thought she might vomit herself. Her mother would not take this news well, and Hannah couldn't explain to her that it was thrilling to go somewhere. Together, they went nowhere. When her mother came to the phone, Hannah said bluntly: "So. I'm in Gettysburg.

"Excuse me?"

Hannah imagined her mother standing in her dental hygienist's uniform, her hair an explosion above her taut face.

"Gettysburg. Site of the most definitive battle in the Civil War. A turning point—"

"Yes, I know what Gettysburg is."

"Fran surprised us."

"You're telling me that psycho up and took you halfway across the state without your mother's permission?"

"I guess so."

"Put her on the phone."

Fran spoke in a voice meant to soothe. It was her best impression of mother to mother, friend to friend. She ignored the simple fact that she and Hannah's mother were not friends. They had been acquaintances, briefly, by default, when Sam and Hannah first became close, two single mothers losing their closest—their only—companions to adulthood. Two women who'd gone through bitter divorces. Early on, they shared grasshoppers and pink ladies at Jim Dandy's Saloon while Sam and Hannah coursed the mall's wide thoroughfares, Orange Julius shakes in hand. Once, the four of them shared an awkward Chinese takeout dinner, pupus spread across Fran's glass coffee table, shrimp toast and duck sauce, brittle rice. Bitter tea for the girls, chardonnay for the mothers. Their camaraderie had been a momentary hiccup in time, followed by Hannah's mother's realization that they had nothing in common, their situations were far from the same. "That woman thinks her life is so hard. Imagine my life if I didn't have to work. If I didn't have to worry about money and bills. If your father had ridiculous sums of money and paid child support."

"Now, Karen," Fran said into the phone. "The girls are growing up. It's time for us to loosen the reins, let them ride their rodeos. They might get knocked off the bull. They might land on their heinies. Unfortunately, it's no longer about us. We're merely spectators. Our job is to grab ourselves some corn dogs, watch, and wait."

From her spot on the garish floral quilt—it smelled like the motheaten clothes she and Sam tried on at the Dickson City Salvation Army—Hannah deciphered certain phrases in her mother's tirade. "Crazy," she heard. "Faulty metaphor." Her mother asked, "A *corndog*?"

Fran held the phone away from her ear, motioning with her hand to suggest *blah blah blah*, and then the conversation ended because Hannah's mother hung up.

In the few photographs Hannah later saw of this trip, Sam obtruded like something that didn't belong, too pallid, like a piece of broken tusk; she had always hated the sun. There was not a single shot taken of her on the battlefield, where she refused to go. She remained inside the hotel room, wrapped inside the garish quilt, watching television as if she'd never left the basement couch. When Hannah and Fran returned from their first day out—after sniffing the scented candles and admiring the embroidered linens displayed in dimly lit shops; lunch consumed in the hotel's dank dining room; an afternoon in a museum, staring at cannons and reading factual paragraphs etched onto placards—they returned to discover the room filled with stolid white plates and empty glasses dotted with residual orange juice pulp. Hannah counted: Sam had drunk sixteen glasses of orange juice, lining the empty glasses in neat rows along the dresser as if they were their own army.

"*Shh*," Sam said when Fran and Hannah entered the room, still smelling of the Coppertone they'd slathered on one another. Their feet ached. The air conditioning blasted. Sam lay in bed, eyes glazed, watching a program about bees.

"You stayed inside for *bees?*" Fran said.

"I *like* bees," Sam said. "I like bees better than you. I would prefer to do literally anything else than do something with you. I would rather shovel shit."

"Good thing there's no shit to shovel," said Fran, unfazed.

They had saved the battlefield for the following day in the hope that Sam might join them, but no amount of bribery Fran could conceive of, no clothes or concert tickets or food, convinced Sam she wanted to see the site of the most casualties in the Civil War.

"Get the fuck out," she told them. Fran gathered her things while Hannah lingered. She felt claustrophobic in the darkened room, slightly panicked by the stale air, the permeation of Sam's bad mood, like a gas leak threatening to ignite. She stood, immobile. She never knew what to do when Sam turned cruel. Hannah didn't want to leave her alone, but neither did she want to stay with her inside the suffocating walls.

"Both of you," Sam said. "Get the fuck out!" She heaved the tv remote at Hannah, forcing her to dodge it, but when Hannah started toward the door, Sam's voice pierced her back.

"You duplicitous cunt." Sam stared at her with a venomous expression, and Hannah understood she had made the wrong decision. But she'd made it; she could not now take it back.

At the battlefield, the air contained a certain hazy scent Hannah attributed to Pennsylvania summer. She stood, taking it in: late August afternoon, distinct horizon, drone of insects, fathers wearing short shorts and white tube socks, mothers with varicose veins and plastic visors. Bored children, their mouths still smeared with breakfast's wet crumbs.

Four score and seven years ago.

I had a dream.

History, Hannah guessed, was whatever you felt like making it.

Fran, standing too close to Hannah, made an atypical tourist. She wore a dress whose top she'd unbuttoned to expose what she called her "orbs." She'd worn heels to a battlefield. The veined, visored mothers stared as she picked her way across the pocked ground, which Fran seemed surprised to discover did not have the manicured quality of a putting green at the Scranton Country Club. She clung to Hannah's bicep, and something in this clinging suggested to Hannah how fragile Fran was, like the final card placed at the top of a trembling house of them. Together, they gazed across the expanse of battlefield, Fran dabbing her melty foundation with a tissue.

"I'm worried about Samuelle," she said abruptly. "I don't know how she'll fare in this world."

"She'll be fine," Hannah said, and realized it wasn't true.

Minutes passed. The battlefield quivered in the heat.

"Those glasses weren't filled only with juice, you know."

"Oh," Hannah said.

"Oh," Fran repeated, this single syllable plump with meanness. "*Oh.*"

"You brought it," Hannah said, feeling like she'd been accused of something. "You buy it for her."

"So you're saying everything's my fault," Fran said with a glare.

"You give her whatever she wants. You never say no."

Fran's hand landed against Hannah's cheek with a crack. A mother pulling antibacterial hand wipes from a container looked up. A father ceased fidgeting with his fanny pack. In the distance, tourists laughed. Children cried. Fran turned away from her, and their sightseeing was done.

Two weeks later, Hannah said her final goodbyes to Sam and Fran outside their house, her mother waiting in the packed, idling car. Sam extricated herself from Hannah's embrace; Fran clung too tightly to Hannah's elbows. With crimson lips, she kissed and kissed again the hollow of Hannah's cheek, and Hannah knew Fran meant to erase her memory of that slap.

Hannah's mother laid on the car horn. Once, twice. Three staccato bursts.

"Such a charming woman," Fran said as Hannah pulled away from her.

"Sam doesn't stand a chance with that woman as her mother," her own mother said as Hannah slid into the passenger seat. Fran waved at them, blew tiny kisses.

"That's harsh."

"Accurate," her mother said. "It's only accurate."

DEBRA, 2001

*I*n June, we traveled as a family to Monterey. At the aquarium, we studied orange jellies pulsing against a bright blue backdrop, schools of fleeting silver fish, undulating seaweed. Otters cavorted and lazed, wrangled for treats. My husband shifted his weight. He forgot: he had to make a call. Jamie and I later passed him, a stranger, on our way to the penguin exhibit. He sat on a bench, legs crossed, talking into his cell phone. We passed, pretending we hadn't seen him.

At the exhibit, Jamie asked, did I know that penguins were actually cruel? In the photographs of them in the glossy pages of *National Geographic*, penguins standing on icy ledges, staring into the ocean's dark depths—those photos were misleading. In actuality, that crowd of penguins had most likely pushed a sacrificial penguin into the water below. Yes, Jamie said. The callous mass chose a sick, unwanted penguin, shoving it into the water to see if it was devoured by seals. If this penguin was in fact devoured, the mass on the icy ledge knew the water was unsafe. They shrugged, moved to a different icy ledge. If, however, the penguin survived, the water was proven safe. The others jumped in, frolicked and fished.

"If the water is safe," said Jamie, "probably that sacrificial penguin just wishes he'd died. Now he has to stay with them, knowing they don't give a shit about him."

I touched his cheek. "Penguin bastards. Do you want some ice cream?"

My son did not want ice cream. He was low-maintenance—like a succulent, or a cat who prefers sleeping in a closet—and I wondered if we'd made him this way by not giving him enough attention to know he needed it. We found our way back to my husband, who appeared stiff from sitting but remarkably cheerful.

Returning home, I recounted everything to Colleen Crane: the discontented sharks; the large octopus, elusive on past trips, who emerged from the rocks to gaze penetratingly into my eyes. A video had shown an aquarium keeper handling an octopus in a shallow pool. If I looked quickly, it appeared as if they waltzed together: a man smitten with an octopus, a man in love. This trip—which I'd proposed—had felt like a rummaging attempt to salvage something. Octopuses, it turned out, distinguished one human from another by the texture of their skin. "Amazing," I'd said while my husband checked his watch.

Colleen Crane and I discussed our fear of sharks, her love of commemorative pressed pennies. She pressed pennies in every place she visited; had pressed a penny on Cannery Row, which yielded an image of a sea lion that might have been confused for old man winter. Cannery Row led us to Steinbeck. She preferred *Grapes of Wrath*; I preferred *East of Eden*. We discussed driving though Steinbeck country, with its vegetables strewn along the shoulders of the roads, its unwanted lettuces and broccoli. The hunched backs of the fieldworkers, the slanted sun. There was safety in not being proximate to someone; I told Colleen Crane things, knowing I'd never see her face to face. We talked about George Bush. How, in moments of concentration or stress, he looked constipated. We talked about earthquakes, unfolding everywhere like staccato warning notes in Peru and El Salvador and India. About our own experiences with earthquakes: our preparedness, our lack of preparedness.

"My ex-husband is LAPD," said Colleen Crane. "We had earthquake kits in our house and in our cars in case we were on the highway when disaster struck. We had spare athletic shoes in our trunks in case we needed to outrun seismic activity."

"We have nothing," I said. Once, in the middle of the night, awakened by a small jolt, fearing a larger one, I went into the kitchen, panicked. I filled countless glasses of water, lined them on the kitchen island. I told her my husband believed us above disaster. He believed, in times of catastrophe, we'd knock on the doors of the prepared people, buy their jugs of water, their tins of Spam. Money would solve the problem of our own ineptitude.

Summer evolved. The media declared it the summer of the shark (a boy bitten by a bull shark in the shallow water near Santa Rosa Island, the leg of a New Yorker taken in the Bahamas, footage of sharks massing off the southwest coast of Florida). Andrea Pia Kennedy drowned her children in a bathtub, one by one. "Now, *there's* a man who believes money will buy anything," Colleen Crane said regarding Dennis Tito and his voyage into space. "He played *billiards*," she said of Crown Prince Dipendra and the Nepalese Royal Massacre. "By *himself*. Before he murdered his entire family." Details of Timothy McVeigh's final day emerged. He showered. He napped. He watched news stories of himself on CNN. He consumed, for his last meal, two pints of mint-chocolate-chip ice cream.

We talked about our own last days, what they'd be if we could choose them.

"Knowing me, I'd spend the day worrying," Colleen Crane said. "I'd worry, and then I'd die."

"I'd lie on the beach with Jamie," I said. "Shoulder to shoulder. I'd close my eyes and feel the sun on my face and know he was safe. We'd go waist-high into the ocean. We'd jump into the waves, and no sharks would maim us."

Colleen Crane said, "Don't be so sure." She asked, "What would you *eat*?"

"It would be summer," I said. "In this alternate reality, I would have a garden. My last meal would be vegetables from my own garden. Heirloom tomatoes and fresh basil and squash blossoms and green beans, beautiful aubergines."

"I had a flower garden," Colleen Crane said. "In Los Angeles. Until my husband's girlfriend brought an entire bachelorette party to my house and they ruined it."

"What?" I laughed.

"That's how I found out about the girlfriend. These women in tiaras, in dresses that barely covered their crotches, frantically ripping out my zinnias." Her laugh echoed mine, then she sobered. "If you want a garden, you should have one."

"Our neighborhood has restrictions on things that might make a person happy," I said. "I touched a tomato plant once, if that counts."

"That smell," she said, "is as good as the scent of freshly ground coffee. Is as good as the scent of poblano peppers roasted in the oven. Is as good as the scent of cilantro."

I asked, "What would *you* eat?"

She hesitated. "Anything your father wanted to cook. Anything he wanted to bake, but especially his biscuits. I'd eat an entire plate of his biscuits."

"Are you some sort of biscuit connoisseur?" The question felt tangled with anger. "I thought he burned his kitchen to the ground. Isn't that how this thing started?"

In the beat of silence, I knew she considered the phrase *this thing*.

"I'm sorry," she said.

"How does he bake without a kitchen?"

"He uses mine."

A pause as I registered this.

"Any day now he'll move out of the Extended Stay America and back into his house. We found a girl to live with him."

"A girl."

"So he's not alone."

"It's not my fault he's alone."

"He wants to see you."

"He's a smidge late."

"He—"

"You have no idea about any of this," I said, and we didn't speak for a week, the longest we'd gone without talking. She did not mention my father again.

At some ambiguous point in this strange summer in which sharks attacked people and George Bush vacationed at Crawford Ranch—pointing at nature with a constipated grin that suggested he did, in fact, comprehend its beauty—she ceased being Colleen Crane and became, simply, Colleen.

Colleen. I repeated her name, a mantra, as I drove on the highway. As I practiced downward-facing dog and rested in child's pose. As I scrambled eggs for Jamie's breakfast. Inside Jamie's baby name book, I located the name Colleen and read: *Derived from the Irish word cailín meaning "girl." Not commonly used in Ireland itself, but used in America since the early 20th century.*

Colleen, whose soft laughter reminded me of the bamboo I'd once heard rustling in someone else's yard. Not my own yard, because bamboo was an invasive species, banned by our neighborhood association, as were vegetable gardens and aboveground pools, solar panels and concrete-slab driveways, garden figurines.

"We should meet halfway," Colleen said. "San Luis Obispo or Pismo Beach. It would be nice to talk in person. We could have lunch and drink too much."

"Yes," I said, then invented excuses to ensure we would *not* do that. Dental appointments, dermatology appointments, gynecology appointments; no woman dared argue with another woman's gynecological care. I claimed country club fundraisers and bridge tournaments, stints volunteering in Jamie's school library.

"Are you afraid?" Colleen asked.

"Why would I be *afraid?*" Fear rattled inside me like china during an earthquake I would not be prepared for.

"I guess you wouldn't be," she said.

In late July, she came to Los Angeles for her parents' anniversary. "I've cleared out Friday afternoon. I made a lunch reservation. I'll call you when I get in on Thursday." Her voice contained a schoolgirl giddiness. The week of her arrival, I let the machine take the calls. I counted the hang-ups: fifteen.

"What happened?" she asked, having returned to Oakland. The question was concerned, not accusatory. "Is everything okay?"

"Yes," I said. Her kindness pained me.

In mid-August, she came for her mother's birthday.

"I'll stop by," she said. "Maybe Monday? We can have tea, or I'll bring takeout. Chinese?"

"Sure," I said as my panic rose.

She read the menu over the phone in her languid voice.

"Hot and Numbing Combination sounds intriguing," I said, though I had no intention of being hot or numb with her. Lies poked my innards like the branches of a shorn tree.

Three Lucky Treasures. Jingjang Duck. Cold Fun with Sesame Paste.

"Stir Fried Dough Stick with Cucumber," I said, and sensed her writing everything down, determined to get it right.

"What about Jamie? What would he like?"

"Jamie," I said.

"He's vegetarian, right?"

"He is," I said, and wanted to cry: that she remembered this about Jamie, that she cared to bring him something he could eat. That she would not be meeting him. That he would not be eating Ma Po Tofu or Hunan Tofu or Princess Tofu, none of the tofus, in the presence of Colleen Crane because I lacked the courage to let this happen. Because I was fearful—she, ever-knowing, had called it—and there was no circumventing this fear.

On Monday, I found Jamie in bed, reading a book in the darkened room.

"Get your bathing suit." I whisked the curtains open. "We're going to the club. It's summer. You can't fritter your life away in this room."

"It's the *end* of summer."

"You need sun," I said. "You can have a Shirley Temple."

"Shirley Temples ceased being persuasive when I was five."

"This isn't a negotiation."

"Yes, *Dad*," he said.

At the country club pool, we withered in the sun. The lounge chairs with umbrellas had been taken by the people skilled in pool-going, those who arrived early, with sunscreen and snacks, water bottles with which to spritz their flushed skin. Jamie and I were decidedly unskilled in pool-going.

"Oh, Jaim." I reached for him. "You need sunscreen."

He shoved my hand away. "I thought I needed sun."

"Let's talk," I said.

"If I can't say something nice," he said, "dot dot dot."

"Let's swim."

"I hate swimming."

"You don't hate swimming!"

"I severely dislike swimming."

As a child, he'd learned to swim in this very pool, his skinny boy arms encased in green floats imprinted with the smiling faces of frogs. A blonde teenager had given him a board, instructing him to kick, *kick*! Jamie had kicked doggedly across the length of the pool, looking miserable; but wouldn't any child, in relation to those happy frogs, that effusive teenager?

"*Please.*"

We entered the water slowly: toe, ankle, knee, thigh.

"Why are we here?"

"I told you."

"You hate this place," Jamie said.

"I don't."

"Okay." He submerged.

I *did* hate this place, with its clean white furniture and heated water, its tanned, effortless women. I hated the men who sauntered in after rounds of golf to join these tanned women, their wives. They shouted at waiters taking drink orders at the opposite side of the pool, men plump with confidence and entitlement, as if they had not just shot bogeys on ten out of eighteen holes.

Jamie's head popped up, hair stuck thickly to his forehead. "It's a good thing we celebrated your birthday here, then."

"Your grandmother spent a lot of time making that party special."

"Well, I hate it here." He submerged again. I watched his back moving just beneath the surface, his skin speckled with reflected sunspots. When he came back up, shaking his head, sending out fleeting beads of water, he said, "I'm done." I watched from the pool as he collapsed on his lounge chair, covered his face with a towel.

We spent the day inside the flamboyant sun. The flamboyant sun smiled at us with vaseline-rubbed teeth, a beauty queen, my mother. I closed my eyes; the sun remained. I consulted my watch. Surely, we were out of the woods and into safety. I stalled, ordered snacks. Jamie sighed heavily over nachos.

"Please," he said. "Can we go?"

On the ride home, I saw that his ears, burnt to a crisp, looked like something given to dogs to gnaw on.

"Jaim," I said. "I'm sorry."

He touched his ear. "Consider it a souvenir of the fun I just had."

I tried to imagine a life in which I could take anything he said at face value, a life in which I provided the things he needed. I'd used my own son as an excuse. I'd brought him to a place he hated, had exposed him to the possibility of skin cancer. Despite being a grown woman, I'd not been able to tell another grown woman I had no interest in seeing her. That we weren't friends. Weren't acquaintances. Had no history, no kinship. No need to *lunch*.

"There's, like, a homeless person sitting on our steps," Jamie said as we pulled into our driveway.

A woman watched as we rolled to a stop. I understood the plastic bag she held contained the Chinese food I'd selected when she'd read the menu to me in her sleepy voice. She sat on my steps, holding a bunch of Cold Fun, packets of duck sauce and hot sauce and soy sauce. She smiled a kind smile, even though I'd been mean. I was afraid, but she was brave. I was avoidant, she persistent. As we exited the car, she stood. In another generation, Colleen Crane might have been considered an ephemeral beauty, but in this generation, her skin was too pale, the translucence of the rice milk Jaimie had recently been asking me to buy. Her broad forehead gave her other features the suggestion of being too small. And yet, seeing her, I felt the quickening of my pulse. Colleen was *here*, inside my world with its lack of gardens and above-ground pools. As we approached the steps, she waved.

"She thinks she knows us," Jamie whispered.

I constructed a number of quick lies inside my head, each of them insufficient to explain Colleen Crane's presence on our stone steps. I whispered, "She does."

"You *know* her?"

"I do," I said. "That's Colleen."

WEBB, 1941

Ummer 1941, Webb perfected pound cake, sponge cake, angel cake. He learned every kind of filling: coconut, whipped cream, maple cream, marshmallow cream. He made caramel for burnt sugar cake, soured his own cream for sour cream cocoa cake. His mother instructed: "Webster, love, remember to use a low temperature. Otherwise, my sweet, a crust will form while the cake remains undercooked. Never grease the pan. You want the cake to cling dramatically to the sides—as if for dear life!—as it rises."

In the dead heat of July, his mother tutored him in the art of the Christmas fruitcake. Webb measured ingredients carefully: nutmeg and mace, molasses, citrus rind.

"What the hell?" his father asked when Webb's mother placed it on the table after dinner. "Should we set a place for Santy Claus?"

His mother filled his father's glass with bourbon. "Oh, Genie! I had the most inexplicable hankering for fruitcake in July!"

His father pushed aside the cake. "*I* decidedly do not."

Webb's singular joy that summer was baking with his mother. Afterward, in the kitchen's bright light, they squeezed lemonade, put up their feet, listened to the radio. He felt a rosy pride when his mother served whatever they'd made to his father. Compliments, his father said, made assholes of people, but he shoveled Webb's cakes into his mouth. A fickle man, he soon grew bored of cake. He asked Webb's mother, would it kill her to make a goddamn pudding? Webb then progressed to tricky custards, soft and plain baked and rennet and blancmange and crème brûlée. It pleased him to see his mother torch the ramekins with her typical dexterity, but his father, forgetting he had demanded pudding, soon asked, "What's with all this goddamn baby food?" Webb then moved on to pastry and yeasted breads.

"Finally, you made decent dinner rolls!" his father told his mother, and Webb, blushing, lifted his glass of milk to cover his face.

Eugene Willet Jackson had no idea his only boy had made these eclairs, this pain au chocolat. Had no idea his only boy had set the table for dinner, leveling the fork and knife with the bottom of the plate. His boy, who preferred to play waiter rather than football, folding a napkin into the crook of his arm as he served pretend tables with impeccable posture. *Let me recommend the coq au vin.* His boy, who played housewife, donning an apron, fluttering his hands before the open oven as if to catch the wafting scent of his imaginary roast. His boy, whose favorite apron was the floral one with the wondrous ruffle bottom. When Webb caught his reflection in the mirror wearing this apron—when he bore witness for the first time to his possible beauty—his heart stilled. Beauty, beautiful. The apron was a bib apron, the closest he'd gotten at this juncture to a dress. The rose pink of it enhanced his skin. Mesmerized, he stared.

"Webster, love." His mother took him by the shoulders. "Why do you want to play at being a woman?" She smoothed his dark hair. "One day, you'll be glad to be a man so you can leave this kitchen and this house and *accomplish* things. Whatever you want to do, you'll do. And because you're a man, people will respect and commend you, and I, as your mother, will be proud of you."

"I love this kitchen," he said. "I love this house."

She took his chin in her hands. "You are my dear, darling boy, and I understand. This is a special thing about you. But others will not be so gracious. Sometimes we want things that make our lives harder, and the truth is that we must often be very quiet about the things which make us happiest. We must pretend to be the people others expect us to be, so we might survive this world unscathed. Do you hear what it is I'm saying to you?"

Unsure he did, Webb nodded.

His mother said, "When men stand before God, his judgment of them is an expression of his omnipotent power. He evaluates what they've done with what he's given them. If they've frittered away too much of their brief time on earth, he tosses them into the fiery mouth of hell. Webster, one day you will be a man, and it will be important for you to *do*."

"Why doesn't He evaluate the women?"

"What?"

"You said He evaluates the men."

"He doesn't *need* to evaluate the women. The creator understands the predicament of women. He already knows we have too much time on our hands. He knows, regarding time, our hands are tied."

One Sunday in late summer, Webb sat at the kitchen table, drinking coffee and eating drop hermits as he paged through his mother's favorite cookbook. He studied the recipes and photographs, charmed by their cheerful captions: *While marmalade escorts scones on their short life, Sally Lunn is turned out of the pan to face a hungry world! The ring mold, whether of noodle, vegetable, or chicken mousse, is the delight of family and friends!*

"Webster." His father grabbed his collar. "Boys don't spent Sundays reading cookbooks with their mommies. They go outside. They play football."

Outside, the land of men, held little interest for Webb. Football, he hated. Hated running until his lungs threatened to burst; hated the exertion of catching, tackling. Sweat, the inherent outcome of football, gave him the shellacked feeling of a mollusk. Each time his hands touched the ball, he thought of the other snotty, germ-laden hands that had already touched it. He preferred the kitchen, where one was expected to wash.

The Lordly Lobster is still the aristocrat of the festive occasion.

"Webster," his father said, "you're going outside until your mother calls you for dinner."

Webb asked, "What about lunch?"

"What about it?"

"I'll get hungry."

"I don't care how hungry you are! You'll stay outside and play!"

Webb looked to his mother. She floured the counter for biscuit dough and said, "What your father says is true. A boy needs fresh air."

His father stood on the front steps as Webb walked down the street. When Webb was certain his father no longer watched, he retraced his steps to his own backyard, where he folded himself behind the branches of his mother's hydrangeas. He would sit here, behind these pink and blue and violet flowers touching his face like a duster, until dinner. He waited a long time with closed eyes, imagining dinner parties: if he were a woman throwing such a party, what would he serve? What would he wear? He would offer standing rib roast to a crowd of appreciative guests. He'd wear turquoise, the most beautiful color in the history of colors. Dessert would be platters of pastel petit fours, impeccably arranged.

When his mother finally called him in, Webb took fistfuls of dirt, rubbing them over his pants so it would appear he'd either been tackled or had tackled. He waited several minutes for added effect, coming dramatically through the back door with feigned exhaustion and labored breath.

"Love!" his mother landed a kiss on his cheek. "A little roughhouse with the boys did you well." Webb thought, *Sometimes we must pretend to be the people others expect us to be.* She handed his father a glass of bourbon. "Genie, you were right! If he plays every week, he'll be a football star just like you!"

"I doubt that."

"The world is filled with surprises!"

His father said, "There are no surprises." He turned as Webb settled at the table. "Webster. You enjoyed playing football?"

"Yes." He added, "Sir."

"What position did you play?"

"The one that runs."

His father studied him. "You say you played running back?"

"Yes, sir." Webb committed to the lie. "I scored a touchdown."

His father's mouth turned down. "A *touchdown.*"

"Yes, sir."

"Webster, no one likes a liar."

"Genie!" Webb's mother said. "He scored a touchdown!"

"Like hell he did!"

"Genie!"

Webb's father asked, "How was your afternoon, son?"

Webb mumbled at his fork.

"Webster, what have I said about enunciating your words?"

"Good."

"What was good?"

"I had a good time playing football."

"You did a nice job of roughing yourself up, making it look like you played football. Didn't you?"

"Yes, sir."

Webb braced himself for what came next. This was undoubtedly something he'd be lashed for. He hadn't gone to play with the neighborhood boys. He'd lied. He said a prayer to the God who didn't care how women spent their time, asking that the punishment be over quickly.

His father leaned across the table to Webb's mother. It looked like he would soothe her cheek, but instead he grabbed it. He tugged her cheek as if it had snagged on something and he wanted to loosen it. His mother's eyes teared.

"Tell your son. A boy shouldn't lie. A boy doesn't read cookbooks and bake cakes. A boy goes outside. He plays football. Will you tell him?"

His mother's nod was slight.

"I didn't hear you."

"Yes, Genie."

He released her cheek, which went from white to deep red. "Tell him, then! What in God's name are you waiting for?"

"Webster," his mother said in a choked voice. "Boys don't lie. They don't read cookbooks and bake cakes."

"*And?*"

"Boys go outside. They play football."

"I guess now we're in agreement," his father said.

His mother closed her eyes. "Yes," she said. "We are."

His father rattled his empty glass. "Now, where's dinner in this goddamn house?"

Here is a flash in our newsroom, announced the radio months later. *The Symphony number one in F minor by the Russian composer Shostakovich begins this afternoon's Philharmonic program. Japan has attacked Pearl Harbor, Hawaii, and Manila, the Philippines, by air.* His mother, scrubbing the sink, cried out, her cry reminding Webb of a doll he'd coveted in a shop window but could never have. Dolls, like kittens, were girls' things. The doll's undergarments were neat rows of ruffles like pale lettuces. If a person squeezed the stomach hard, the doll opened its eyes wide and cried, *Mama!* The doll's cry indicated to Webb the convoluted nature of relationships. You harmed someone, but comforted them; you failed them, but made amends. In relationships, a person possessed both the poison and the antidote. His father wrenched his mother's cheeks. He drew her close and kissed her.

Remain calm and avoid all unnecessary confusion because of hysteria. Coolness will accomplish more than anything else.

It would soon be difficult to sort the rumors: talk of Japanese ships thirty miles off the California coast. Talk of soldiers taking up posts on the Golden Gate Bridge, digging trenches at the Presidio on San Francisco's bluffs. In the crux of war, Webb would hear that Boy Scouts had been sent to guard the Bay Bridge. A boy in his class, as ruddy-faced as a middle-aged drunk, said he would guard the bridge in his Boy Scout's uniform. He would stand before the railing, holding his father's pistol, looking through the fog for signs of an imminent Japanese invasion, though Webb had once seen him cry like a baby over a dropped Valomilk cup.

Keep watch for spies and saboteurs.

As Webb listened to the radio with his parents, Eleanor's voice once again gave him the feeling of bobbing on a raft in the swollen ocean—a speck too small to disappoint those who loved him, so small his secrets didn't matter. He and his secrets, like flotsam on the great expansive sea. Surely, they hurt no one.

III

COLLEEN, 2001

Colleen watched the footage on the television, replayed countless times: one airplane flying into the Twin Towers, and then another. On the screen, pandemonium, news anchors trying to comprehend the unfathomable, while in the background sirens reverberated and people rushed in and out of the frame. Finally, she grabbed her purse and her keys from the kitchen island. She didn't brush her hair or her teeth; didn't put on nicer clothes. She didn't turn off the television. She got into her car and drove.

She didn't know *where* she was driving. Maybe through stop-and-start traffic to Berkeley. Maybe west, to the state's craggy edge. Maybe east, to its forgotten middle. She drove south, toward San Jose. Passing San Jose, reaching the cutoff for I-5, she understood where she'd always been going. Not to see her parents, vacationing in Palm Springs for the month: her father with his strong calves, her mother, taut, like a dried wishbone. Colleen pictured them lunching after a round of golf, eating unwieldy club sandwiches, clanking sun-dappled glasses of iced tea, unaware that airplanes had been flown into buildings, that everything was different now. When they heard the news, they'd greet it with the same surprised syllable they used for anything unanticipated. *Oh!*

Little traffic clogged the highway to Los Angeles. Colleen kept the radio off, striving for a meditative silence. She was driving to Debra because she couldn't say what she wanted to say without looking at her head-on. She hadn't phoned first, fearing Debra would say, *No, don't come.* Would say, *Sorry. There's nothing here for you. No comfort, no respite, no sanctuary.*

She'd seen Debra in person only once, after waiting hours on her steps in the heat, smelling the Chinese food she'd picked up. Gardeners eradicated weeds. Heavily made-up women, their lips unabashedly red in the bright sun, walked dogs. The inhabitants of passing cars eyed her suspiciously, acknowledging she was a stranger. Finally, a BMW turned into the driveway. Debra and Jamie emerged, sunburnt and with chemically frazzled hair, emitting the scent of chlorine. Hadn't Colleen joked once about BMW owners being assholes? She felt a rush of shame.

"This is Jamie, my son," Debra said, fumbling with the house key. "Jaim, this is Colleen."

As Jamie hesitantly shook Colleen's hand, something inside her snagged: the boy possessed the same aquiline features as Webb, the same broad shoulders. How very handsome Webb must have been; how beautiful his daughter was.

"Jaim," Debra said when they were inside. "You don't need to stay with us." She kissed the still-damp crown of his head, but Jamie shrugged, sat at the kitchen table while Debra poured cold drinks and Colleen unpacked the Chinese food. Debra didn't own a microwave; Colleen cooked everything inside a microwave. They ate the food luke-warm and congealed, laughing at how overboard Colleen had gone with ordering. They nudged one another to pass various containers, joking about the names of the dishes.

Of course, Debra laughed like Webb. She contained his DNA, was of his body and blood. It was rare, Webb's laughter, but it contained the same buoyancy Debra's did as she overfilled their glasses of wine. The surprise of this caused a sharp stitch in Colleen's side. The stitch wasn't pain; it was joy. They were sipping their second glasses when the husband arrived, eyeing the mess of containers with a frown. Everyone fell silent, then Debra spoke into the void. "This is my friend Colleen, from the club; Colleen, this is James."

James shook Colleen's hand as her mind reeled. From the club. Of course Debra couldn't tell him the truth; he knew nothing about Webster Eugene Jackson.

"Nice to meet you," Colleen said.

"Hmm." he nodded before slipping away to his office. She saw in his eyes he'd already forgotten her, that she was not important enough to relegate to memory.

The day after the airplanes were flown into buildings, a palpable heaviness still bowing her shoulders, Colleen summoned the courage to call Debra, to say she was in Los Angeles. If it were possible, she'd like to see her.

"Please," said Debra. "Come over." Jamie was at school, the husband at work. Her volunteer meeting at the YMCA had been cancelled. Together they spent the afternoon on Debra's couch, sipping mint tea with too much honey and watching the continued news coverage. Colleen tried to imagine it was *their* couch, *their* home, but she knew they'd never choose a home like this—dark, showy, abundant with brass and leather, the furniture as ponderous as fat kings. Their home would be small, with white walls and colorful, carefully chosen objects. It would have good light, a gas stove. A yard with flowers and bees. They would plant an herb garden, a vegetable garden, the residual intoxicating scent of tomatoes on their hands after they'd picked them for dinner. They'd cook together, laughing, mincing garlic to whatever music Jamie wanted to hear. Slayer, Jane's Addiction. In this alternate reality, they'd eat without the television's distracting noise. At night, Colleen would reach across the span of the bed, touch a hand to Debra's upturned hip. The bed would not be a California king like she'd once shared with her husband. It would be a queen, small enough that she might feel Debra's presence beside her.

"You're very beautiful," Colleen said spontaneously.

"I don't *feel* beautiful."

"Well, you are."

"My mother always suggested otherwise. I should do this, I should do that. In high school, she'd ground me for not plucking my eyebrows."

"That can't be true," said Colleen. "Eyebrows are so inconsequential."

"Nothing physical is inconsequential to a former beauty queen. When I was twelve, she put me on a diet. I ate cottage cheese and burger patties. We'd go to the club, but she wouldn't let me swim. Wouldn't let me be seen in a bathing suit. My weight would reflect poorly on her. Kids made fun of me because I was the girl wearing long sleeves and pants at a pool party."

"That's cruel," said Colleen.

"The kids or my mother?"

"Both."

"It's who she is. She can't help it. And anyway, it's too late for change."

Colleen had never kissed a woman. Perhaps the thought had risen inside her—touching a woman's slight waist, pulling her lips towards Colleen's own—but she'd been stopped by the idea of her parents' reaction. Her staunch Republican parents, who believed women loved men and men loved women. Who believed in the Bible, the laws of God and man. Maybe she'd wanted to kiss a woman, but she'd been too frightened by the core of need inside her, pulsing like a reactor. Her fear had sent the desire skittering away. If she acted on her impulse, how would she deal with the ensuing wreckage? It was far easier to push things deep, to steer clear of the sharp precipices of emotion. Settle for what felt wrong but was easy.

"I'm afraid," she told Debra. "Terrified."

"Oh, God," said Debra. "Me too. *Fucking* terrified."

In the aftermath, they laughed at their hesitancy, how like teenagers they'd been, and Colleen, watching Debra's wide-mouthed laughter, felt emboldened by the flush of her own happiness, but not so emboldened as to trace Debra's perfect clavicle and tell her, *You. You laugh like your father.*

BEVERLY, 2001

That terrible morning, Beverly turned the key to her daughter's front door and found herself inside the house's enveloping coolness, alone, as she'd known she would be. On Tuesdays Debra met with the YMCA volunteers—or maybe that was Wednesdays. If it wasn't the YMCA, it was Meals on Wheels, and if it wasn't Meals on Wheels, it was the lonely cancer patients. In Debra's house, Beverly could be proximate to her daughter without the strain of her actual presence. She could leave her husband transfixed by the news on the television. She could be alone, a blessed commodity.

Alone, she made herself strong black tea. On the kitchen television, the channels showed the same news footage. She searched for something superficial, shows her bridge friends watched, shows Beverly had never seen and on which people aired their grievances. *Don't sweat the small stuff*, Erma Bombeck had once declared, but these people sweated everything. On these programs, her friends told her, neighbors confronted neighbors who held karaoke parties late into the night. Husbands admitted to their wives their secret fears: mewling kittens, the guzzling vacuum. On these shows, wives didn't know who had fathered their babies! Or they did, but the babies weren't their husbands'. These women came on the show to reveal secret paternity test results before their husbands and the real fathers of their infants. There were fisticuffs, chairs first toppled then broken, the rushing in of security. When everyone had been wrangled back to their seats, hearts cloven, the truth would emerge: the wife and the husband's best friend hadn't *meant* to conceive a baby that night in the hall closet, but copious jello shots had been consumed, and they had.

Relationships between mothers and daughters provided endless fodder. Daughters accused, mothers cried. Mothers accused, daughters cried. This mother slept with her daughter's boyfriend. That daughter slept with her mother's boyfriend. This mother bought her daughter drugs. That daughter tossed her mother's drugs down the toilet. Beverly gathered toilet bowls were ubiquitous on these programs.

"I can't believe you girls waste time on such nonsense," Beverly said one afternoon after bridge.

"We like to see how the other half lives," said Trudy Sutton.

Carol Reese said, "There's not a secret among us."

"There's always a secret," Beverly said, realizing how little these women knew her. She understood how close they weren't.

"Beverly! Beverly Laurenzi!" a woman had cried out in the supermarket that long-ago summer when Beverly had relocated to Los Angeles. The woman's excitement reminded her of a dog mouthing a spit-soaked tennis ball. The universe, with its unsolvable mysteries and cruel tricks. Its tests. The universe was always demanding, at every inopportune moment, *What kind of person* are *you?*

"Excuse me, do I know you?" It pained Beverly that someone else should recognize her before she recognized herself. Since leaving Webster, she felt as if she'd jumped from a ledge, all the anxiety of held breath, the anticipation of hitting ground. Beverly awaited the blunt trauma of realization—yes, she was *here*—but felt only the ambiguity of suspension: water in oil, egg yolk in egg white, fetus inside the amniotic sac, as she'd once thought of Debra.

"Catherine Benton! Cat Benton! Miss Los Angeles 1956! My God, you haven't changed!"

Miss Los Angeles 1956 now stood clutching cans of Campbell's Chicken Noodle Soup against her chest, which was certainly less buoyant than when Beverly helped grapple it inside a too-small turquoise swimsuit. Beverly remembered that Miss Los Angeles had botched interview, answering the questions with the same frenzy with which she now spoke to Beverly.

"You set my hair for evening wear at Miss California! You persuaded me to pick the pale green rather than the violet! You were right! How's Webster?"

"Who?"

Until Miss Los Angeles 1956 mentioned Webster, there had still been a chance Beverly would acknowledge her. That door slammed closed. Webster. Beverly had kissed him that final morning with her face covered in nutritive cream. She'd felt the swirl of confusion: what was she doing? Oh, God. She could change her mind, stay. No. She steeled herself. Phoned Clive. "He's gone."

"You wore a red swimsuit! You tapped to—."

"You're mistaken," Beverly said and thought, "*Puttin' on the Ritz*."

Cat Benton's confidence dissipated. "You look just like her."

"I've never competed in beauty pageants, though I'll take your mistake as a compliment."

The face of Miss Los Angeles 1956 turned redder than the swimsuit Beverly had worn. She fled with her soup cans. Moments later came the sound of clattering. Beverly imagined her crawling on the linoleum, wrangling the cans back into her possession. She felt a hot, fluttering shame: she had not fooled Cat Benton, but neither could she explain. She was no longer Beverly Laurenzi. She was not Beverly Jackson. She would soon be Beverly Murdoch. Here she was, caught in the uncomfortable caught-betweens. Ensnared, like a bit of prey.

Beverly had, in fact, conducted a highly charged friendship with Cat Benton during pageant week. At the Pasatiempo Inn, they had set each other's hair in rollers, practiced their beauty walks, answered mock interview questions. Cat Benton had watched Beverly exchange vows with Webster that June day in 1957. *'Til death do us part.* She'd given them a beautiful glass bowl from Tiffany's that represented the life Beverly had imagined for herself, the life she'd led Cat Benton to believe she'd have. *Dearest Beverly,* Cat Benton had written in countless fervent letters the first year of Beverly's marriage. *I can only imagine your happiness!* Beverly replied to none of these letters. "She's dead to me," her mother declared after severing relationships with women who'd disappointed her. Her mother's hand sliced the air as she said this, cutting the offender's imaginary throat. In this case, it was not Cat Benton who was dead to Beverly, but Beverly who was dead to Beverly. In her place was a woman disappointed and disappointing, like a chocolate easter bunny that appeared solid but wasn't.

Her dismissal of Cat Benton might have been fodder for the talk shows.

Now Beverly sat in Debra's kitchen, sipping her tea and watching other women's cheap tragedies unfold on the television. Finally, she stood to go. She would leave signs of her visit. Like Goldilocks. Or was it Hansel and Gretel? Having never been a woman who read her daughter bedtime stories (*this* was surely a topic for the talk shows), Beverly didn't remember. She left the teacup on the kitchen table, the kettle in the sink. On the counter she found an open bottle of wine. It was ten o'clock in the morning on a difficult day. Beverly poured herself a glass. She drank it, poured another. Tipsy, she wandered through the house. Imbued with courage, she entered Debra's bedroom, her sitting room. She stood before Edna's turquoise jewelry box; imagined sitting with Debra on a stage before a studio audience, asking her daughter: *Who are you? Why do you insist on remaining that person?* She imagined Debra staring back at her with Webster's square jawline. This image compelled her to hoist Edna's jewelry box from its spot, carry it downstairs and out to the car. She obscured the box inside the glove compartment beneath an assortment of maps.

She intended to drive home, but without thinking she merged onto the highway headed north. She would get off at the next exit, she told herself. She would turn around. Passing the next exit, and the next, she realized she was driving to Santa Barbara. To her childhood home, a place she hadn't been since her father died and her mother, shaken with dementia and delirium, had gone to live in a rest home.

In that house, she'd been a girl with a promising future. In her bedroom, curlers pinned into her hair, she had regarded herself, doe-eyed, in the vanity mirror; had applied powder, practiced the purse of her kitteny lips. Beneath the pink canopy of her bed, she pined for boys, conjured possibility.

She should stop at a payphone, call Clive. Surely, he was worried. She hadn't said she was going anywhere; had simply disappeared, like the Twin Towers this morning, leaving their residues of ash and smoke. She imagined Clive calling Debra. *Have you seen your mother?* Debra, too, would worry. Motivated by their worry—she yearned to be missed, she yearned to be yearned for—Beverly drove without stopping. On the radio, male voices jockeyed to be heard. When men talked in this vying clamor, Beverly retreated to a distant place where she might sit, silent and pretty, until she herself forgot who she was.

She intended to drive past the house. Instead, she pulled into the long driveway, where she idled, studying its worn facade. The house was a shell, stripped of its former glory, like an aging actress or a restaurant whose lights were dimmed to hide the scuffs and skittering bugs.

Inexplicably, Beverly turned off the ignition and got out of the car. She would just stand at the edge of the grass. She would look quickly and leave; but then she was walking up the front lawn, trekking the distant edges of the grass to the back lawn.

Upon her mother's decline, when she couldn't manage by herself and had been ushered into a senior living home, Clive had sold the house to a childless couple at Beverly's request. She hadn't wanted children drawing on the walls, peeing on the carpets. ("My dear," Clive had said with exasperation, "you're thinking of dogs. Children don't pee on carpets.") That couple obviously no longer lived here. Strewn about the yard were assorted toys: an upended plastic wagon, a construction site's worth of Tonka trunks. The backyard, once meticulously maintained—the gardeners had come weekly, with their clippers and rakes and lilting Spanish—now suffered dandelions, bald patches. On this very lawn, which had seemed at the time more sweeping, less contained, wedding guests had spilled, cocktails in hand, congratulating her. How beautiful she looked! What a wonderful wife she'd make! What happiness lay in store for her!

"Can I help you?" A young man approached, slobbery baby at his hip.

Beverly didn't understand young people these days. First, the young man's question, posed with little deference. Second, what was he wearing? A knitted hat suggested he was cold, while shorts suggested he was hot. His shoes were untied, either a fashion statement or a sign he'd rushed outside to accost her, an older woman wearing black and white, standing on his grass like a Holstein at pasture.

Moo, Beverly thought. She said, "This was my childhood home."

"Okay." He bounced the baby. His was an ugly baby.

"My wedding reception was on this lawn. Right here." She pointed. "Beneath a beautiful white tent." The young man said nothing. Was it possible, Beverly wondered, to elicit more than one syllable from this person? "How long have you lived here?"

He shrugged.

Now it was a syllable game, and she'd lost one. "Do you like it?"

"Sure."

Here, she gained one. "It's a wonderful neighborhood."

"It's fine."

"The schools are very good. I was my class's valedictorian."

"Cool."

As typically happened when Beverly felt hurt, she narrowed this hurt into a meanness she might hurl like a javelin. She said, "It's a shame you've let everything go."

He stared at her.

"Once, it was beautiful place, but I see under your care, it's become a tenement."

"A *tenement*."

Four syllables. "Not to mention what your children have done to the lawn. I suppose you're too busy making ugly babies to keep things up."

The young man's passive face hardened. "You're trespassing. Leave or I'll call the cops."

"You'd call the cops on an elderly woman?" Her use of the word *elderly* shocked her. "Today?"

"It's been a long, hard morning for everyone," he said. "I'll give you five minutes to make your peace, or whatever it is you're here for."

He turned toward the house, shoelaces dragging through the grass. From the kitchen window, a blonde watched them. She clutched two other wide-eyed infants. How many babies did these people have! (*Three*, Clive would have told her, scarcely looking up from the newspaper.) The woman's eyes met Beverly's. The curtains fell, and she was gone.

At home, Clive slept on the couch, neither waiting for her, nor worrying over her absence. His right hand rested inside the waistband of his pants. Hint of a snore. She'd disappeared down the rabbit hole for hours on a day when terrible things had happened. She'd provided neither breakfast nor lunch, and this man, her husband, didn't care.

Sitting beside him, she touched his hip. On the television screen, the news still unfolded. Beverly longed for a normal day, Clive's normal programming. Wrestling men in brightly colored leotards lunging and grappling, hurling insults. Clive loved wrestling, whether legitimate or illegitimate.

"It's just theatrics," she told him. "It isn't real." Still, he sought it out. Grown men in decorative plumage hoisting other grown men in decorative plumage. Grown men attempting to unscrew the heads of other grown men like lightbulbs.

She jabbed at Clive's hip, trying to wake him. She wanted to talk about the airplanes, the smoke and panic, the falling paper that was not confetti. Wanted to tell him about that young man's disrespect, wanted to tell him how badly she'd behaved. There were countless things she wanted to say to him, but talking to Clive—*admission*—was something she had no idea how to do.

In the shifting light of the television, Beverly reached over and pinched Clive's nose closed. This was something she often did at night, when he snored beside her and she wanted him to stop. She held his nostrils closed for a beat longer than normal; for a beat longer than that. He would wake, she thought. They would talk. He only shuddered in his dream state and kept sleeping.

BEVERLY, 1955

LIGHTER POPS, BEAUTY QUEEN CRASHES! the *Santa Barbara News Press* declared. It was true: the car's lighter had popped out of its socket, and Beverly, a beauty queen, had crashed her car into—through—a billboard advertising Arden's Diced Cream. Her father would claim the accident had been caused by the malfunctioning of the lighter, which was not true, but he was a lawyer who spun persuasive stories, twisting them into whatever amalgamation of truth and bullshit suited him. In reality, Beverly had pushed the lighter into the socket herself, cigarette lolling from her mouth, waiting to be lit, as she steered with the opposite hand. She'd lost control of the car, as happens when one drives recklessly. The lighter popped out of the socket, ready, just as she drove off the road and through the billboard, the impact sending the lighter careening into her thigh. There, it left a perfect burned circle, a giant O of shock.

That day, she'd left the house after an argument with her parents. In the kitchen's morning light, over dry toast, she'd told them she wanted to quit pageants to focus on school. She wanted to go to college. She wanted her degree.

"Your *degree*," her mother said, as if Beverly had announced she wanted to live inside a thatched hut in the jungle. "I knew nothing good would come of chess club. Now you want to use your brain?"

"Yes," Beverly said.

She could study her brains out, her mother said. Her father would not be wasting his hard-earned money on college. "You're a *beauty*." Her mother nibbled toast. "You don't *need* college to find a husband like the ugly girls do. What use will college be when you have a family? College won't help you pack the children's lunches, or clean their crumby mouths, or soothe their ailments. It won't help you put dinner on the table, or keep dinner warm nights your husband comes home late after a long day at work. If you'd like to attend cooking school, your father and I would support that. Debby Wainwright's daughter just completed the Sears program. Janet now makes a delicious tuna noodle casserole."

"I do *not*," said Beverly, "care to learn the intricacies of tuna noodle casserole."

"Pray tell," her father said, "what is it you care to learn?"

Beverly ignored her father's patronizing tone. Just as a woman coaxed dough into a coveted latticed pie crust—as one doubtless learned in the Sears Cooking Program—she believed she might coax her father into anything. Smiling the coy smile she practiced before the mirror, she said, "Biology."

"*Biology.*" Her father's lips twitched.

She continued, "It interests me to know how things live. I appreciate knowing *why* things do what they do." (She thought Miss Margaret would be so proud of her.)

A laugh escaped her father before he composed himself, but tears glimmered in the corners of his eyes. This was the first time she felt betrayed by a man she loved.

"I'm intelligent," she said, her own eyes smarting.

"If you were intelligent, you'd have said the humanities," he replied. "The sciences are out of the question." Then he asked, "Are you finished?"

Beverly laughed a hollow laugh that would soon become a staple in the repertoire of her laughter. "Yes. I was being silly."

"There's my good girl." Her father rustled the newspaper. Her mother nodded, glad to have survived this debacle.

Beverly stood from the table. She walked through the hallway and out the front door to her convertible, parked in the cul de sac of the driveway. Turning the key in the ignition, she drove down the long driveway to the street. Safely away from her house, merging onto the highway, she located the hidden pack of cigarettes inside the glove box. She pulled a cigarette from the pack, pushed the lighter into the socket, then wiped her wet cheeks as she crossed the yellow lines. A moment later, she swerved off the road, through the billboard, as the lighter ejected, landing against her thigh just below the hem of her short white shorts. The ferocity of her cry surprised her.

The car rolled to a stop on the other side of the billboard, in a circle of tall grass, its engine hissing like an angry beast. Though she'd been crying minutes earlier, Beverly found herself devoid of tears, stepping past the threshold into the bleakness beyond feeling. She'd bitten herself in the crash. Touching her finger to her bottom lip, she drew it away dotted with blood. As she waited for help, she watched the tall grasses as they shook, communicated something incomprehensible.

HANNAH, 2001

For weeks, they occupied the same house without speaking.

Lying in bed nights after she'd returned from work, Hannah listened to the man moving about his kitchen as she'd listened to Hot Tan's late-night ramblings. Clatter of measuring spoons against the countertop, clank of a whisk. The opening of the refrigerator; its closing. The sound of an egg cracking. One morning, she discovered a poundcake—perfectly golden, barely eaten—nestled inside the garbage bin. Days later, she discovered a pineapple upside-down cake, its cracked top resembling a stained-glass window. Another day, an angel food cake. This was what her life had become: she lived with a man who baked cakes, unabashedly wasted them. Sam was gone. Fran was gone. The person she herself had been was gone. Reaching into the garbage bin, she pulled off a clean hunk of angel food cake, ate it. She was this person now, a person who ate cake from the garbage.

And then, waking one morning with the expectation of cake, Hannah came downstairs to the news that a plane had flown into the World Trade Center. A plane, and then a second plane. Both towers had fallen.

She went straight to the man's bedroom, knocked on his door.

He answered dressed in a lilac peignoir, something Hannah's mother would have dismissed as too womanly, too sexy. *Slutty*, her mother would have said. The peignoir's lace neckline drew a mesmerizing *V* across a pair of foam breasts. Its lilac color soothed her, like pills swallowed down, pharmaceutical and lulling.

In the morning's lackluster light, the man appeared substantial, hewn. She'd lived with him for eight weeks—enough weeks to form two months, one sixth of an entire year—but hadn't seen him since the interview at the

Extended Stay America. At the tiny table, they'd drunk tea from plastic, like children playing. Wearing stiff denim and stiffer flannel, he'd reminded her of a large dressed doll. They'd avoided one another's eyes, had let the woman named Colleen do the talking. Hannah had known he didn't want to live with her. He'd known she didn't want to live with him. She'd felt there was a mutual silent understanding that they would respect one another's aversion; they would let each other be.

"Yes?" he said uneasily, focusing on a point behind her head.

"Something terrible has happened."

In the living room, the television rattled out its confusion. *In medias res.* This was a phrase Hannah now understood. Plunged suddenly into the madness, she felt herself cracking jaggedly, like a coconut. She made some sort of sound, and then the man, sitting beside her on the couch, took her hand, pressed it against his foam bosom. It should have been a shock, but his hand was comfortingly cool, like a rock shucked from dirt. Hannah registered the beat beat beat of his heart. She imagined what existed beneath that faux bosom, the things swirling inside the man's chest: histories and loves, losses. There were these things; there was nothing at all. His hand palmed hers, smoothed it. She'd always thought how a person dealt with another's unadulterated emotion was terribly revealing. Past experiences leapt to mind: her mother, shoving boxes of tissues at her, shortening Hannah's name into a single staccato syllable: "Han, don't cry." Sam's apathy. Her hostility. Fran's coddling; her comfort stifling, like air inside a tent on a humid day.

Hannah let her head drop to the man's shoulder.

"My girl," he said. "I'm ashamed I don't recall. What's your name?"

"What's yours?"

In the darkness of the living room, television flickering, they laughed, though nothing was funny.

Webster Jackson—Webb, he said, two b's—set card tables before the sofa and served pancakes made from scratch. He brewed strong coffee, set out pristine sugar cubes and tiny bottles of cream. In this living room, he said, he'd heard the news of Pearl Harbor on the radio. Saw his mother's restrained panic, his father's swollen anger: "We'll bomb their Jap faces in." Now, this. The voices on the tv were drowned out by the ringing telephone.

My mother, Hannah thought, but no. On the line was the goateed manager; Hannah need not come to work today.

"You walk there, don't you?" Webb asked. "All the way to Berkeley."

"Yes."

"It's a long way."

"I have nothing better to do."

Webb studied her. "She was a slight woman, but you're about her size."

"Who?"

"I have something for you."

Hannah followed him outside to a shed. She'd not yet been in the backyard; it was bigger than she'd imagined. Overgrown, with clamoring vines, their flowers straining for end-of-summer light. Rose bushes in their many-hued beauty. Hydrangeas, her mother's favorite. Vegetable beds racked with weeds. An excess of ceramic fairies. Hannah had never considered fairies. She'd never realized that people placed such things, decoratively, in their yards; that people wanted to see the diminutive faces, the wide eyes and shapely limbs.

Having manhandled the lock, Webb was stepping into the shed's pressing scent and malformed light. "Can you ride a bike?"

"It's been years."

"They say you never forget."

"They," said Hannah.

"You walk home at night. This will be safer . . . faster."

"I doubt that," said Hannah. "In high school, I failed gym."

The bike, hidden beneath a tarp that Webb carefully removed, was a vintage Schwinn.

"It looks new," said Hannah. "Barely ridden."

"Oh, it's been ridden. She loved this bicycle, took excellent care of it. *I* have taken excellent care of it, for her. It calms me to clean the spokes and grease the chain, to fill the tires with air. It focuses my mind to take things apart and clean them, reassemble them. Keep them working."

"It's pretty," said Hannah.

"Orange was her favorite color, though she told me once that Marie Antoinette loathed it, forbade the color in her presence."

Who was this *she*?

"There's two." Hannah pointed. "Do you ride?"

"Not in years."

"They say you never forget."

Hannah watched with the fairies, intimidated, as he pumped air into the tires. Pushing the bicycle onto the street's cracked asphalt, Hannah found it heavier than she'd imagined it would be, stolid. She straddled it as she'd been taught to do. Inhaled, pushed herself off. Her legs quivered on the first pedal rotations. They drew their slow circles, muscles reverberating, straining from the effort. Concentrating on their movement, she imagined that, like a child's music box, they produced a sonorous noise. She gained speed, felt the push of wind at her face, felt her heart clattering inside the hollow of her body.

Hannah rode the length of the street while Webb Jackson, the man she'd avoided speaking to until this terrible day, stood, smiling faintly at her in his lilac peignoir. She would be sore tomorrow. The good kind of sore, people said, but was there, actually, a good kind of sore? Soreness was just soreness. The body's nagging reminder of something not being right.

In the following days, Hannah rode the orange bicycle to work, taking Shattuck Avenue through downtown Berkeley, turning left onto University Avenue toward the water. She rode to the grocery store, stuffing her Grape Nuts and skim milk into her backpack. Then she ranged farther, with no clear purpose. She'd not known she liked riding a bicycle. It had never occurred to her to ride one for the simple sake—the enjoyment—of riding it. Now, making up for lost time, she expanded her imperfect sense of East Bay geography, pedaling north through stop-and-start traffic to Albany and El Cerrito, foreign places with wide spaces between houses, the rattle of the Bart on the tracks above. She rode through empty streets south toward downtown Oakland, to Jack London Square, where she stared across the glassy water at a silhouetted San Francisco. Riding east over the hills would, her coworker told her, drop her into a town called Orinda, where the weather was warmer, the sun brighter.

On a bike, she could concentrate on the present. She could not think about Sam, about Fran. In her everyday life, time was not linear but a spectacular mass, memories begetting memories. Riding a bicycle required being present. It was concrete, actual. Pedaling, she drew a straight line across time and space; nothing existed beyond this line, this physical exertion. Sweat accumulated behind her knees. Dripped from her forehead onto her tongue—salty, like the ocean she hadn't visited since that day with Sam— and still she pedaled, grounded in this exact moment.

She decided to ride into the hills like the cyclists who passed her on the road in their bright and speckled spandex, like parrots on wheels. They refused to make eye contact with her, a girl riding a Schwinn, wearing jeans.

"You'll never get that heavy-ass bike into the hills," her coworker said.

She'd never considered the weight of her bicycle, only that it was hers now, having once belonged to a woman Webb had loved. With the falling of the towers, the silence between them—their avoidance of one another—had dissipated. Hannah, returning home from work, sat with Webb at the kitchen table talking late into the night, watching as he baked things. Listening. Webb had ridden a bicycle in tandem with this woman. She'd sewn him beautiful clothes. Some of her own clothes still hung in Hannah's closet. She'd had, apparently, ten wardrobes' worth. On the closet's floor was a gilded leather trunk. Opening it, Hannah discovered dozens of scarves folded into neat squares. She removed these scarves, laying them across the bed, where she traced their patterns with her finger, admired them. She pressed them against her cheek, tied them around her neck.

"The woman whose clothes hang in my closet," said Hannah as she sat in the kitchen with Webb. "The woman whose bike I ride. What's her name?"

Webb stared at a corner of the kitchen ceiling. "It was Hila P. Firestone."

"What does the *P* stand for?"

"Anything you want." He said, "You like riding a bike."

"I do."

"Would your friend like it?"

Her friend. The dirty handsome cook. She'd learned his name was Sean. Sean, who'd attempted to drive to California but whose car had broken down before it even left the state of Missouri. He slept on friends' couches. He didn't have a bank account or a telephone. He had moved here for a girl he believed he would marry, and when that had broken down as irrevocably, as irretrievably as his car, he'd stayed.

"Why did you come here?" Sean asked as they pedaled together on their bicycles, leaving work. "Did you dream of California?"

"Definitely not."

"But you came."

"I'd been planning to move to Maine, before."

"Before?"

"Before someone changed my mind."

"Who?"

She pedaled faster, as if she hadn't heard him.

HANNAH, 2000

S am was living in a house on Martin Luther King Jr. Way in Berkeley, on whose gate someone had printed TOFU! in screaming neon. Weary palm trees rattled in the front yard, annoyed to have been carted here from their distant homelands. A gauzy backdrop of hills rose in the distance, pretty, but failing to meet Hannah's expectations regarding the rumored beauty of this place. People, promised oranges and prosperity, had left their homes and traveled here. *California!*

Sam shared this house and its irrepressible scent of decay with five vegetarians. The refrigerator was stocked with a startling number of soy products, including soy fashioned into frozen salmon filets with faux scales and faux beady eyes. These faux eyes stared up at a person, demanding to know why she hadn't made a better selection at the grocery store, *actual* salmon, with its omega-3 oils, its B vitamins, its magnesium and phosphorus. On the kitchen counter were loaves of dense seeded bread. Hannah unearthed crumbs of this bread from between the leaves of the dining table, from inside her bra. She plucked them, bloated, from her water glass. Along with the crumbs were more ants than Hannah had seen in her lifetime. They disappeared into cracks in the walls, emerged from crevices in the kitchen cupboards. Inside the freezer, piles of their dead bodies collected by the soy ice cream. Ants formed a neat line down the kitchen drain. They marauded the cat food. They hoisted onto their backs crumbs of that goddamn bread they'd foraged from the countertops.

Fran had visited this house only once. She spent the entire trip cleaning, Sam said. She refused to see Alcatraz, the Golden Gate. She didn't want to eat chowder from a bread bowl or gawk at the seals on Fisherman's Wharf. Even the most tedious people wanted to do these things, but Fran wanted only to scrub the kitchen, the bathroom. She found a ladder. Washed the walls, dusted the light fixtures. She asked how Sam could live in this filth, with these dirty, jaundiced people? Sam mimicked Fran's voice: "Samuelle, the house smells of flatulence. There's too much fiber in those vegetarian diets. Do these people even shower?"

Hannah was in California because Fran had asked her to come; had said please, live there. Watch our girl.

"I can't just *live* in California."

"Please, Hannah."

"I don't have the money."

"I'll give you whatever you need. I'll give you more."

"She says she's good. We should trust her."

"Trust," Fran snorted, as if Hannah had said the stupidest thing imaginable. "There's no such thing."

She arrived on a rainy Tuesday in March. Regarding rain, Hannah learned, Californians were moody and impractical; it rained, and the world stopped. Rain exacerbated the stink in Sam's house; the windows remained closed. Rain still fell on Sunday, when they walked to the Thai Temple for lunch. They walked through the downpour and, beneath an awning billowing in the wind, shared papaya salad and tofu spring rolls, mango with sticky rice. Hannah picked at sticky rice, unable to shake the sense of there being something wrong. Everything appeared fine: Sam sat across from her, intermittently guzzling Thai tea and chewing the inside of her cheek. Their forks clacked accidentally as they both reached for papaya. Something inside Hannah loosened. Then Sam said, "I found you a place to live."

"A what?"

"A place. To live."

"I thought we'd live together."

"We both know that's a terrible idea," said Sam, though Hannah did not.

"Where will I be living?" Hannah asked with sarcasm. "*With whom* will I be living?"

"I don't know them," said Sam. "A friend of a friend of a friend of a friend. The house is in Oakland."

"Oakland. That's an entirely different city."

Sam shrugged.

"I want to live in Berkeley."

"Well, you'll be living in Oakland."

"I don't want to live with strangers."

"After a day or two, they won't be strangers anymore."

They walked home from the Thai Temple, Hannah keeping pace with Sam under a veil of anxiety. She wasn't sure what had just happened, why Sam was making decisions for her. Why she was letting Sam make these decisions. She was still considering this when a boy stopped them to ask the way to the Thai Temple. Sam, who would have once scoffed at the stifling scent of patchouli entrenched in this boy's clothes, pointed. Yes, that way. Yes, you could get papaya salad without fish sauce. You could make it as spicy as you wanted. When had he arrived here? Where had he arrived from? Hannah stood, impatient, at the periphery of this discussion. Then something indiscernible happened, and they were walking with this perfect stranger through the rain to someplace called the Essex Hot Tub.

This hot tub was located in the private garden of a man's house. Sam did not actually know this man. No one did. She punched a number into the security system, and they and this boy pushed through the gate into the man's yard. These things didn't happen in Pittsburgh: you didn't meet a strange person on the street and bring him to an even stranger person's hot tub. Women were allowed to use this man's hot tub, as long as they knew the gate code and followed the guidelines on a mimeographed paper. Only women received the code; men were allowed with women who'd vetted them. Before entering the tub, you had to shower, lathering yourself thoroughly with the lumpy brown soap provided. You had to be naked. You couldn't take photographs, couldn't speak.

Sam and the boy stripped down to nothing. Hannah possessed zero inclination to see this boy's lean body, his prominent ribs, his penis. But here these things were, like scenes from a B-grade porno. The boy constantly lengthened and smoothed his goatee into a point between his thumb and forefinger, a nervous tic. Sam stepped with this boy into the scrubbing-off shower. When they emerged, the fleeting image of Sam sliding into the tub jolted Hannah. Sam was thinner than she'd ever been. She was herself, diminished by a third. How had Hannah not noticed this until now?

Inside the shower, Hannah scrubbed and scrubbed. She would have remained forever beneath the frigid water, but people—*strangers*—waited to use it. Moments before, she'd feared living with strangers; now, strangers averted their eyes when she stepped out of the shower and into the tub. Across from her, Sam sat, shrouded in steam. With her dark hair and outstretched arms, she resembled a saint printed on the wrapping paper they'd sold, along with stale hoagies and chocolate that tasted like cardboard, to raise money for their trip to Little Flower Camp. Her breasts, white with dark areolae, appeared above the water line. Inside the rising steam, the boy playfully pinched Sam's right nipple with the motion of a gardener deadheading a flower. He did this twice more. Hannah yearned to be in Pittsburgh, where people merely nodded in passing on the street, where they kept their clothes on and didn't touch each other's nipples. Where they treated homemade soap with derision. They were a heartier people who didn't cry over spilt milk or rain.

The boy walked them home with a smile that refused to be eradicated. Midway there, he and Sam ducked behind a jasmine bush in someone's front lawn, Sam's dark scalp moving up and down in the empty space between leaves. The boy emitted a shrill yelp, like a tiny dog that had been kicked. Moments later, they emerged from the jasmine, the knees of Sam's jeans dampened with muddy circles.

"What *was* that?" Hannah asked when they had returned to the ant-infested house, its scent clamping them like a vise.

"What was what?

"He was *gross*. You didn't even know him."

"I'm *happy*," Sam said. "That made me *happy*."

"That wasn't happiness."

"You know nothing about my happiness."

That night, they ate dinner with the housemates. A lumpen loaf made with texturized vegetable protein. A salad, but no one had washed the grit from the lettuce. The loaf was specked with curious chewy flakes that Hannah picked out, banished to a pile at the edge of her plate while everyone else ate happily. She drank terrible red wine from a mug with a ring of coffee residue while Sam took small, neat sips of soda splashed with cranberry. Hannah felt proud of her for maintaining sobriety under these obviously trying circumstances.

"Wine glasses," a housemate with strong body odor said, "are for bourgeois bitches!"

"Hear, hear," the other housemates said. Mugs cracked together in a toast, and an endless discussion ensued regarding something called Burning Man, and the benefits of *Cannabis sativa* versus *Cannabis indica*.

In Berkeley the next day, Sam pointed out the apartment on Benvenue from which Patty Hearst had been kidnapped.

"Cinque and the SLA burst into that apartment with guns," said Sam as they paused before it. "They beat Steven Weed to a bloody pulp. They shoved dear Patty inside the trunk of a car. One minute you're an heiress eating chicken noodle soup and tuna fish sandwiches, watching *Mission: Impossible*. The next, you're an urban guerrilla eating mung beans and robbing banks."

The return of the mung beans seemed ominous.

That afternoon, they attended a meeting in the spare room of a dusty church. There, a man in a suit told a story about a wreath stolen from his front door. A bird had built a nest inside this wreath, and when he'd left the house earlier, not only was the wreath gone, but several dead baby birds the size of the man's thumb lay on the concrete. One bird remained, barely alive, its tiny bird heart pushed from its chest. He'd had no choice but to take the faux rock by the front door—*Welcome!*—and crush the bird beneath it. He'd placed the bodies in a small white box. There, in the church, he produced this box from beneath his seat, held it with two hands.

At meeting's end, everyone formed an imperfect circle, clasped the sweaty hand of the person beside them as they vowed to move on with their days intentionally, one at a time. The man in the suit held the hands of no one. He extended the box into the circle.

As people gathered their things to leave, Sam pushed her way to the man in the suit. For a moment, Hannah believed she would be kind to him, a belief that dissipated as Sam tapped his shoulder.

"Did you seriously bring dead baby birds to a fucking meeting in which people are trying to feel better? What the *fuck*? What the actual *fuck*?"

"I'm sorry." Hannah tugged Sam away from him. "I'm so sorry," she said, and then they were outside, Sam wresting herself from Hannah's grasp.

"Don't ever apologize for me."

"You were mean."

"That meeting was a piece of shit. A waste of my fucking time. I need help, solutions, not an asshole who loses it over some dead birds."

"That man was having a hard time."

"*I'm* having a hard time."

"I thought you were happy."

Sam speared her with a sharp glance. "What do you know about it? You've never had a hard time in your life."

"What do *you* know about it?" Hannah shot back. "You have a mother who's given you everything you've ever wanted. You're a spoiled brat."

Sam's hand landed audibly against Hannah's cheek. The memory rose up: Fran, Gettysburg. The bees, the glasses of orange juice lined across the dresser.

"I hate her," said Sam.

"You hate her?" Hannah told Sam's receding back. "You're exactly like her."

The day Hannah moved to Oakland, she loaded her things in the car and Sam drove them out of Berkeley to a place named Bolinas. In Bolinas, she said, the locals removed the road signs, not wanting tourists to discover their little town.

"I'm not sure *why*. There's nothing special here, only beach and dogs," Sam said as they stood on the hard sand, avoiding each other's eyes

Later they pulled off Route 1 and hiked up Mount Tamalpais, Sam lingering five paces behind Hannah, with her, but also not. At the top, breathless, they stared across a valley of fog so dense it seemed solid, like it possessed physical features. A person could run her hands across this fog, deciphering it the way a blind person reads another's face.

"The group, the church," Hannah said, remembering the meeting. "What if you don't believe in God. A higher power?"

"The *group* is God. The *group* is my higher power."

"Even the guy with the dead birds?" Hannah asked.

"Even that unfortunate fuck," Sam said.

You were an asshole to him, Hannah wanted to say, but didn't. Relaxing into the fog as if it were a mattress, she said, "It's like we're in another time, another place."

"No," said Sam. "We're still just here."

They drove down from Mount Tamalpais through Marin and over the Golden Gate Bridge. When they arrived at the yellow-painted taqueria, mariachi played on the jukebox. Rainbow foil snowflakes and papel picado fluttered as people passed beneath them, reminding Hannah strangely of an undersea scene, jellyfish pulsing through cold waters. Hannah drank horchata for the first time. For the first time, tasted cilantro.

"To some people—" Sam burrowed into her burrito. "—cilantro tastes like soap."

"You like living here," Hannah said. It was either a statement or a question. The mariachi had changed to Zeppelin. *You need coolin', baby, I'm not foolin'. I'm gonna send ya back to schoolin'.* On one side of them, a man dabbed at salsa stains on his shirt; on the other a couple argued heatedly in Spanish.

"I do."

"Fran hates it. It's hard for her to have you so far away."

For the first time since the meeting, since its aftermath, Sam met her gaze. "Did she tell you that?"

"No."

"I know that's why you're here. Fran asked you to come. It wasn't your overwhelming love for me."

Hannah looked away.

"There's no escaping her. When I die, I'll walk inside one of heaven's blank white rooms and there she'll be, waiting."

"You're being histrionic."

"Nice twenty-five-cent word," said Sam coolly. "Check out the big brain on Brad."

"She wants what's best for you."

"We did it together, you know."

"Did what?"

"Heroin. The first time."

Hannah stared at Sam. "No. You didn't."

"In the basement of the Clarks Summit house, before I left for college."

"You're lying," Hannah said, not because she believed this, but because she wanted to.

"I don't lie. Unlike you." Sam pushed her burrito aside. "You only see the convenient parts of things."

Hannah shook her head.

"I hate you for coming here," Sam said.

"I came here for *you*."

"You came here for *her*. Because she told you to. Because you're compliant. How's that for a word, Brad?"

"I felt sorry for her," Hannah said.

"You chose her."

"I don't know what you're talking about."

"In Gettysburg. You went with her. You left me there alone."

"You threw a television remote at me. You told me to get the fuck out!" Sam stood. "You shouldn't have come."

The drive to Hannah's new house was a silent one, though the wind rushed noisily through the windows, whispering indecipherably in Hannah's ear. She guessed the wind was saying Sam was happy; or it was saying she wasn't. She closed her eyes.

They did not speak after this. Sam neither answered her calls nor returned them. When Fran phoned, Hannah made up stories about the places they'd gone, the things they did. "We went hiking and climbed a giant hill," she told Fran. "We saw the ocean. We rode bikes down University to the marina. We drank acai smoothies at an outdoor hut. We shared calamari with too much squeezed lemon. She has a tan for the first time ever. She's put on weight. She looks good, healthy. She's taking care of herself. They're fixing the ant problem in the house. She cleaned the kitchen."

"Thank you, Hannah," Fran said.

"I haven't done anything," Hannah said, and knew it for the truth.

"You've watched our girl. You've kept her safe."

WEBB, 1973

ebb was not new to accidental discovery. Accidental discovery was unavoidable when a man did secret things. It was inevitable that a man's wife should find the silken primrose panties he'd hidden beneath the mattress—she was a snoop, had always been a snoop—inevitable she should throw these panties into his lap, accuse him of having an affair with a fat woman. Inevitable she should, early one morning, barge into the bathroom to discover him applying her lipstick, tilting his head before the mirror like a quizzical bird. Afterward, there would be frostiness at dinner, Beverly saying, "Webster, don't forget to bring the garbage out. That seems like a task for the *man* of the house, don't you think?" Or, "*Oh!* I saw a beautiful sapphire brooch in that jewelry shop on College Avenue. I'm not sure the price, but a blank check will do." She would stare at him with cool aloofness from across the dining table. She was not his wife, but a crisp piece of lettuce. Iceberg, devoid of nutrients, like the "salad" she served once she'd made her biggest demand and his mother moved out. For this salad, Beverly quartered a head of iceberg lettuce. She chucked a quarter onto each plate, shaking bottled thousand island dressing onto the hunks. Webb sawed through the iceberg with a steak knife and yearned for his mother. Yearned for the salad she made in the height of summer, picking butter lettuces from the garden, tossing them with crème fraîche and herbs, lemon. She served these salads with an open hand, offering fresh pepper like they did in restaurants. He loved that salad! But he'd been caught wearing a women's brassiere, stuffing it with tissue as if he were a teenage girl, and one paid for such indiscretions. His mother had warned him of this, and his mother—not he—had paid.

Nights following these discoveries, Beverly came to him with unquenchable desire. She climbed on top of him. Rode him. Slapped his face until he cried out. Bit his shoulders, yanked his hair. With moonlight glimmering menacingly through the blinds and across her face, she looked at once indefatigable and demonic, like a deranged gerbil. He clamped his eyes shut, but she took his face between her hands and cried, "Webster!" as if to remind him who he was. In the morning, he would leave the blank check on the counter with his too pretty signature betraying his desires.

The afternoon Hila uncovered the truth, Webb was in the bedroom wearing a pair of minuscule lace panties that left residual markings like Braille against his skin. He preened before the mirror like either Mick Jagger or a peacock. *Like a peacock*. A problematic metaphor. Only the males preened, showing their glorious and unabashed selves to the world. If he were a peacock, he could be both beautiful *and* male. He could be both decorated in finery *and* loud about it.

On this particular occasion, Webb had watched from the window as Hila eased the car out of the driveway and onto the street. Knowing she would not return for several hours, he went to his drawer of special things. Mesmerized by the polite, pleasing scratch of lace against his genitalia, he'd not heard her return. She'd forgotten something innocuous but needed; sunglasses or lipstick.

"Oh!" she said, as if she'd barged into an occupied bathroom stall. "Excuse me!"

He found her waiting at the kitchen table. Her legs, contained by black hose, were crossed not once but twice. She'd made coffee. She motioned him to the table, handed him a mug.

"Webster," she said. "First, I'd like to apologize for startling you."

Her words were measured and meticulous. He waited to hear what she wanted, prepared to meet her demands.

"Webster, do you like wearing women's clothing?"

This, he had not expected. He dropped mumbled words into his coffee like sugar cubes.

Hila lit a cigarette. Her smoking in the house made clear the seriousness of this discussion. "Webster," she said. "I'm not trying to make you uncomfortable. I'm only trying to understand this situation in which we find ourselves."

"No."

"No, what?"

"No, I don't."

"Don't what?"

"What you said."

"Webster, certainly you should be able to say it."

"No, I do not like wearing women's clothing."

"So let me understand. A genie whisked her wand and said *presto change-o*, and suddenly—*oops!*—your corduroys went missing and you found yourself before the mirror clad only in a pair of lace panties."

"Genies don't have wands."

"Excuse me?"

"Fairy godmothers have wands. Genies reside in bottles."

"I cannot fathom that you are arguing with me over the magical implements of imaginary characters at this moment in time. Fine. Allow me to rearticulate. You're saying that a fairy grandmother waved her wand and said, *Give this dear man some lovely lace panties. Make them nine sizes too small, for that is his destiny!* And voilà!"

"No," he said. "Yes."

She exhaled cigarette smoke.

He said, "I'm not homosexual!"

"I don't believe I said you were. Also. That's an offensive thing to say. You're implying there's something wrong with men who prefer men, or that your own predilection and need is superior to theirs."

He said nothing.

"I find that sentiment offensive. I'm especially pained you feel the need to say such a thing to *me*. I believe I'm the closest person in this world to you, and as such, I would never judge you. Yet you act as if I do. As a result, we're entangled inside this . . . this quagmire of deceit, because you've refused to be honest both with yourself and with me."

Here, his face must have betrayed him.

"If you don't like the words, Webster, maybe a fairy godmother will wave her magical wand once again and change them. Until then, we find ourselves inside a landscape of treachery because you are hiding the truth. You're treating the truth like something unsavory, and as a result, Webster, you have made the situation needlessly dirty."

Tick tock tick went the grandfather clock.

"Webster, do you want to be a woman?"

He clasped his hands to keep them from shaking, felt the residual tremors deep inside himself.

"No."

"Yet I did not imagine you wearing panties just now."

"No."

"So, you *do* like wearing women's clothing."

"Yes."

"Yes, what?"

"Yes, I like wearing women's clothing."

He'd never uttered it aloud before. He braced himself, as if for an inevitable crash.

"Okay then." Hila shrugged.

His voice was tiny enough to slip through a crack. "I'm sorry."

"Webster. Please. Don't ever be sorry for who you are. Be sorry for hurting someone, for causing pain. Don't ever be sorry for trying to get what you want from this life. It's yours, to do with as you want. The only thing on this wide, beautiful earth you'd ever need to apologize to me for is not living this life the way you want to live it."

She came to him then. Knelt between his legs, pressed her face to his inner thigh. He heard the rush of the ocean in his ears. He would have preferred her outrage. In the lean shadow of her anger, he could have drawn a tidy and finite line between them: him, her. He could have made her the antagonist against whom his desires pounded their fists. Her understanding frightened him.

"I'm sorry." He strung the words together like pearls on a necklace Beverly might covet in his greatest moment of guilt. *Sorrysorrysorrysorry-sorrysorrysorrysorrysorry.*

Hila told his knee that there was nothing for which to be sorry. "Love," she whispered. "Shhhhhh."

That night, in bed, starting at the rough soles of his feet, she worked her way upward, kissing the various parts of him: slightly ticklish large toes, pinky toes, indeterminate other toes, the ball of each foot, his inner ankles, the knobs of his knees, the pale flesh of his thighs, the soft crease where thigh met pelvis. She kissed his pelvic bone, the dip of his stomach. Kissed his right hip, his left hip, his navel. Kissed her way along his side, lingering, it seemed, on the indentions of rib. He had the sensation that she anointed him; conveyed his body to him, as if it had previously been missing. He felt in her kissing that she accepted all of who he was, his particularities and predilections, his tics and foibles, his yearnings, both guarded and uttered. Him, she accepted *him*. Beverly had cringed at the expression "to make love." He'd reach for her, speaking with a throaty eagerness—*Make love to me*—and she'd turn away. Hila had never quaked over the concept. Quietly, she made love to him, and afterward they lay, awed by the magnitude of what they'd made.

Neither did Hila quake before the realization that Webster Eugene Jackson, who'd once appeared as quintessential man, preferred frothy dresses and silken slips, minuscule panties. A doer and a maker, she promptly began sewing his clothes.

"I won't have you wearing things you've shoved yourself into, like sausage inside a casing." Kneeling to measure for whatever dress or skirt she was making, she kissed his strong calves.

They went together to the fabric store. Women eyed him curiously; they'd seen so few men in these environs. He saw in their eyes: they believed he should be off wielding a hammer to great effect, eradicating weeds from the lawn. He should be caulking things in need of caulking; men caulked! The world's leaks and rickety fences and rodent infestations could all be blamed on a man who spent time in the fabric store. The quilters in particular stared at him over bolts of discounted holiday fabric as the turkeys on cotton blend ogled him.

He and Hila selected fabric for a fictional woman they called Shasta, a name coined one late night when they had no mixer for their gin except Shasta black cherry cola. Her name suggested she was the sort of woman who wore little clothing while dutifully stirring a cauldron of beans over a campfire. Because Hila believed women felt plain without the romance of a middle name, Shasta became Shasta Jane.

"I *do* believe Shasta Jane should avoid colors reminiscent of ballpark condiments," Hila would say over a bolt of satin. "I know she's fond of mustard yellow, but truth be told, that shade makes her look sallow, like the poor girl needs a transfusion." Or, "I know Shasta Jane isn't inclined toward busy patterns, but her midsection is unfortunately *not* her strong suit. These geometrics might be dizzying, but the chaos will help the good people understand she isn't pregnant. We don't want them thinking Shasta Jane has had *relations*."

"Shasta Jane isn't that kind of girl," said Webb.

"She most certainly is *not*." Hila's laughter billowed like a sheet hung to dry.

One evening, as Hila sewed the geometric fabric into a dress that would obscure Shasta Jane's ample midsection, they turned on the Emmys. They cared less about the awards; they wanted to see the gowns. They dissected the women in their sequined chiffon, debating their hair and accessory choices. And then an envelope was opened, a winner announced, and Webb saw *him*. Clive Murdoch, caught in a web of men clasping one another's shoulders and hands and elbows, nodding effusively at one another with the oh-golly-gee surprise of fishermen who'd ensnared a marlin.

"That's him!" Standing, Webb nearly upturned his card table.

"Alan Alda?"

"Clive Murdoch!"

Hila, blank-faced.

"*Clive Murdoch*, the infamous Missouri wrestler. The magnificent surf-boarder. *Mr. Beverly Laurenzi*."

"Oh!" said Hila. "Oh, *oh*!"

Webb wore a ruffly pink nightgown Hila had sewn for him, having insisted that flattering nightwear was the cornerstone of a person's self-confidence. He gathered up its lace hem as if he were accepting an award of his own and, walking to the television, tapped Clive Murdoch's befuddled face as he ascended to the stage. Clive Murdoch fidgeted in the background as a man more important than he gave a rambling speech. A taller man stepped before Clive Murdoch, obfuscating him from view.

"Sir!" Hila said. "I beg you, move!"

And then, music played. The gaggle of chattering men walked offstage together, Clive Murdoch the little red caboose of their fraternity.

Hila—wonderful Hila!—disintegrated into laughter. The sight of her hilarity caused him to join her, and Webb laughed too, then coughed up a sob, then hiccuped.

"I'm not sure what's funny," he said, having exhausted his combination platter of emotion.

Hila gathered his face between her hands. "One thing is certain. Clive Murdoch no longer has a wrestler's physique. That cummerbund was a bit snug!"

Those were the beautiful years: Hila, measuring and sewing, biting her bottom lip in concentration.

Hila sewed late into the nights. "I can't stand to see you dressed in a muu-muu every day! You certainly knew what you were doing when you chose the home economics teacher. Maybe you found yourself attracted to the biology teacher, with her dewy skin and scientific disinclination towards brassieres, but you realized a dissector of frogs couldn't properly tailor clothing."

His lips brushed hers. "The dissectors of frogs are nothing beside you. I feel terrible for the poor, useless dissectors."

She worked with one pin held at the side of her mouth. Her pincushion—she'd sewed it herself years before as a Texas teenager—was a plump tomato made of now lusterless velveteen. "It's not as beautiful as the ones *we* grow!" she'd say, pushing pins inside it. When the plants' yellow flowers made their first appearances, she'd cry, "Webster, our tomatoes are coming!" Hila, sentry of tomatoes. Still dressed in pajamas, coffee mug in one hand, she touched every tiny blossom to welcome it. One evening, drinking Pimm's cups in the yard, Hila toasted their tomatoes' heady scent, saying, "From here on out, whenever I smell a tomato plant, I'll think of you, Webster, and this exact moment in time, as if there's never been a moment before or after *this* one, with its rosy setting sun and the trill of that bird. I'll remember the itch between my toes, your beautiful blue eyes, and you, Webster. I'll remember *you*."

Nights, watching their favorite television programs, Hila taught him to apply makeup. She gave him manicures and pedicures. Between sips of bourbon, she filed, soaked, cut. He marveled: she could have been a professional manicurist, a makeup artist! She could have been anything: an astronaut, a haughty French chef, a scientist as disinclined toward brassieres as the biology teacher. An activist, a bank robber.

Patty Hearst had just robbed the Hibernia Bank with her rifle and ugly beret. "Poor Patty," sighed Hila. "Once, she was in the society pages. And now, look at that hideous hat." Hila, Webb knew, would look good wearing a hideous hat; she looked good wearing everything. He marveled that she was his, though he dared not say this to her. Male ownership made her bristle, as did the constant pawing of men. Once, at a dinner party, a drunken friend had wrapped his arm around her waist. She'd flung it aside, saying in a voice chilled by ice cubes, "If I want you to manhandle me, I'll say, *Please, Mark, manhandle me.*"

"That ship has sailed!" Hila declared when Webb expressed an interest in powder. "I'm sure Beverly-the-whore was powdered to high hell when she stood on that beach bandstand lusting for her bejeweled crown, but the fifties are a distant memory. It's the seventies, my love, and *au naturel* is the look. Fortunately, you're a great big hairy man, as *au naturel* as one can get." She applied a sheer coat of foundation to his face. He reveled in the motion of the brush against his skin. "We'll find that tenuous place where *just enough* resides, but I can assure you it doesn't involve powder."

Just enough. *Au naturel* would do for others, those endowed with genuine feminine gifts, but he longed to look like what his mother had called doxies.

"I respect that you want to look like a woman." Hila's face was somber and long. "But here. This is the first lesson: there will always be a contradiction between the things you yearn for and the expectations others have for you. Yes, occasionally I wanted to dress like a hussy, wear a white t-shirt without a bra. Wanted to sit bare-chested in the back of some handsome rogue's pickup, flapping my breasts at the cows, but I couldn't because my daddy's heart would cleave."

He closed his eyes, relished becoming other as Hila tweezed his eyebrows into thin lines. She curled his lashes, applied mascara. ("Your eyelashes *are* unfortunate," said Hila. "As if a penis isn't enough adversity to deal with!") Under her ministrations, Webb felt the coaxing tug of beauty, so different from the transformation of the football locker room, hub of testosterone, with its slapping of sweaty asses and snapping of towels. Its grappling with pads, donning of straps.

Afterward, he regarded his resplendence in the mirror. It was like leaping off a precipice. Like flight.

Hila interrupted his rapture. "If you truly want to be a woman, Webster, I ask you please beat those emotions down. Actually, never mind. The mascara I just applied will see to it you do."

Webster. Here's how to shave without nicking the skin. Here's how to put on hose without ripping it. Here's how to remove hose without ripping it. Here's how to fix the run in a stocking at a party because you've ignored my earlier instruction—though it's best to carry a spare pair in your bag. Here's how you wash the hose in the sink. Here's how you hang it to dry, surreptitiously. Men want women to be beautiful, but they'd prefer not to see how it happens. Oh, is this too much information about a pair of hose? Welcome to womanhood and the necessary belaboring of banal detail.

Webster. Walk toward me. Walk away. Pick up that book. With a straight back. No, straighter. Marie Antoinette's mother insisted she climb countless stairs whilst carrying heavy objects. No doubt she walked beautifully to the guillotine. Webster. Your legs are falling open when you sit. Remember, you're wearing a dress. The children and grandmother sitting at the next table would rather not see your splayed baubles. Bend over again, this time without flashing your ass. Oh, is my constant needling annoying you? Well, let me welcome you once more to womanhood.

"No, Webster, women don't hold their arms out like that."

"Like what?"

"Like Frankenstein's monster stumbling off the lab table."

Webb, irritably: "Maybe this woman does."

"No one cares about *this* woman, Webster. There's only the mass of us, like holiday lights you can't untangle."

The beautiful years.

Parties, once again, took place in his home. Not the formal dinners of his mother's era, but the casual and impromptu, promiscuous parties of the seventies. Hila served fondue in ceramic pots at the coffee table, guests sitting on strewn pillows. Rising laughter, vibrato of voices. *Mary-jew-wanna,* as Hila called it, kissing him. *I do. I do wanna.*

Potlucks affronted her. "If a person insists on throwing a potluck—and I really wish they'd refrain—it must be highly organized to succeed. Otherwise, there will be ten green bean casseroles when one green bean casserole is one green bean casserole too many."

She planned their parties in a black-and-white school composition book: who was invited, what would be served. What projects she'd make, what clothes she sew Webb for the occasion. For a luau, she made a magnificent orange dress embroidered with white plumeria. For a casual backyard barbecue, a ruffled ankle-length bohemian skirt. For a French-themed dinner party celebrating her birthday, a simple black dress with a higher than usual hemline. "Vavavavavavavoom!" she cried. "There aren't enough va's in this world for you, Webster. The world is countless va's short!"

The night of the French party, he'd yanked constantly at this dress, more tailored than he was accustomed to. She'd confited duck legs for cassoulet and baked madeleines and crème brûlée. She'd set the tables with hydrangeas from the bush he'd hidden behind as a child, put blankets outside for guests who grew chilly. He'd not seen anyone this thoughtful since his mother. After a bottle of Provençal rosé, he tried to remember his mother in better times, but all he could conjure was the final image of her in her stark white apartment.

The guests kissed his cheeks, asking him to turn so they might admire him. "Hila! You've outdone yourself!" In this way, he was reminded—he already knew—all things circled back to Hila. She tethered him to the harsh reality of the world, like a rubber ball tied to a post—that game Debra liked to play.

Oh, Debra.

He remembered this party not for all these reasons—though the memories of his dress and the food and Hila's ringing laughter as everyone sang happy birthday came to him, years later, persistent, both in dream and waking states—but because at this party, Webb met Hollis, Hila saying, "Webster! This is Hollis, the new senior chemistry instructor."

Hollis, his mouth looking like he'd swallowed a teaspoon of ipecac, shook Webb's hand. Moments later, cheeks flushed with wine, Hila expressed her pleasure that Webb had finally met Hollis. Her joy surprised him. He hadn't thought much of the man.

"He looked at me," Webb said, "as if I had leprosy."

"That's just Hollis," said Hila. "He's Virgo. You know how they are."

"He's in love with you," said Webb.

"Hollis loves any woman who talks to him."

Later, Webb saw them, tucked into a corner of the living room, lost in conversation, a testament to Hila that she could be friends with someone so dour. But Hila was friends with everyone. It was Hila who befriended the drag queen in San Francisco after seeing a performance in the Mission. Hila who'd invited this drag queen to dinner, the drag queen nodding at Webb over the bedraggled remains of the steak he'd made. Vivienne—*not* Vivian, she declared—took him upstairs to what had been his childhood bedroom. She would teach him, she said, the art of tucking.

"Of who?" Webb had never heard of such a thing. He removed his pants, as per Vivienne's request.

"The act," said Vivienne in a melodic voice, "whereby a man sends his testes back from whence they came, so his package doesn't ruin the lines of his stunning dresses."

She sat on her hands, wobbling her ass back and forth to warm them, adjusting a cheek on each hand, chattering about the weather as she did so. How cold it was even for this fine summer day! Mark Twain was right when he said the coldest winter he ever spent was a summer day in San Francisco.

"We're in Oakland," said Webb. "Also, Mark Twain never said that."

"Well, he should have." Vivienne slid her hands from beneath her ass and reached for Webb's genitals in one fell swoop. When Webb donated blood, he could not watch the filling of the vial, and Webb also found he could not bring himself to look as Vivienne manipulated his testes. He instead focused on her face, the place where the foundation blended with her skin, where illusion met reality. Her voice took on the cadence of the ocean, thrusting itself toward and then away from shore. "You cannot do if you do not watch. If you cannot watch, you should not do."

Afterward, Hila served dense chocolate cake and strong coffee as if he and Vivienne had been upstairs busying themselves with needlepoint. His testes had been shoved back into the inguinal canal for the first time since they'd dropped down, like ripened peaches falling from a tree, when he was a teenager. Webb chewed cake without tasting it.

The next morning, Hila passed the gaff she'd sewn him over the breakfast table. He'd been reaching for a muffin but now held a gaff. He asked, "Are there things you're afraid of?"

She dropped sugar cubes into her coffee. "Apocalypse. Threat of aliens. Women with necklaces so large they hide the beauty of their clavicles. Food prepared without salt. Certainly, I'm not afraid of *life*. I understand this tendency toward the gilded past. The past gets us through. It gets us by. Still, one cannot sacrifice the present to it."

"You need balls," he said, "to get rid of balls."

Hila's cascading laughter. "Yes, I suppose you do."

Soon after this, he and Hila returned home from luncheon at a friend's house. The neighbor, watching Webb extricate himself from the car in a silken kimono, shouted, "We don't want fairies here!"

"Excuse me?" Hila asked.

"Get out, fairy!" said the man's wife, standing beside him. Her mouth opened wide, like a sinkhole. "God will make you pay!"

Webb felt confused; when had God stepped into this scene? Hila lurched a step toward them. He clasped her wrist. Inside the house, she raged: "Who does that piece of shit think he is? I don't want neighbors who drink tall boys with their ass cracks exposed. I'd prefer my neighbor wasn't a bleached bimbo."

He'd never heard Hila speak derisively of another woman besides Beverly.

"That woman borrows my sugar," Hila said. "And smells of Aqua Net doing it."

Hila left early the following morning. She returned laden with bags and accomplishment. Inside the bags were countless ceramic garden fairies. Where had she found them? Glistening blue-winged fairies and violet-and-pink-winged fairies. Smiling fairies, mournful-eyed fairies, demure fairies. Silvery fairies. Fairies with pigtails. Old men fairies bedecked in shimmery purple, wearing grave expressions, like authors who'd posed for photographs on book jackets. Fairy babies curled sleeping on ceramic leaves. Hila made a great show of placing them in the lawn, saying loudly enough for the neighbor to hear—he tinkered on his car, the way men who feared fairies often did—"Webster! The fairies are infiltrating the neighborhood!"

The following week, drinking gin in the privacy of their yard, Hila said, "At first, I worried I'd wake up and discover the house covered in glitter. You know how impossible it is to clean glitter."

"I do," said Webb and thought of Debra.

"But now, I've grown so accustomed to them. A life without fairies would be lonely. Did you know," Hila said, "in fairyland, mortals are sometimes magically compelled to dance with the fairies?"

"I did not," said Webb.

Eyes aflame, Hila continued, "Captured by fairies, mortals are forced to dance all night long, until they collapse from exhaustion. Webster, my wish is to see that grease-drenched neighbor dance naked around a fire while the fairies laugh and poke his ass crack with their wands."

"One can dream," Webb said.

"One can," said Hila.

Weeks later, she roused Webb from a deep sleep.

"Webster," she said. "Wake up. Be quick."

An ambulance idled in front of the house next door. He and Hila watched from the lawn as the neighbor's body was carried out on a stretcher, his wife weeping.

Hila, not typically merciless, shrugged. "Thank you, fairies," she said, patting a slight fairy on its head as the stretcher was loaded into the ambulance.

"It's been thirteen years," said Hila on Debra's birthday, which for thirteen years Webb had treated like a day of mourning. "We'll drive to Los Angeles and fix this."

"Thirteen is an unlucky number," said Webb. "It's best to wait another year."

Hila said, "In Italy, thirteen is a lucky number."

"I'm not Italian."

"You like pizza margherita. That's sufficient. Your daughter is now an adult. Every year, Webster, she turns older on this day and every year on this day I bear witness to how much her absence hurts you. Your daughter is old enough to decide if she wants you in her life. A grown woman, maybe married. Maybe a mother! Webster, you might be a *grandfather*. You'd ignore the unfolding of generations, deny their existence because you're afraid of Beverly, that dirty whore?"

Be a man, Beverly the dirty whore would have told him in this situation.

"Los Angeles is a large city. Shall we go door to door, knocking?"

"I hired a private investigator."

Webb stared at her. "You what?"

"I did what I had to do. Webster," said Hila. "Please. I know what your heart needs. I have the exact address."

Hila, obsessive Scorpio, persisted until he could no longer stand the sound of her voice. When words failed, she threw a champagne flute against the wooden floor. "Goddamn it! Your daughter needs you. You need her. Make this right!"

That evening, she wore a dress, floral and fluttery and declaring, in its lightness, that she refused to be fettered by him. She held an overnight bag. She said, "Call me when you've changed your mind."

He expected she'd return before dinner the following day; an entire week passed. Finally, he dialed her number. She answered the phone with her lilting *hello*.

"Fine," he said. "I'll go."

They left on an early June morning, sky swathed with fog, fog hanging like men's beards from the trees. The pea-green Impala tunneled into and through the suspended wisps until eventually the sun burned into a crisp sky. Hills a mirage disappearing periodically into the blue backdrop, Webb drove. This incessant disappearing act of the hills made him dizzy. Anxiety buzzed at his ear, tugged his heart. He tasted its sourness on his tongue. Soon he pulled to the side of the highway, where he retched into the tall grass beneath the gaze of several despondent cows.

"I love cows!" Hila proclaimed when he returned to the car. "I'd like four stomachs of my own! I'd eat a French dinner, an Italian dinner, a Mexican dinner, and a second Italian dinner."

"What's there to be so happy about?" he asked.

"Webster." She touched his neck. "I'm proud of you for doing this."

He found himself unable to speak. His tongue was the weight attached to the body thrown into the river so that it might sink into the deep. Hila's cheerfulness agitated him. She held her hand out the window to feel the pushing air, sang the songs playing on the radio.

She's a beauty.
One in a million girls.
She's a beauty.
Why would I lie?

Hila retorted jauntily, "You'd lie because you're an asshole! A goddamn unreliable piece of shit, that's why!"

Webb's stomach had filled with darkness. It spread, polluted his insides, turned his heart and liver and spleen and everything pink and healthy inside him into black withered things. Driving towards the disappearing hills, he knew: seeing Debra was an impossibility. He lacked the courage for it, just as he lacked the courage to tell Hila he lacked the courage. He would never, in this lifetime, have the courage. Terror threatened to cleave him in two. For thirteen years, he'd been capable only of inaction, and now inaction defined him.

Reaching their hotel room, Webb collapsed onto the wide bed with its cool sheets. In the bathroom, Hila marveled at the shell-shaped soaps by the sink, the darling containers filled with shampoo and conditioner. She rejoiced over the exorbitant number of pillows strewn across the bed. Sitting on their tiny balcony, she narrated the events transpiring on the beach below: pinprick of a man flying a kite in the distance. Beautiful bronzed sunbathers. "A possible lovers' quarrel. She's throwing up her hands and walking away! He's tripping across the sand to reach her!"

"Webster," Hila said. "Famous rockstars have probably vomited from this balcony."

The topic provided an opening.

"I'm sick," he said. "I think I have a fever."

Pressing her hand against his forehead, Hila said nothing. She ordered room service, and they ate dinner inside the sprawl of bedsheets, watching something called Music Television. Encouraged by the placard beside the phone, she periodically called the front desk to ask questions. What would tomorrow's weather bring? Where was the closest bowling alley? She finished dinner and ordered up dessert. Their first twenty-four hours in Los Angeles passed like this. He noticed her studying him when she thought he wasn't looking. Yes, he was sick! With anxiety, with the possibility of imminent rejection, with guilt. Sick about the persistent, pressing future. What could he possibly say to Debra? How did a man explain his absence to a person he loved more than he loved himself? There was no explanation for such a thing. No words. Webb smashed his face onto the cool pillows and slept.

On the third day, Hila yanked the curtains open. Bristling light besieged him.

"Webster," she said. "I know you're not sick."

He manufactured a cough.

"Please. Spare me the dramatics."

He coughed again.

"What will you wear to the Oscars when you accept your golden statue?" asked Hila. "You best find yourself an excellent seamstress who isn't myself. You're pretending to be sick, Webster, rather than tell me your feelings. It makes me feel unworthy of knowing them."

At this important juncture, he could have told her his feelings. They could have salvaged this moment, this trip, their future. Yet much later, with the perspective the thickness of accumulated years gave to things, he would wake in the night with a start, knowing that sharing his feelings had never been an option. He'd always been a fragile man; Beverly's leaving had broken him.

"Why would I lie?" he chose to say.

"You're kidding."

"What?"

"I'm trying to have a conversation with you—I want to know what you're thinking and what you *feel*—and you just quoted a *song lyric*."

"You like that song!"

"I can't save you," she said.

"Do I need to be saved? It's wrong of you—fucked up—to assume I need saving."

Nodding slowly, she said, "You're right."

Encouraged by her admission, he said, "I never asked to be saved. I never fell to my knees and cried out, *Please! Save me!* I'm not your damsel in distress."

Coldly, she said, "Don't be histrionic."

"I'm telling you my *feelings*," he said. "You want to know how I *feel*."

"Careful," said Hila. "You're scraping the bottom of the barrel."

This conversation fell within the length of the video playing on Music Television: "She Blinded Me with Science," a song Hila claimed gave her the heebie jeebies. The song ended, and a rocket blasted into space. A pulsing

MTV logo then appeared on a flag planted in the moon's surface. An astronaut stood as if mesmerized by this flag. Webb remembered a time, so long ago now, when astronauts had been like gods. What had happened? Why did no one care anymore? What had just happened *here*, between him and Hila?

Without another word, she went into the bathroom. He heard her using the vials of things. Heard the rush of the faucet. She left without saying she was leaving. He lay mummified in bed, watching Music Television. She returned several hours later, calm and collected. They ordered room service and ate together politely. She sat across from him on the bed wearing crisp black, hair pulled into a taut bun. She resembled a poet; had she gone to a museum?

"I was thinking we'd leave tomorrow," he said.

Hila nodded, and Webb felt relief this brief debacle had ended. They could put it behind them. Go home, return to their life. *Turn around, bright eyes*, went the song playing on the television. *Every now and then I fall apart.*

The next morning, he woke to discover her gone.

But they ate breakfast together every morning! They'd eaten breakfast together for thirteen years! Where would she have gone without breakfast? She'd expressed interest in watching the sunrise from the beach. The sun was already high and bright—he'd slept late, for she always woke him—but he dragged himself onto the balcony to look for her. He scanned the beach, squinting to discern if any of the happy, cavorting flecks were Hila. Unable to distinguish between flecks, he went to the minibar, where he selected a minibottle and downed it. He selected another. Summoning his strength, he dragged a cowl-necked sweater over the nightgown he'd been wearing for days. He pulled on a pair of argyle knee socks and his black dress shoes, the only pair he'd brought. In this ensemble, he crossed the angry road separating the hotel from the beach. Weak-kneed and tremulous, he traversed the sand lodging itself in his socks, chaffing his skin. The cowl-necked sweater was too warm for the overt midmorning sun. He threw it onto the sand, removed his shoes and socks. He was then a man in a nightgown walking barefoot on the scalding beach. He hadn't showered since arriving in Los Angeles. Hadn't brushed his hair or teeth. Beachgoers stared. He felt only a frantic need to find Hila. To embrace her. To declare, *I am in this world, wanting you! I am in this world because of you!*

She was not among the people frolicking at water's edge. She was not any of the people building inadequate sandcastles, nor any of the women coaxing children to apply sunscreen. Thunderous panic overtook him. He focused on the beach umbrellas. Hila, pale-skinned, took great precaution to avoid the sun. Yes, she must have rented an umbrella.

The first umbrella shielded a family eating sandwiches. They laughed when he poked his head under and said, "Hey, wrong umbrella!" He trekked determinedly toward the next umbrella. A college-aged boy yelled after him, "Nice nightie!" The second umbrella was empty, its inhabitants having gone to splash in the ocean. They'd left only their beach blanket, its corners anchored with sandals and unopened bags of snacks. Beneath the third umbrella, a young woman clutched a baby to her bare breast. Seeing him, she gesticulated wildly. "Out! Get out! I'll scream! I have no money! There's nothing here for you!" and Webb stumbled away, backward and blinking, into the hot sand and sun.

HANNAH, 2001

hat bike. Motivated by her coworker's belief that she could not accomplish such a thing, Hannah rode Hila's bike though downtown Berkeley with the intention of climbing into the hills. Taking her coworker's advice, she traveled light; had left the house without her backpack, which would weigh her down. She'd brought only one water bottle. Water was heavy. She'd seen it countless times on television, battering coastlines and knocking down doors, sweeping unsuspecting people out to sea. Water filled ships, sent them to the ocean's haggard bottom.

The climb began like a lackluster handshake, gently. Hannah pedaled past a modernist church on her left, the remains of what had been an abundant summer garden on her right. Fifteen minutes later, her heart knocked inside her chest like a fist against a door. In a horror movie, this was the moment before a zombie climbed through a window or a bat lashed across the screen. As the meat of the climb hit her, Hannah suddenly remembered the small town in Pennsylvania where Max had once driven them. Every night, a crowd gathered to watch a throng of bats fly from an abandoned church's steeple. Anticipating the sight, Hannah had imagined the bats frenetically beating their way into the dusky sky, but the bats had proceeded from their belfry in an orderly fashion, one after the other, like catholic schoolchildren maintaining neat lines; like she and Sam in their plaid skirts walking to morning services in the brisk air, the nuns speaking sharply when Sam lollygagged: "Samuelle!"

Hannah gripped the handlebars. Bits of sweat fluttered into the ether. She pedaled and thought, *I hate this*. This exertion, this pressure gripping her heart and lungs. Vomit lunged inside her throat. She swallowed it down in a rancid swallow. Memories and images pushed against her as she climbed:

Webb's crooked bosom and sad knees, chocolate cake in the outdoor garbage bin, crumbs at the bottom of the Grape Nut box. Sean's dexterous handling of the tongs as he grilled shrimp for linguine con gamberoni. Fran, voraciously drinking boxed chardonnay. Sam's foul-smelling kitchen, its ants hoisting breadcrumbs, her housemates drinking soy chai around the dirty table. Fran's howl when she called to tell Hannah Sam had died. "You bitch, Hannah. You said you'd watch her. You promised!"

Hannah promised her pink and pounding, fleshy heart that she would not get off this bicycle. She'd sworn she would do what her coworker had said she couldn't. "Use the entire pedal stroke," he'd advised. Hannah hadn't known there was an entire pedal stroke, an up as well as a down. For weeks now, she'd ridden across town pushing down, down, down. Pulling up was an impossibility without the shoes she saw people wearing, their bikes with special pedals; she hadn't known bike shoes and special pedals existed. She would stay on this bike, survive this hill. She would find comfort in this singular physical act. Hannah saw herself reflected in her mind's eye, as if her image stared back at her from a puddle of rainwater. She'd remain on this bicycle or she wouldn't. She'd quit or she wouldn't. Little ambiguity remained. There was no navigating various iterations of the story: Fran's version, Sam's version. No negotiating, interpreting.

At the top of the hill, heart threatening to burst, Hannah threw herself from the bike. Her legs hummed. Her entire body was a plucked strand, like those on the instruments she'd wanted to play as a child and whose lessons her mother had refused. Her innards felt excavated, like pith and seeds from a pumpkin. Before her, the bay stretched. In the time she'd lived here, Hannah had not seen it from this vantage point. San Francisco, the Golden Gate, Marin. Mount Tamalpais ached in the background, the place where she'd once stood with Sam, staring into the phantom fog. One day, she knew, she would have lived here longer than Sam had. One day, she would have—she hoped—lived longer than Fran.

She stared for a long time at the bay's interconnected beauty, breathing in, in, in. She gradually slowed her heart. And then, she rode home.

It took several tries to conquer Claremont, another hill her coworker had told her she'd never make the top of. One afternoon, heart cramping, muscles reverberating, she cracked it. Wind against her face, she smoothed the ragged edges of her breath. Tasted the sweat, salty, on her lips as she descended through residential streets. She emerged at the bottom of the hill in a foreign place, a land she'd never been, like Dorothy in Oz, a place greener and brighter than Oakland. She'd descended east rather than west, into fabled Orinda. She laughed into the dry air.

At the Baskin-Robbins, she asked the girl behind the counter to please fill her water bottle. The girl rolled her eyes as she walked to the sink. Hannah asked, "How I do get back to Oakland?"

"Seriously?"

"Yes, seriously."

The girl waved in the direction of the hills before turning away. A man licking a chocolate cone intervened. "Ride that way about a mile and a half. Use Wildcat Canyon, off the left-hand side of the street. It's less steep."

"A mile and a half," Hannah repeated.

"Maybe two," the man said. "Flat until you reach the climb."

"The climb."

"It's not bad as far as climbs go."

Hannah pedaled the two miles to Wildcat Canyon slowly, conserving her energy. Turning onto the road, she found a single policeman motioning the traffic away.

"What's this?" Hannah asked.

"Road closed," the officer said. "Fire."

Hannah's laughter erupted before she could stop it.

"That's funny?" the officer asked sharply. "Fire in this weather is funny?"

"It really isn't," said Hannah. "I was laughing at myself."

"Do you want a repeat of 1991?"

Hannah knew nothing about 1991, remembering only that it had ended with Fran and Sam. "No," she said.

She pedaled back to Orinda. The Orinda BART would take her to College Avenue, walking distance to Webb's house, but at once she realized her stupidity. She'd left her backpack in Oakland. She had no money. No credit card. No way to buy a ticket. She considered her options. In the lobby of the BART station was a payphone. Hannah picked up the receiver and called Webb collect.

He came for her in the pea-green Chevrolet, emerging from the car in a yellow kimono whose hem dragged on the asphalt, following him like a dog. He'd not worn a slip underneath. His legs appeared through the sheer fabric, thinner than she'd realized. Hannah thought of Sam at the Essex Hot Tub; her obtrusive ribs, the way that boy had yanked her nipple. She helped Webb wrangle the bike into the car. He'd brought ice water inside a thermos, knowing she'd be thirsty. He'd brought a dampened towel for her face. Handing it to her, he said, "Imagine how Jesus felt when Mary Magdalene gave him that towel."

"You believe in those things?"

"What things?"

"Jesus, Mary Magdalene. God."

"I believe in mopping a sweaty brow."

Another memory: Sam, raising her hand in seventh-grade catechism.

"Sister Grace?"

"Yes?"

"There is no God."

"Samuelle, why would you even say that?"

"Look around. Look at us."

"God made us."

"We're all miserable."

"We're here, Samuelle. That's God's work."

"Then this misery, Sister, is God's work."

Hannah left the house now with identification and money, a credit card. Two water bottles. She bought herself a kit to repair flat tires, bought a tiny pump that attached to the bike frame. She rode through Berkeley, turning right into the hills, riding along the ridge of Grizzly Peak, down Tunnel Road, to Rockridge. She returned home to a hot shower, to the bright kitchen where Webb served peanut butter and pickle sandwiches cut into neat triangles.

"They were the peanut butter and jelly of their time," said Webb. "I adored them. Being the woman she was, my mother would bake the bread from scratch. Once it had properly cooled—never before!—she'd slice it into even slices, slather them thick with whipped butter. She'd cream the peanut butter with whipping cream, spread a beautiful layer of that on top of the butter. Dust each half with coarse salt. Certain recipes called for the pickles to be finely chopped, like a relish, but my mother always used the cucumbers she'd pickled. Ones she'd grown in our backyard. She would slice the pickles thicker than paper, but quite thin. Not even Hila possessed my mother's knife skills. Sliced like this, the pickles gave the sandwich a necessary crunch that relish could never provide. I would eat my mother's peanut butter and pickle sandwiches and believe myself whole."

"Are we ever?" Hannah asked.

"Ever what?"

"Whole."

"Occasionally," said Webb. "For a moment, yes."

Fall was a foreign thing, hotter than the ones Hannah had experienced as a child, less punctuated with colorful brilliance. At night, in the softened light just before sundown, they talked or didn't. Shared stories, or didn't.

"I think," Hannah said. "We should take a walk sometime."

"A *walk*?"

"Something easy, just around the block."

"Why?"

"It's important to stay limber."

He laughed. "That ceased being important long ago."

"When you see your daughter," said Hannah. "You won't want to appear *old*."

"Debra," Webb said.

"Yes."

On nights Hannah didn't work, they walked around the block. Webb dressed for these occasions in clothes Hila had sewn years before and that Hannah marveled at, dresses with bright colors and careful stitchery. They walked shoulder to shoulder, slowly, Webb grasping Hannah's arm, and Hannah remembered, with a tightening of her chest, bearing Fran's weight in the Pennsylvania battlefield's humidity.

One evening, while they were making their slow round, the red face of the woman across the street appeared in her window. Hannah waved. The woman scowled, disappeared.

"She hates you," Hannah said.

"She does."

"It's a compliment."

They walked, hills to their right.

"Hila lived there." Webb paused, pointed. "Up there. She kept the place even when we were together. Loved it. The house is gone now." His finger lingered.

Hannah squinted at the silhouetted hills, at the tip of his finger.

"Once," he said, "It was right there."

IV

BEVERLY, 1983

The year had been fraught with tension. Debra would be married to James at the end of June, and she and Beverly agreed on nothing, arguing over every minuscule detail: which font to engrave on the cocktail napkins, what color mints should fill the swan favors. To flambé dessert, or not to flambé dessert. A rainbow-hued bridal party or no rainbow-hued bridal party.

It was mid-May when Violetta came to Beverly. Violetta cleaned James's parent's house as well as Beverly's—Beverly had recommended her to James's mother, singing her praises over iced tea and undressed salads. Now Violetta shifted her weight as she stood before Beverly, afraid to speak.

"Yes?" Beverly said.

Violetta, it turned out, had been cleaning one of the Johnsons' upstairs bathrooms earlier in the week when she'd heard a loud thump. Here, Violetta paused.

"*Yes.*" Beverly looked at her watch. "You heard a thump."

"A thump, against the wall. I went to look."

"*Yes.*"

"I'm not sure how to say it," said Violetta.

"In my experience, it's usually best just to say the thing," Beverly said, though saying things directly was not actually a practice of hers.

"Well, Jimmy had her against the wall."

"*Who?*"

"A vulgar girl. She must have stayed the night with him. I think she was trying to leave before anyone saw her. She was wearing one of those skirts the girls wear these days. I have panties larger than this girl's skirt—"

"Yes, I understand. A miniskirt."

"Jimmy had her against the wall, right next to Mrs. Johnson's wedding portrait, the one where she's admiring herself in the mirror, holding her bouquet, while her mother is reflected in the background, smiling at her—"

"You're a budding novelist, Violetta."

"His hand was up her skirt. His fingers. Right by the photograph."

"Thank you, Violetta," Beverly said, more crisply than she intended. "You've painted quite the picture."

"Poor Debbie!" Violetta's lip quivered.

"Yes," said Beverly. No one called her daughter Debbie.

"Weeks before her wedding! What a lowdown dog!"

Watching Violetta's warbling mouth, as if the woman might cry over her daughter's plight, Beverly realized Debra and Violetta had become close.

Beverly said, "Certainly, he's a lowdown dog who should be kicked."

Violetta's eyes widened. "Dogs should never be kicked!"

"It's a figure of speech. But since we're talking, there's something I've been wanting to discuss with you. Just last week, Clive invited a gentleman to our home, a television producer of a show I know you watch. Clive found a quarter inch of dust inside the highball glasses when he served this fine man a drink. The only things Clive ever wants to see in his highballs are gin, tonic, and freshly cracked ice."

"Oh!" said Violetta, ashamed.

Clive had mentioned no such thing. Clive wouldn't notice if all the world's dust stuffed itself inside his nose. Beverly needed to change the subject from James's dalliance with the short-skirted slut; needed to plant the seeds for Violetta's dismissal. She couldn't risk Violetta telling her daughter about her future husband's adroit fingers.

"I checked with Mrs. Johnson. She mentioned she's had similar issues. *I* recommended you, Violetta, and so of course I feel terrible. I'll talk to Debra about the *incident*. It's best she hears it from her mother. You concentrate on getting dust out of the glassware."

Beverly now understood how Debra had snagged James. She'd snagged him with her plainness. Such plainness, James knew, would make Debra insecure and agreeable, never delving too closely into matters for fear of his leaving. He was a lowdown dog, but with Debra his leash would be long.

At dinner that evening, Debra ate a meal of iceberg lettuce and cottage cheese, wanting to look as beautiful—*thin*—as possible on her wedding day. James this, Debra said. James that. Debra recounted tedious stories of her fiancé with the glow of a girl on the precipice of marriage. What had Beverly said to Violetta? *It's usually best just to say the thing.* Beverly hadn't even told Webster she was leaving. Her sudden absence, she'd decided, would do the telling better than her meager words could. She'd once been good with words. Her high school English teachers had told her so.

Across the table, Debra vigorously chewed lettuce while Beverly planned her chat with James regarding discretion. She poured herself a second glass of champagne. Privately, she toasted herself, congratulated herself on the preservation of her daughter's happiness.

Two weeks later, Beverly was organizing the seating charts for the reception, an act akin to wiring a bomb so it wouldn't explode in your face, an act demanding ingenuity and a firm grasp of the individual underpinnings of the invited group. There were squabbles to consider, jealousies and grudges, not to mention the divorces. One wanted to put distance between the first and second wives, but it was paramount to avoid seating the first wives at the same table. Their potential to draw animosity from one another, combined with alcohol, could prove combustible. When the front door chimed, Beverly walked through the echoing hallway, thinking, *Men and their lack of control, their inclination toward nubile secretaries.* She opened the door without looking to see who was there.

A woman stood on the steps, regarding Beverly expectantly. Her delicate features reminded Beverly of a china teacup.

"I don't want anything," said Beverly. As she began to close the door, the woman said, "Beverly Murdoch."

Beverly accelerated the closing of the door. How did this woman know her? Why was she staring like that?

Even with the door shut, Beverly heard the woman say, "Beverly Murdoch, formerly Jackson, née Laurenzi. Miss Santa Barbara 1955. Runner up to Miss California 1956. Married to Webster Eugene Jackson in the year 1957, divorced in the year 1971."

Beverly opened the door an inch.

The woman said, "I'm acquainted with Webster Jackson."

Beverly saw it now. This woman had taught with Webster at the high school. She and Beverly had intersected briefly at faculty parties, those dreadful affairs with slung-together punch and too many deviled eggs. Beverly had once watched the chemistry teacher pour two bottles of booze into a bowl, stir the mixture with the upended neck of a bottle, and declare it punch. Beverly drank this concoction; how else to endure hours of insipid talk about the mathematics curriculum, and which poor soul would oversee the dreaded prom committee?

Despite having never spoken to this woman, Beverly remembered her. Of course, Beverly always remembered the attractive ones. She was an expert at sizing up the competition. This one had offered Webster a platter of deviled eggs with that particular glint in her eye. Beverly had known: this woman wanted her husband. Worse, people, *men*, had liked her. They teased her, rushed to find her a napkin, refilled her punch. Beverly was typically the center of attention; but here was *this* woman, with her rising laughter, with the prettiest birdlike wrists and ankles.

She still possessed an ethereal beauty. Beverly remembered being jealous of her thinness. She gave meaning to the expression Beverly had seen in books, *a slip of a woman*, and her clothing was impeccably tailored; she was a slip of a woman who knew what looked right on her body. And she had that elusive quality Miss Margaret had yammered on about. Poise. You could thrust a cider block into this woman's arms and she'd still have that posture.

"No," Webster later swore. "I don't know her." In their bed, his mouth on her nipple, the residual sting of punch flushing her cheeks, he said, "She looks like a French teacher."

"She does *not*," said Beverly, "look like a French teacher."

Beverly wanted her to be the school librarian, reprimanding children for not returning their books in a timely fashion. Or the cafeteria lady, collecting dimes for milk, scooping slop onto trays, wiping her greasy hands against a stained apron. But Webster had it right; she looked like a French teacher.

And now, this woman—*this* woman—stood in Beverly's doorway.

"Hello," the woman said cheerfully.

Beverly noted with satisfaction the loss of elasticity in her skin. "Do you need something?"

"Would you like to ask me inside?"

"I would not." To emphasize this, Beverly stepped outside, closing the door behind her.

"Here will do," said the woman. "Certainly, I've arrived unannounced, and it would be inhospitable of me to force hospitality." Her words had an ironic sharpness, but she smiled through them as Beverly had once smiled her way through difficult pageant interviews.

"I'm sorry, why are you here?"

"I've come to ask that you declare a truce with Webster. A moratorium, if you will, on the silly silence of the past thirteen years."

"Webster and I are divorced, an act of separation recognized by the courts. People divorce for a reason, and *silly silence*, as you call it, is the logical outcome."

"I understand that you and Webster are divorced."

"And yet. Here you are. Standing on my veranda."

The woman laughed the same ringing laughter of years earlier.

"I'm unclear what's so funny."

"You would, of course, be drawn to the word *veranda*."

Beverly felt flustered. She hadn't felt flustered in years. "We're standing on a veranda."

"The word *veranda* denotes a sensibility to which you'd be drawn. Genteel, superior. This is a porch, not a veranda, though I'm not here to quibble over vocabulary."

Beverly's face burned. (*Why wasn't it a veranda?* "A veranda," Clive told her when she asked later that night, "has a roof. What we have is a porch.")

"At least it isn't a stoop!" the woman said. "You don't seem like a stoop woman. And yes, you are divorced, but I believe Webster should have a relationship with his daughter."

"Webster sent you," Beverly said, "his lackey, to perform his menial negotiations."

"Webster has no idea I'm standing on your fine veranda. We drove here together. He intended to speak with you himself, but he's afraid. He judges himself harshly for not making things right before now. With Debra, I mean. He doesn't say it, but I know it hurts his heart. He doesn't want to disrespect you, or the life you've created here. I, however, care very little if

I disrespect you, or the life you've created here. I don't give a fuck. I care only about Webster."

"Charming," said Beverly. She understood that this woman loved Webster, as she most likely had since she lifted that platter of deviled eggs to him. She couldn't risk Webster showing up so close to Debra's wedding. What if he insisted on coming! What if he believed he should walk her down the aisle! The past was the emphatic past. You couldn't have it bleeding into the present.

"You should know," Beverly said, "that Webster has contacted me as recently as this year. He's made declarations of love. He'd take me back in a heartbeat. I'm sorry, but you're embarrassing yourself."

The woman laughed, distracting Beverly with her pretty white teeth. "I'm not stupid," she said. "And I don't play games."

Beverly gritted her own teeth. Every woman played games. Some liked to think they didn't, but they did. "Fine," she said. "I'll tell you the truth."

"Yes, tell me your version of the truth."

"I suspect our versions are similar."

The woman smiled.

"You'll never fix him."

"Webster isn't some broken toy, in need of repair."

"You would be one for semantics. Let me rephrase. He'll never change."

"I don't *want* to change him."

"But you do. You want to change the situation."

"No—"

"You're here," said Beverly, "trying to change it. You want to repair his relationship with his daughter, and in turn you want to repair him."

"I love him," the woman said fiercely. "I accept everything that makes him who he is."

"Of course you love him," said Beverly. "I see it. It's even touching. But if you accepted everything, you would not be here."

"You have no idea what kind of woman I am," the woman said. "He loves *me*."

"Even if he loves you with the entirety of his heart, it won't be enough. Having once been the recipient of Webster's love, I *do* know what kind of woman you are."

"And what kind is that?"

Beverly stared at the woman's thin face. "Patient. Hopeful."

Something indecipherable passed across her sharp features.

"I'm sure you've waited years for Webster to snap to. Be present and accountable. You've waited for him to make amends with his daughter, to get out into the world and *live*. Let me tell you," said Beverly, "he'll never live in the world. In a moment of panic, he might make a desperate gesture to prove his love. But that's all it will ever be. A desperate gesture. He stole the neighbor's swing set for me once. It changed nothing. I know what kind of woman you are because *I* was that woman, stuck inside that house waiting for Webster. We were supposed to travel to New York City on our honeymoon—a glamorous trip, with dinners and shows!—but no, we spent our honeymoon in Oakland, with his mother."

"Boo hoo," said the woman. "So you didn't eat caviar and watch Broadway shows."

"We'd agreed to live in Santa Barbara, but we stayed in Oakland. It wasn't a discussion. We'd get our own house, he said, whatever I wanted. But there was no new house. We stayed with his mother in hers. Our bedroom was the bedroom he'd grown up in. And that was our life. Staying home, watching television, sitting on the couch with his mother between us, like two teenagers with a chaperone. We never went to the ocean, never touched the sand. Never went to movies or to dinner. He couldn't deprive his mother of joy, couldn't leave her. What about me? What about *my* joy?"

"I guess that was your big monologue," the woman said.

"As a woman speaking to another woman, I can tell you: the only thing that got a rise from Webster was my leaving. If I could have left every week of our lives, dramatically, we would still be married. Where is Webster now? Let me guess. Cowering inside the hotel room."

The woman's expression didn't change, but Beverly saw. She'd taken this woman's heart, rolling it like a hard-boiled egg along the countertop until hairline fissures appeared. You couldn't break something whose integrity hadn't already been compromised. The chair broke beneath the person, yes, perhaps because the person was heavy, but the chair itself had proven weak. If she'd cracked this woman, it was because she had already considered, somewhere deep inside her, the things Beverly said.

"If Webster told you he was sick," said Beverly, "he's as sick as apple pie."

The woman said nothing.

"I left because I wanted things I knew I'd never have with him. And I don't mean a large house, or a new car every year and a vacation every season. I wanted obscure things, but eventually I had the sense to know he'd never give them to me. Not because he didn't want to, but because he was incapable."

Standing on her veranda—*porch*—Beverly imagined Debra pulling into the driveway in her Datsun. She imagined the three of them pushing aside the seating charts, settling at the dining table to drink coffee. Eating the Stella D'oro cookies Beverly put out, the woman would see Webster clearly in his daughter: his aquiline nose, his blue eyes. Debra looked nothing like her. Debra *was* nothing like her. She had her father's dreaminess, his predilection for random observation. "Look at that cloud," Debra would say as a teenager, a time when Beverly would have preferred she talked about makeup. "It's a sad man hunched over, crying!" What response was there to such a comment? Debra would say something about the preternatural brightness of the world's colors after an afternoon storm, an observation Beverly was sure she'd heard Webster make. His language had been different, but the sentiment was the same, as though across the distance Webster were placing the thought in his daughter's mind. A song Webster loved would play on the radio—a song he'd loved long before Debra had been born—and Debra would declare her own love for this song, singing the lyrics with an assuredness her speaking voice lacked. Her daughter hadn't gotten her voice from Beverly, but from Edna, who'd moved about the kitchen, singing with beautiful clarity.

Daily, Debra reminded Beverly of the power of genetics, the tug of DNA. This was the undeniable truth presented to Beverly nearly every day she looked upon her daughter's face: Webster was inside Debra's blood, her body. This fact could not, against all strength of trying, be denied.

She'd known it even when Debra was a child. Her mother had intervened when Beverly had informed her she planned to leave Debra with Webster. "Mothers don't leave their children behind. What kind of woman are you?" Beverly had believed leaving Debra was the right thing to do. She'd known it in her heart, which had been almost eradicated during her marriage, but which still possessed a slight, discernible beat. She had never wanted to be a mother, a thing she admitted to no one. Motherhood had happened to her like a snake bite, sudden, but with a creeping poison. In the end, she'd lacked the courage to leave Debra with Webster, just as she had lacked the courage to attend university despite her parents' refusal. She was the sort of woman who, at the end of that first summer with Clive, told her daughter that Webster would be coming to visit. She had watched her daughter's blooming joy, her anticipation over his arrival, with a keen jealousy she hadn't felt since her pageant days. Of course, Webster had not come, because he had never been coming. When the day of his arrival came and went, when it became clear he would never arrive, Debra had cried with such stark, unabashed ugliness that Beverly felt frightened by it. Still, the lie achieved what she wanted. Debra never expressed her desire to see Webster again.

The woman had started down Beverly's front walk. Beverly considered calling out to her, telling her what she'd always known: she'd been wrong, *wrong*, to take Debra from Webster. With distance between them, with Webster's guidance, she and Debra might have salvaged their relationship. She watched as the woman climbed into her car. Flash of knee, flutter of black dress. Beverly's words had struck this woman's down. She considered chasing her, tapping the window, saying Webster was a broken man, it was true, but a good man. It had been years since they'd seen one another. Perhaps this woman had changed something inside him, had altered him in all the ways Beverly hadn't managed. Perhaps this woman had been the necessary missing link between Webster and the entirety of the world.

Beverly did not chase her. She watched as the woman climbed inside her car. Beverly's car! What had been her actual car, with its paint the color of a queasy leprechaun, its lack of air conditioning because Webster had insisted it wasn't necessary. Flash of knee, flutter of black dress, level chin. Beverly's words had struck this woman down. She arranged her expression into a perfected aloofness. As she'd been taught, she squelched her emotions, willed herself silent, and watched the woman drive away.

"See, Mother?" Beverly would have said, had her mother been standing beside her. "Let there be no doubt about the kind of woman I am."

BEVERLY, 1963

*B*efore she'd quit to devote herself to pageants, Beverly had been a member, briefly, of the high school chess club, which met in the echoing gymnasium after school on Wednesday afternoons. There, Beverly sat with her perfect posture, ankles crossed, surveying the board. The thrill of plotting a plan—of *executing* it—tingled her spine, the tips of her fingers. She'd smooth her skirt, sigh in faux frustration before taking Joseph O'Brien's queen, acting, always, as if her maneuverings were happenstance. *Oops!* Afterward, the club members walked to the drug store for cherry Cokes. Taking long draws on their straws, they discussed what they might have done differently. Beverly returned home high on sugar, following her mother around the kitchen as she recounted the story of besting Joseph O'Brien or Vincent Dunn, Judy Dean. Joseph O'Brien was quite the savant, so deft in his decisions that Beverly could ignore the acne pocking his chin as he sat across from her. Congratulating her, he possessed a firm handshake; looked into her eyes in a way that made her knock-kneed, not because she yearned for Joseph O'Brien's lips against her neck, but because he seemed to appreciate her *brain*.

And then, one night at dinner, over her usual Monday dish of Johnny Marzetti, her mother said that if she was serious about pageants, there wasn't time for chess.

Beverly said, "I *like* it."

"You're old enough to know *that* doesn't matter."

"We pay a lot of money for you to do pageants," her father said. "And we need to know, you are committed? Are you delivering on our investment?"

"And anyway," her mother said, "isn't that time you could use for calisthenics? For reducing?"

The machinations with which she got rid of Edna years later reminded Beverly of those chess-club meetings, minus the camaraderie and Coca-Cola, Joseph O'Brien's firm handshake. Beverly saw a clear path to taking the queen—whose back was turned, whose arms were elbow-deep in gizzards—and she took it. Rome wasn't built in a day, went the saying, and neither was the ousting of Edna Jackson from her home. Beverly planted the seeds, a few at time. As if she'd ever gardened! As if she'd ever cared to watch a seed grow! Pregnant, she'd hated her swollen body, lugging it to and fro like an overpacked duffel. From hers and Webster's bedroom window, Beverly watched Edna kneeling gracefully beside the tomatoes, speaking nonsense to the peppers.

The first time Beverly discovered Webster, she'd walked humming into their bedroom—she'd been in an unusually good mood that day, clear-headed, her depression dissipated—and found him, lipstick smeared on his lips, lying in their bed squeezed into a pair of her pink panties. She'd wondered where those panties had gone, had swept her hand beneath the dressers and bed, searching for them. Well, she'd found them. She thought, *I am large enough for my husband to fit in my panties.* She latched onto this: her magnitude, her own monstrosity.

"You're supposed to be shopping!" he said, and suddenly the discovery became her fault rather than his.

She fled downstairs.

Dinner that evening was frosty, like glassware placed in the freezer for martinis. Beverly stirred herself a martini before sitting down. Dirty, extra olives. She drank with what felt like rapture, like she imagined she was expected to feel when she drank from the gilded goblet the priest held to her lips.

"Well," Edna addressed Debra as they sat at the table, "your mama can't whip potatoes, but at least she can mix a cocktail!"

Webster reached for her hand; Beverly shooed it away.

Edna passed the salad. "Our Beverly is out of sorts this evening, isn't she? Dear, maybe you should lie down."

"Mother, you can't get rid of me *that* easily," said Beverly, and went to mix herself a second martini. Drunk, she carried the jar of olives to the table, eating them from the jar with her fingers as Webster waxed poetic about the chicken marinade.

That night, when her husband reached for her, Beverly straddled him, hoping to convey *she* was the woman here. Not him, but her! Her! She stared down at this man beneath her, who had hours before smeared lipstick upon his lips like a clown. This man who'd told her, Beverly Laurenzi, she who had placed second in the entire state of California—a large state filled with impressive beauties—that perhaps the cut of her dress widened her waist too much. That she shouldn't have worn red during swimsuit! That the hang of her pearls had been wrong!

Wrong, she was wrong. Evidence proved her so. Later she found the tip of her favorite lipstick flattened; the tube of mascara left slightly open, drying; the four-inch heel broken off the left shoe she'd worn to compete in evening wear all those years ago. Her favorite ruby teddy, vanished without a trace! She understood the behavior would not soon end; would never end.

She made her demands quietly at first: a new dress, new heels, a sapphire brooch. She watched Edna shaving a pig's snout in preparation for headcheese, and in her own head, she marked Edna's slight back with an *X*.

One day she left her lacy brassiere out as if it were Snow White's tantalizing apple. She made a show of leaving for the store. She returned to find him wearing the brassiere as she'd known he would be, standing before the mirror, stuffing the cups with tissue.

"It's time, Webster," she said, once he'd dressed himself properly. "Your mother needs her own apartment."

"My mother? An *apartment?*"

"Yes, an apartment."

"My mother doesn't *want* an apartment."

"Have you spoken with her? Do you *know* she doesn't?"

"She absolutely *does not* want an apartment."

"Perhaps she's afraid to tell you. Perhaps she'd like some independence but doesn't want to hurt your feelings."

"Mother has lived in this house for decades."

"Yes," Beverly agreed. "For an excessively long time."

"We'll buy our own home," he said. "Whatever house you want!"

"This moment," said Beverly, "has a smattering of déjà vu."

"Beverly." Desperation pinched his features. "I can't ask my mother to leave her home. I can't."

"All I'm saying," Beverly said, "is that you should ask her. See what she says. She might surprise you."

Part deux involved Edna herself. Late spring turned to summer. Webster tying up loose ends at school, Debra elsewhere, playing dolls or coloring. Beverly found Edna in the kitchen, mincing with deep concentration. Beverly pulled the vodka from the freezer, the ice. She reached into the refrigerator for some dry vermouth and, beneath Edna's critical gaze, mixed a martini.

"Drinking in the afternoon!" said Edna. "I hadn't realized things were quite so desperate!"

"Things have been desperate for some time," said Beverly.

"In any case, don't let Debra see."

Beverly sat at the kitchen table, ankles crossed like Miss Margaret had taught her. Ankles crossed, like she'd once played chess in the school gymnasium. She drank from the martini glass as if she were the queen drinking earl gray from bone china. She watched Edna, dexterously making an onion smaller. "Would you like help?"

"No, thank you."

"Didn't think so." The onion became still smaller; the martini became smaller still.

"Beverly," said Edna. "Is there something you *need*?"

"No."

"You don't usually spend extraneous time in the kitchen."

"I was wondering," Beverly said. "Tell me about Charlotte."

"*Charlotte.*"

"Yes, Charlotte. Webster speaks with great feeling about her."

"Webster speaks about Charlotte?"

Beverly heard the softening in Edna's voice. She set her knife down.

"Frequently," said Beverly, even though he did not, except to say, "Charlotte made excellent gougères that pleased even my father." When Beverly asked, what did Charlotte look like? He answered, "My father thought she resembled a titmouse, but she wasn't completely unfortunate-looking."

"I suppose he would," said Edna.

"He says you were very close when he was growing up."

"Charlotte was like an aunt to Webster."

"That," said Beverly, "would make Charlotte like a sister to you."

"Charlotte was *very much* like a sister to me."

"Did you have that relationship with *all* your sisters?"

Edna paused at the question, as if sensing a trap, then continued. "Well, Frances died when she was quite young. But yes. We were very close."

"Did *Frances* bring you to ensuing ecstasies?"

Beverly would never, for as long as she lived, forget the look on Edna's face. Her eyes widened; her mouth caved in like a failed soufflé. She soon smoothed her shock back into normalcy, rendering herself as immobile as a Roman statue in a museum, but Beverly had seen it. Then Edna took up the onion again, as though to steady herself.

Beverly continued airily, "Did your lips travel the private crevices of Frances's body, or just Charlotte's? Are you an explorer of *all* women's crevices?"

Beverly waited for Edna to grip the edge of the counter, as she'd seen in television shows when mothers learned their sons had lost limbs in war, or died in car crashes; when they learned they themselves had been diagnosed with cancer and had only months to live. Edna merely continued her chopping. When she'd finished, she turned to face Beverly. She studied her wordlessly.

"I found your letters," said Beverly.

Edna said, "So I surmised."

"I read every one. They were certainly smutty. Come," Beverly patted the chair beside her. "Let's talk."

Edna sat. Without asking, Beverly mixed two more martinis, placing Edna's before her with care.

"I think you prefer a twist, but since you're not in a position to barter, I took the liberty of giving you an olive."

Over the rim of the glass, Edna regarded her warily.

Beverly asked, "Does anyone know? I mean, of course, besides me?"

"Of course not!"

"Would you like them to?"

Drawing herself up, Edna replied with dignity, "You know the answer to that."

"Webster is going to ask you if you'd like an apartment," said Beverly. "I'm going to recommend that you consider it."

There was a long pause before Edna responded. "An apartment."

"Yes. In Berkeley."

"Berkeley," repeated Edna, her expression stony.

"I've found a very modern place. There's no yard, but I'm sure you don't need the inconvenience of *that*."

"I see," said Edna.

"Very clean!" said Beverly. "Filled with all the latest trappings. I know how you love amenities."

Edna lifted her chin. "My son will never ask me to leave my home."

"I think he will." Beverly smiled, eliciting another long pause.

"Who's to say anyone will believe you?" Edna finally ventured. "Who's to say you're not lying?"

Beverly reached over to pat Edna's hand. "You might want to hide those letters," she said, "before someone snatches them. Or perhaps someone already has."

The place she found Edna! Any modern woman would have been pleased. Wall-to-wall carpeting. Freshly painted walls. Brand new electric range. New refrigerator with a squeaky-clean plastic smell. A galley kitchen she wouldn't have to kill herself to clean!

"It's so square," said Webster when he saw it.

Beverly had indeed chosen the squarest apartment she could find. She had imagined slipping Edna inside it as if it were a cage, Edna nothing more than an animal.

Webster said, "It's so *plain*."

Beverly answered, "It's a blank canvas! It's an opportunity! Your mother can make it anything she wants!"

Edna took very little with her to the new apartment, as if she'd already begun plotting her departure from the earth and was shucking the burden of objects. Webster loaded her few things into the car, his face drawn with guilt, his hand constantly reaching to touch the small of his mother's back. Edna turned from him with a newfound coldness.

"Kiss your grandmother," Beverly instructed Debra, who buried her face in Edna's legs.

Beverly did not wave them off, but rather stood stoically as the car pulled down the street and turned the corner. Edna was gone—*finally!*—from their daily lives. Setting her daughter before the television, Beverly took up Edna's good scissors—the ones used *only* for fabric—and strolled to the garden to cut the blooms from Edna's prized rose bushes. Snip, snip. Snip, snip. Stem after stem. The blooms collected in a heap in the grass. When she'd finished with the roses, Beverly sliced through the baby lettuces in the raised bed, she chopped up the herbs. *Chiffonade* was the word Edna would have used. She ripped the tomatoes from the vines; so many tomatoes. Imagining herself a baseball pitcher, she chucked them as far as she could throw them. She went through the green bean plant, finding each pod and cutting every one neatly in half.

Surveying her handiwork, she felt some satisfaction. Not enough. Not nearly enough. Beverly then took Edna's gardening shears, the ones used *only* for the rose bushes. She retrieved Charlotte's letters and carried them and the shears to the driveway. There, she made a chiffonade of Charlotte's letters, slicing frantically, maniacally. The wind frittered the pieces away, carted them off like confetti. She watched them, buffeted by the wind, and understood she'd been overzealous in her optimism. There was as yet nothing different. There was as yet nothing to celebrate.

BEVERLY, 2001

This morning, Debra had called, coughing into the phone.

"This is the fourth time you've cancelled lunch," said Beverly.

"You're counting?"

"Of course not."

"I'm *sick*."

"You have a tickle in your throat."

"Mother, it's flu season."

"Have you gone to the doctor?"

"I haven't."

"If you're on death's door, perhaps you should visit the ER," said Beverly.

"I'm not *on death's door*."

"Then we can meet for lunch."

"I'm sorry," said Debra. "I can't."

"I'll bring you lunch," Beverly said, a thing she'd never in her life offered. "Broth and ginger ale. Tea. Things sick people like."

"No," Debra said. "No, thank you."

Debra wasn't sick, only avoiding her, though Beverly couldn't guess why. Her daughter had cancelled four lunches (*yes*, Beverly had counted). This did not include the rash of excuses Debra had used to avoid making plans in the first place: a bake sale at Jamie's school, a fundraiser that involved cycling on a stationary bike for three hours during lunch on a random Wednesday, a special yoga class that would help open one's heart, an appointment with the gynecologist.

"You scheduled such a thing during *lunchtime*?"

"It was the time available."

"Thursday, then," Beverly said early last week.

"Mother, I'd love to, but I'm chaperoning Jamie's field trip that day."

"Where to?"

"What?"

"Where are you taking the children?"

"The La Brea Tar Pits."

"Isn't he a bit old for that?"

"His class is going with a younger class."

"I see."

"It's an exercise in building interclass morale."

"Interclass morale! Did you just make that up?"

"Of course not!"

"Well, then. Interclass morale. What a lovely concept. Friday, then."

"Friday, I'm having lunch with James."

"You're having lunch with your *husband*."

"People do that, you know."

"You don't," said Beverly.

"He's trying."

"Well, isn't that nice," Beverly said. "So many nice things! Where are you lunching?"

"It's a surprise."

"How lovely!"

"Yes," said Debra.

Debra had never been particularly adroit at lying. When she lied, her face grew red, her voice became shrill. Beverly had once pulled her aside to say she needed to stop. Not because lying was *wrong*, necessarily, but because it did nothing for her appearance.

"Next week," Debra said. "All right?"

Hanging up, Beverly paged through the phonebook, searching for Jamie's school. *No*, the office woman said. There was no scheduled field trip to the La Brea Tar Pits in any grade.

On Friday, Beverly drove to Debra's house. She discovered it decorated for Halloween, a holiday Beverly found odious, with its arched black cats and glowering pumpkins, its openhanded children barking for candy in their makeshift costumes. Debra had hung countless tissue-paper ghosts from the trees on the front lawn. She'd hung the silhouettes of bats. Beverly traipsed across the yard to examine them. They were *homemade*! Debra had spent time *crafting* such things! She lacked time for lunch but had enough to carve pumpkins; they adorned the front walk with their toothy grins and mis-shapen eyes. Debra's wasn't the only house on the street decorated for the holiday, but the tackiness of the decorations stood out like severed thumbs. A car Beverly didn't know was parked in the driveway. Not the cleaning woman's car; Nina came on Tuesdays and Thursdays. Beverly continued to the back of the house, let herself in through the garage. James's car was absent, but Debra's car remained in its spot. Liar.

In the kitchen, Beverly found dishes still piled in the sink. Chinese con-tainers had been left on the kitchen island, plastic forks still stuck in their half-eaten contents. Nothing offended Beverly—nothing screamed abject laziness—like plastic cutlery, people eating prepared food straight out of containers when plates and silverware were at hand. A half-drunk bottle of sauvignon blanc remained on the counter. It was barely one o'clock! Beverly poured herself a glass.

In the family room, throw pillows had been tossed from the couch. A crumpled blanket remained on the cushions. Two empty wine glasses sat on the coffee table. Beverly pushed these glasses aside, set her own glass down. She sat on the couch. Listened, waited. She'd sit here until her daughter came downstairs. She'd ask, what did she have against lunch? What did she have against her *mother*? Beverly crossed her legs. Recrossed them. She consulted her watch. The house's silence proved deafening, but occasionally Beverly thought she heard something. Voices, laughter. Muffled, as if one were hearing them underwater, through the murmur of the ocean. Then everything grew silent again, suggesting she'd heard nothing at all, had only imagined it. Bored, she finished off her wine. Soon, she found herself climbing the stairs to investigate.

Nothing doing in Debra and James's bedroom; it remained as dull, as in-nocuous, as always. Beverly examined her reflection in the formidable mir-ror. There was no denying it: she looked *old*. Age had come for her, finally. Or perhaps it had come for her long ago, and she'd avoided the truth of the matter. The lighting in this room exposed everything, like the lighting in a low-end department store's dressing room. Beverly tilted her chin this way and that, trying to find an angle that didn't cause a rising panic. And then she heard it. *Laughter*, coming from one of the guest bedrooms. She walked quietly down the wide hallway. The laughter came from behind a closed door. She strained to hear. Her daughter's voice and another voice. Certainly not James's voice. A woman's, chilling Beverly's insides. *Miss Real Cool*. She held her breath. Words sounded as if spoken into pillows, things she lacked the fortitude to decipher. Beverly slipped into a strange, floating reverie as she listened, like a child succumbing to a lullaby in the strongest moment of fatigue. What shocked her back to reality was Debra's laugh; Beverly could not remember the last time she'd heard it. And here was Debra, laughing a deep, throaty laughter, a foreign sound, as if she'd become suddenly fluent in another language—French, Italian, Russian—and Beverly could only listen without comprehension, without response.

In the car, she took herself away as quickly as she could. She drove, considering the situation. How to proceed. She could return to Debra's house, force a scene. In front of a strange woman with whom her daughter lay in bed, Beverly could explode: *What was Debra doing?! What was she thinking?!* The men on talk radio talked, talked, and Beverly settled a bit. She could explode or she could disappear; she could wait it out, like she'd waited out countless other phases of Debra's life, feigning patience. Debra was the queen of phases. Beverly needed the fingers of both hands to count them all: the time Debra wanted to play a musical instrument, the time she took painting classes, or the time she wrote poems. "Listen, Mother. Listen." (Beverly, sighing over the newspaper, would say, "Why all this creative expression? No one is as interesting as they think they are.") As an adult, there had been the costume jewelry phase, the yoga practiced in the heated room. Something called pilates performed on a strange contraption. The time she passed out at the club on the sixth day of a lemon-and-chili cleanse. The time she'd started meditating. The entire year she'd believed in mantras. The time when her mother discovered her in bed with a woman, pretending to be someone other than who she was, a married woman with a son, a family. She'd taken Halloween to depths Beverly hadn't believed possible.

The only consolation, Beverly realized, was that her daughter was not a woman to *actually* change things. She was too fearful to pursue her own happiness. She might consider it. She might flirt with the notion. But when push came to shove, nothing would actually move her to action.

She was like her father in this, in so many, ways.

WEBB, 1983

*L*eaving Los Angeles, Webb drove, alone, back to Oakland. Hila had gone, but left the car. Had she taken a bus? Surely, she would be waiting at home for him. Letting himself into the house, he called into the stillness, "Hello! Hello?"

She wasn't there. He guessed she'd gone to her apartment in the hills. Fine, she needed space. Alone in her tiny apartment, she would realize her presence was a condition for his survival, as his was for hers, as essential as air and food and water. Together, they were symbiotic. Two halves forming a necessary whole. Hila loved him with the ferocity of a protective animal. Her return was inevitable. As such, he found temporary respite in her absence. It took such energy to love and be loved; to constantly toss emotion back and forth like a hot potato. In her absence, he exhaled, skirted the ever-present sense of accountability. ("Yes," she would have said, tickled by his language, "of course you *skirted* it.") He donned the beautiful clothes she'd made him and cooked boeuf bourguignon, potatoes dauphinoise, cassoulet. He set beautiful tables for himself, poured wine they'd selected together. He relished the lack of pressure to give, to explain, to delve.

For three weeks, he lived without her. And then one night, pouring wine into the coq au vin, the realization of her absence swept in. The pain of missing her swallowed him like a black and parasitic thing. *Oh*, he never wanted to eat coq au vin without her. He dropped the wine bottle onto the linoleum with a thud. It rolled to the nether space beneath the table as he reached for the phone.

"Webster!" Her voice contained an underlying thread he couldn't decipher. A muffled sound came through the line.

"You're laughing!"

"If you want to call it that. It isn't as simple as laughter. It's just, I know you so well."

"You do!" Encouraged, he asked, "When are you coming home?"

"I *am* home."

This statement, spoken firmly, made him uneasy, but he reasoned she'd always been persnickety about language. "When are you coming back *here*?"

"I am never," she said, "going back *there*."

A tendril of alarm snaked through him. "But you love me!"

"There aren't enough words to explain my love for you," she agreed.

"Don't you miss me?"

"I will always miss you."

Her tone, definitive, shook his heart. Alarm blossomed to full-blown panic. "I need you," he said.

"Need is irrelevant. Suspicious." Her voice had grown lean. "Please, anything but need."

"I love you!"

"Webster. I will not be returning to you. Nothing you say will persuade me."

"You need time."

"Decades will not change my mind."

"You're being histrionic."

Silence swelled between them like a bite. Fine. They would be silent together in the easy way they'd often been silent, and in the span of this silence, she would realize she loved him and he loved her and that leaving him would be a mistake.

"I coddled you," she said finally.

"You didn't," he said, and knew she had.

"I believed I was doing a good thing. It gave me such pleasure to coddle you. But it's done neither of us favors. Webster, I'm getting off the phone now."

"No. Please!"

"Goodbye."

Days later, still bereft, he took the large dictionary down from the bookshelf in the living room. He looked up *coddle* and read: *1. To cook (as in eggs) in liquid slowly and gently just below the boiling point. 2. To treat with extreme or excessive care or kindness, pamper.*

Mollycoddle, a synonym for coddle, the dictionary informed him, origi-
nally meant a person who coddled himself; or it meant an effeminate man.
Herein lay a paradox: yes, maybe Hila had coddled him, seeing his need,
seeing he'd never been as effeminate as he'd yearned to be. Without her, he
never would be. Despite his longing, he'd only played at being other than
he was. In reality, there had never been anything except indecision inside
him. Hila had tried to show him the way, but he hadn't allowed it. He had
not changed himself.

In the ensuing weeks, he realized he might have won her back. ("Knowledge," Hila liked to say, "never wins awards for its punctuality.") He should
have driven to her apartment, banged the door down, knocked things over,
swept her up in a tumultuous passion. Should have taken her by her thin
shoulders and kissed her, kissed her! He'd called her as if phoning in a pizza
order. That call had been the defining moment in a previously ambiguous
situation; had been the reason she laughed. It proved to her who he was.
Egocentric, devoid of self-reflection. Neither an adequate man nor an adequate woman, only a failed, muddled version of both. He resided neither in
the body he wished for nor the body he possessed. Hila understood: snagged
in his chronic ambivalence, Webb would never give her what she deserved.
Overshadowed by his yearnings, her own would always be forgotten.

She'd been gone a year when Webb, beneath the residue of the night's
alcohol and angst, woke with a start remembering her heady declaration
years earlier: *A life devoid of fairies would be a life without meaning.* She'd not
taken any fairies when she'd gone. He would bring them to her.

Wrangling himself from bed, he looked up her address in the telephone
book, ashamed not to know it. Ashamed he had never insisted: *give up
that damn apartment. Live with me.* Was this where the crack, now cleaving
them, had originated? He plotted. His would be a covert operation in the
night. He would transport the fairies from his yard to hers in a definitive
proclamation of his love. To win her back, he must act.

In his yard, he took fairy inventory. He counted fairies and ceased counting fairies because too many fairies existed to count. He located fairies in
the crevices of the yard and carried them to the car, arranging them in the
backseat of the pea-green Impala like obedient children. He lay them on the
floorboards and packed them in the passenger's seat. Locked them inside

the trunk: sorry, fairies! When Hila did a thing, she did a thing. When Hila committed herself to the purchasing of fairies, she committed herself to the purchasing of fairies. When she committed herself to Webb, she committed herself to Webb. Hila was not, had never been, the problem.

In the darkest part of the night, he drove the fairy-filled Impala into the hills. The sky was clear and starry, an anomaly. He pulled to the side of the road and clambered out. Across the bay, San Francisco blinked with lights. What beauty! How many years ago had he and his mother taken the ferry there? They'd shopped in the department stores and afterward lunched at Blum's, drinking dark coffee and eating coffee crunch cake. To the left was the Golden Gate; to the right was Mount Tamalpais sheathed in fog. The wind tossed up Webb's dress, chilled his bare legs. The bay's beauty squeezed his heart. Like relegating cake to the garbage bin, he pushed his emotions down, *down,* and climbed back into the car.

Hila's apartment was on the bottom floor of a quaint stucco duplex with a small yard. Seeing her car on the street, his pulse quickened. It was three o'clock in the morning. No light shined from the rooms. There were no lights in the yard. He disapproved of this lack of lighting. Once she'd returned to him, he'd reprimand her for this. It wasn't safe! Men could hide in her bushes, waiting to ambush her. Here *he* was, a man toting ceramic fairies into her yard in the dead of night.

He'd brought a flashlight. Careful not to shine the beam at the dark windows, he surveyed the terracotta pots and their plants spilled across the grass. Small signs in Hila's penmanship declared what the plants were. Exclamation points followed the names, implied her joy at having grown these things in these containers. *Mint! Tarragon! Japanese Eggplant! Zucchini Squash!* Tucking the flashlight under his armpit, he plucked the herbs she'd planted, breathed the scent of them. He lifted his dress into a makeshift receptacle, and inside it he placed two eggplants and several zucchini. He took these things because they were Hila's. She had grown and tended them. Holding his dress as a basket, exposing a length of white thigh, he carried his goods to the car.

"Mallowfruits are fairy cheeses," he remembered her saying. "And dogwood fruits are pixie pears. Saffron is fairy salt and cherished by all."

He arranged fairies on the outdoor bistro table. Nestled them inside the curl of garden hose. Amongst the tangles of ivy, the tall grasses. He lined fairies on the back porch steps, formed a cancan of fairies across the cement patio, like those Rockettes Beverly had wanted so badly to see. He sat fairies in chairs. Rested them in votives atop melted wax. Tired, he sat for a moment in an Adirondack chair, holding a forlorn fairy. He stared at Hila's duplex. She was inside those walls; this was the nearest he'd been to her in an entire year. He imagined breaking the door down, rushing inside to love her.

The next thing he knew, dawn stabbed the sky, and a man shook him awake.

"Webster!" Hollis loomed over him. Hollis, wearing a plaid flannel pajama set and moccasin slippers, like a middle-aged parent in a cartoon strip. Webb tried to move, but his limbs were stiff from cold. His dress had ridden up to an embarrassing height. At the corner of his mind flashed that morning, long ago, in which he'd woken to Clive Murdoch's vise grip on his ankles. He felt frozen.

"You need to leave," Hollis said. "Before she sees you."

"She's with you." The statement came out as an accusation.

"Yes, Webster. She's with me."

How had this happened? His mind and body thawed, roared back to life. In his hand was the weight of the forlorn fairy. Webb clenched the fairy and raised it up. A weapon? An offering?

"Put the fairy down, Webster," said Hollis.

Webb's hand shook.

Hollis pried open Webb's fingers and removed the fairy. Gently. With care. Was this what Hila saw in him? That Webb, having never coddled her, left her needing to be coddled?

"Please," said Webb. "Can I see her?"

"She doesn't want to see you. Let her go."

Hollis did not invite him inside, serve coffee and danish. What he did was collect the fairies and load them once again into the car. After a while, Webb lifted his head to watch. When all the fairies had been rounded up and stashed in the Impala, Webb stood, walked to the car, slid behind the wheel.

As he drove away, his eyes caught Hollis's in the rearview mirror. The man stood in the middle of the street in his flannel pajamas and moccasin slippers and did not wave goodbye.

Webb later received two letters from her. The first arrived in 1985, a textured aubergine envelope he couldn't stop touching. He smoothed its bent corners, its stamp—an image of a New England neptune, or wrinkled whelk. With a fingertip he brushed the return address: *Hila P. Firestone, 543 Charring Cross Road*.

"What does the *P* stand for?" he'd asked years ago.

"Nothing," she said. "Everything. Anything. I made it up because I liked the sound of it. Today I feel like Patricia. But tomorrow I could be Pamela or Pinna or Phoebe or Paige or Penelope or Piper or Pandora."

"Pandora?"

"Yes, Pandora."

Opening the envelope seemed akin to opening the mythical box. Webb could not bring himself to do it. She loved Hollis, a dullard with an expression suggesting chronic constipation. She was writing to say: *Webster, I love Hollis*. Not wanting to read these words in her lovely handwriting, he tucked the letter in his dresser drawer, under his special things.

The stamp of the second letter, which arrived five years later, bore the image of a common dolphin. He'd never before considered whether dolphins were common or uncommon. He laid the second letter beside the first, comparing them. Hila formed letters differently depending on which letters neighbored them, on whether the letters began a word or were sandwiched inside that word. How had he never noticed this? The penmanship on the second letter seemed different, though he couldn't pinpoint how. Both letters sang their siren songs to him. *Open me*. But once he did, he would have only the stark truth before him. It was easier to know nothing, to pretend, to relive the accumulated memories, dwell in the thickness of the years past.

"Just think of all the things," Hila used to say, her beautiful mouth carefully forming the consonants and vowels. "The things that make up a life. All the tiny beauties that make it yours."

For those thirteen years with Hila, there had been beauty. Countless beauties. Now he plodded forth as though harnessed to a wagon, aware of the gap between what he'd imagined and what had come to be.

One Sunday among many indistinguishable Sundays, as Webb drank coffee, trying to break through the haze of the alcohol he'd consumed the night before, he thought he smelled something burning. He then heard the distant sirens and turned on the television. On the screen, the Niners played Detroit. Joe Montana was on injured reserve with a neck injury. This Steve Young character would be starting at quarterback. Barry Sanders posed his usual threat. John Madden called the game, and it was Madden who mentioned the six-alarm fire across the bay, in Oakland. The camera cut to the image of the sky over the stadium with its smoldering halo. Ash was falling onto the field.

Opening the front door, Webb stepped into thick smoke. Fluttery bits fell from above. The sun loomed, odd and orange, a formidable thing with blurred edges. How long had it been since he'd stood outside with Hila, her pointing him to the location of her apartment on the hill above them, a spot now billowing and black. "There. I live there."

Inside, he dialed her number. The phone company's polite recording declared it out of service. He located the cumbersome phone book and found Hollis's number. Dialing it, he heard an insistent buzzing. He dialed it and dialed it again, then dialed it once more. Finally, he heard no dial tone, only ominous silence. He went into the bathroom and vomited into the toilet bowl. He then poured himself bourbon and sat dialing "Mary Had a Little Lamb" on the phone, as Hila had once taught him: *3212333 222.399.32123333322321.*

Nothing remained except to drink bourbon and watch the television, merge the images on the screen with the dark, pressing reality outside his door—the circling helicopters, the swell and retreat of sirens. Webb dragged the telephone cord across the living room, sat with the phone in his lap. He waited for it, like a man concussed, to come to. On the television, people ran frantically, cars drove over flaming debris. Women cried. Men shouted. Residents sprayed their homes with garden hoses. Trees combusted. Trees fell.

Once, hiking in Redwood Regional Park with Hila after a storm, they came upon a downed tree blocking the path. "Look." Hila pointed. "It's treemageddon."

Hila's number remained out of service when the phone lines opened. Pacing, Webb tried Hollis's. The man answered hesitantly, as if worried what terror might exist on the other end of the line.

"Hollis!" Webb cried into the phone. "Hollis, it's Webster!"

"Yes," said Hollis, as though confirming Webb was Webb.

Webb said, "Hila! Have you talked to Hila?"

Silence followed.

"The phone line is still down!"

"The phone line is *disconnected*, Webster."

"You've spoken with her?"

"Have you been drinking?" Hollis asked. "Are you drunk?"

"Of course I haven't been drinking!" Webb banished his glass of bourbon to a distant corner of the table where he could forget he'd ever poured it. "Goddamn it, Hollis. I'm asking about Hila. Is she all right?"

"She's dead."

All of Hollis's overwrought words began with *D*: *disconnected, drinking, drunk, dead*. In the aftermath of this statement, inside its clattering confusion, Webb's knees buckled. He asked, "In the fire?"

Twenty-five people had died. The fire chief had died, as had cats and dogs and birds. Cameras and silverware had melted. Papers and books had disintegrated, their remnants traveling though the wind, across the bay to San Francisco, ash settling like snow.

"No, Webster. Not in the fire." Hollis spoke without inflection, as though reading the news. "She passed some time ago."

"That's not possible," said Webb. He would have sensed it. Felt the difference in the atmosphere, the earth. Had he truly been walking around on an earth bereft of Hila and not known? Anger rose in him at this injustice. Rage bloomed behind his eyes, blurring his vision. "How?" he demanded. "Why didn't anyone tell me?"

"Hila told you," said Hollis, an edge creeping into his voice.

"Hila never—"

"She sent you a letter," Hollis said. "I mailed it myself."

Webb hung up. His eyes stung as though burning ash had flown into them, watered as though trying to cleanse themselves of debris. She would have laughed at him: *Oh*, Webster. *If the woman you love sends a letter, open it! Don't hoard it like a drop of water in the desert! Study it like an epic poem, like you'll be tested on its contents! Don't bury it inside a dresser drawer because you fear it, as cats fear snakes and men fear cats.* (Men fear cats? he would have asked her.) *It's so like you to avoid the things you fear.*

He retrieved his bourbon from its banishment, carrying it to the bedroom, where he freed the letters from beneath the silken things in his dresser. He smoothed his thumb along the edges of the first envelope, which was dirty from years of him fondling it, the eggplant color deeper in places, darkened by the oils from his fingers. He turned it over, turned it again. And then, like dunking himself into the coldest of lake water, he opened the envelope and removed the letter, written on the prettiest marbled paper. Her perfect penmanship conveyed what he'd expected:

Webster, love. I want you to hear it from me. I'm marrying Hollis.

He steeled himself and opened the second letter, which said what Hollis told him it would say:

My love. I am dying.

He exhaled, gathered the scattered shards of himself, read on.

Months ago, they staved my illness by taking my breasts. Tit for tat. (Tit!) They carted them off as I slept. Took them like unwanted things, but the truth is I want them terribly, I miss them terribly. I understand, now, your compulsion to have them. You weren't missing anything, I said. I don't need them, don't even want them. Now I'd fight to the death to keep them. I will fight to the death, and still I won't have them. All those times, Webster, you chose plunging necklines and I asked you to please, show restraint. I was wrong; you were right. You saw beauty. You wanted to show this beauty to the world.

It feels Frankensteinian, my love, when they start taking body parts.

Webster, I have a cat now! She sits beside me as I write this, though I yearn for her as if she's already gone. As if I'm already gone. I've memorized the exact feel of my face in her fur, the weight of her body as she sleeps on my chest. I memorize every bodily thing because soon this body will be gone. I miss all of it already. I miss you, Webster.

I read recently that cats, aware that death is near, go off quietly to die. They find a place beyond the reach of their owners' worry. I imagine this place as a tree, and beneath the canopy of whatever beautiful tree they've chosen, they die.

Webster, you would be my chosen tree. I would go to you through the tangle of herbs we planted in the garden, through the glorious tomatoes, and I would lie there, beside the beauty of you, until I was gone.

The letter fluttered to the ground. He'd finished his bourbon but couldn't muster the will or strength to pour another. Instead, he crawled into his bed, pulled the covers over his head as his world burned. He wept.

The next day, he dialed Hollis again. "Who has the cat?"

"What cat?"

"In the letter, Hila says she has a cat."

"I have no idea what you're talking about!" said Hollis, and though the situation was desperate, dire—ah, here were the *Ds* again—Webb laughed.

"I don't understand what's funny," said Hollis.

"You're a terrible liar!"

"No one's lying!"

"It's the last time I'm asking." Webb did his best impersonation of a heavy in a mob drama. "Where's the cat?"

"I'm hanging up now," said Hollis. "Goodbye!"

Webb stood holding the receiver. Finally, it buzzed at him, and he dropped it in its cradle. He felt uncharacteristically compelled toward action, as if Hila stood beside him, whispering into his ear what to do next. Upstairs, he changed into a silken frock she had sewn for him. Loose and lacy, it had always been one of his favorites. Dressed, he went to the dining room and opened the bottom drawer of the china cabinet. Inside this drawer was a box emblazoned with the name of a pastry shop that no longer existed, the shop's name in gilded cursive. This box might have once contained an over-frosted piece of cake. It might have contained the prettiest of pale-pink macarons. It contained, instead, his father's .38 special with its shiny wooden handle. Webb carried the box to the car in both hands, holding tight as though it might squirm free. And then he drove to Berkeley.

Hollis was one of those private people whose street address wasn't listed in the phone book. He lived, Webb remembered, in a tiny house on Grant Street. He'd gone there once, twice with Hila years before. Certainly, he did not remember the number of the house. He conjured its memory: ratty yard devoid of fairies, slanting fence, worn steps. He slowly drove the length of Grant toward University and back again, looking. Cars honked. He waved them around. In his next life, he would remember where people lived. And then. Yes, that one. Webb parked in the drive behind what he presumed was Hollis's car. He took the unloaded gun, decorative but necessary, from the pastry box.

Webb had never threatened anyone with a gun, loaded or otherwise. This was a virgin experience, like his first time with Beverly on the Santa Cruz sands beside the decorative Pacific. He'd told Hila of his icy baptism earlier that day, and she'd cried, "The northern Pacific isn't utilitarian! It's like a figurine one keeps on the mantel. It's the coffee-table book of oceans."

Holding the .38 low at his side, he walked steadily to Hollis's front door and rang the bell. Its quotidian dong provided no forewarning of a madman gripping a firearm on the front porch.

I've become my father, Webb thought. *All this time, I've been my father.*

Hollis opened the door in a bathrobe, his hair wet. "Fuck," he said when he saw Webb.

"I'm here for the cat."

Hollis sighed noisily. "I told you, I have no idea what you're talking about." His bathrobe did not have a belt. He held the door with one hand and tried to cinch the bathrobe with the other. "There is no cat."

"It was Hila's cat!" Webb said.

Hollis shrugged. "I like dogs."

Webb raised the gun from his side. He waved it as he imagined one did for dramatic purposes, circling it through the air as though lassoing something. Then he recalled how his father had pointed this same gun at the neighbor, and Webb aimed the weapon squarely at Hollis's chest.

"Fuck, Webster!" Hollis stumbled backward. "What are you thinking?"

Keeping the .38 trained on the place where Hollis's lackluster heart lived—that paltry organ, that tepid sack of meat—Webb pushed his way into Hollis's living room.

"I don't want trouble," Webb said.

"You're pointing a *gun* at my chest."

"I just want the cat."

"There is no cat!"

Hollis's eyes betrayed him. Webb saw them shift infinitesimally to a corner of the room. Webb's own eyes went there. The cat slept soundly on a rocking chair, paw pressed over her eyes to block the sunlight. When she removed her paw, the golden markings on her face resembled the sun from which she'd shielded her eyes.

"Please," said Hollis. "It's the only thing I have left of her."

"Say your goodbyes."

Hollis's face dissolved in tears. The sound of his crying clogged Webb's brain. Making an effort to focus, he pointed the gun at Hollis's forehead. "Find me a carrier."

"What?" Hollis stopped crying.

"A cat carrier. A thing that carries a cat."

"I know what it is!" said Hollis. "You came to steal a cat without a carrier?" He fisted his hands on his hips, and his bathrobe swung open.

"For fuck's sake, Hollis, cover yourself up or I'll shoot it off."

"You're not going to shoot me over a cat."

"Try me!"

"Save your energy. She doesn't like being transported." Hollis disappeared into the bedroom. Webb heard the opening and closing of closet doors. Hollis returned with the carrier.

Webb fluttered the gun. "I need the cat *in* the carrier."

"This is your deal," Hollis said.

"I'll shoot your lamp into bits!"

Hollis rolled his eyes.

"I'll shoot your eye out!"

"Fine, I have two."

"I'll shoot myself!"

"Please."

"You'll be cleaning bits of my brain from your carpet."

"If you introduce a gun in the first act," said Hollis. "You'd better use it in the third."

Webb said, "You were always insufferable."

Hollis sighed and went to rouse the cat from the rocking chair. Upon seeing the carrier, she transformed at once into a scratching, yowling demon. Hollis attempted to cage her in his arms. As he did, the cat screeched and clawed and pissed on him and onto the floor. Hollis, too, was shouting. His bathrobe fell open. His penis flapped.

"Cover that up!" yelled Webb.

"Fuck!" Hollis screamed. "I'm trying to do a thing!"

Webb saw he had no choice but to put the gun down and hold the carrier steady while Hollis shoved the cat, writhing and arching and howling, into it. When Hollis finally latched the carrier's door and drew his hand away, Webb saw the lashings. Blood dripped onto Hollis's carpet. Webb went into the kitchen for a dish towel and handed it to Hollis, who had slumped to the floor beside the carrier. Hollis pressed the towel wordlessly against his wounds. Webb sank onto the floor beside him and asked, "Why are you letting me take the cat?"

"If you'd been a different sort of person," Hollis said, "I never would have gotten to love her."

Webb stared at Hollis's white wall.

"This dramatic posturing," said Hollis. "The cat, the gun. It's too little, too late. It means nothing. You never came to see her after she wrote that letter. She was dying, and you never came."

"I never opened it," said Webb.

Hollis laughed without humor. "She said you wouldn't. Knew you wouldn't." He fumbled in the terrycloth pocket of his bathrobe for a cigarette, then matches.

Webb watched as Hollis lit the cigarette. "I didn't think you smoked."

"Yeah, well. New habit."

"I think I'll start again," Webb said. He stood. He shoved the gun in his pocket. "By the way, it's not loaded," he said.

In the carrier, the cat cried.

Hollis nodded at it and said, "If you want to gain her trust, feed her tuna fish."

"Hila hated tuna fish," Webb said.

"She loved you. I got to be with her, but she loved you. I hate you for it."

"I hate you," said Webb. He lifted the carrier and left Hollis sitting against the wall.

DEBRA, 2001

Thanksgiving arrived, and I braced myself for the impact of the family gathering. My mother, entering my house, gave my cheek a succinct kiss and requested champagne. My father wanted a manhattan. My husband mixed the latter, the only act he'd performed with gusto for weeks. *Clink clink clink* went the stirring spoon inside the glass. Pretending to need flour, I stood unmoving inside the pantry amid the sugar and beans. The brunt of the holiday lay before me, formidable. When I returned to the living room with canapés, the television blared football. My father sipped his drink and read the newspaper. My husband held a tumbler of whiskey and stared out the window. Jamie sat on the couch playing a handheld device. My mother, believing no one watched, poured herself more champagne.

I'd imagined myself cooking dinner for Colleen. I'd brined the turkey before roasting it, fried the Brussels sprouts until crispy. Colleen loved bread; I made dinner rolls from scratch. She loved butternut squash; I made butternut squash soup, a thing I'd never before served. My husband slogged through the meal, squinting at his soup as if he'd spotted something drowning inside it. Afterward, he tossed his cloth napkin onto the plate, a gesture I found uncivilized for someone who'd grown up eating in fine restaurants. Pushing his chair from the table, he asked, "We're finished here, right?"

"There's still *pie*," my mother said, seeming incredulous at his desertion, though I'd never seen her eat pie.

"Have a piece for me."

"Stay," my mother said. "Eat your own."

He pretended he hadn't heard her. He appeared jovial as he disappeared into his office. Following suit, my son excused himself. Then my father settled in for a nap on the couch, hand shoved inside the band of his pants. My mother and I stared at each other across the wreckage of the dining table.

"It's a holiday," my mother said.

"It is."

"It's important for families to be together."

I asked, "Since when do you care about family togetherness?"

"Always!" she said.

For years, we'd celebrated holidays with countless others at the club. Turkey buffets on Thanksgiving, carving stations on Easter. Champagne brunches for Mother's Day. Even the annual Christmas party—hosted in my mother's home, but always catered—comprised a slew of people unfamiliar to me, making small talk over hors d'oeuvres. Formal affairs, diluted by strangers. My mother hadn't cooked a single holiday dinner for our family, nor cleaned up after one. Until now. I watched as she helped clear the table, carrying plates to the kitchen with two hands as if they might detonate, sending shrapnel into her face.

"Where's Nina?"

"With her family. But also, I let Nina go. She started drinking."

"*Nina?*"

"She would help herself to the open bottles of wine in the refrigerator and on the counter. She'd put them back, thinking I wouldn't notice."

"Nina would never do that."

"Mother, have you ever had a conversation with Nina? Do you talk to Simone? Did you ever talk to Violetta? She cleaned our house for years until you fired her."

"I talked to Violetta," my mother said.

"I never saw you."

"And anyway." She eyed her empty glass. "People drink. Your husband has a basement full of wine."

"I didn't care about the wine," I said. "It was the deception. Also she took something important to me and said she didn't. Something personal."

"What did she take?" my mother asked, but because I couldn't tell her about the jewelry box and what was in it, I went to get the pies. I couldn't explain that Nina had taken a thing my mother didn't even know I possessed. "Pack a bag," my mother had said that final morning in Oakland.

I had packed clothes, and though I hadn't consciously known I'd never return, I had packed the turquoise box with its newspaper articles.

"You went overboard," my mother said when I set out the pies. "As usual."

I borrowed her words. "It's a holiday."

"There's pie for twenty people."

"There is." Baking had calmed me, like pranayama practice in yoga. I cut butter into neat cubes, measured flour, sifted it. Sliced fruit, toasted nuts. Immersed in the meditation of making, I hadn't stopped.

"It's excessive," said my mother, ever the hypocrite.

"Better excess than a regime of denial." This was something my father— not Clive—would say when she judged him for eating decadent things. With a sly smile, he'd swoop to kiss her cheek as she pushed him away.

My mother rolled her eyes, but her color rose. "The person who said that was wrong."

I passed her a fork, which she gripped like a weapon.

"It isn't something you need to defend yourself against," I said, gesturing to the pies. "What kind?"

She hesitated, cleared her throat. "Apple."

Hiding my surprise, I cut her a generous piece. She tapped her fork against its crust with the hesitancy I'd once seen in Jamie, fearful of touching the snake someone held out to him at the zoo.

"You can do it," I teased, expecting a sharp retort, but she surprised me again by nodding, as though taking the encouragement to heart. And then we were eating pie together, a thing that had never happened in my forty-two years. When the pieces on our plates were gone, we moved on, shunning formality, digging into the centers of the pumpkin, the chocolate merengue. My mother burrowed her fork into pecan pie as if she'd waited her entire life to eat it.

"It's good," she said, "very good," and something inside me cracked. I poured us each champagne. We both drank it down. Under the buzz of the alcohol, I reached over and touched her hand.

She said, "You need to get your home in order. I have reason to think your husband is cavorting with that blonde number."

I drew back my hand.

"His business partner's wife. The one with the horsey mouth."

"Janey?" I said. "Janey Walsh?"

"Yes, her."

I waited for emotion to strike—outrage, jealousy, self-pity—but there was nothing. I wasn't numb; I simply didn't care. "She used to model," I said, eating another bite of pie. "She follows a raw diet. She has good muscle tone and a rigid skin-care regime. I think you'd like her."

"Debra, if you don't get this situated, your husband could leave you."

"So?"

"So!"

"He doesn't seem very happy with our marriage," I said. "I know I'm not."

"Happiness is irrelevant."

"It wasn't when you wanted it."

"That was different."

She dismissed me with a wave, and my temper stirred. "Are you saying your happiness matters and mine doesn't?"

"I'm saying, it's different. I was in love."

"Fine. I'm in love." I said this flatly, but it was true. Wonderfully, beautifully true.

"With your husband." My mother nodded, attempting to lead me along her path. Expecting me to fall into line behind her.

"Not with my husband."

She turned a flinty gaze on me, staring, trying to piece the puzzle. Finally, she asked, "Who is it?"

"Her name," I said, "is Colleen Crane."

My mother said nothing. I knew she was trying to find the right words, but as a rule my mother wasn't a woman who believed in discussion. The earth, daily, continued its unfettered movement around the sun. It did so whether you spoke about it or didn't. When I'd first gotten my period—the shock of blood on my underwear, the initial quaking cramps—my mother simply showed me the belt and box of Kotex she'd bought in preparation. She said nothing about those irritating birds and bees; to explain those, she left a book beside the Kotex. From then on, the necessary materials simply appeared in my bathroom closet.

My mother said in a neutral tone, "You love this person."

"Yes."

"This woman."

"I do."

"Not like a sister, but romantically, the way you vowed to love your husband."

From the living room came the sound of the television. My father, I knew, was asleep on the couch, hand still shoved inside his waistband. "Yes," I said. "I love her."

"It's a phase."

"It's not a phase." My voice contained a guttural emotion that surprised me.

For once, my mother appeared shaken. "You want to be *with* this person."

"Her name is Colleen," I said.

"You'd destroy your family for this person."

"My family is hanging by a thread."

"Then *fix* it."

"It's not a toy."

She asked, "How do you know her?"

This question proved hardest to answer.

"That weird heated yoga? Did you meet her while you were learning heart opening?"

Her derision gave me the strength to say, "She's my father's neighbor."

Confusion registered on her face.

"My father," I said. "Webster Jackson."

She swallowed visibly, as if choking down this information. "You've talked to him," she said finally.

"I haven't."

"You've gone behind my back." For the first time in our conversation, her voice rose.

"She reached out looking for his family. He—"

She stood from the table. "This is your grandmother's fault."

"What are you talking about?" I said, lost.

"It's in your genes," she accused.

"The way I feel isn't *genetics*."

"If you'd break up your family for a woman . . ."

"Finish the sentence," I said. "Say what you need to say."

She shook her head.

"Say it!"

"That would be the end of our relationship." She turned and walked away from the table.

As she reached the archway leading to the living room, I said, "You're my *mother*."

She didn't look back. I didn't follow her. I imagine she roused my poor father—the one whose genes I had not been given—from sleep. I imagine she snapped her fingers impatiently, informing him they were leaving; that he followed her, hazily, from the house. She left me with the pies strewn about the table, their centers slumping, their crumbs scattered, a testament to the fact that *yes*, disaster had occurred here.

HANNAH, 2001

ecember eased in.

Hannah pedaled her bike home from work, riding on back streets in the quiet dark through Berkeley to Oakland. She arrived home, where every night Webb moved lightly about the kitchen, baking something different, every night wearing a new nightgown: chartreuse chiffon, billowing when he moved quickly from refrigerator to counter; a ruffled number exposing foam décolletage as he leaned to crack an egg. He wore white cotton overrun with tiny flowers like measles, something her grandmother might have worn. He wore oceanic blue, soothing mint, blood-colored lace.

"You are," said Hannah, "a greatest hits of nightgowns."

"Stop," he said. "You'll make me blush."

It was December, cookie season. He baked drop hermits, his favorite. Baked sugar cookies and oat cookies, gingersnaps.

"A greatest hits," said Hannah, "of nightgowns and cookies."

They sat at the kitchen table, eating warm cookies and drinking milk late into the night. Mornings, Hannah discovered the cookies packed neatly inside boxes. She carried these boxes in her backpack to work, where she left them inside the wait station and kitchen, the manager's office, where the bug-eyed manager drank quadruple shots of espresso, consuming cookies in quick succession.

"People eat them?" asked Webb, pleased.

"All of them," said Hannah. "Every last one."

When, in the thick of holiday season, she complained about the demanding women who brought large parties to the restaurant, refusing to tip extra or gift even the smallest slices of cake to their servers, Webb switched from cookies to cakes. He baked pineapple upside-down cake, the recipe handed down by his grandmother. He baked something called a charlotte russe, the very cake, he said, his mother had buried in the neighbor's garbage can when she'd been displeased with the final product. He baked the fruitcake he'd once served his father in the dead of July; baked burnt sugar cake and devil's food cake, afterward driving Hannah to work in the pea-green Impala, the cakes held carefully in her lap. She shared them with her coworkers after shifts.

"This," he said once of the pineapple upside-down cake he'd just taken from the oven, "this is my favorite cake. My mother baked it as a reward."

"A reward!" said Hannah.

"For playing sports like a boy, behaving like a boy. My mother's pineapple upside-down cake was also my father's favorite, and so my mother baked it Sunday afternoons when I returned from whatever dreadful football game I played in. My father and I would sit down and have large slices and pretend, for my mother's sake, that because we loved this cake, we loved one another. Sometimes, for a single moment, eating that cake, I believed it, but before too long, he'd find something to criticize: the cake had too little sugar, or too much. It was either too dry, too moist."

"A regular Goldilocks," Hannah said.

"Always. About everything. But that singular moment of peace before his censure struck was a beautiful respite. I hated him," said Webb. "I thought my hatred for him would overtake me. That I'd disappear into the black hole of it and there would be nothing left of me *but* my hatred. And then, finally, he died. I felt only relief. Happiness. I thought my mother would be sorry—she'd married him, spent half her life with him—and I knew even then a person could be sorry without being sad. He died, and she wasn't sad or sorry. She'd been waiting for his death just as I had, patiently, just biding her time until it happened."

"How *did* it happen?"

"On the couch," said Webb. "Listening to the radio. His heart quit."

"A peaceful death," said Hannah.

"As peaceful as one's heart seizing up can be. That day, I'd come home and seen him napping in his favorite chair. My mother sat in her chair beside his. They sat like this every afternoon. I went into the kitchen. Maybe I drank a glass of milk, or ate something because I was in college then, playing football and always hungry. My mother couldn't bake things quickly enough, which pleased her. It gave her a feeling of accomplishment to watch me eat everything she made. When I returned to the living room, they both still sat in their chairs. Everything looked as it should look, as it always *had* looked. On the side table beside my father was a glass of bourbon, as there always was. My mother said, 'Webster, your father died. He's dead.' Just like that, like she was announcing there'd be chicken for dinner.

"We buried him in the Mountain View Cemetery, where the family plot was, without shedding a single tear. No funeral. My mother didn't run his obituary in the paper. She let him fade into obscurity. In time, no one at all would remember Eugene Jackson. All that pomp, all those stories and tall tales. The Berkeley conflagration, the building of the bridge, his supposed heroism on the police force. She let his life—she let the stories he told about it—disappear into the ether. Her only mention of him in years to come was an apology: she was sorry my father had not added to my inheritance, but that's what happened when a man didn't finish his degree. And actually, it has been enough money for someone like me to live on. Of course, I have the house."

"I love this house," said Hannah. She and her mother had always rented apartments, tidy units in drab buildings, sad hallways thick with scents of other people's cooking. She loved everything about Webb's house: the morning light in the kitchen, the dappled view of the hills from the front bay window. She loved the vintage tiled bathroom with its deep and beckoning clawfoot tub. She loved the house's dark wooden floors, the vocalizations of the staircase when she climbed it. She loved the single square patch of grass in the front, the solitary camellia tree planted by Webb's mother decades before. She loved the backyard, a private place inside this city, a former paradise that had once contained roses, a Victory garden. She loved returning home with her orange bicycle through the side gate, loved the satisfying clank the gate made as she eased it shut behind her.

"Since I was a child," said Webb. "I have loved this house. Sometimes in the night, I wake up, sweaty and terrified, imagining my mother saying, *Webster, you haven't repainted! Where's my garden? What's happened to your relationship with the neighbors?*"

"If she knew them," Hannah said, "she might say don't worry about it."

"She'd tell me to fix it. She'd say, *You have to do better*." He paused. "I should have done better. For Debra. One day, it will be her house."

At the kitchen table, eating cake, they studied photographs. Here, the house in its prime. Late 1940s. Postwar. Webb and his mother standing in the foreground. His mother with coiffed hair, squinting into the sun, her hands resting on Webb's shoulders, already too broad for a boy his age. The camellia still a neat twig in the front yard.

Hannah, squinted. "What are you holding?"

"That is my medal of valor."

A photograph of Webb as a naked baby with a dimpled bottom. A photograph of Webb, searingly handsome, unsmiling in his senior picture. A photograph of his mother staring wistfully into the camera, pale-skinned and slender.

"Who's this?" Hannah, tapping on a woman's face. Webb's mother sat, laughing, beside her.

"That," said Webb, "is Charlotte."

"Who's Charlotte?"

"Charlotte was a surrogate sister to my mother. A surrogate aunt to me. My mother's biological sister died when my mother was young. When Charlotte died of cancer, they were both in their thirties. My mother never fully recovered. That was the worst of her bouts. She stayed inside the bedroom with the blinds drawn. She didn't prepared breakfast, she didn't cook dinner. Finally, my father yanked her out of bed, dragged her downstairs and stood her before the stove. She went through the motions after that."

"Your father," said Hannah, scanning the photos. "Where's he?"

"Those pictures are gone. One day they weren't here anymore. I imagine my mother picking through them, stuffing them into the neighbor's trash like she did with that charlotte russe. Burying them forever."

"Do you remember what he looks like?"

"I can't forget."

"I feel that way about Sam," Hannah said. "And Fran. Both of them."

December brought the first winter storm. They stood beneath the roof's overhang, watching water soak the trees, rush the gutters. One dramatic night brought crashes of thunder, flashes of lightning. In a nightgown the color of succulent berries, Webb marveled and laughed. Clapped his hands.

"It's just a storm," Hannah said.

"We don't get thunder and lightning here."

"There it is," she said. "Right there. Thunder and lightning."

"An anomaly. Remember this. Take it in. One day, you'll see. It won't happen again any time soon. Ten years will pass, and you'll still be waiting."

"That can't be true," Hannah said.

"It is," said Webb. "You'll see."

That night, hail fell, clattered. Hannah watched as Webb ran into the yard, collecting hail in his outstretched hands, filling them as easily as a grandmother filling a candy dish. He returned sodden, nightgown clinging to him like a starlet in a movie scene.

During the Blizzard of 1993, Pennsylvania had declared a state of emergency. No one was to leave their homes under any circumstances. When the snow began falling, Hannah was at Sam's house. Fran was supposed to drive her home but waited too long—intentionally, Hannah now realized. Hannah's mother couldn't drive the mile between their houses to retrieve her. *Too treacherous!* declared the news anchors, via the government officials, and Hannah spent the entire weekend at Sam's house. Snow fell, fell. Fran appeared pleased to hold them hostage. She stood cheerfully at the microwave, heating milk for hot chocolate, dumping a packet inside each mug and swatting at the emerging clouds of cocoa powder.

When Sam shrugged disinterestedly at the cocoa, Fran served them toddies in snifters, offering them on a lined tray, like a waitress in a fancy restaurant. She leaned forward, extending the tray with a theatrical dip of the knees.

"Why are you *curtsying?*" asked Sam.

"I have style," Fran said. "I have panache."

"You have nothing," Sam said.

"I have *you*, Samuelle." Fran took Sam's angular face between her hands. Sam shook her away. "Please. Don't remind me."

That night, drunk off toddies, Hannah and Sam ran barefoot into the snow, crushing their way into the yard's quiet stillness. They stood, arms outstretched, chins tilted to the sky, trying to see who could gather the most snow on her outstretched arms, the crown of her head. Who could stand longest, feet frozen, without flinching? Hannah succumbed first. She stood dripping on the kitchen tile as Fran crawled at her feet, drying the collecting puddle around her like the men Hannah had seen on television buffing the floor of a basketball court.

The following morning, the snow had declared a truce. Hannah and Sam emerged into air so cold it made Hannah feel, on inhaling, like she'd sucked a throat lozenge. The outside world held a stark, mesmerizing purity; it felt disinfected, like a hospital room before surgery. Her and Sam's footsteps were the first to crack the snow's surface. The cold whipped their cheeks, turned them ruddy. *Les cerises;* in three months, Hannah would win the French award by default. In six, she'd leave for college. Together, they collapsed backward onto the snow, which formed a protective wall around their bodies.

"I could sleep right here," said Hannah, closing her eyes. "Like this."

"I could die right here," said Sam. "Like this."

"I wouldn't let you."

"Yes," Sam told the wall of snow between them. "You would."

COLLEEN, 2001

*D*ebra didn't call. The days burgeoned, became, passed.

Sleigh bells ring, are you listening? In the lane, snow is glistening, sang the car's stereo as Colleen drove through Oakland. Christmas had ramped up early this year, everyone desperate for tidings of good cheer. Colleen had once been a woman who'd inadvertently heard Christmas songs while standing in line at the grocery store; she'd become a woman who sought them out. Colleen considered this proof: every woman became her mother. She considered Debra. She considered Beverly, Debra's mother, a woman Colleen had never met, had only heard stories about. It seemed impossible that Debra could become her mother, but who knew? A week ago, Colleen couldn't have imagined that Debra wouldn't return her calls.

The weather outside is frightful, sang the radio, but after December's first storm, nothing frightful existed; the weather settled into a pleasant malaise. Colleen passed Salvation Army workers ringing their bells with bare arms and open sandals. Inflated Santas smiled from dry lawns. In the store windows were displays of candy canes and garlands, faux Christmas trees listing in their stands. Colleen had not bought a tree. Weeks ago, she'd dared herself to imagine Christmas with Debra and Jamie: the three of them choosing the tree in the lot, trimming it with a disparate mix of ornaments, a motley collection of colors and shapes. Her husband had preferred white lights, steady and innocuous, but she and Debra would agree on colored. They would string their own popcorn, kernel by careful kernel. Debra would make eggnog, as she made everything. Jamie, obliging them, would listen to Christmas music, as Colleen had once obliged her mother. He'd sing carols with his own mother, whose voice possessed an expansive beauty that Colleen had heard only by accident as Debra boiled water for tea.

Colleen had marveled. "You can sing!"

"I can't, really."

"I just heard you!"

Colleen yearned for a tree; its intoxicating scent, its blinking lights. She wanted to sweep the fallen needles into an orderly pile, pour water into the tree's basin each morning. She wanted these things, but she wanted them with Debra and Jamie. Without them, the things themselves mattered little. In the rush toward Christmas, Colleen waited for Debra to call. Days passed; she waited, neglecting to shower, wearing the same pair of sweatpants around the house, to the grocery store and bank. She microwaved frozen food for dinner—pizza, compartmentalized meals, burritos—but drank expensive wine out of the crystal glasses she'd claimed in the divorce. She kept the curtains closed, poured herself wine in the dead of afternoon. She sniffed the abrasive scent of her armpits and listened to Christmas songs certain to make her cry. *You're a bum / You're a punk / You're an old slut on junk.* She had not felt this badly when she got divorced. Then, she'd felt only stupid. Affronted. Her heart had not splayed open like a chicken breast pounded flat against the countertop, something likely to spread infection.

My heart, Colleen wanted to tell Debra, *won't take* no *for an answer.*

One night, drunk, she dialed Debra's number. She'd intended to hang up before anyone answered, but Debra's husband picked up the phone.

"Hello?" he said.

Colleen flung the receiver away as though it had sprouted thorns.

Moments later, her own phone rang. Debra's number appeared on the caller ID.

"Hello!"

Debra's husband asked, "Did you just call here and hang up?"

"I'm sorry," Colleen said. "Wrong number."

"Watch your dialing!" The phone slammed down.

Colleen thought, *What a charmer.* She thought, *She chose him.*

In mid-December, the doorbell rang. Colleen peered through the peephole. Hannah stood on the steps with a person Colleen had never seen, a boy wearing awkward-length shorts. Colleen had been wearing the same clothes for days. She smelled. She'd been drinking. Unable to answer, she watched as Hannah and this strange boy walked back down the path, knocking shoulders. When she felt sure it was safe, she opened the door to discover a sad little evergreen planted inside a pot, a box of cookies. Attached to the box of cookies was a note written in Webb's erratic penmanship. *We miss you!*

I miss myself, thought Colleen. She missed them too, but she'd avoided him and Hannah for weeks, though she'd watched his house from her own, kept tabs. From her kitchen window she saw Hannah leaving for work through the side gate on a clunky orange bicycle. She heard Hannah's returning hours later, saw the kitchen lights burning late into the night. She should go to him. Tell him the thoughts constantly needling her insides. *Your daughter is a remarkable human. I love her. I thought she loved me.*

Late one night, unable to sleep, her breath catching, Colleen opened the front door for some air. She found herself walking out, standing barefoot in the street. It was two o'clock in the morning; Webb's living room light was on, the curtains open. Colleen investigated.

Remembering those girls who ripped up her camellias, she stopped halfway up the front walk beside Webb's camellia. Through the window she saw Webb and Hannah sitting, talking with that boy from earlier, Hannah making expressive movements with her hands. Their friendship gave Colleen a sharp pang of jealousy. What did they possibly have to talk about, this man and the girl Colleen had bullied him to live with? Not bullied. Deceived. She had *lied,* then distanced herself. And now she had become this lurking woman, swatting at bushes in her pajamas, spying. Of course they'd grown close; she'd been elsewhere, distracted. In love. Hadn't she wanted him to have a caretaker—a friend—so she would not feel burdened by him? She'd gotten what she'd wanted, and she hadn't. This seemed to be how things worked. You could have some of the things, the universe declared, but you could not—you would not—have all of them.

When Debra finally called, Colleen cried, "It's been weeks! Three long, terrible weeks."

"I'm sorry."

"Twenty-one days."

"I know."

Colleen let out a breath she felt she'd been holding for all that time. "I just meant I've missed you."

"I've missed you," said Debra.

"I was afraid you hadn't. You didn't."

"Of course I missed you."

"I wanted to give you time, whatever you needed."

Debra said, "I can't, actually, do this."

"What's this?" The meanness in Colleen's voice surprised her.

"I have a family. A husband, a son."

"You're afraid." Colleen's own fear threatened to swallow her.

"It's easier for you," said Debra.

Anger flared inside Colleen. "Because my husband already left me? Because my womb dried up and I don't have children to consider?"

"No."

"What then?"

"Because you're braver."

"Right."

"You are," said Debra.

"My braveness. Does it change anything?"

The silence between them swelled. Colleen's mind felt curiously separate. A thing apart. She thought of balloons released into the sky, the accompanying hope as they rose to their quiet destruction. And yet people insisted on joyously releasing balloons into the sky. Colleen imagined herself released, floating away in a blissful daze, only to come to naked and confused in another country's dense forest, a random California woman, brought by the wind.

"Does it?" she asked.

"No," said Debra. "I guess it doesn't."

"So why call?"

"I wanted to tell you," Debra said. "Like an adult."

"Well, thanks," said Colleen. "Thanks for that."

That night, again unable to sleep, Colleen walked once more into the street barefoot, in pajamas. Webb's house was dark; she detected no immediate signs of life, no motion at the peripheries. Opening the side gate, she walked along the house to the door that led into the kitchen. Months ago, nearly a year ago now—it felt like a lifetime—she had stood with Webb watching as this house, this kitchen, burned.

It was three in the morning. She hadn't expected to find anyone awake, but a faint light shined from the window. Inching closer, Colleen peered through the glass. Hannah and Webb sat at the table talking with the boy from earlier. They were eating *cake*. Colleen wavered. She could turn away. They'd never know she'd shown up in disarray, wanting to admit her lies and failures, wanting to tell Webb about his daughter, beautiful and fearful. Their lives could continue their separate trajectories.

Because you're braver, Debra had said. She *believed* Colleen was brave, a thing Colleen had never in her life been accused of. She *believed* Colleen was a person who could address the unpleasant truth, accept responsibility for it. She rapped the door's square pane.

Webb approached in a flowing tangerine peignoir. If he was surprised to find her at his door at three a.m. after weeks of silence, he didn't show it. He said, "We were just eating some cake!"

The tears Colleen cried on his steps were ugly things unleashed.

His arm surrounded her waist, and he ushered her inside.

HANNAH, 2001

olleen had come to Webb's door like a sudden bird, tapping on the glass window.

Her face was the stunned face of a woman on a documentary, recounting her run-in with an alien. *I was lying on a table. Five gray figures poked me. When I came to, I was lying in a field.* Colleen cried into the lace neckline of Webb's peignoir—tangerine, the color of amiable citrus—and Hannah saw that she was barefoot, wearing misbuttoned pajamas. Finally, Webb extricated himself to boil water for tea, and Colleen, who'd grown thin, trembled in her skewed pajamas without speaking. Hannah realized: she was here to talk to Webb.

"I guess we'll turn in," Hannah said, and in her bedroom above the kitchen, she lay in the dark next to Sean, trying to discern their words. Their voices were not the overt voices of Hot Tan and his houseguest. She strained to listen and fell asleep straining.

In the morning, over coffee, Hannah touched the lip of her tiny milk bottle and asked, "Is she okay?"

"She's heartbroken," Webb said. "She'll be fine eventually."

Hannah imagined Colleen's once-upon-a-time husband, conjuring someone broad-shouldered and thick-necked, the sort of man whose shirts, too small, strained his biceps. The sort who refused giving foot rubs but who accepted them willingly; who sighed heavily at dishes left overnight in the sink. Who pointed at someone cleaning something and said, *You missed a spot.* The sort of man who grunted when you asked him what he'd like for dinner, who never cooked a meal but always criticized the things served.

"She needs to put that guy behind her," Hannah said.

"Yes," said Webb. "She does."

Several days later, as they took their daily walk, Webb said, "She told me something else. Colleen."

He gave no outward sign it was bad news, but Hannah had learned to read him. "Okay," she said cautiously.

"Debra, my daughter, won't see me."

Hannah sought his eyes, but he evaded her gaze. "She said she would," Hannah argued. "She said if you got a caretaker, she would see you. Here I am. I'm right here. You did what she asked."

"I guess she changed her mind," Webb said evenly.

Anger rose briefly, but just as swiftly drained away. "I don't know what to say."

"I wasn't sure I ever believed it," said Webb. "You can't ignore a person for thirty years—. You can't disappear from their lives and expect they'll forgive you."

"Are you *okay?*" She placed a hand on his arm.

"Yes."

"You're not," said Hannah.

"I'll never be okay," he said. "I made peace with that long ago. I've done the things I've done. I can't change them."

"True. But."

"You can't make a person come." He studied her with his blue eyes. "You can't make a person stay."

"No," she said. "I guess not."

"Not Beverly, not my mother, not Hila," he continued. "Not Sam, not Fran."

Not you. The thought occurred to Hannah, quick, rushing into her head before it, like Sam, like Fran, was gone.

When Hannah saw Colleen again, she appeared, not fine, but serviceable, like a plain white platter. There had been a shift Hannah couldn't pinpoint. Colleen had returned to them, but she was somehow also far away, Webb touching her shoulder, calling her back from wherever she had gone as he offered her the first cookies out of the oven, served her peanut butter and pickle sandwiches.

"Thank you, no," said Colleen with characteristic politeness.

Hannah insisted, "No. You have to try them."

"Really," said Sean. "You do."

Together, they spent a subdued Christmas at Webb's house, Hannah and Colleen lounging on the couch, listening to Christmas music, Webb and Sean cooking dinner. In the doorjamb, Hannah stood, taking a mental picture of a man in a peignoir, chopping, a man in awkward shorts, mincing. She played Hila's game, committed the moment to her memory, detail by detail, knowing it was something she might one day want—*need*—to recall: the scent of roasting ham, the pungent smell of garlic, Webb's jutted-out hip as he sighed before the refrigerator. It came to her with a start: her first Christmas in California! Last year, she'd gone home to please her mother; had been stranded for hours in Cincinnati due to snow.

They gathered in the rarely used dining room to eat. Hannah had lined the silverware and plates carefully, setting the polished forks and knives and spoons as Webb instructed—as Edna had done many years before.

"It's lovely," said Colleen. "Thank you."

"Edna measured the hang of the tablecloth," Hannah admitted. "I only eyeballed it."

"Slacker," said Sean. "It isn't straight."

Webb, touching her elbow, said, "It's perfect."

V

WEBB, 2001

*D*uring the war, his mother had converted the neighborhood social meetings into the local block neighborhood chapter. The attendees discussed blackout procedures and home nursing, health and nutrition and other air-raid precautions. In their skirts and heels, they donned gas masks, performed drills. His mother instructed in her level voice, "Ladies. If you're outside and bombs are falling, lie on the ground, face downward. On your elbows, please, hands clasped behind your head, chest raised slightly to avoid earth shock. Leap for shelter only if it can be reached in a single second." Wearing her green cowl-necked dress—Webb's favorite, for its green was the color of the deepest forest—she lay on the ground, demonstrated. (Was there anything, Webb asked later, that could be done in a single second? "You'd be surprised," his mother said, "how *long* a second can seem under duress. One day, when you're older, you'll look back and realize you've lived an entire lifetime of seconds. You'll want every lengthy second back.")

The women had removed their gas masks, laughing at their lack of prowess, their certain inability to survive disaster. With disheveled hair, they ate his mother's teacakes baked with hoarded butter and served on dainty, flower-strewn plates. They sipped strong coffee, whispering: had everyone *seen* Peggy Edmund's new sapphire brooch? "Nothing declares a husband's guilt like a pricey brooch gifted on a random Monday in wartime," declared a woman with powdered sugar on her chin.

His mother, hater of gossip, smiled. "Oh, Connie. You're such a sage."

Connie blushed at the compliment. Webb would never forget the ease with which his mother refilled Connie's coffee cup, the quiet, nearly imperceptible quality of the insult, handed out as casually as the sugar caddy.

His mother had been destined for things larger than those she'd been given. She lived an incorrectly sized life, squeezing herself into it as Webb later squeezed himself into women's panties. His mother could have had a career. She could have been a leader. She didn't, she wasn't. She pinned her hopes on him, but the truth was that he too was destined to feel ungainly in this life, dissatisfied. Waking in the night, unable to breathe with the memories assaulting him—*No*, he told Hila, memories weren't *all* rosy nostalgia, they weren't *all* tiny beauties—he considered his daughter, girl born of his own DNA. Bearer of his DNA, she too had likely suffered. She had suffered, but he had failed her. He had offered no counsel, no tips on survival. He'd allowed her to simply manage. As his mother had managed, as she had allowed him to manage.

It was summer, the height of July. He had not yet received his tarnished medal of valor, but soon would. He and his mother first heard the chirping as they left for their morning walk. His mother dragged the kitchen stool out front, clambered up, and in the soffit discovered a nest of baby birds. When she'd finished admiring them, Webb took his turn. Sweet darlings. Feathery wisps with needy, too-large mouths.

For several days, the birds remained their secret. As Webb and his mother ate the night's pot roast or chicken, as they washed the evening's dishes or sat with his father in the living room, listening to the radio in their separate microcosms, they did not speak of the birds, though they followed the comings and goings of the parents from the nest. As the babies grew, they became more vocal, bold in their bids for bugs and worms.

On Sunday morning, their calamitous chirping woke his father, who came padding down the stairs in his fur-lined moccasins and red pinstriped pajamas. These lent him the appearance of a man who was cheerful, who was comfortable and kind. In everyday life, his father's hair was a barometer for his emotions, his tolerance for human dealings. If his father had not yet applied his pomade—if his hair still had the fuzzy, untended look of a hamster's rump—Webb knew not to speak, to avert his eyes, awaiting the pomade and his father's acquiescence to the existence of mankind. On this morning, his father's hair was all frenzied static, emitting its unsubtle warning. The baby birds chirped. He stormed outside to investigate.

"Come now, Genie," Webb's mother said when his father located the nest. "Let's have breakfast."

"It's sleep I need, not goddamn breakfast." His father went mumbling to the shed, talking at his own feet like the downtrodden people Webb saw on trips to the department stores downtown.

His mother tried again when he returned. "Genie, shall I pour some coffee?"

Her forced cheer dissipated when she saw Webb's baseball bat. "Genie!" she shrilled. Without preamble, Webb's father hit the nest with the bat, striking it again and again like a drunk hitting a piñata at a quinceañera.

This went on for interminable seconds—a lifetime of seconds; yes, they were unfathomably long—until finally Webb's father tossed the bat with a clatter against the front steps. Wordlessly, he returned to the house, leaving behind blood and wing, tendon and brain. Bile rose inside Webb's throat. His legs trembled as he stumbled away from the gore.

His mother snapped into action. In the kitchen, she filled a bucket with hot water and bleach. She donned gloves, collected the residual bird pieces in a trash bag. Kneeling on the stone, she furiously scrubbed the steps, determined to eradicate the physical evidence of what had just occurred there. Webb, paralyzed, felt only rising panic. Air chaffed his lungs, burned his eyes. He ached to his very bones. Suddenly his mother was shaking him by the shoulders. "Webster. Your father cannot hear you crying. Do you understand?"

Yes, he understood. He was fourteen, too old to cry.

His mother shook him hard, harder. "Webster. You'll wake your father again. And then what?"

"Yes. And then what?" His father had appeared in the doorway, hair wildly askew.

Webb steeled himself for what came next. Would he be punched? Thrashed with a belt? Would his father box his ears? Rain obscenities over him?

His father passed him. He stood instead before Webb's mother, whose face he took between his hands. With mustered momentum, his father slapped his mother's right cheek. He turned her face and slapped her left cheek. Slapped her right, slapped her left. Back and forth—left, right, left, like an army marching. A memory: his mother telling her story about the

Berkeley conflagration. How her own father had slapped her mother into silence. *Oh, Webster, that you never experience such a thing.* He'd thought she meant the fire, its suffocating smoke and terror, but perhaps she'd hoped he'd never see his father strike her; never see how men hurt women.

His father said, "Tell your son he has no business acting like a little girl."

His mother nodded.

"I didn't hear you."

"Yes."

"Yes, what?"

"Yes, I'll tell him."

"Tell him what."

"Not to act like a little girl."

"I need to hear it with my own ears." Taking his mother by the shoulders, his father positioned her before Webb. "Go ahead. Look him in the eyes and tell him."

"Webster, you shouldn't act like a little girl."

"Tell him you're sorry for raising him to be a fairy."

"I'm sorry," his mother said, "for raising you to be a fairy."

"Tell him there will be no fairies inside this home."

His mother repeated, "There will be no fairies inside this home."

His father said, "I guess now I'll get some sleep. I expect you'll wait for me, so we can eat breakfast as a family."

"Of course," his mother said, and his father climbed back upstairs to bed.

When all was quiet, Webb placed his hand on his mother's shoulder. She shook free of his touch.

"Webster. You are at a crossroads. I cannot help you."

He knew then he would play football. He would not cook. Would not bake. Would not wear his mother's frilly aprons. He envisioned himself in a steamy room while all around him boys snapped towels and told tasteless jokes. He imagined his fatigue and accumulated bruises, the locker room's acute stink. His life as he'd known it was over, and the person he'd been before this morning was gone.

Summer nights with Hila, drinking gin and tonic garnished not with lime but lemon because it pleased her to pluck lemons from the tree, he'd considered telling her about the baby birds. Every time the impulse rose, he lacked the courage. He'd concentrate instead on *her*, sipping gin, squinting her eyes as she committed to memory every detail of the evening they'd just lived together, saying, "I might someday need this memory the way other women need Tupperware. I might, for instance, feel sad—I might, in fact, be on my death bed—and only the memory of this flawless clafoutis with its perfect cherries will lure me from the edge of sadness. Experiences are always prettier in the remembering. Sweeter, pinker. Gilded, like a baroque door. But these cherries. When I remember them, I will know they were perfect."

He could have told her experiences weren't always prettier in the remembering. They weren't always sweeter, pinker. Instead he asked, shrapnel of lemon between his teeth, "Have you always played this game?"

"I've played it more since knowing you. So I can remember all the things."

"What things?"

"I remember pressing my face into the old tortoiseshell cat's fur, its softness against my cheek. She lived to be eighteen. That girl was old enough to vote, and believe me, she would have made the right choice. I remember Texas evenings in the neighborhood, tall men in white t-shirts drinking beer from tall cans. The largesse of my hair in the humidity, bigger than a mushroom cloud."

"Me," he said selfishly. "What do you remember of me?"

"I remember two hours ago when we blistered poblanos in the oven and their scent was intoxicating, as lovely as cilantro or freshly ground coffee. *Coffee*. That time we brought thermoses of it into the hills at dawn—see, Webster, how memories beget memories?—and drank our perfect coffee as the sky lightened around us. When we drove into Santa Cruz and stood with our bare feet in the warm sand until it grew too hot for our wee pinkies and we walked into the cold ocean in our clothes, and afterward you kissed me and we drove home on the 17 and I stuck my face out the window like a euphoric dog as the sunlight came though the trees. And that time, on the Fourth of July, when your face went purple and blue in the light of the fireworks."

She poured more gin. The ice whispered and crackled. "You should play! Tell me what you remember."

But he had not played. He'd been either too lazy or too drunk. How many things he wished he remembered now, about her and Debra both. Starting with the exact moment they each came into his life. Debra, red and squalling. Hila, in the high school theater, dressed in sleek black, with plum lips, staring at him across the auditorium as if to say, *I see you.*

He remembered everything, he remembered nothing. Couldn't know, in the haphazard remembering, if he made memories prettier or uglier: his mother inside her modernist cube of an apartment chosen by Beverly. White walls, white wall-to-wall carpet. Flimsy lacquered cabinetry, also white. Tiny square windows like those offered to prisoners. Upon moving her in, he'd stood at the center of the galley kitchen, arms open. His wingspan stretched from cabinet to wall. His mother watching him, he who had once been her beautiful boy, saying in her voice vibrating with irony, "How wonderful! An electric stove!" Weeks later, months, his mother opened the door on Thanksgiving Day still wearing her housecoat. She had not brushed her hair, which resembled a bird's nest, which in turn made him think of birds, of crossroads. He'd steeled himself against emotion. She would not remove the chain from the door. He'd coaxed, "Please. Come to dinner. We miss you. Your family misses you."

"Webster," she said thinly.

"Yes."

"I'm tired."

"We'll find you a nice space to rest. Someplace quiet, until dinner."

"*You* have made me tired."

"Mother?"

"My whole life, Webster. So tired." Her face had grown narrower as she closed the door, and no amount of knocking—no amount of cajoling—persuaded her to open it. Driving back to Oakland, he had known this would be the last time he'd see her, her gaunt face disappearing inside the crack of the door's closing, slipping away as she'd slip from this reality into the next.

Don't leap to shelter, he remembered her saying, *unless you can do it in a second.*

If you introduce a gun in the first act, he remembered Hollis quoting, *you'd better shoot it in the third.*

You couldn't explain to someone the fatigue inside your own bones, as if you'd been dragging them, grinding them against the concrete. In his and Hannah's many talks about the people who'd left them, he'd wanted to tell her how he felt, how ready he was to be elsewhere, how frequently he thought of the company he'd keep in this foreign place he'd not yet traveled to, but he found the details too personal, necessarily private. *Sometimes*, his mother had said, *we must pretend to be the people others expect us to be, so we might survive.*

Sitting with Hannah at the kitchen table this morning, watching as she ate the croissants he'd made—his last laminated dough of this lifetime—he knew he had not fooled her. She had always recognized these feelings in him, even when they remained unspoken. He wore his turquoise robe with its careful embroidery. "Fit for Marie Antoinette!" Hila had declared, pin at the side of her pursed mouth, as she stitched it. "Fit for you, Webster Eugene Jackson." Staring across the table at Hannah, he said nothing, concentrating instead on the details of this unfolding morning: his croissant, his beautiful dark coffee. He poured Hannah a tall glass of whole milk as he'd once done for Debra, milk rich with nutrients meant to fatten his daughter for the future, *her* future, her beckoning life. In these last months, Hannah had grown from a diminutive ghost into this person beside him, tanned and strong, in search of hills to climb. He watched as she mapped her ride, something about mama bear, papa bear, baby bear; three hills around the Briones Reservoir. A hard ride, the longest she'd attempted. Soon, Hannah was clattering out the side door, and he realized the moment to tell her things was lost, a moment like all the others that could not be gotten back.

He carried his plate to the sink, where he stood looking at Colleen's yard, remembering when he and Debra dismantled the neighbor's swing set in the dead of the night. How, together, they'd stared at the sky.

"Everything you do for the rest of your life should be with her in mind," his mother had said, holding Debra for the first time. "I pray you don't disappoint her."

He recalled sitting at the kitchen table, pieces of his father's gun lined neatly on its surface. How he cleaned them as Debra sat watching. They did this one weekend Beverly traveled to Santa Barbara. Guns frightened Beverly; she would not have allowed this gun inside the house had she known. Surely, she would not have let her young daughter fondle its pieces between her slight fingers. "Don't tell your mother." Webb lifted the parts one at a time and explained them to Debra, all those tiny pieces that formed a formidable object. "This was your grandfather's gun," he told her. He could see she was mesmerized by its power without yet understanding what it was capable of. *Just another terrible thing passed down from your grandfather,* he didn't say. Of course, his father had taught him to maintain it. It was, he said, a man's responsibility to keep his family safe. He instructed Webb on how to take it apart and clean it every few months. Keep it ready for use. And Webb had—in secret, except for that one time with Debra. Afterward, he always returned the gun to its pink patisserie box, a thing Beverly would never deign to touch, pastry more dangerous to her than even guns. He slid the box inside the bottom drawer of the dining cabinet, tucking it beneath table linens that had once been his mother's, and as such, things Beverly would never use.

Holding the gun now, he imagined crossing the threshold between here and there as like the trip to Los Angeles all those years ago with Hila: how the fog hung heavy, hazy and swirling, a makeshift tunnel through which they'd driven. How, when they emerged into the radiance on the other side of that fog, Hila placed her hand over her heart and exclaimed at its beauty. Dying would be like that, except it would not be the light that greeted him but Hila herself, appearing through the parting fog to say, *Oh, Webster.* Hila, reaching her hand to him, pulling him into the sun. His would be a quick rush to safety. It had taken a lifetime; it would take a second. He knew nothing with certitude except that in the instant where the fog parted and the second elapsed, Hila waited.

DEBRA, 2001

As a family, we performed the motions of Christmas Day. We endured it with affixed smiles, proclamations of heady joy. My husband surprised me with a sapphire-and-diamond brooch, watching with a smug expression as I opened the box.

My mother spotted it immediately upon our arrival for her holiday party. "Just beautiful!" she declared. Her voice implied *He loves you very much.* But when had I ever worn a brooch? He'd pinned it to my dress awkwardly, like a boy pinning a corsage on his prom date. It glinted at me from various mirrors, pricked me whenever I reached for something. A thing to endure, like all the others. Like Colleen's absence, which I had insisted upon because I felt too frightened by her presence.

My mother had greeted us at the door with glasses of champagne, miserable winter strawberries at the bottoms of our glasses. Carolers dressed like characters from a Dickens book sang jauntily at us, men with their top hats askew, women with faces framed by severe curls. The carolers moved about, arranging themselves in inopportune places, caroling their hearts out while blocking access to the hors d'oeuvres. My mother had requested that everyone wear red. Guests flowed through the house like blood that refused to be staunched after a bludgeoning. On mantels and consoles, tiny Christmas villages sprawled, with cotton pulled apart and fluffed into makeshift snow, ceramic reindeer and cozy houses and bundled-for-winter figurines. Mistletoe hung from myriad door jams. When the party had ended, my father stood beneath a twig of it and asked, "Who are they kidding? The only time our married friends kiss one another is once a year at this party."

"You and mom," I said, "saving marriages one Christmas at a time."

279

"Quick!" My father reached for my mother's waist. "Let's kiss before everything falls apart!"

My mother swatted his hand away. "You're both so funny." When he'd gone, she narrowed her eyes at me and said, "*Yes*. Marriages are things to save."

"I don't remember you saving any."

"When did you become this person?" my mother asked.

"I've always been this person."

"I'm not sure . . ." my mother began.

"Not sure of what?"

"I'm not sure I like it."

"Yes," I said. "I know."

Two weeks after Christmas, Colleen's number appeared on the caller ID. I stared at her flashing name and let the machine pick up. Colleen never left messages, worried James would hear them and wonder; but the beep sounded, and then her voice spoke through the machine. "Please, Debra. Pick up."

She called ten more times, hanging up every time with a resounding click. Finally, she left a second message. "I don't want to say this on your machine, but it's about your father—"

The machine screeched loudly when I picked up the receiver. "*Yes*." I spoke like a customer service representative fielding a complaint.

"Your father," Colleen said.

"You mentioned that. What is it?"

"He's dead."

I'd been prepared for her to say many things. I was not prepared for this. "How?" I asked.

My father, Colleen said, had shot himself in his bedroom with a .38 revolver.

"My grandfather's gun." I remembered holding its pieces in my hand, remembered my father's face, creased in concentration as he cleaned them.

"No one knew he had it," Colleen said.

"Who found him?"

"Hannah."

"Who?"

"The girl who moved in with him."

"Right," I said.

"He left a note, taped to his bedroom door, saying please don't come inside, please get the police. She came here, to get me."

Silence pressed between us. Emphasized the jagged edges of Colleen's breath.

"I barely knew him," I said.

"I'm sorry," she said, picking up on something I myself was unaware of. "I know how similar you both are."

"Were," I corrected.

"I know how similar you both were."

"I need to go," I said. "I have plans."

For the duration of the day, I longed to tell someone the story, whatever it was. To unburden myself of feelings I had not expected to feel. James was at the club. I could call there, ask someone to find him. I imagined his eye roll when they handed him my message. James was bad at conversations he'd prepared for; forget those rushing at him unexpectedly. There was no easy way to explain to him about my biological father, whose existence he'd never heard of.

I brought the phone into my sitting room and called my mother. "There's something I need to tell you."

"I'm on my way out."

"Colleen called."

"Colleen," my mother repeated.

"Mother, you know who she is. At least don't be disingenuous."

"Fine," my mother said. "I know who she is."

"She called—"

"*Yes?*"

"My father died yesterday."

A pregnant moment passed. "Your father is at home," my mother said. "Sleeping on the couch."

"You know what I mean."

"No, I don't."

"You do."

"Everyone dies," she said finally.

"He shot himself."

"It runs in the family. Depression. Bouts."

"I have no idea what that is," I said. "I have no idea what you're saying."

"He had problems."

"Mother."

"We hadn't spoken in years."

"You were married," I said. "You had a child together."

She said, "You *want* something from me."

"Of course I do."

"Go ahead. Tell me what you want."

"Why can't we talk?" I said. "Why can't we have a conversation?"

"We speak frequently."

"That's not what I mean."

"I don't know what to do when you're like this," my mother said.

"Like what?"

"Sensitive."

The day continued like a steep uphill climb. My husband, sawing through the steak I'd made for dinner, noticed nothing. Jamie regarded me from across the table. "What's wrong?"

"I'm fine."

"You don't seem fine."

"I'm great."

"All right," he said, ironically.

"Really," I said.

"You must have low standards." He shrugged and excused himself.

The next morning, a letter arrived, addressed to me, the handwriting unfamiliar. I stared at it for a long time, considered not opening it. I turned it over, turned it over again. I could keep it like a talisman, I thought, something sacred and near. I could never read it, never know what it said. I touched the stamp. And then, as if plunging into an ice bath, I opened the envelope and read.

"I knew you weren't fine," Jamie said when I knocked on his door.

I stood, saying nothing.

"What's happening?" Jamie asked.

"Can I come in?"

Inside his dark room, he turned down the music. Together, we sat on his unmade bed.

"I don't know how to explain it," I said.

He asked, "Are you leaving Dad?"

"I'm not leaving Dad," I said.

"Oh."

"You sound disappointed."

"I am," Jamie said. "You should."

We sat together silently. He asked, "Did someone die?"

"No," I said. "Yes."

"That's decisive."

"Someone died. But no one you know. No one you've ever met."

"Who?"

"There's a bit of backstory."

"I have time," he said.

I told him my biological father was a different man than the man he called his grandfather. My father wasn't the person who slept on our couch after too many manhattans, his hand shoved under the band of his pants. He was some-one Jamie had never met, who lived—or had lived—in Oakland. I'd spent the first twelve years of my life there, with him, until my mother left him to marry Clive. I hadn't seen him, hadn't spoken to him, since the evening be-fore that April morning, nearly thirty-two years ago, when Clive drove us to Los Angeles. Months ago, Colleen had called me, saying he wanted to reunite.

"Colleen knows your father," Jamie said.

"That's how I met her. She called me, looking for his family, looking for someone to care for him."

"But you didn't go," he said, piecing it together. "You didn't see him."

"No."

"You never said anything. Ever."

"I wanted to, so many times, but your grandmother wanted to forget it. That life was done for her. She put it behind her, and that was that."

"Does Dad know?"

"No."

Again we sat saying nothing.

"You look like him," I said.

"My grandfather?"

"Yes. You remind me of him."

"How?"

"Your sensitivity," I said. "People will tell you sensitivity is a bad thing, and it's not."

"What else?"

"Your reserve. Your stoicism. Also, your humor."

"I'm stoic?"

"Yes."

"I'm funny?"

"Wonderfully funny," I said. "You didn't get it from me, and you certainly didn't get it from your father."

"Why did grandmother leave him?"

"She was unhappy."

"Grandmother is always unhappy."

"She was trying to make things better for herself," I said, and realized for the first time that she was.

"Was he sick?"

"He shot himself," I said.

"He killed himself," Jamie said.

"I hadn't seen him in thirty-one years," I said. "But I remember there being a sadness about him, a heaviness, and sometimes I see that in you, too. It hurts me that you have that, that you feel like that, and I can't help you. It hurts me that I've never told you where it came from, that there's an entire history you know nothing about, and it explains these pieces of you."

"Do you remember the last time you saw him?"

"I do."

My son waited.

"It was the night before we left. I didn't know it at the time, but it was. Your grandmother cooked a special dinner."

"Grandmother cooked?"

"She cooked a special dinner that she ruined. Something called pampered beef filets. It had a mushroom sauce. She burnt the filets to a crisp in the oven and over-seasoned the mushroom sauce. It tasted like ocean water. And she'd baked something called King Kamehameha's pie. This should have clued us in that something strange was afoot. Your grandmother never served dessert."

"She doesn't," Jamie said. "Ever. But she should."

"The filling was supposed to set, but your grandmother botched the recipe and there was just a pool of liquid in the center of the crust. It looked radioactive."

"Radioactivity looks like nothing," Jamie said.

"It looked like it could kill a person," I said. "To save her feelings, my father poured it into glasses, and we drank it like it was a magical concoction. Then we watched television, and I went to bed. The next morning, my mother woke me and said I wasn't going to school. There was a moving truck outside, and we were leaving."

"No goodbye, nothing."

"No," I said. "That dinner was the last time we spent together."

"I would have put up a fight."

"You would have," I agreed. "I was a different sort of child. Acquiescent. I did as I was told."

"You've never been back?"

"Never."

"We could get into the car," he said. "We could drive there right now. There's no one to stop you. Us. You know that, right?"

I remembered with clarity that final supper. Pampered Beef Filets and something called Piquant Carrots, then the liquid pie for dessert. An ordinary discussion about moon flight, Apollo 13 floating in the night sky above us, carrying its three men to Fra Mauro. The next day, the astronauts would broadcast live from space. Space flight entranced my father. He liked the daily, mundane details behind the glamorous veneer of exploration. He cared about rockets and propulsion, risk and discovery, but what he really wanted to know was how did the astronauts use the restroom? What did the astronauts *eat*?

"This astronaut business is old hat," my mother said, poking at a blackened filet.

No, my father said. It wasn't old hat! He'd read, for instance, that on Apollo 11, the astronauts ate thermostabilized cheddar cheese spread and hotdogs, packets containing such precious delectables as sausage patties and pork with scalloped potatoes, chicken stew. NASA had, for instance, provided fifteen cups of coffee for each astronaut on the mission, not quite two cups of coffee a day. Not enough! How did these men perform their difficult tasks without caffeine? How did they perform such tasks without sleep? Because who, under these circumstances, could sleep? On Apollo 11 there had been, my father told us, shrimp cocktail, each shrimp selected individually for its ability to squeeze through a food packet.

"Shrimp cocktail!" my mother exclaimed with feigned interest. I watched as she pushed away her Piquant Carrots.

"The very first meal eaten by man on the moon was bacon cubes coated with gelatin to combat crumbs!" my father said.

"Really!" my mother said.

"Even the moon men like their bacon."

"Bacon is terrible for us," said my mother, who rarely served it.

"Bacon," my father said, "is essential to happiness!"

"You can't be happy if you're dead." My mother gathered plates and said, "I want your life to be happy and long."

Later, I would consider these words the most magnificent lie I'd ever witnessed. Or perhaps they weren't a lie at all. She had said nothing about our collective lives, the whole of them. Perhaps it was her final message to him: be happy. Or perhaps it was a message to herself, an incantation, a desperate, tugging plea: *happy, be happy.*

HANNAH, 2001

*H*annah had not called 911. Leaving the note on Webb's bedroom door, she'd crossed the yard to Colleen's house, where Colleen, calm in a crisis, dialed the numbers. Afterward, they sat unspeaking, waiting for help to arrive.

There had been, in the aftermath of Webb's death, the swarm of police and the filling out of reports. The answering of questions. Hannah, salty-skinned from her bike ride, stood hugging herself, inhaling the stink of her underarms as Colleen, her voice as crisp as a ship captain's, handled the pragmatic tasks Hannah hadn't known to handle: the removal of the body, the scheduling of a cleaning crew.

"You'll stay with me tonight," Colleen said. "Please."

Inside Colleen's shower, Hannah scrubbed herself raw, watching the grime from her ride swirl down the drain. She held her face to the water and marveled at the hollowness inside her. She considered barren things: deserts, dusty farmland, women. Colleen had made the bed in her guest room. Clean sheets, soft blankets.

Hannah woke at dawn. She sat on Colleen's front steps, staring at the hills, listening as birds' cries cracked the lightening sky.

His daughter arrived days later with her son, a teenager who resembled Webb in the photographs he'd shown Hannah of him as a young person, large and fine-jowled, handsome. The daughter had Webb's languid movements, his propensity to stare into space, to gnaw at his bottom lip; she possessed his forehead, his nose, his blue eyes. She did not look how Hannah had imagined a beauty queen's daughter.

She had not announced she was coming. She rang the doorbell of the home she'd once lived inside but had never visited, clutching her son's arm as Hannah opened the door, keeping him close as they navigated rooms together. Hannah shut herself inside her bedroom. She listened as the daughter and her son opened and closed doors, their footsteps echoing in the hallway. Finally, the daughter knocked, asking if she'd join them for tea? Hannah did not want to join them for tea. She feared what they might say to her, what they might ask of her, but this was the reality of the situation. Here was where they'd found themselves. Here was where they'd arrived, inexplicably, together.

The tea was made when Hannah arrived in the kitchen, and the daughter poured the three of them cups of strong earl gray, set out sugar and milk. At the table, Hannah clutched her mug with both hands. The daughter paused, as though building the courage to say what she wanted to say.

"We were thinking," the daughter said. "Wondering."

She's asking me to leave, Hannah thought.

"We'd like to stay for a few days, if that's all right with you. We didn't know we wanted to. But."

"It's not my house," Hannah said. "It's not my place to say. It's your house now."

"You live here. This is your home. We'd understand if you'd rather we didn't."

"I can leave," Hannah said. A sharp panic rose inside her.

"Of course not!" the daughter said. "No!"

She and the son took Edna's old room. It seemed sacrilegious to disturb Webb's, the room where, days before, he had taken his last breath; the same room where, he'd told her, he'd pissed into a pickle jar when she'd first arrived, fearful of seeing the girl who'd moved into his home. Even when they'd become friends, Hannah had never entered the sanctuary of his bedroom. She had respected the imaginary line, talking to him from the doorjamb, never stepping over the implied boundary. That day—the day he'd put a gun against his temple and pulled the trigger—she'd entered the empty kitchen, sweaty from her ride. Under a strange umbrella of silence, she climbed the stairs. The note had been taped to his bedroom door: *Please do not enter. Please call 911.* Even upon his death, she had not entered. Even upon his death, he had been polite; had been fastidious, considered details.

The coroners told her he'd laid tarp across the floor, wanting to contain the inevitable mess. A contained disaster.

She did not tell the daughter and her son any of this. Simply watched as the daughter marveled, remembered: this room had once been her grandmother's. Here was her grandmother's armoire, with the lion pulls. Here was her grandmother's bed frame, made of solid, beautiful walnut. Here on the walls were watercolors of the sea her grandmother's good friend had painted at Sea Ranch. The daughter recalled that once her grandmother moved to Berkeley, wanting space and independence, her mother had removed these watercolors from the walls, threatened to throw them into the garbage.

"He kept them! He rehung them!" the daughter said. She ran a finger along each of the frames, stepped back to admire them.

The morning following their arrival, Hannah found the daughter in the kitchen frying bacon.

"Your father loved to cook," Hannah said. "He loved to bake."

"He did. When he got the chance."

"My favorite was his tarte tatin."

"When we were alone on weekends, he'd cook all of the Julia Childs recipes. I remember the tarte tatin. My mother wasn't much of a cook. She'd eat Stella D'oro breakfast cookies in her bathrobe. Right there, at that table. Well, whatever table was there at the time."

"Your father told me," Hannah said, "how she'd sit there, reading the *TV Guide* in her Noxzema."

"He told you things."

"Eventually."

"What do you mean?"

"We avoided each other for months. We lived together, here in this house, and didn't speak." She surprised herself by laughing. "We were afraid of each other."

"That sounds about right." In a gesture seemingly borrowed from her father, the daughter—Debra—filled Hannah's coffee mug. She said, "You know things."

"Not much."

"More than me."

"Just different parts," said Hannah.

"Tell me some of them?"

Hannah told her, striving to remember every detail: his mother had moved out, to the modern cube of an apartment Beverly had chosen for her. An apartment in Berkeley; Beverly wanted ample distance between them. In the days following his mother's departure, Beverly had begun planning Thanksgiving dinner, even though it was summer. Tomato and bean season, corn season. A season whose bounty should not be squandered. For weeks, she'd cut recipes from his mother's old magazines, collecting the pictures first in a tiny heap before storing them inside an envelope marked First Thanksgiving! Of course, it wasn't their family's first Thanksgiving. There had been six before this one.

Beverly collected recipe after recipe. Flash of scissors: hot tomato bouillon, roast turkey and oyster stuffing, whipped potatoes, giblet gravy. Webb had doubted Beverly could identify a giblet in a lineup, but here she was, planning giblet gravy. Gourmet onions and brown-and-serve rolls, though he doubted she'd ever risen finicky yeast. Blue cheese Waldorf salad and California Waldorf salad—*all* the Waldorf salads—and gelatin mold and broccoli with easy hollandaise *and and and*. She'd clipped a photograph of, and intended to make, a turkey wearing a pastry suit jacket. The turkey in the photo was indeed a formal turkey, with pastry cuffs on its fine turkey legs, a pastry bowtie. A real carnation boutonniere had been placed at its pastry lapel. Webb had merely looked on, a passive observer as her notebook of ideas filled, as her envelope of recipes swelled.

Thanksgiving arrived. He'd gone to retrieve his mother, to bring her home for the holiday dinner, the first she hadn't orchestrated since marrying his father. He hoped she'd be happy to kick her feet up, relax with him and Debra, but when he knocked on her door, she still wore her housecoat. She refused to leave the apartment. She latched the door.

He'd returned home without his mother. He'd entered his kitchen, heavyhearted, to find an incomprehensible scene. Covering the kitchen floor, the countertops, like winter's first snow, was flour. On the linoleum lay the turkey, legs splayed. Strewn beside it were the various other components of the failed dinner—apple slices, already browning; thick quarters of onion; smaller round onions Beverly had called *cheepolleenee* with an intimidating amount of zeal; puddles of tomato bouillon like blood at a crime scene.

"Our turkey," Beverly sobbed.

"Did you turn him away," Webb asked, "for being improperly attired?"

Beverly, herself covered in flour, shrilled, "You're so funny! You and your funniness!"

Her hysteria, like a dinner bell that would not stop ringing, frightened him. He said, "It's just a turkey, my love."

These words drew fresh hysterics. "Are you that stupid?

"What?"

"It's not just a turkey!"

"What is it?" he asked, dumbly but sincerely, as she sobbed, periodically interrupting her sobbing with gasps for air. She had, he noticed, snot on her cheek, which she swiped into her hair. And then, shoulders shaking, she did the most remarkable thing. She *sat down* in the wreckage. Simply sat in the mixture of onion and flour and apple as if it were a snatch of grass in a park. And then, as though sitting were too demanding, she folded herself up on the linoleum. She lay crying in a fetal position in a puddle of tomato bouillon.

"What did you do?" Hannah had asked.

"Nothing," he said. "I did nothing."

"You didn't ignore her, lying on the floor."

"But I did," he said. "I was thinking of my mother, how she hadn't brushed her hair. I was thinking about how she'd latched the door to keep me out. I stepped around my wife, and then I salvaged what I could salvage of dinner. I remember slicing potatoes and being annoyed that they weren't as thin as I wanted. And at some point, while I sliced potatoes, she got herself off the floor and went to take a bath."

This, he'd told Hannah, was an example of the insurmountable gap between what he'd done and what he should have done, exhibit A in the case of the manifold wrong choices he'd made throughout his life. He might have lain beside his wife in the puddle of tomato bouillon, pushing aside the scattered onions to spoon her on their kitchen floor. He might have kissed her floured cheeks and hair. Might have smoothed her heaving chest beneath his hand. He might have changed their entire trajectory had he done this single thing.

Hannah told his daughter what he knew, and what she now knew: you couldn't keep a person where they didn't want to be. You couldn't tether them to an unwanted world. Hannah had known he would leave. Known he was mostly already gone. Like Sam, existing bodily but not in spirit, a person perpetually longing for a place different from this one.

Hannah told his daughter: on the afternoon of what would be their last walk, he opened the mailbox's slot and slipped the letter inside.

"A letter to Debra," he'd said.

"How do you know where to send it?"

"I have my wily ways."

"I guess you do."

"Always," he said.

She hadn't asked, *Why now?* There was no use in asking questions you already knew the answers to. There was no use in wasting energy you needed for other things. Cycling long distances had taught her the need of preservation, the necessity of storing surplus energy and resolve, knowing you'd need them more later. She'd need them for afterward, the aftermath, the rest of her life.

"California is a place without history," her mother had said. "I give you three months. You'll hate it."

Now, Hannah knows this was absurd. Every place has a history. Early in the days after Webb's death, as she told his daughter and grandson the stories she knew, she understood his history had fused with hers, had fused with Sam's. Their histories had become her singular history. The neighborhood where she now works was once the field Webb set ablaze. The man who eats truffle salad without bacon, shakes his glass at her for more iced tea, owns the Chimes Pharmacy, where Webb sat with his mother on its once-new swivel stools. There, where the theater once existed, is a place she often sits with her husband eating burritos.

Years after Webb's death, she and her husband will enter the bar of the restaurant where they met, the final night of service in a restaurant that was not, had never been, a revolving door. The bug-eyed manager will go home with the picture of himself wearing the speedo; others will leave clasping clay pigeons to their chests.

"Oh, God," her husband will say. "Remember the time I put that pan on that box and started the fire in dry storage?"

Things revolved, things evolved. *She* evolved.

And yet. She will always be the person who lived with Webster Eugene Jackson before he died. She will always be the person who pedaled away from his house that morning when she might have done something differently. That house, the place where his mother had held him in her arms for the first time, had given him life, praying that it would be a bounteous, beautiful life. Believing it would be so.

Occasionally, Hannah will make herself peanut butter and pickle sandwiches in fine afternoon light. She'll witness thunder and lightning after years have passed and grasp, finally, the anomalous beauty of that stormy day with Webb.

One day, hiking on Mount Tamalpais, she and Sean will take a wrong turn, find themselves at the top of a steep hill they hadn't meant to climb, a hill whose view will take Hannah's breath. She will realize *this* was the hill she'd climbed with Sam on their last day, in a time even before her time with Webb. She and Sam stood *here*, right here. The sea of fog will appear both exactly as she remembers it and completely different. She'll close her eyes, imagine herself elsewhere. She'll open them and think, *I've lived longer than Fran.*

"Thank God," she'll say.

"Thank God what?" Sean will squint into the sun, shivering, touching her hip as another memory rises: Colleen Crane, finding Debra in Webb's kitchen. Reaching to touch Debra's hip, to prove her existence.

"You're here," Colleen had said. "Right here."

Debra, tipping toward her, had answered, "I guess I am. I guess we are."

ACKNOWLEDGMENTS

I learned, in the process of creating this book, that writing a novel is a near impossible task. I have relied on an essential cast of characters to reach their collective hands out and pull me through to the other side, as Hila does for Webb. This cast of characters has grounded me countless times I was hanging by a gossamer thread.

Lena Bertone has read every story I've written since we met in Kathleen George's introductory playwriting class twenty-five years ago at the University of Pittsburgh. Our conversations about writing and the difficulties of being a writer in a world that makes it nearly impossible have sustained me. She reminds me (daily!) that we humans need language and stories. We artists need one another.

For over twenty years, Michelle Wenzel has cooked countless Sunday dinners on my behalf. She's mixed the negronis, poured the Robert Sinskey vin gris; she's shelled pounds of fava beans, provided much necessary laughter. For over twenty years, Isabella Stryker Lisitza's careful, studied approach has countered my reactionary nature; our conversations have challenged and anchored me, as have morning hikes with Doug Hamilton, who unfailingly points out the poison ivy before I stumble into it. I have relied on Roger Feuer's perfectly scathing cynicism and clarity of vision, his unfaltering advice. Andrea Gough is the greatest energetic sister I could ask for. To think I met all of these people in the same place astounds me; I am indebted to Venezia's doorway at 1799 University Avenue in Berkeley, which I walked (dubiously) through in 2001 and where I found many things I needed without knowing I needed them.

Beyond necessary has been my mother's undying belief in me when I couldn't muster it for myself. Beyond necessary has been her unconditional love.

My husband's quiet steadiness almost convinces me I'm doing things on my own (I'm not). He cooks dinner, he builds our furniture, he cleans literally everything better than I do. He tells me when I'm wrong, which is frequently. When I first met him in 2001 (at Venezia, of course), he shared a house in Rockridge with a man who wore foam breasts and lace negliglees. This man loosely inspired the character of Webster Eugene Jackson. Jay, I am indebted to you and to the life you lived; I am grateful that you are forever woven into the fabric of my California history.

For years, I remained at the top of my grandmother's novena list. I eventually worked my way off, but I am thankful for those years of prayers. It is she who asked, "Is your book a love story?" With this question, she uncovered what I hadn't known. It is indeed a love story.

The Grateful Dead provided me, at every turn, the emotions that shaped this book and lent inspiration to it at varying points during an interminable process: "Wharf Rat," "Peggy-O," "The Eleven," "Standing on the Moon," "Row Jimmy," "He's Gone," "I Bid You Goodnight."

Nicola Mason. Your insight leaves me speechless. You are an honest, sharp reader, and I am eternally grateful this book found its way into your orbit.

Excerpts of this novel were published elsewhere: "Gettsyburg" in *Fiction*, "Mr. Industry and Miss Real Cool" in *Alaska Quarterly Review*.

Lastly. Kiki and Bud, my loves. This is for you.